Brig-Wallis Preparatory School for Boys

Book One of the Osiris Plan Trilogy

Drew Fisher

ISBN: 1974520676
ISBN 13: 9781974520671

for Toril

1

BRIG-WALLIS

Brig-Wallis Preparatory School for Boys sits nestled among the mountain hillsides of the Alps in the southern Swiss canton of Valais. Though Brig-Wallis is little known, it serves the same population whose high-school-age boys might attend the more famous schools of Harrow, Eton, and Charterhouse in England; Exeter, Andover, and Choate in America; or Le Rosey, Beau-Soleil, and Brilliantmont in Switzerland. Brig-Wallis graduates rarely become famous, and they often do not attend college. The school does no advertising. It accepts no applications.

Entry to Brig-Wallis entails a series of interviews performed by school representatives with individual boys who have been identified by alumni as "potential candidates." The first interviews take place at the boys' families' homes and at their schools, as the admissions officers prefer to see the boys "in action" in the context of their routine surroundings. There follow some unannounced observational visits before favored candidates receive an invitation to visit the school in Switzerland. There, they must sit for an interview with the school's headmaster and/or staff. Once admission is achieved and attendance begun, the two-hundred-year old school does its best to help nurture the full realization of each student's potential.

The first day at Brig-Wallis for first-year students is fairly low key. Student arrivals are spread out all over the day due to the vast variety of directions from which they are coming. Many of the students are traveling from brief family-oriented mid-September stays at resorts or in cosmopolitan centers that have been wisely orchestrated in order to try to cut down on the stress of traveling from larger distances. Most of the newcomers arriving throughout the day turn up alone, with taxi or limousine delivering them to the front gate. Though Americans dominate the mix of students arriving on this particular day, three of this year's incoming class—the Class of 15-18, according to the school's rather unorthodox accounting system—hail from the East—from China, Indonesia, and Australia—two are coming from South America, and five are from either England, France, or Germany. The rest are Americans: nine, in fact. There are eighteen in total.

The arriving students are greeted outside the school's front gate on Polenstrasse by members of the second year—who have already been on campus for a week. Two members of the incoming class are even met by second-year students they know: Londoner George Paul "Joe-pa" Taylor by his "cousin" (third cousin once removed), Albert "Bertie" Chatto; and American Peter Vandenhof by fellow American Bronson Rumsey, whose family, like Peter's, is a member of "The Big Club" on Fishers Island. Peter and Bronson were, thus, occasional childhood "playmates"—that is, they were often grouped together for tennis, swimming, and sailing lessons.

At 2:35 p.m., a taxi arriving from Zurich Airport pulls up to the curb in front of the large double doors that are recessed beneath the massive stone Gothic arch of the Brig-Wallis Gatehouse. The driver gets out of his old Mercedes sedan just before the slight frame of an average-looking boy sporting a head of unruly dark hair emerges from the back passenger door.

The two move toward the trunk of the car just as a door within the school gate opens. A uniformed wiry young man of similar age sprints forth to greet them.

"Peter!" says the out-of-breath young man, thrusting his right hand out toward the shorter boy.

"Bronson?!" responds the new arrival, shaking his greeter's hand. "You go here?"

"Yeah!" answers the taller boy. "Second year!"

"I didn't know—" Peter starts.

"It doesn't matter," responds Bronson, looking into the taxi's trunk.

"You got a lot?" he asks. "Not too much," Peter answers. "Just two suitcases and my carry-on," he says, indicating the bag strapped over his shoulder.

"Cool!" breathes Bronson. "Some guys come with *so much* stuff!"

The taxi driver gets the second bag out of the trunk, shutting the trunk as he moves to place the bag curbside next to its companion.

Seeing Peter begin to rummage around for his wallet, Bronson steps forward and presses a wad of Swiss francs into the driver's hand.

"Thank you very much!" says the driver with a nod, tipping his hat as he backs toward the street.

"That wasn't necessary," says Peter.

"School policy," Bronson says with a shrug.

"What?"

"Yeah," Bronson explains. "School pays for everything. Including taxis and limos."

Peter raises his eyebrows before moving to grab his suitcases.

"I can get one," Bronson says as he rushes in to grab one of the two suitcases. "That's what I'm here for!" He starts for the still-open door-within-a-door before adding over his shoulder, "Well, that and taking you to your room."

Peter follows his gangly companion through the door, closing it behind him. In a few steps, the two boys emerge from the shadows of the archway into the sunshine and the beautifully manicured lawn of the school's courtyard.

"The Quad," Bronson says, nimbly executing a 360-degree spin with Peter's suitcase flying out beside him. "You know your way around?" he asks as they cross the empty courtyard. "I mean, you know: from the interview?"

Peter is not sure if he does—it was six months ago and the end of winter when he visited the campus for his final interview. "I think so," he says.

"Food and showers to your left," Bronson says, indicating the corner where two of the three-storied Collegiate Gothic-styled buildings come together.

"That's Engineering Hall, or 'EH,' as we call it," he says, indicating the building to their immediate left.

Now waving his arm to his right, he says, "That's Châtelaine." He then adds, "Classrooms upstairs. Workout and gaming rooms on the RC." Turning to look back to Peter, he adds, "That's '*rez-de-chaussée*,' in case you didn't know."

Peter nods, though absently, as he is mesmerized by the gorgeous play of sunlight and shadows within the surroundings of the Oxford-styled Quad around him.

As they reach the other side of the courtyard, they enter the shade of a stone-floored colonnade hallway. Open to the elements behind them, Peter finds himself feeling rather comforted by the rather monastic feel that the cloistered hallway gives the school.

"This is Aubrey," Bronson says, indicating the building around them. "Residential and Music," he says before turning left to walk down the hallway. "Aubrey has two staircases to get you upstairs—one at each end of the hallway. I'll take you up this one so you can see the Dining Hall and the shower rooms."

Beginning to feel a little more relaxed, Peter says, "I remember the Dining Hall." Then he adds, "It's on the RC of EH, right?"

"Good job!" says Bronson, acting impressed. "We've got a live one here!" And then, "We'll *skip* the Dining Hall, then!"

As they reach the end of the colonnade, they turn right to start climbing the wide stone staircase in front of them.

Peter takes a moment to look back down the way they came. He finds himself thinking, *That is* truly *an impressive hallway.*

At the top of the stairs, Bronson waves his hand toward a set of doors on the right. "Bathroom and showers," he says. Then, pointing to a door around the corner, he says, "Oh, and that's Laundry."

He turns left and heads down a hallway that runs the length of Aubrey Hall's first floor on the Quad side of the building. This hallway is much narrower than the grand hallway on the ground floor but still maintains the look and feel of a medieval cloister, as it employs a regularly spaced arched-and-pillared Gothic-style window in a tracery-less tri-part form over its entire length. In contrast to the grand hall below, these windows are set with glass and are relatively small, stretching to a height of less than a meter from their waist-high sills to the peak of each arch, while only spanning perhaps a little more than a shoulder's width, each one. Still, Peter notices, the bank of windows offers an impressive and continuous view of the Quad below, as well as of the other buildings encasing the courtyard.

Opposite the twenty-four-meter-long Quad-side window bank is a continuous wall in which three doors and three curtained-from-the-inside windows are set. These are the first-year student living quarters. Bronson leads Peter through the second, most centrally placed, of the three doors.

The room that opens before them is modest, comfortable looking. It contains several plush sofas and couches and a hearth-style fireplace. There are three boys sitting on two of the couches.

"Hey, guys," chirps Bronson. "This is Peter. Peter Vandenhof."

"Hey, Peter," chime the three boys.

One boy jumps to his feet and extends his hand. "I'm Jimmy. Jimmy Perry."

Peter meets Jimmy's handshake and then turns to the other two boys, who have followed Jimmy's lead. "Quattrone," sounds an unmistakably New York accent from one of the boys. "Adam," he adds.

They shake hands.

"Fabrice Takazaki," states the third boy—a small Japanese-looking boy with deferential eyes in his narrow face. Peter shakes his hand.

"You've got three beds to choose from," says Jimmy, motioning with his rather large head toward the hallway behind him. "Better stake your claim while you've still got some choices."

"Thanks," Peter says as he maneuvers to break from his three suite mates to head toward the indicated hallway. Bronson is already ahead of him.

"Clothes go here—on hangers," Bronson says, indicating the open closet spaces on each side of the short hallway. "'Cept for underwear, socks, T-shirts, pajamas, and the like," he adds as they emerge from this brief passage between the commons area into what is obviously a dormitory-style sleeping area. Before him he observes three bunk beds: one on the left wall; one straight in front of him, set between the room's two small and rather simple windows; and a third on the wall to his right.

"Two dressers for six guys, one drawer each," Bronson says. "You gotta make do."

Peter hesitates while considering his bunk options: two tops and one bottom.

"Well," starts Bronson, "I'm gonna go back up to the front gate. See if there's anybody else needs welcoming."

"Oh!" says Peter, snapping out of his thoughts. "Sorry, Bronson! Thanks so much for...for everything!"

Bronson smiles. "No problem." Then, hesitating before leaving, he adds, "Unless you need something else? More touring—"

"No!" Peter shakes his head. "No! You've been great. Thanks so much. I'll take it from here!"

"Awesome," says Bronson. "I guess I'll be seeing you around!" He turns and starts to walk out of the suite. "See you guys!" he says to the three boys in the lounge area. "Have a great year!" And he exits.

That was weird, thinks Peter. *He said that like we'll never see each other again!*

He decides to throw his computer bag onto the top bunk on the left and go out to talk to the others.

"Nice enough guy," Jimmy says as Peter comes out to join them.

"Yeah," Peter says, settling himself into one corner of the couch, opposite Jimmy and Adam and next to, but distant enough from, Fabrice. "He is," he says, before adding, "I know him from back home."

"Oh!" and "Oh," are the other boys' responses.

He decides to change the subject. "I didn't expect the school to pay the cab fare! That was nice!"

"Yeah. I guess the school pays pretty much for everything," says Adam in his delightful Italian New York accent.

"I wonder what *that's* all about?" Peter wonders aloud.

In the next suite over, a similar conversation is going on between another newcomer, Californian Nathan Ambrose, and his new suite mates.

"If I understand right," a large, athletic blond is saying in a slightly accented English, "The school is completely paid for—all expenses. Even travel!"

"It's a good thing!" says Nathan. "Otherwise, *I* wouldn't be here."

"Really?" asks the tall blond, Harry Hagen.

"What d'you mean by that?" asks Bryce Packer-Meares in his cheery Australian accent.

"My parents aren't rich," Nathan divulges matter-of-factly. "I don't even know why I got recruited to come here. There's no way my folks could afford a boarding school *any*where, much less one in Switzerland!"

"So, your dad's not, like, a banker, politician, or CEO somewhere?" asks Bryce.

"Not even close!" Nathan responds. "My dad's a middle school principal, and my mom's a librarian."

"Private school?" asks Harvey Belin from behind the knees of his lanky legs.

"Excuse me?" Nathan asks.

"Your dad," clarifies Harvey. "Is he a principal in a public school or private?"

"Oh! Definitely public." He turns the questions to the others. "What do *your* parents do?" he convulsively scrunches his shoulders up. "Oh! That's so rude!" Then, correcting himself, "Where are you guys from?"

"No worries, mate," excuses Bryce. "I'm from Sydney. My dad's a telecom billionaire."

"Whoa!"

"My dad's a banker," says Harry. "In Hamburg." Then he adds, "Germany."

"I'm from Boston," says Harvey. "My dad's in government." He pauses before adding, "And banking."

"Oh," says Nathan. "Now I *real*ly feel out of place."

"Well, whatever, Nathan," says Harvey. "Whatever brought you here, you wouldn't be here if the school didn't want you."

"Yeah," says Bryce. "That interview process was a bitch!"

"I didn't think it was so bad," says Harry. "Just long. And unusual." Nathan notices that, despite being German, Harry is virtually accent free.

"That's for sure!" says Harvey. "None of the other schools I looked at had anything like it."

"Yeah," says Harry with a laugh. "Usually a nice check from Daddy is enough to get the job done!"

"Or even a letter!" affirms Bryce.

The boys laugh—sprinkled with a couple of "yeahs."

2

PATTERNS AND RHYTHMS

Sunday begins with few or no expectations placed upon the boys. This is due partly to the fact that not all of the first-year class had arrived and partly to the fact that that is the way at Brig-Wallis: Sunday is the only day of the week on which nothing is required of the boys (except reasonable decorum).

At breakfast Maestro Garibaldi—who would be the boys' Psychology teacher—announces that he will be leading a walking tour to Brig in the late morning. Any interested participants are asked to meet in the Quad at 10:00 a.m. Then the Headmaster stands up to go over the Student Handbook with the boys. (Copies of the Handbook had been left on a side table for the boys to have in their possession if they wished.) Most of the students had at least glanced at the document when they had received it at home over the summer, so they were at least familiar with it. Still, the Headmaster is very thorough in his presentation, elaborating in some areas and taking questions freely from students throughout.

The Headmaster follows the Handbook review with a presentation of the day's schedule—which, he says, was to begin the following day, on Monday. Several of the boys express some surprise when the Headmaster reveals that the "academic day" will take up *six* of their weekdays, not five as most boys had been used to in previous school settings. In his final statements of the morning, the Headmaster announces that several of the areas of the campus are to remain off limits to the first-year students. Today only, the classrooms, the Music Room, and the athletic/workout facilities will be closed due to it being Sunday. But it comes as a real surprise when he announces that the school's second floors and Merchant House are to remain respectfully off limits to first-years *throughout* the school year!

"What?" responds Bryce. "That's where the upperclassmen all live!" he whispers to his suite mates sitting at the table with him.

After the Headmaster sits down to finish his breakfast, the ensuing buzz of the conversations among the first-year boys focuses on trying to divine the reasons for this last interdictum.

"How're we supposed to learn the ropes?" Bryce complains.

"I guess they want us to figure it all out on our own," is Nathan's submissive reply.

"We still have the staff to learn from," says Harry, prompting some upturned noses.

"Oh, well," says Bryce with a purposefully stereotypic Aussie sarcasm, "we'll be great."

A majority of the boys opt for Maestro Garibaldi's tour of the town. John Marchaud and Adam Quattrone ask if they can stay behind--if they can, in fact, go back to bed--as they both claim to be suffering from jet lag, but when the tour group returns after being gone a little over two hours, they walk into the Quad to find John and Adam barefoot on the lush green grass enjoying a little game of hacky sack with another boy--a first year who had apparently arrived while the tour was en route.

"Michael Paine!" announces Adam to Maestro Garibaldi's returning group. "From Redmond, Washington."

A few of the boys ask if they can insert themselves into the hacky sack circle. They are enthusiastically welcomed, while some of the others go off to bathrooms or elsewhere.

"Sunday Meal will be at three o'clock!" announces Maestro Garibaldi before walking off toward Merchant House.

"What time is it?" asks Michael.

"Almost one o'clock," says Harry after looking at his watch.

"Geez! It's four a.m. back home!" spouts Michael. "Man, is my internal clock gonna be off!"

The boys laugh as each of them takes a turn sharing the time change they're adapting from.

"Where I come from, it's...one o'clock!" Harry says in mock alarm. The boys all laugh.

Several of the boys seem quite good at the game with the little sack. Though a few are struggling, they seem intent on trying their hardest.

Several minutes later, Benji Hartono appears with two badminton rackets and a shuttlecock. "Anyone wish to hit the birdy with me?" he asks.

Adam and Emil, two of these weaker hacky sack players, dart off to join Benji in another part of the Quad.

As Benji hands a racket to Adam, the first boy to catch him, Emil asks, "Do you have more rackets?"

"No, but we can take turns," says Benji, backing away from Adam and launching a shuttlecock into the air.

"Okay. Thanks," says Emil, weighing his options. He decides to return to the hacky sack game.

The Sunday Meal—which has been traditionally placed in the middle of the afternoon for longer than anyone can recall—is cherished by all, as it is the one meal of the week in which the entire school community is present. Teachers, building staff, Headmaster, second-years, upperclassmen, and even the kitchen staff take seats at the long room-length table that has been put together especially for this meal. Though the upperclassmen are not very talkative, the first-years notice, it is nice to be able to put faces and numbers to their new "family."

At the end of the meal, Meneen van Oort announces that the Music Room will be opened for a one-time special extended period over the course of the evening. "The staff and upperclassmen will be helping me to demonstrate proper care and use of the instruments in our school's rather precious collection," he says. Herr Giorgiadis also takes a moment to serve notice of his special opening of the Gaming Room—which elicits an excited response from the student body.

Just before 9:00 p.m., the final first-year student, a rather small boy with curly white-blond hair named Loïck Adolphus de Rothschild, arrives. He is coming all the way from his family's vacation home on a privately owned island in French Polynesia. Loïck walks into a rather loud and loose scene, as live music is being played in all corners of the campus, shouts and cries are emanating from the Gaming Room, and boys are running to and fro around the lawn of the Quad—many bearing cups of frozen yogurt or yogurt cones that have been procured from the Dining Hall. Though barely any of the other students at play notice his arrival, Loïck is rather surprised and quite pleased at this "reception": he had a preconceived notion that Brig-Wallis was going to be a rather "stuffy" and boring place.

Soon after Loïck's arrival, both Messrs. Garibaldi and van Oort announce the closing of their respective rooms. They remain present to oversee and aid in the safe and proper return of the games and musical instruments, respectively. The campus gradually quiets down as the boys move to their appropriate sections of the campus. The first-years, rather wound up, as one might understand, all congregate in the three lounges of their living areas—some boys flitting in and out of their own lounge to check on the goings-on in either of the other two lounges.

At 10:00 p.m., the lanky form of Monsieur Montechenin breezes into each of the lounges to announce that "lights out" will be occurring at "precisely" 10:30—which sets off a whole new scurry of motion as the boys scurry to and from the shower rooms.

When 10:30 arrives and not only the lighting but the electrical connections to Aubrey Hall are shut off, some of the boys are caught a little off guard. Having checked their cell phones and laptop computers with Herr Giorgiadis, the experience of utter darkness is a bit unexpected. With the curtains and shutters open, some light from the night sky is able to illuminate parts of their room, but, for the most part, it is dark. The cool night breeze coming down from the mountains coupled with the gentle night sounds help relax the boys. In the end, it does not take long for most of the boys to fall asleep. A few of the others—the more jet-lagged contingent—struggle awhile, but soon the sounds coming from the Brig-Wallis student body are limited to a few snorers and heavy breathers.

When the morning wake-up of "lights on" occurs at 5:30 sharp, there can be heard several groans of complaint. Of course, this is understandable, as most of the boys are going to require a bit of time to adjust to the school's rather formal schedule. And yet, all eighteen of the boys manage to scramble into the Chapel on time for Morning Song and Morning Meditation—though some are still adjusting their black ties, tucking their white shirt tails into their black trousers, or adjusting their necks and armpits to their new crested black wool blazers as they find seats in one of the two columns of wooden pews.

At 6:00 a.m., Choirmaster Weston Vox de Mournay stands to lead the opening chant—which is traditionally a monophonic "Gregorian" chant intended to warm everybody up. Three minutes later M. Vox de Mournay leads them into another short piece, this one by Phillip Ledger. Most of the first-year students do their best to follow along, though it is obvious that this untutored "performance" is a little unexpected. When the next song commences—a more complicated polyphonic song by the Italian composer Palestrina—most of the newcomers stop singing. At the front of the Chapel, standing with the Choirmaster, is the inspiring figure of a very enthusiastically engaged Headmaster. Peter and his peers all take notice of their headmaster's strong tenor.

The rest of the staff and upperclassmen are dispersed throughout the pews. All seem equally absorbed, some singing with their eyes closed, others using their toes and swaying bodies to display their level of engrossment.

On this very special day of the new school year, it is tradition that the choirmaster prepare his seasoned veterans for a "welcoming concert" for the new staff and students—this is the main reason the upperclassmen have been on campus a week longer than the first-years. It is during the course of the third song—the one in which the first-year students find themselves truly "out of their league"—that the rest of the community members begin to move out of the pews, into the aisles, and into positions that create a circle around the first-year students. Facing the newcomers, the practiced cast run through an impressive string of songs: Bach and then Mozart and then a beautiful Rachmaninov Vespers—which puts on display the remarkable talents of one particular upperclassman in the *basso profondo* role. Several of the first-year students find themselves actually moved to tears. But the climax of the "concert" is the finale, in which the entire group of singers surrounding the first-year contingent performs a credible and very animated Balinese *kecak*, or Ramayana Monkey Chant—complete with the theatrics of the collective arms flailing skyward and then, suddenly, shifting toward the students in the center in an eerie, almost threatening way.

Spirits are so high after the concert ends that the Headmaster moves into Morning Announcements before Meditation instead of the reverse, as would be his normal custom. This, of course, is to give people a few minutes to calm their hearts and quell the flow of adrenaline.

"Welcome! Welcome all," projects the sonorous voice of the Headmaster. "Welcome to the beginning of another year at Brig-Wallis Preparatory School." Nodding toward the Choirmaster, he says, "I wish to extend a *ve*ry special thank you to Monsieur Vox de Mournay and the returning school community for working *so* diligently to pull off that *ex*quisite performance of some *ve*ry special music!"

Nods and claps fill the Chapel. Headmaster Visconti next turns his eyes to focus on the cluster of first-years in the middle of the room. "In welcoming the incoming class of first-year students—a rather exceptional group, I might add—I would like to bestow upon you a little gift of my own wisdom.

"You would do well to look at every single member of our little community here at Brig-Wallis as a peer—as a family member. That would include everyone from our esteemed Groundskeeper, Mawlawi Pahvlavi"—he nods in the direction of the front pew, toward a middle-aged man dressed in European-style teaching robes, like every other staff member present—"to our extraordinary cook, Chef Novelli," he continues, nodding toward one of the younger staff members—this one dressed in kitchen attire, "and his staff." The Headmaster nods emphatically, waving his hand toward the pew nearest the exit. "As well as the leaders of our Housekeeping and Engineering departments, Signore Avarti and Mister Holt—without whom the campus buildings would be unkempt, unsanitary, cold, and dark."

A few soft laughs, chuckles, and even claps emerge from the audience.

"But also to your teaching staff," the Headmaster continues, "the upper-class students"—nods and clapping—"and last and certainly not least, yourselves." He pauses to scan over the faces of each of the individuals in the group of first-years. "If the stars continue to shine in the night sky, and if the sun continues to rise and set each day, these eighteen young men will be your support for years to come. Do *not* hesitate to call on them.

"And now, for the benefit of the whole, let me introduce to our family its newest members." Then, in a softer voice directed especially to the first-year students, he says, "Please stand as I call your name."

Now standing tall and projecting his voice for all to hear, he calls out:

"From Pasadena, California: Nathan Ambrose.
"From Boston, Massachusetts: Harvey Belin.
"From Santa Clara, California: Emil Frederick.
"From Hamburg, Germany: Harrison Hagen.

"From Kudus, on the island of Java in Indonesia: Benjamin Hartono.
"From Hong Kong, China: Li Zihou.
"From Fairfield, Connecticut: John Marchaud.
"From Rio de Janeiro, Brasil: Enrique Osorio.
"From Sydney, Australia: Bryce Packer-Meares.
"From Redmond, Washington: Michael Paine.
"From Jackson, Wyoming: James Perry.
"From New York City: Adam Quattrone.
"From Paris, France: Loïck de Rothschild.
"From London, England: Thomas Russell.
"From Canterbury, England: Robert Somerset.
"From Lima, Peru: Fabrice Takazaki.
"From Guildford, England: George-Paul Taylor.
"And, from New York City: Peter Vandenhof.

"Gentlemen, I give you our incoming class of first-years." The Chapel echoes with clapping—which is followed by the Headmaster's gentle directive, "You may be seated." The Headmaster then walks over to the side of the sanctuary, where he pulls a simple wooden chair from its place along the sanctuary wall to a spot at the front and center of the sanctuary platform. Sitting down onto the chair, he closes his eyes and assumes the posture of a meditator.

"Find a comfortable position, feet on the floor. Or, if you prefer to sit Indian-style on the floor, feel free to do so—find a place in the aisles."

Several students move from the wooden church pews to the worn but clean rugs at the front of the knave and in the aisles.

"Now, close your eyes," continues the Headmaster. "Bring the focus of your attention to a point between your eyes. A point slightly above the bridge of your nose, a point that exists inside you, a point that is within you and yet allows access to all that is with*out* you.

"Some call this point the Third Eye or the Mind's Eye. Some call it the *Ajna*, or the brow chakra; others call it the pineal gland or even the muddy pellet. It is the window to Other Realms, the perspective of the Higher Consciousness.

"Try to keep your focus on this point. Try to remain focused on this single point. Don't struggle with it—as elusive as it might be; just rest on it; allow your self to be *in* the point, to *be* the point. It is the source of your healing, the source of your wisdom, the source of your strength. Eventually it will feel warm and welcoming, even comforting. It is your home."

The Headmaster allows silence to engulf the room for a few minutes. The silence and stillness are inconsistent with the internal struggles going on within each of the room's individuals—especially most of the first-year students.

"As we close today's meditation, I will take you through a prayer as old as the Cosmos—though it has only been rendered into English recently. Follow, if you will, with me:

"I have a body, but *I* am much more than the atoms and cells that make up this body.

"I have emotions, but *I* am much more than these feelings and reactions.

"I have a mind, but *I* am much more than these thoughts, this intellect.

"I am an individuated spark of the Divine, a wave in the Great Ocean of Cosmic Creation, a cloud in the vast Sky of Higher Mind. I am an agent of Intelligent Design.

"*Hong sau*," he says before falling into another extended silence.

After perhaps a minute, a rustling of clothes and wooden benches begins as individual members of the assemblage come out of their meditations with stretching, twisting, and yawning. Eventually, all rise to their feet and slowly head for the exit.

Breakfast is a simple and light affair that takes place, as do all meals, in the Dining Hall within Engineering Hall. Various preparations of eggs are offered in the hot-meal line next to oatmeals and other grain-based gruels; otherwise the students are left to find and seek their own sources of satisfaction. Scattered around the kitchen end of the Dining Hall are several do-it-yourself stations: one for instant cereals, hot and cold, and granolas and yogurts; one for bread toasts, bagels, muffins, or croissants and their condiments; and a third for fresh fruit juices and teas.

"Hey! Where's the coffee?" can be heard coming out of first-year Michael Paine as his classmates slowly make their way through the food-table lines.

"You'll find no coffee here!" responds an accented, Indian-looking boy with dark curly hair. "Nor will you find any sugared sodas or alcoholic beverages," he adds.

"Why not?!" asks Michael.

"They're discouraged at Brig-Wallis for 'distorting man's natural perceptions.'"

"What?!"

"Yeah!" chimes in another upperclassman. "They interfere with clear thinking!"

"You're serious!?" asks Michael.

"Totally!"

"Ask anyone!" seconds the original respondent.

"I'm asking you!" says Michael, obviously frustrated.

"I mean, ask a teacher," says the dark-haired boy. "Or the Headmaster!"

Michael shakes his head before directing a comment under his breath to the boy next in line, his suite mate, John Marchaud, "Can you believe this shit? I don't know if I can go without caffeine! I'm from Seattle!"

First Period opens with a two-hour block in the Language Lab on the second floor of Châtelaine Hall. While Latin, Ancient Greek, Arabic, and Mandarin Chinese were the school's "languages of choice" for first-year students, it is a fact that virtually every student accepted into Brig-Wallis is already fluent in three or four languages. This common trait is due to the fact that all of the boys have lived and traveled extensively in several foreign countries over the courses of their young lives. Still, a familiarity with as many languages as possible is believed to be a useful tool for the Brig-Wallis graduate. Thus, language studies have become a firm and central part of the Brig-Wallis curriculum.

The Language Lab is used on Mondays, Wednesdays, and Fridays to focus on teacher-led explorations into Greek, Latin, Chinese, and Arabic. Though M. Montechenin's pedagogical rationale might seem dubious, he allows each day's language of choice to be dictated by the class members. Accordingly, each morning begins with a short discussion in which the boys choose their language of the day according to group consensus. At the beginning of the first year, this process is sometimes messy and arduous, as individual egos are more prone to get in the way of the decision-making process. But, eventually, the process becomes smooth and virtually effortless.

"Consensus," recites M. Montechenin from time to time, "is the most desirable means to any effective cooperative group dynamic." Somewhere in a past Brig-Wallis instructor's education, a copy of *Developing Effective Classroom Groups*, by Gene Stanford, made a powerful impression—so much so that its philosophies and methods quickly won over the school's headmaster and his staff, enabling the "group dynamics" style of classroom management to become instituted as a foundational component to all instructional approaches on the campus ever since.

"Consensus building is a brilliant way for individuals to build up the forensic skills necessary to articulate themselves accurately and fully to the world," Weston Vox de Mournay—forensics teacher by daylight, choirmaster by dark—is often heard repeating.

Once a consensual decision is made for the day's language of choice, M. Montechenin's lessons and materials are *very* organized. On Tuesdays, Thursdays, and Saturdays, M. Montechenin allows the students to explore the Language Library individually. Here, many students choose to go into media forms of languages that are already familiar to them: audio tapes, written documents or literature, and even film and YouTube videos are available to the students, so long as they don't abuse their freedoms with impromptu forays into the Internet's "inappropriate" resources. For the most part, once the boys get the hang of the system and their options, they are fairly self-disciplined.

Another phenomenon common to the "open lab" language periods is the ad hoc formation of small study groups. Students interested in honing or even beginning study of a language that is new to them might pair up or sneak into small groups of like-interested classmates. This, then, usually leads to small splinter groups forming around a fellow student or school staff member who has more advanced skills (perhaps even fluency) in that particular language—which then moves to an extracurricular evening meeting time in one of Engineering Hall's upstairs meeting rooms. It is, in fact, routine and even encouraged for individual students with particular language skills or native languages that are desirable to others to take over the leadership or "teaching" of these small splinter groups—some of which become quite large. By midyear it is commonplace to find almost all language studies being overseen and facilitated by students. This pattern of student leadership can be observed to fall into place in many aspects of school life—especially academic learning subjects.

For example, Iranian second-year student Dariush ("Darius") Tabrizi came to Brig-Wallis fluent in Arabic despite Farsi being his native tongue. As is school custom, he was required to attend the Arabic classes. It turns out that this was precisely for the role his own experience and expertise could play in assisting the learning and mastery of Arabic for others. Likewise, Chinese-born first-year Li Zihou was asked to help out in the Mandarin classes. All other foreign language pursuits remain open to the students, but the school asks that student choices be limited to individual need and/or desire. Thus, Old Icelandic and Evenks are not often languages of choice, while French, Spanish, and German are.

Interestingly, as the year progresses, M. Montechenin is found less and less present leading language study groups. This happens to be an intentional outcome of the Brig-Wallis philosophy of education: that students often find themselves being led—being taught—by one of their peers instead of an adult pedagogue. In the two specific cases cited above, the books, workbooks, assignments, conversations, and multimedia presentations all became the welcome and enthusiastic responsibility of student teachers Tabrizi and Li. Similarly, the Fitness Room and the physical fitness pursuits of the first-year class quickly came under the leadership of their resident jock, Harry Hagen. A first-year "gaming" club came under the passionate coleadership of Nathan Ambrose, who was an avid enthusiast of Pokemon as well as a wizard at finding his way around the Internet, and Emil Fredericks, who excelled at mathematics, computer programming, and chess. Though physical education and game playing are not considered academic subjects at Brig-Wallis, they are required activities for all campus residents, as they are strongly believed to improve overall health and well-being.

Between First and Second Periods, the boys have ten minutes before they are expected in Headmaster Visconti's "Philosophy" class. Another two-hour block, the class's name stems from the absolute broadest possible definition of the word "philosophy." With the Headmaster's approach, the class's daily, weekly, and even monthly topic of discussion and study could shift radically as it, too, is driven by student interest—to what topics prove most engaging to the students—to the ebb and flow of their "love of wisdom."

A typical day in the Headmaster's class might take one through discussions of topics as far ranging as current events, history, cosmology, conspiracy theory, archeology, botany, Andalusian cuisine, the poisonous snakes of Australia, Italian yacht building, and particle physics as much as the more typical rudiments of the academic discipline that we call "philosophy." Headmaster Visconti is a genius to watch as he effortlessly, almost imperceptibly, draws each student into the discussions in a most Socratic way, with a seemingly unending barrage of questions. The Headmaster is also quite adept at ensuring that each and every day's discussions move in and out of more specific and traditionally expected areas of philosophy while guiding them "safely" through topics like abortion, religion and religious differences, politics and political theory, and cosmology and astrology, as well as theoretical and quantum mechanics. Never dull, these discussions; the students always seem to enjoy the Headmaster's class and often find themselves carrying the class's discussion topics out into other parts of their day.

After morning classes comes the school's Midday Meal. At Brig-Wallis, this is the central and hardiest meal of the day—the one for which Chef Novelli goes all out in displaying his world-class culinary skills. The meal is usually presented in five- to nine courses, depending on the time of year and availability of fresh foods, and it may last for a full hour of the Midday Break.

The second half of this two-hour midday break is called "Repose." It is intended to allow the entire school community a respite time in which to collect oneself, relax, and/or (as is strongly encouraged), nap. Though silence is not "demanded" *per se* of the student body, it is practiced as a show of respect to others. Still, the odd game of hacky sack or Frisbee invariably pops up on the Quad, while many first-year boys choose to use the period to read or take a walk. Eventually, however, the vast majority fall into the time-honored routine of taking a twenty- to forty-five minute restorative nap, as the Brig-Wallis day is long and demanding.

At the two o'clock hour, students are expected to matriculate to their first afternoon class. For the first-year students, this means Psychology Class with Giuseppe Garibaldi. Once again, the course name, as printed in school materials, proves a bit misleading: if one were to assign a course title that might express more accurately the subject of *actual* learning that is taking place in the ninety minutes with Maestro Garibaldi, one might find the school's motto a better descriptor: "*A posse ad esse, mens agit molem. Fiat lux*," which, in Latin, is intended to translate into English very closely to, "From possibility to reality, mind creates matter. Let there be light," but, if you ask Maestro Garibaldi, he would say the meaning is, "The world is an illusion; everything in Creation is just information, and all information is metaphoric."

Huge chunks of Psychology Class are spent discussing the possible meanings of dreams and symbols and "archetypes." Maestro Garibaldi's classroom is littered with books of all shapes, sizes, and ages that claim source knowledge of symbology, mythology, world religious interpretation, shamanic traditions, theosophy and occultism, mandala, tarot, I-Ching, Tao Te Ching, fêng shui, bioenergy studies, folk literature, and more.

It is quite typical for Maestro Garibaldi to start the day's discussion by asking for a student volunteer to share a recent or memorable dream. It is also not out of the ordinary to walk into "Psych Class" to find the students enthusiastically engaged in a Sufi dance of "whirling dervishes" or to find the lights dimmed for some shamanic journeying or to find the class intently watching a cartoon video (which would later be discussed in depth) or to find all of the students lying on the floor in the darkened room as loud bass-exploding trance music is playing (an attempt at achieving the Holotropic breathing experience).

Outside of Psych Class, the boys talk about its topics and experiences with enthusiasm and amazement, and yet they also wonder at the point of its content—and they question its relevance to their future careers. It can often be seen that these informal review or gripe sessions turn into animated laughter fests as the boys' conversations devolve into contextual language of psychedelia, drug trips, and the like. As a matter of fact, by the end of the first term, almost all of the first-year boys were referring to the class as "LSD Lab" and to their beloved teacher, Maestro Garibaldi, as "Timothy Leary" or "Carl Jung" or "Joseph Campbell" or some creative combination or permutation of the three. Regardless of the boys' teasing banter outside of class, each one of them finds his experiences in "LSD Lab" fascinating and highly rewarding; it is rare to see anyone miss a single class.

At 3:30, the boys move downstairs to the Game Room for ninety minutes of "Mentastics"—which is intended as a combination of the words "mental" and "gymnastics." Here Herr Giorgiadis orchestrates a room of many games that are meant to develop critical thinking skills. Chess, checkers, Stratego, Battleship, mah-jongg, and Pokémon, as well as a vast number of other known, lesser-known, and unknown board games are part of Herr Giorgiadis's teaching repertoire, yet he also uses card games—from solitaire to euchre to bridge—and puzzles of all kinds: 2-D and 3-D visual piece puzzles, word puzzles, crossword puzzles, Sudoku, koans, Psalms, poetry, religious texts, song lyrics, and even the I-Ching, tarot, and magic tricks. Video games are also occasionally employed—any and many pursuits or activities that might test and expand the synaptic wiring patterns of individual brains.

Once again, numerous small special-interest groups spin off from this class, becoming extracurricular clubs. The most popular club, the Chess Club, is run by Herr Giorgiadis himself, as he had once achieved grand-master status while competing within his native Switzerland and throughout Europe, though Nathan and Emil's Gaming Club also gathers a strong following.

At 5:00 p.m., the boys are "released" with the expectation that each of them use part of the next two hours for the pursuit of some kind of physical exercise. There is a fully equipped workout room next to the Gaming Room, but students are not limited or confined to the Workout Room for their exercise. In the basement of Merchant House, there is a room for fencing, as well as two squash courts and an indoor archery range. The Quad, of course, is the focal point of such pursuits as hacky sack, Frisbee, fencing (when the weather is conducive), badminton, and Tai chi and Qigong. There are several students who choose to use part of their five-to-seven block several days a week for walking, running, or hiking in the mountain hills behind the school. Over the course of the school year, most every boy falls into his own personal pattern of physical activity—though there are always a few who are quite fond of variety and who seem to dislike regularity or "predictability."

A few of the first-year students who join Brig-Wallis have experienced success at or have even learned to self-identify with a particular sport or physical prowess. This usually deters consideration for admission into Brig-Wallis, as the staff and admissions team know that pursuit of a profession or even obsession with a particular sport will serve neither the individual nor the school's "leadership" goal in the long run. However, as in every incoming class to Brig-Wallis, this class has a few "stars." Benji Hartono had achieved a fairly high ranking in badminton in his native Indonesia. His Brig-Wallis badminton club proves fairly popular in September when the weather is still nice, but the Headmaster soon finds himself banishing the club from the Quad, as the seemingly permanent badminton court that Benji had meticulously constructed is doing quite a little damage to Mawlawi Pahvlavi's beautiful grass lawn. Despite the setback, Benji is quick to bounce to his next favorite sport: ping-pong, which proves much more suitable for the season's changing weather, as it can easily be set up in a part of the large space of the Workout Room.

There are several football (soccer) enthusiasts who find themselves disappointed to find out that football is not allowed on the Quad (for the very same reasons that badminton is now banned). The Headmaster is always genuinely apologetic—and encouraging of the students' searches for alternative playing fields off campus. (The boys do find a park in Brig in which there are always pickup games going on all day on Sundays.) The sanctity of the grounds and facilities is always paramount in the Headmaster's decisions—as it should be. "Try something else," or "Branch out," and "Challenge yourself to something new and different" are some of the Headmaster's pat comebacks to the students' pouts or groans.

The challenge posed to all Brig-Wallis community members is to fit in not only their exercise but also a shower (if they desire) *and* evening meal or "Supper" into the two-hour block of time. Though several of the food stations in the Dining Hall remain open and stocked throughout the evening, the hot or prepared food items are all taken down around 6:45 each evening. Salad bar, sandwich bar, soup bar, and the ever-present yogurt and granola bars are the most typical fare, as this meal is expected to be much smaller than the Midday Meal. But it isn't: the appetites of teenage boys—especially teenage boys working as hard as these boys are—require surprisingly large caloric intakes; the supper smorgasbord turns out to be more like the site of a killing feast for a pack of voracious wild animals. This description proves remarkably apropos, as it is quite common for groups of boys to descend upon the Dining Hall as late as 6:40 or even 6:50 in order to try to shovel in copious amounts of food before they are required to be in Study Hall at 7:00 p.m.

Over the course of the first two months of school, the boys experiment with many variations on ordering their activities into the two-hour exercise-supper block. Some try an early meal, at 5:00 p.m., followed by their exercise and shower; others come to the Dining Hall straightaway from exercise without showering and perhaps save their shower experience for the last half hour of the evening before the 10:30 "lights out." This latter pattern comes to be favored more by those boys participating in exercise forms that are less sweat producing, like yoga, Tai chi, or walking. The other factor driving some of these time-management experiments is the sudden loss of hot water in the shower rooms when all students happen to choose the same time to invade them.

By the time Halloween rolls around, the majority of the boys have discovered patterns that work.

At 7:00 p.m., students are expected to be transitioning to and focusing on homework or, with permission, "club" meetings. Clubs form and disappear weekly as student learning interests wax and wane—and some are formed precisely as study groups for specific upcoming tests. Yet some clubs persist for months, if not years. The aforementioned Chess Club is one such perennial group. Clubs that form for the study of individual languages are also typically long lasting.

The only rules applying to using Study Hall for club meeting times are that the club has to be teacher approved, it has to have been generated during the core academic classes (of which exercise period is not one), and it has to be scheduled in writing on the all-school Activities Board, where individual meeting-room schedules are posted. If your club has forgotten to enter its name into a time slot for a particular meeting room, then it is not allowed to meet (that day). If a club signs up for a particular room at a particular time, then it is expected to be there, in that room only, at the designated time. If a club fails to show up at its designated time and place for more than three consecutive absences, then that club is unceremoniously disbanded and will have to go through the process of formation all over again.

Though most students are involved in multiple clubs, most clubs meet only one to three nights a week and, so, rarely conflict with one another. Individual absences from scheduled club meetings are understood and indulged as there are myriad other pursuits and assignments that each student might prioritize more highly than the subject of the club.

Around 8:30 each evening, members of the staff begin to show up at the Music Room on the ground floor of Aubrey Hall. Once the strains of music begin snaking around the school campus, the students begin to flock. Though the staff members begin disappearing around 9:30 or 10:00, "lights out" isn't officially until 10:30—though this is inflexibly prompt and, it seems, never expected.

Thus are the routines that the first-year students get used to over the course of the ten-month school year. They have vacation breaks for three weeks around the Christmas-New Year's holidays and another one at the end of the Winter Term at the end of March/beginning of April, and then a ten- or eleven-week summer vacation starting at the end of June/beginning of July.

3

"WHY ARE WE HERE?"

Six teenage boys rest under the warmth of their respective down comforters after their first full academic day at Brig-Wallis. Though the boys are tired—some are still trying to recover from jet lag from their arrivals the day before—and the lights were promptly extinguished at 10:30, they all find themselves a little wired due to the novelty of everything in this day.

"Why do you guys think we're here?" asks the boy on the top bunk closest to the door, Adam Quattrone.

"I dunno," responds the boy in the bottom bunk closest to the door, Enrique Osario. "Because our fathers are rich."

"Is your father rich, Rique?" asks Adam.

"I think so," responds Enrique. "I don't really know what he does."

"Do you have a mansion with servants and staff?" Adam continues.

"No. No mansion," says Enrique. "We've never lived in a house."

"What?!" blurts a top-bunk boy from the opposite side of the room, Emil Frederick.

"Rique's homeless!" laughs one of the other boys across the room: Jimmy Perry—Emil's bunkmate.

"No, no! That's not it!" Rique says. "We've moved around a lot—"

"Me, too," chimes in the boy on the top bunk of the room's middle bunk, Fabrice Takazaki.

"Us, too," adds Emil.

"But we've always lived in cities—in apartments or homes within the city blocks," Rique continues. "But we do always have servants."

"Does your dad have a jet?" comes from Fabrice. "Or a helicopter?"

"We had a helicopter when we lived in São Paolo," Rique responds.

"Cool!" says Jimmy.

"Two," Rique adds.

"What!" Adam reacts.

"Yeah," Rique continues. "Everybody did! You see, at that time—when we lived in São Paolo—the streets were so dangerous—from crime and trash—that people used helicopters to get around."

"What?" asks Adam. "You'd fly from rooftop to rooftop?"

"Exactly!"

"But you still had cars, right?" asks Jimmy.

"No. We didn't. We only used helicopters."

"And a lot of people did this?" asks Adam.

"Everybody I knew."

"Whoa!" breathes Jimmy.

"Freaky," says Fabrice.

"Were there a lot of crashes?" asks Adam. "Like car crashes?"

"Well, yes," answers Rique. "But not very often."

There is a brief stillness as each of the room's other three occupants tries to imagine life using helicopters to get around instead of cars.

"Two helicopters," ruminates Jimmy Perry out loud. "Your family must be rich."

"How about your family?" asks Rique.

"Yeah, we're rich," answers Jimmy. "Three houses in Wyoming—one for skiing, one for getting away—an apartment in DC, and a condo in St. Bart's. But nothing very glamorous, I don't think."

"My family has many homes, but I have a very big family," says Fabrice.

"What do you mean?" asks Adam.

"We move around a lot. Yes," Fabrice clarifies. "But we live in our family's homes."

"How many times have you moved, Fabrice?" asks Jimmy.

"Oh. Many. Hundreds."

"What?!"

"We go where my father is needed."

"What does your father do?" asks Jimmy.

"He fixes things for other people," says Fabrice. "Problems and things."

There is another brief pause.

"Anybody's family famous?" asks Jimmy.

"I have a cousin who's an actor," answers Emil. "As a matter of fact, his two sisters are actresses, too."

"American actresses?" asks Jimmy excitedly.

"Yep."

"Famous actresses?" prods Jimmy. "I mean: would I know them?"

"Yeah, I guess so," answers Emil.

"Who!" Jimmy insists.

"I'd rather not say," is Emil's response.

"What?! Why not?" says Jimmy.

"It doesn't feel right," answers Emil.

There is a pause before Jimmy speaks again. "Okay. That's cool."

"Man, I want to get to know beautiful American actresses!" spouts Fabrice.

"Emil never said they were beautiful," says Jimmy.

"Are they, Emil?" asks Fabrice.

"They're okay," Emil responds. "One of them gets sexy roles and the other one gets the roles for the brainy, nerdy, nice girl."

"Dog!" spouts Jimmy.

The others chime in with laughter and barking sounds.

"Hey!" defends Emil. "She's been nominated for an Academy Award!"

"Whoa!" breathes Rique respectfully as the room quiets down.

"So what do you guys think of the Headmaster?" asks Peter Vandenhof—the one boy who, until now, has not said a word.

Peter's question is met with silence.

"Come on," Peter prods. "We've all met him."

"He's okay," says Fabrice.

"He's sharp—" starts Emil.

"Yeah! He doesn't miss a thing!" bursts out of Adam.

"I think he's kind of creepy that way, if you ask me," adds Jimmy.

A little nervous laughter creeps out of several boys.

"What do you think of Hagen?" asks Peter.

"The big guy?" asks Rique.

"Yeah."

"The pretty boy?" asks Fabrice.

"The Hunk!" bursts from Jimmy.

Laughs all around.

"Yeah, him," continues Peter.

"Why?" asks Jimmy. "You wanna date him?"

More laughter.

"No," Peter responds coolly. "It's just that…he doesn't really fit in, does he? I mean: he's like a footballer or a Greek god…not like…the rest of us." Then he adds, "I mean: seriously. We're all kind of normal. Plain. Unexceptional."

Some snickering and playing on the word "unexceptional" erupts.

"But he's," Peter continues, "different."

Peter's topic starter is met with silence.

"Maybe he's in trouble and his dad paid extra to get him in here," says Rique.

"Yeah! So he doesn't have to see the likes of him anymore!" jokes Jimmy.

"Isn't that why we're all here?" Adam speaks softly. "'Cuz our parents don't want to see us anymore? So they can be free to do whatever they want whenever they want without having to worry over us?"

There is an awkward silence.

"I was told that Brig-Wallis has no tuition," says Jimmy.

"What?!"

"Is that true?"

"Yeah," continues Jimmy. "Nothing. Once you're in, everything is paid for. Some kind of school endowment pays for all of us."

"No way!" exhales Rique.

"It's not like this is the Waldorf Astoria!" jokes Adam.

Everyone laughs.

No, but it is a Swiss boarding school, thinks Peter. *Rich boys in an all-expenses-paid boarding school…*

4

HARRY, THOMAS, AND THE FRUSTRATING AVATAR

Harrison Hilford Hagen, Jr., is walking down the hall away from the classroom wing of the school.

"Harry!" comes a call from behind him. "Wait up!"

Slowing but not stopping, Harry looks over his shoulder to see that it is Thomas Russell hailing him. *The polite kid with the piercing blue eyes that never blink when he looks at you,* Harry thinks. *'Thomas,' not 'Tom' or 'Tommy,'* and then, *creepy kid.*

He stops. Waits.

"Hey, Harry!" the pale, dark-haired Thomas blurts out as he reaches Harry. "So, what do you think of our grand and esteemed headmaster?"

Harry feels the need to be wary, protective. "Why does it matter what *I* think?"

"Oh, but it does!" says Thomas obsequiously. "Everybody here looks up to you, Harry! You know that!" he oozes.

He's being sarcastic, the little bastard...I wonder what he's really after... I'll just try to play along. "I think Headmaster Visconti is an interesting man."

"I'll bet he's got some stories!"

My thoughts exactly! How'd he do that? Or does he even know that he just read my mind...no. How could he? Of course that would be the common response. Everybody would be curious to know more about such a wise old man like the Headmaster. "Yeah," Harry says.

"The trick is: how to get him to *tell* us some of his stories," continues Thomas.

Harry notices Thomas flushing a little. *He didn't mean to say that out loud, did he? What is he up to? What is his game?* "I don't know," Harry responds. "I guess just ask him. That's what I'd do." *Ugh! That was stupid! I'm so stupid! I've just done it again: reinforcing my 'dumb jock' persona...but it was the truth. That* is *what I'd do...why fear? Why hesitate? Why not go after what you want?*

Harry looks over to find Thomas studying him, smiling. *What? Is he reading me? Into me?*

"You would, wouldn't you, Harry?" says Thomas softly. "You really would."

"Yes, I would!" bursts from Harry. "And now, if you don't mind, I'd like to get changed so I can get down to the Workout Room." He turns and steps into a brisk walk toward the student living area.

He catches Thomas's raised voice coming from behind him. "Perhaps I can help you get your question out, dear Harry! 'Harry the Hunk'!"

In the workout gym, Harry is at home. His athletic prowess has become a key to his self-confidence. There were some schools that he looked at that were trying very hard to recruit him for some serious sports training. Football, water polo, lacrosse, and rowing—those were his sports. Football he was able to let go of because of the stress it placed on his body—and because he had heard too many stories from former athletes about brutal injuries and the ensuing life of pain management. Water polo was fun but ultimately a bit boring. Lacrosse was probably the one sport in which he most excelled, and at a young age, but it, too, was pretty hard on the body.

And then there was rowing. Harry loved rowing. Even more than swimming, rowing pitted one man against the elements, against his own mental stamina. And it pitted the mind against the body. "Who is the master here?" captures the essence of the struggle going on during the row. That is what Harry loved most about sports and having a human body: the struggle to see what extraordinary feats can be extracted out of these amazing bodies we are born into.

So how did Harry Hagen end up at Brig-Wallis—a school with no competitive sports programs? It was the admissions process: the interviewers, the teachers, the Headmaster. They all intrigued him; they all seemed different from any other school representatives. They seemed as if they were interested in getting something different out of Harry, something that he couldn't pinpoint but which he felt strongly—and strangely—attracted to. Harry felt that, at Brig-Wallis, maybe he didn't have to be known for his brawn—that maybe they wanted him for his brains. Or something else: something... more important. Something that even *he* didn't know about himself. And yet, once in the flow of campus life, he quickly threw himself into the activities that served him best. Perhaps it was a crutch, but athletics, physical fitness, came so naturally, so easily. And they brought him a lot of joy and satisfaction. Plus, the sudden notoriety and respect he received from this new group of "strangers" didn't hurt either. But this strange "dance" going on between him and Thomas was new. It was different. Harry found it alluring and exciting yet disturbing and unsettling. The unintentional competition that arose between them became the provenance for their budding, though circumspect, friendship.

The target and primary thread of their interactions had become the "mysterious" Headmaster. Each day the two would exit the classroom just before noon in the greatest hurry to compare notes, to review and commiserate (and laugh) over their failures at getting Headmaster Visconti to divulge anything about himself. Invariably, whenever a student would ask the Headmaster directly for an opinion or personal perspective, the wise man would manage to skirt or deflect the probe—usually by quickly returning or redirecting it to some other member of the class. In fact, Vittorio Visconti proved to be such a master at subtly deflecting a discussion away from himself that Harry and Thomas were unable to gain any insights much less facts with regard to the venerable man's personal beliefs or story. It was frustrating yet exhilarating. Above all, it was bonding. Though the two would go deep into discussion, sharing their tactics, they would *never* open up about their most deeply private motives or feelings.

The rest of the class picked up on Harry and Thomas's little game—and, so, too, did the Headmaster—as the school found out in mid-November when the two boys were summoned to the Headmaster's office. They had both been in the Headmaster's office before—during the final stage of the process by which they had earned their invitations and admissions to Brig-Wallis—so there was little or no dread or intimidation factored into their summons. Contrarily, they both found themselves intrigued, excited, even a little flattered that they were being singled out and given 'an audience' with their esteemed leader.

The boys arrive at the door to the Headmaster's office only to find the ornate, richly hand-carved wooden door already ajar in its recessed stone wall setting. Harry decides to knock anyway—to no avail: there is no response. Unabashed, Thomas decides to forge ahead—whereas hesitation is quite visible on Harry's face. Thomas pushes the door open.

As the door swings further inward, a small, well-decorated room is revealed. Floor-to-ceiling bookshelves are encased within the wall opposite the boys. To their left sits an old, heavy wooden desk and chair set in front of a horizontal panel of four beautiful stained-glass windows that are recessed into the thick stone wall. At the other end of the room, to the boys' right—which they can only lay eyes on once they have entered the room—sits, in a state of deep Indian-style meditation, their headmaster... floating three feet off the ground!

The boys both freeze in their tracks, as if trying to study and make sense of the apparition before them, but also in respectful and embarrassed stillness. As Thomas settles back onto his heels, Harry turns and flees from the scene. Thomas remains a moment longer—as if studying this vision before him, seeking some deeper, hidden meaning—before turning to leave. Just before Thomas's visual field passes out of view of the hovering avatar, he could swear he catches, out of his peripheral vision, a glimpse of the appearance of a smile on the Headmaster's face: in the wrinkles around the corners of his eyes, even on his lips. But Thomas is too shaken to stop and turn back. He finds his thoughts racing on his brisk walk back to his living quarters. *Was I* meant *to see that smile? Was that a smile? Was any of that real? Was there something there that I missed? How was he doing that?* Was *he really doing that, or was it a hallucination?*

These and many other questions haunt the two boys over the night. They both sleep badly and, sadly enough, both boys choose not to speak of the incident—not to each other: not to anyone. As a matter of fact, it is several days before the two boys are able to open up a conversation between them—and when they do, it is strained, awkward, and bumbling. Their bond, their common ground, has been ruptured. How, neither of them can figure out. For a long time, they both find themselves wondering whether this might have been the Headmaster's intention.

Though both Harry and Thomas continue to observe their headmaster with the utmost attention and curiosity, it is Harry who finally musters up enough courage to confront him.

As class lets out one day before lunch, Harry eschews his usual pattern of rushing for the cafeteria. Instead he lingers behind. To a fly in the room, it would be obvious that the Headmaster can see what is unfolding: a slight smile forms on his face as he pretends to be focused on gathering his papers and books from the desktop.

"Headmaster Visconti?" Harry manages to squeak out with a crack in his voice.

"Yes, Master Hagen?"

"I was wondering if I could ask you a question."

"And what does your wondering tell you?"

"Hunh?" Harry grunts. "What?"

"You said that you had been wondering—for some time or a little time, I'm not sure, as you did not say—you had been wondering whether or not you could ask me a question."

"Yes, sir! That's right!"

"And, so, I asked you what it is that your wondering revealed to you."

"Hunh? Oh! Yes! *Yes!* I get it! My wondering revealed to me that I *could* ask you a question—I *did* ask you a question!"

"Did you?" The Headmaster's face looks quizzical. "I must have missed that part."

He's enjoying this...this torture! Harry is thinking.

"What question was it that you think you asked me?" asks the Headmaster.

"I think I asked you...whether or not I could ask you a question." *Aarghh! This is* so *frustrating!*

"No, Master Hagen. You never actually did ask me that." The Headmaster looks on impassively.

Harry stands a moment, dumbfounded. Then he decides to bulldoze ahead. "What did Thomas Russell and I see in your office the other night?"

Now it is the Headmaster's turn to look dumbfounded. "Master Hagen, I could not *possibly* tell you what *you*—you and Master Russell—saw in my office the 'other night.'" As if to sympathetically ease Harry's suffering, Headmaster Visconti adds, "What is it that you *think* you saw in my office the other night?"

Harry summons all his courage and strength as he tries to formulate his word choices in a way that will enable him to avoid any further humiliation. "I saw you, seated, in a meditative state, floating nearly a meter above the floor."

Headmaster Visconti looks either amused or impressed. "Very good, Master Hagen. Now I'd like you to go. But I'm going to give you an assignment." Harry looks eager to please. "I want you to try to figure out *why* it was that you saw—or *think* you saw that vision. I, I am sorry to say, must hurry along as I am already late for a previously scheduled meeting."

"Yes, sir. Thank you, sir," Harry says before he slinks out of the room. Though he leaves no wiser than when he entered, Harry walks down the hall flushed with a feeling of utter and total relief. He commends himself for his bravery—and for the fact that the Headmaster did not deny what he said he had seen. *Why did I see that vision? Why do I* think *I saw that vision? What the fuck!*

If there is one positive outcome from Harry's 'confrontation' with the Headmaster, it is that it gives him the desire and drive to reopen communication lines with Thomas. Accordingly, Harry strides into the cafeteria, right up to the table at which Thomas is sitting.

"It's true," Harry says, leaning over the table toward Thomas. "What we saw. It's true."

Thomas says nothing but motions to Harry to sit down in the seat across from him. Complying, Harry leans across the table to continue in a whisper. "I just confronted the Headmaster," he says, a little boastfully. "He confirmed it."

Thomas's eyebrows arch.

"Then he told me to take some time to 'try to figure out why we saw what we did.'"

"We?" Thomas reacts with surprise. "He wanted *us* to try to figure it out to*gether*?"

"Well, not exactly," Harry wriggles in his chair, a little flustered. "He said it to *me*—for *me* to try to figure out. But I think he'd tell you to do the same thing. If you were to ask him." And then, "Why don't you go ask him?"

"Somehow, I think it dangerous...or...maybe presumptuous to predict what the Headmaster might do. In *any* situation," Thomas replies.

"Yeah," says Harry. "I guess you're right." Then, leaning back in, he says, "Still. What do you think it meant? I mean, it's not like you haven't been thinking about it, right?"

"You may be certain of that, old chum," Thomas affirms. "Truth be told, there's little else I've been *a*ble to think about—"

"So, what do you think it means?"

"It could mean something as simple as the fact that our headmaster knows how to manipulate the fabric of space and time—"

"Or, at least, his body's relationship to…things."

Thomas casts a condescending look to Harry before saying, "Or something like that."

"But maybe it isn't something he does himself! Maybe it's something he did to us!"

"What?!"

"You know, like planted something in our minds! Caused us to see something that no one else would have seen—something that he wasn't actually doing—"

"Or maybe a curtain."

"What?!" Harry is confused.

"How could he plant the exact same vision into two different minds at the exact same time?"

"Yeah, okay. I see your point," Harry concedes. "But then, maybe he can?" Harry takes a moment. "My point is: the Headmaster seems to be inferring that what we saw was something that *he* did—and that it was for us—*just* for us!"

"But, *why?*"

5

SOMEONE TO WATCH

One day in early November, as M. Montechenin's Language Lab is letting out, Peter Vandenhof remains behind. The teacher appears busy with the clearing of his desk, moving papers and books into his soft leather briefcase. Peter seems to wait patiently before finally deciding to speak.

"Monsieur Montechenin? Why are there so few upperclassmen at Brig-Wallis?" Peter asks.

"Attrition," is the tall, slender teacher's hurried response. "Survival of the fittest," he adds in accent-free English. Then, turning to look Peter in the eye, yet sounding a little curt and impatient, "Because they got kicked out," he says, adding, "though most leave of their own accord." He returns to his briefcase.

Peter is nonplussed. "But why? The schoolwork isn't so difficult. The rules and regulations aren't so strict."

"No. But the skills and talents necessary to *finish* at Brig-Wallis are sometimes, shall we say, weighed down by the foibles and habits of the ego, aren't they?"

"Are they?" Peter asks in pure innocence. "What does that mean: 'foibles and habits of the ego'?"

"Another time, Vandenhof," M. Montechenin says, and he seems to be trying to get rid of Peter.

"But isn't the ego necessary for survival?" Peter forges ahead.

The tall, stilt-like man turns again to face and look down upon Peter as if looking at him and really seeing him for the first time. He studies Peter for a few seconds. Then, as if finished with his summation, he says, "One would think so, Vandenhof, wouldn't one?" before starting for the door.

"Then, it's not?" Peter blocks M. Montechenin's clean passage through the exit—prompting a near collision.

Montechenin stops, collects his balance, and looks sharply, and yet with interest, upon Peter. "I fear you may be a bit young for this conversation, Vandenhof—"

"I'm fourteen!" Peter blurts out—with far more emotion than Peter would ever have wanted if he could do it over.

Montechenin relaxes his shoulders. "Yes, well, you're also a newcomer here." He slides by Peter through the door to the hallway. "Why don't we wait to have this conversation at a time a little farther in the future," he says over his shoulder. "Once you've had time to settle in better." He casts a final glance back to Peter—as if in hopes of capturing Peter's reaction.

Peter is roiling inside. Ever so curious, ever so piqued by the cryptic comment Montechenin had just tried to use to so obviously brush him off, trying so very hard to suppress his feelings of frustration, anger, and even outrage, he can see in the teacher's eyes that Montechenin had caught all this; he can see Peter's internal struggle for control. This realization makes Peter squelch it. All of a sudden, he finds himself filled with a detached calm. *All in due time,* are the words his mind produces.

"Yes, sir," he says aloud. "Thank you, sir!" he yells down the hall. Then he repositions his backpack on his shoulder and begins to saunter down the hall toward the student living areas.

Two minutes later, M. Montechenin enters the Headmaster's office.

The Headmaster is seated behind his desk. He looks up from the papers before him to his visitor. "Rémy? What can I do for you?"

The tall, lanky teacher with a shock of unruly black hair on his head appears to be not much out of his twenties. He appears uncomfortable, perhaps a little nervous.

"Headmaster, there is a first-year who is starting to stand out for me, sir," he says in a deferential tone. "A boy who stands out not only for his ability to go unnoticed but for some rather remarkable characteristics of self-control that I've seen glimpses of."

The Headmaster leans back into his chair, lacing his fingers behind his head. "And who is this remarkable and yet invisible boy from the first-year class?"

"Peter Vandenhof."

"Ahh. Yes. I know who you are talking about. He is an enigmatic one, isn't he?" The Headmaster speaks as if to himself. Then, looking back to Montechenin, "And you think there is something special about him?"

"I do, sir."

"Then we shall be watchful," he says slowly. Then, in a kind of dismissive tone, "Thank you, Rémy."

"Of course, sir."

"Oh, and Rémy?"

"Yes, sir?"

"Why don't you and I sit down some evening soon and discuss all of the first-years. Would that be amenable to you?"

"Yes, sir. Of course, sir. I look forward to it."

Later in the very same day, Maestro Garibaldi enters the Headmaster's office.

"What can I do for you, Giuseppe?" asks the Headmaster.

"I have come in order to relate an unusual event that took place in my Psychology class today."

"Go on."

"Well, I had chosen the day for dream sharing. A student brought a dream that I thought you would be interested in.

"One Peter Vandenhof—a first-year—began to relate a dream—a dream that he said he had had the very night before. In this dream Master Vandenhof says he found himself a member of a group of combat soldiers who were suddenly trapped in an ambush of gunfire. He says that they knew that there was no escape from their situation and that he watched as all of his group—including himself—were killed. It was a bloody, muddy, and quite prolonged and detailed mess that he related. He even went into great detail in describing how thoroughly and completely he felt he was experiencing the thoughts, feelings, and flood of life experiences of the particular soldier in the group whose body he was occupying. He experienced the futility the situation that he and his troop were in and then of his eventual death by gunfire and bleeding out. And then, Master Vandenhof says, after leaving the body of one soldier—in quite a detailed out-of-body death experience—he found himself inside the body and mind of one of the other soldiers in the group—reliving the exact same scenario, only from the perspective of thinking and feeling patterns, life history, and individual and *different* death experiences of this *other* person!

"Master Vandenhof went on to say that he was able to freely 'step into' the bodymind of each and every member present in that slaughter—and that each and every one of the soldiers had a completely unique history, thinking pattern, and way in which he interpreted and sought to avoid and fight off his death, as well as a completely different 'world' that he receded into after his death. Master Vandenhof experienced the complete life review of each and every one of the nearly twenty soldiers!"

"That is remarkable, Giuseppe," the Headmaster comments. "Did Master Vandenhof have any idea of the meaning or significance of his dream?"

"None. That is why he chose to share it in the class—to see what the others would be able to make of it."

"Were there any insightful interpretations forthcoming?"

"No. None."

"Did you reveal the significance of the dream, Giuseppe?"

"I thought it premature to do so, Headmaster."

"Yes. I suppose it is. Still, as I surmised, this class may be a special one."

"Yes, sir. I just thought you'd like to know."

"Of course! And you were exactly right! Thank you, Giuseppe. We must keep a watch on this Peter Vandenhof. If he is already becoming aware of visits to the Akashic Library, his spiritual perspective may emerge more quickly than most."

"Yes, sir. I agree, sir.

The very next day, at the beginning of Philosophy Class, Headmaster Visconti enters the room late—something the first-years had never seen before.

The Headmaster's entrance is actually quite theatric. He rushes into the room with a few long strides before suddenly stopping, as if frozen in place. Slowly he pans his gaze around the room, looking from one face to the next, one by one, until he has connected eyes with every student in the room.

"Master Vandenhof," comes out of the Headmaster's mouth as he turns his back to Peter.

Peter almost falls off his chair. "Yes, sir?"

"What…interests you?" the Headmaster says with great clarity and deliberation.

"Excuse me, sir?" Peter responds.

"What kind of topics do you find yourself interested in?"

"I don't know, sir," Peter responds—obviously trying to avoid engagement.

Headmaster Visconti swirls on his feet, robes flaring out for a second as he turns to face Peter directly. "Oh, come now, Master Vandenhof. There must be something that interests you. Something that—"

"Okay," Peter interrupts. "I've thought of something."

The Headmaster fixes his gaze. "Yes?"

"This school."

A few quiet gasps can be discerned from Peter's classmates. Even the Headmaster appears caught off guard. "Brig-Wallis?" he responds.

"Yes, sir."

"Okay. Good!" he says, having regained his composure. "What is it about Brig-Wallis that interests you, Master Vandenhof?"

"I am interested in figuring out why it exists. Why we're all here. Why you're here, Headmaster. What this...unusual curriculum and its...unusual teaching styles are all about."

The Headmaster pans the room again. His probing gaze is met with several nods and a lot of hungry eyes.

"That is quite a load of questions and curiosities, Master Vandenhof," he says, interlacing his fingers behind his back and beginning a small circular pacing around the room. "And, by the looks on the faces of your peers, it appears that you are not the *only* one with this interest." He stops pacing. "Is there anybody present who knows why Brigs-Wallis exists?" he asks. "Or why I am here?"

There is no response from the students.

"Does anybody have any guesses?"

"To teach us how to fly?" comes the droll witticism from Thomas—which results in more than a few half-suppressed sniggers—as well as a stern look from the Headmaster.

"That is certainly one possibility—thank you, Master Russell," he responds. "Anyone else?"

"To become teachers?" comes Rique's guess.

"'To become teachers,'" repeats the Headmaster. "And why, Master Osorio—what makes you think that?"

"I have noticed, sir," begins Rique's answer, "that in each of our classes some one of us has been slowly empowered to lead our learning—to become, in effect, one of our teachers."

"Very astute observation, Master Osorio. And one that is not far from the truth." The Headmaster looks around again. "Anyone else?"

"Well," begins Adam. "I can't help but think that part of the reason we're here is so our parents don't have to take care of us—so they can be free to do whatever they want."

"I'm sorry, Master Quattrone, that your opinion of your parents is so low," speaks Headmaster Visconti from beneath arched eyebrows. "But I will tell you that that is *de*finitely *not* one of the reasons you are here or why this school exists."

"To weed the garden," blurts out Peter—which incites such a swift movement from the Headmaster that the room suddenly turns frigidly cold—cold, still, and silent. The Headmaster is now staring at Peter with such an unusual look—and for an uncomfortable amount of time—that it seems as if everyone in the class has suddenly held his breath.

With a feigned disinterest, Peter meets the Headmaster's stare.

"What do you mean, Master Vandenhof?"

"I've been watching," Peter responds. "Listening. Everybody here is pretty amazing: very intelligent, quick learners, highly independent and yet very good at collaboration, and very attentive. There are no dummies here—"

"Speak for yourself," someone manages to sneak in beneath Peter's speech—which provokes several snorts and sniggers.

"I think Brig-Wallis is grooming us for something, while, at the same time, getting ready to weed out…some of us," Peter finishes.

Headmaster Visconti again takes a little longer than expected before responding. He takes a step back and stands a little more erect while loosening his shoulders before broadcasting his sonorous voice to the recesses in the room. "Master Vandenhof is quite right, Gentlemen. Brig-Wallis *is* grooming you for something." The room erupts in small movements, fidgeting. "And Master Vandenhof is correct about another one of his observations," continues the Headmaster. "You are all—*all* of you—exceptional—some might say 'gifted' human beings." More fidgeting. "Our job, however, is to find, uncover, and amplify—even exploit, if I may use such an aggressive word—those gifts."

"But to what end?" asks Loïck de Rothschild.

"So that you can be of service to humankind, Master Rothschild," is the Headmaster's response.

"Service?" comes from Li Zihou.

"Yes, Master Li. Each of you has talents that could be of great help to the course of human history."

A stillness floods the room as everyone seems to be trying to take in what is being said. Peter is the next to break the silence.

"And what course of human history are we talking about here, Headmaster?" he asks. "'Cuz there are many courses to choose from."

Once again Headmaster Visconti's probing, penetrating gaze is planted upon Peter. "That, my dear Master Vandenhof, is for *you* to discover." Then, returning his eyes to a span of the whole group, "It is my hope—it is your *parents'* hope—that you will gain significant insights into your own individual strengths and talents while here at Brig-Wallis, as well as discover various ways in which to *use* your particular talents to help move humankind in a direction that *you* value or desire."

"Do Brig-Wallis students go on to college?" asks Emil Fredericks. "That was never made clear to me during the admissions process."

"Yeah," Peter chimes in. "I remember clearly that the issue was cleverly skirted several times."

The Headmaster again pauses. It seems that he is this time trying to *avoid* looking at Peter. "Of course Brig-Wallis students go on to college. Many go on to attend some of the finest institutions in the world."

"But where are the upperclassmen?" Peter continues. "I mean, I can't help but assume that the junior and senior classes started out with numbers as big as our class. So what happened to them? And why don't we ever get much time to interact with the sophomores—"

"We like to refer to what you call 'the sophomores' as 'second-years,' Master Vandenhof," Headmaster Visconti interrupts.

"Yes. Sorry." Peter is trying to not to get flustered. "My mistake. I know better. But why is this? I mean: we're on the same campus. We share a lot of extracurricular time. But it always feels as if the second-year students are, I don't know, somehow closed to us—as if, at a certain level, they're off limits to us."

"The time-tested curriculum at Brig-Wallis has long observed the benefits of keeping the different years separate," responds the Headmaster. "Believe me, this is for your own best interest."

"Why? How is it in our best interest?" continues Peter.

"Because the second-year students are experiencing a very different curricular focus than the first-years," answers the Headmaster with a sense of calm that only serves to make one wonder if he is bored by this conversation. "The second year at Brig-Wallis is *quite* different from the first year."

"But where are the upperclassmen?" asks Jimmy. "Like Peter asked: What happened to them?"

"There are many reasons for leaving Brig-Wallis, Master Perry," begins the Headmaster. "Despite the rigorous admissions process, Brig Wallis does not always prove to be the best fit for each and every individual who comes here." Then he adds, "Or for their families."

"So none of the previous class members were dismissed by the school?" asks Peter.

"Of course, Master Vandenhof, there have been students whom we have had to ask to leave," answers the Headmaster, squaring up to Peter. "You have read the Student Handbook. You know that there are many possible causes for dismissal. But please know, because of our very rigorous admissions process, we feel quite confident that we bring in with each and every new class individuals who will fit perfectly with Brig-Wallis standards." He then adds, "More often than not, the decision to leave Brig-Wallis comes as the result of mutual accord. Each student knows if and when it is time to leave."

The room is engulfed in silence, though some fidgeting can be observed. Eventually the Headmaster breaks the silence. "So, Master Vandenhof—and first-year classmates: Have I satisfied your curiosities about our school?"

"Some."

"What have I missed?"

"You, sir," says Peter. "How did you end up here? *Why* are you here?"

"Is there somewhere else you think I belong?" the Headmaster asks with intended levity—which works, as several members of the class snicker softly.

"No, sir," says Peter, a little flustered. "I mean, I don't know, sir. I don't even know you."

"What would you like to know?"

Peter recovers his composure. "Where are you from?"

"How long have you worked here?" asks Harry.

"Are you a Brig-Wallis graduate?" from Peter.

"How long have you been headmaster?" from Harry.

"Are you married? Do you have any children?" from Nathan.

"Have you had other jobs?" from Peter.

"Do you ever leave the school?" from Joe-pa.

"Do you have any pets?" asks Rique, which evokes some laughter.

"What's your favorite food?" jokes Jimmy.

"Do you have a television?" from Bryce.

The Headmaster raises his hands, signaling his desire to have the questions cease. "Okay, okay"

He is smiling. "The questions are becoming a little puerile." He puts his hands down. "I will try to answer your questions the best I can.

"I am from Milano—Milan, Italy. I did attend Brig-Wallis. Over sixty years ago! I was a part of the faculty here at Brig-Wallis before I became headmaster. I have never married and thus have no children—though I think of you all as my children. But, no, I have no biological offspring in this lifetime. No pets. No television.

"Of course I leave the school. How else would I get these robes?" Everybody laughs, as the Headmaster's rather tattered and faded teaching robes have already become a source of some good-natured joking among the first-years. "And, oh! My favorite food is pasta!" which evokes another round of laughter and animated faces. Headmaster Visconti uses the tension release as a window in which to redirect the discussion to something more in line with the object of his Philosophy class—which everyone allows to pass, seemingly happy for the diversion.

At the end of class period, the Headmaster brings the students back to their previous subject.

"Before I dismiss you to your Midday Meal, have I satisfied all of your questions regarding Brig-Wallis?"

Nathan Ambrose raises his hand rather timidly. "Excuse me, sir. But I still don't get it: Why are *we* here? How did we get chosen?"

"Yeah," chimes in Jimmy Perry. "How did you even find our names?"

"Why this group of eighteen?" adds John Marchaud.

The Headmaster pauses a moment before addressing the questions: deliberating over his responses. "You were all—each and every one of you—recommended to me by past graduates of Brig-Wallis."

The room falls into silence as the boys sit there with stunned looks on their faces.

"But," begins Harry. "I don't know any graduates of Brig-Wallis. I'd never even *heard* of Brig-Wallis before I began being recruited."

"Most Brig-Wallis graduates keep a rather low profile, so there is a very good chance that they may be in your lives and you don't know it," responds the Headmaster. "In some cases, you might not even know them."

"But why?" asks John. "What is Brig-Wallis looking for that we have? What makes us so...*spe*cial?"

"Or weird?" adds Michael Paine—which elicits some low-level laughter.

Peter brings the group back on track. "What is Brig-Wallis all about? What are you trying to do here? What is it you're hoping to... *create* with us?"

Headmaster Visconti pauses again, formulating his words very carefully. "Brig-Wallis is trying to help nurture the growth and development of certain individuals who might serve in a particular kind of leadership role." Once more he pauses to carefully consider his next words. "You have *all* been singled out and chosen because you show tremendous potential to grow into—to become—*lead*ers of the future." Another pause. "The school exists to try to help you discover and actualize this potential—to realize those traits and characteristics that make this particular kind of leader."

"Exactly what kind of leader is that?" asks Benji Hartono.

"The kind who can lead from behind," is the Headmaster's ready-made response. He then adds, "The kind of person who can lead without needing or demanding to be the center of attention." He pauses a second before continuing, "The kind of leader who can make things happen quietly."

"Are we being trained to be spies?" asks Harvey Belin half seriously.

Laughter breaks out.

"Yes, double-oh-seven," jokes the Headmaster—evoking more laughs.

"I wanna be Ethan Hunt!" Harvey says.

"I'll be Thor!" shouts out Harry.

The Headmaster raises his hands to calm the uprising. "No. I'm only joking," he says. "You are not being trained as spies."

There is a brief pause as the boys seem to be expecting the Headmaster to continue. He doesn't.

Joe-pa Taylor takes a turn to keep the discussion going. "I still don't get it. What does Brig-Wallis have that Eaton or Exeter or Le Rosey don't have?"

"That is a very good question, Master Taylor—and one that we tried to help you understand during the admissions process. But I shall be happy to give it another try." He pauses again before continuing. "Brig-Wallis is the *only* place—on the *planet*—that is training the special kind of leaders of which I spoke. The other schools you mentioned—as well as many, *ma*ny other fine institutions around the globe—have their very special and important places as well. Brig-Wallis just happens to serve a...*dif*ferent population."

Nathan redirects the conversation a bit. "Is it true that no one—that none of us—pays to come to Brig-Wallis? That all our expenses are paid? Every single one?"

"That is true, yes, Master Ambrose."

"How is this possible?" Nathan asks. "I mean: it must be expensive to run and maintain this place! And then there's all the transportation costs."

"This is true," answers the Headmaster in a steady voice. "When Brig-Wallis was created, it was set up with a monetary endowment that was intended to be self-perpetuating. With the additional contributions of numerous alumni, the original vision for the school has been able to remain consistent."

"I still don't get it!" says Nathan, his emotions getting a little out of his control with each sentence. "How and why did you choose *me*? My grades were nothing extraordinary. I'm no special talent in terms of athletics or the arts. And I'm way too young to have discovered any kind of 'special leadership qualities.' I don't get how you found and chose me. I mean, what are there? Eighteen of us?"

The Headmaster steps in. "That, my dear Master Ambrose, is what we hope *you* will discover for yourself through your experience here at Brig-Wallis." Then, turning to try to catch each student's eyes, "It is our most sincere desire that Brig-Wallis will help each and every one of you to discover those special qualities—the ones that I and others saw in you over the course of the admissions process."

"Qualities that have not yet been fully realized," adds Robbie Somerset, seeking clarification.

"Correct, Master Somerset," says the Headmaster. "That is e*xact*ly the point."

"Thank you, Headmaster," says Peter, seeing a place in which the class might break.

"So? Are we in a good place to break for the Midday Meal?"

Nods and rumbling all around as the boys start to get up from their chairs.

"Enjoy your day, gentlemen!"

"Thank you, sir" and "Yes, sir" or "We'll try, Headmaster," trail behind the exited boys.

6

MUSIC AND THOUGHT

Though cell phones, iPods, Gameboys, and other electronic devices are not allowed at Brig-Wallis, music proliferates. Not only are all of the boys proficient in at least one instrument before they come to Brig-Wallis, but the school has at the students' disposal a rather surprising collection of musical instruments, stored in a rather large room at the southeast corner of the lower level of Aubrey Hall. On pleasant, sunny days, it is not unusual to see several students on the Quad with horns or woodwinds or stringed instruments. Occasionally one might even catch the sound of an accordion, zither, or Spanish guitar.

The pursuit of musical "experience," as the Headmaster likes to call it, is helped by the active and avid participation of the teaching staff—some of whom are so proficient that they participate in several local Brig-Glis musical organizations. The teachers invariably wander down to the Music Room late in the evening—sometimes as late as 8:30 or 9:00 p.m. There they start something either individually or collectively. At first these "impromptu" sessions start rather loosely, with the teachers practicing together in small groups or individually, but eventually the students learn that they are not only welcome but encouraged to join in and, of course, lead where they feel so inspired. Some of these sessions evolve into the formation of dedicated practice groups—ad hoc trios, quartets, quintets, combos, and the like. The sessions usually break down around 10:00 p.m. as teachers excuse themselves to go to their bedtime rituals. Occasionally, at first sporadically, but by year's end, weekly, the boys might request a performance time (and, it is insinuated, an audience), which is always granted and often staged in the courtyard or in the Chapel.

The Chapel had been very well maintained, if not embellished over the years. Built in the mid-seventeenth century during the town's heyday, when Kaspar Stockalper's salt mines and silk factories employed ten times the current number of city residents, the Chapel was an old community church of rather drab style, both architecturally and in interior decor. It served the school as a place of gathering and a quiet place to come to pray or meditate, as well as the home, practice place, and performance hall for the school's renowned men's choir. Singing in a style that is comparable to (and, perhaps, modeled after) Britain's Tallis Scholars and Austria's Choralschola der Wiener Hofburgkapelle, the choir experience was instituted and perpetuated because it helped provide such a lift for the community, both spiritually and psychologically (and even physically). Many Brig-Wallis alumni recall choir practice and performances as one of the high points of their entire school experience.

Rehearsals are four mornings a week. They are totally voluntary—though, once a "regular," it was hoped that the student would respectfully commit to regular attendance. Chant is used as the morning warm up before moving to the more complex forms and pieces. Though mostly practitioners of Gregorian chant and Renaissance & Baroque polyphonic styles, the choir was also known to experiment with more modern composers, like Rachmaninov and Arvo Pärt. And, though student initiative occasionally prompted the exploration of non-Western singing styles, the efforts rarely met with success for the large choir. This would result in the break out of small splinter groups of vocal enthusiasts who would initiate and organize practice schedules of their own separate from those of the school choir. Throughout the school's history there had been several small groups of dedicated individuals who had been successful in dabbling into eccentric musical forms like Tuvan throat singing, Tibetan overtone chants, Andean folk song, Siberian Shamanic Healing Chant, and, of course, the Balinese Monkey Chant. Though public concerts are rare (perhaps two or three times per year—and rarely in the school chapel), school performances, to which the school community always looks forward, occur regularly—sometimes two or three times a month.

As mentioned earlier, choir is not required of students (or staff). One such nonparticipant was first-year student Peter Vandenhof.

Peter had a good musical ear—he had trained on several instruments from the classical European repertoire, including piano, oboe, and viola. But, for a long time now, he had found himself uninterested in vocal music. And yet, Peter found himself gravitating nearly every night to the evening jam sessions. He even found himself happily engaged in several group productions that he was reluctantly dragged into. But the thing that most interested Peter in the music department was Brig-Wallis's rather extraordinary collection of instruments. Under the loving and proud supervision of the school's Curator of Musical Acquisitions and resident musicologist, Willem Martin van Oort, the collection included a large number of the known modern orchestral instruments but also quite a number of old, antique, and even "ancient" instruments, as well as an equally large collection of indigenous folk instruments from all over the world. Peter found that he had a virtually insatiable curiosity for the overwhelming number of options of musical instruments at his fingertips. Each night, while the others were working in small groups, Peter would do his best to clandestinely "steal" one of the rare and unusual instruments from the music library and sneak off to one of the private practice rooms that lined the hallway on the first floor of Aubrey Hall. There he would pour himself into trying to find and extricate from each instrument the inborn secrets that he knew made each and every one of these instruments treasures to some culture, some tribe, someone in human history.

This nightly pastime quickly became a source of true joy and passion for Peter, a part of his day that he cherished and never let pass.

Night after night, Peter would slink into the Music Room among the trickle or rush of other students and, if he could manage it—if he could successfully retain his "cloak of invisibility"—he would sneak off to the collections of ancient and indigenous instruments, pick one up, and then disappear into one of the many practice rooms. Didgeridoo, berimbau, talking drum, hurdy-gurdy, recorders, oud, shamisen, hand drum after hand drum, pan flutes, shakuhachi, dulcimers, Celtic harp, balalaika, Chinese and European zithers, koto, gongs, tuned percussives, and even krumhorns—some instruments would occupy Peter's attention for several nights, some for only twenty or thirty minutes. Once Peter was satisfied that he had been able to unveil an instrument's particular magic, he would return the borrowed heirloom to Meneen van Oort with a show of reverence that was both authentic and intentional (he knew that he wanted to stay on the good side of the school's purveyor of his joy). The two would invariably share a brief conversation about the instrument in question, its history or uses, or whether or not any music or modern performances were ever seen for the instrument, but, polite as he tried to be, it was difficult for him to hide his desire to get to the next instrument.

There were four instruments that came across Peter's hands during that first year at Brig-Wallis that beguiled him in ways he never expected. It started during the Winter Term when Peter progressed to exploring the school's surprisingly extensive zither collection. (Mennen van Oort had cordoned off an entire "closet" (a twelve-by-twelve-foot storage room) just for storage and care of zithers and large stringed instruments). The Japanese koto, Indian sitar, and Chinese guzheng each took turns engaging Peter's fascination, frustration, and rapture.

An avid meditator, Peter reveled in the sense of "communion" he was able to attain with these instruments. It didn't matter whether he was working with the lap or floor or mounted versions of these instruments; they engaged him equally. In fact, each instrument took its turn evoking such a devout level of infatuation from Peter that, at times, it seemed as if he might be in danger of losing himself, as if he were falling into a state of manic obsession. Many times over the course of a day, he would find himself distracted by the infiltration of musings over his instrument du jour. His performance at simple tasks like paying appropriate attention in class, reading and writing, and even eating and sleeping, began to suffer. Fortunately, each time he took on a new instrument, he was able to 'conquer' the mystical allure of said instrument quickly enough to avert any serious effects to his psyche.

Perhaps it was a good thing that Peter had "tested" or "girded" himself through the lessons afforded him with his study of the previous three zither-like instruments, otherwise the fourth instrument might have proved his undoing.

Brig-Wallis possessed an exquisite Lyon and Healy 85 CG "grand pedal" concert harp. At 187 centimeters in height, the gorgeous instrument was taller than Peter. It took Mennen van Oort's help to carry the eighty pound instrument to and from a practice room every night. After a little time, Peter was able to convince the Curator to dedicate one practice room to the storage of "his" harp so they wouldn't have to carry it around every day (and risk injury or damage).

Through the harp, Peter was able to experience many moments of pure exultation. Majestic and elegant, rich and sonorous, the Lyon and Healy harp enchanted Peter to such depths that he found himself nearly as satisfied with the acts of tuning, restringing, or cleaning and polishing the instrument as he was during the hours he spent playing it. But nothing compared to the effect playing it had on him. Slowly he learned how to tease the myriad sounds and effects out of the instrument. To Peter, these sounds felt "Divine"; they seemed to evoke in him feelings or "memories" of spiritual, celestial, or theosophical experience—otherworldly, other-dimensional, perceptions of heightened awareness, of raised consciousness. Consequently, he created his own term to use in order to try to describe the beauty he experienced through the harp: he called its sound "God-speak."

After several weeks with his new obsession, he noticed that a rather strange phenomenon began to take place: while listening to the sounds vibrating from the harp, Peter started to become aware of various "noises" emanating from within—from within *his own body.* He became intimately aware of the sound, or feeling, of blood rushing in his ears, the rhythms of his breathing, his heartbeat, his digestive movement, the pulse of his lymph flow and cerebrospinal fluid flow. He even thought he was becoming aware of the exchange of nutrients and wastes among his body's cells and organs. His sensitivity to vibrational movement became so acute, so sensitive, that he began to feel as if he were privy to "conversations" going on between and within cells, molecules, and atoms. After observing this for a while, Peter intuitively began feeling impelled to use his voice to try to enhance, modify, or direct vibrational effects inside him. (He was actually quite unaware of the first time he started to do this; it was a day or two before he noticed that he was singing along with the harp.) So, he began using his voice intentionally in tandem with certain harp sounds to observe what effect it would have. Finding that the addition of his voice did in fact change the cellular or molecular or subatomic responses or "behaviors" that he was seeing from the harp alone, he continued with his experiments. At first he could only perceive shifts in *degrees* of "happiness" or "sadness" in the structures of the micro world, but eventually he came to be able to "read" a much greater "vocabulary" of responses—all due to the effect of the music he was creating with the harp and harp combined with voice.

One day he simply stopped playing the harp; he went *solo voce*—using his voice alone to try to affect cellular and atomic and metabolic "behavior." And it worked! Peter could "see" or "feel" the responses to all of his vocalizations, directed or undirected.

It didn't take him long to understand that all sound—not just a voice or a harp—could have this effect on metabolic, cellular, and even subatomic events and patterns. With the arrival of spring, Peter found that he had become a keen observer of the effects that *all* sound—that all *noise*—had on his being, at many levels. It was during

Spring Term that he also learned that he could direct or cause a particular effect or event through the particular and specific use of a particular and specific note or tone or pitch or chord—that he could use sound to manipulate processes in his own body! To Peter, this was a huge leap. To have figured out a means of using sound to intentionally cause an effect—a planned, orchestrated, intended effect—was at first startling but, once he got used to it, fascinating and, of course, empowering.

One night while lying in bed sleepless, Peter came up with another idea: *Could the effect of sound be projected—and received—by thought... alone?*

He spent the entire night sending recreated or remembered tones and sounds to parts of his body, to cells and DNA, to molecules and atoms, to neurotransmitters (he'd been doing some research in the school library on human anatomy) and his adrenal glands, and even to the atoms and their component parts that currently "chose" to reside and participate in the cooperative health and composition of his "Peter Vandenhof" body. (Peter had also recently learned that 99 percent of all the atoms in a human body at any given time will have been replaced in one year's time, which, to Peter's active mind, implied—no, *screamed*—"intelligence!") And it worked! Peter found that he was able to recreate the same responses within his own body that music, voice, and ambient noise had created! But more: Peter discovered that through thought, he was able to do *more*—that he was able to issue very specific "commands" (though to Peter these were more like respectful requests) to systems and structures and get responses.

It did not take him long to hone his skill so that the responses attained through his "directed thought waves" were more and more fully aligned with his desires and intentions.

Needless to say, Peter was very excited about his findings. As private and shy as he was, Peter longed to tell someone. But he didn't. The school year came to an end. The students went home. The teachers traveled or studied. The Headmaster put his energy into the selection process for the next incoming class (among other things).

7

PETER'S SUMMER

Peter Vandenhof's summer after Brig-Wallis was full of unexpected events, unexpected feelings, and unexpected thoughts. Though comfortable in the Manhattan apartment that his parents kept on the Upper East Side, their "country" home in Westchester County, and their "cottage" on Fishers Island in Long Island Sound, these places no longer felt like "home" to Peter. The rhythms of movement and behavior of the people inhabiting these "worlds," while comprehensible, felt suddenly foreign to him.

Peter's parents had always fostered a sense of independence in their only child. Thus, Peter was given the freedom to move around as he pleased—to spend as much time as he wished at any of the three locations. This he took advantage of, using the family's chauffeur to transport him from one location to the next at his whim and behest. A week in Manhattan, a week at Fishers Island—he even spent a week in Delaware at the coastal compound of his classmate Emil's family—but, even in the company of a Brig-Wallis classmate, Peter was having trouble getting comfortable, relaxing, feeling "home."

Once back at his family's own estate near Tarrytown, he decided to try to take better control of this feeling of restlessness: he came up with the idea of trying to institute for himself some of the now-familiar routines and rhythms that he had found comfort in while at Brig-Wallis. This seemed to work, as, for the first time, Peter was able to feel relaxed and settled. He began to sleep really well. He found himself able to enjoy Nature. He even began to find peace of mind again—to be able to meditate and pick up his sound and thought experiments again. But he had to be creative. And, he found, he had to be disciplined.

This last trick wasn't really very difficult for Peter except for the fact that he also wanted to be deferential to the other humans with whom he had to live: they all had schedules and rhythms in which Peter was always invited to participate, but most often he felt uncomfortable, uninterested, or even repelled by the prospects that each offer held. So, the challenge became how to excuse himself from the myriad other things going on in order to stick to his own desired patterns while remaining polite and inoffensive—without seeming to be too selfish or anti-social. This is how Peter found that the Tarrytown compound suited him best. The Manhattan apartment on Fifth Avenue—and the City itself—had too many distractions, while the Fishers Island "cottage" an entirely different, albeit equally unappealing set of distractions.

At the Tarrytown compound, Peter found himself rising with the sun and going for a long walk on the grounds—usually working in a session of sitting meditation during the course of his walk. He would then return to the house for a simple breakfast, after which he would spend a chunk of the morning in the library among his ancestors' amazing book collection.

Lunch was Peter's favorite meal of the day. Though he had repeatedly informed Staff and Cook that he had chosen vegetarianism, the kitchen staff would invariably slip up with some kind of meat, lard, or meat broth used as an ingredient in the meals they prepared for him. On several occasions, Peter tried his hand at fixing his own meals, as he had found quite a few interesting recipes in the scores of cookbooks in the library, but he usually found himself frustrated by the kitchen's failure to have one or more of the necessary ingredients and thus was never really satisfied with the meals. He had much better luck with his found recipes when he started leaving recipe books on the kitchen counters with their pages open to a particular recipe that he fancied.

Peter's afternoons were spent studying languages and YouTube videos of famous speeches or lauded film performances. He sometimes felt a little guilty for being indoors during the nicer weather, so he would take a walk with one of his language tapes downloaded onto his iPod. Then Peter usually found a way to exert himself with some more vigorous exercise. Swimming in the lap pool was his favorite form, but drilling in the squash court or taking a lesson with the tennis pro or even taking a jog around the grounds once in a while helped break up the monotony of swimming (though monotony was something that really didn't bother a person with such an active, experimental mind as Peter). Exercise was, in turn, followed by a shower, supper, music (which had now taken the form of exercises in what he found was called "toning"), meditation, and bed. To Peter, this was an absolutely idyllic day.

These "perfect" days were usually few and far between, yet they remained the standard, or the template for the standard, to which he aspired. Most every day presented some deviation, some distraction from his *pattern de rigueur.* Still, Peter was able to quickly and easily detach from any disappointment he might feel. Even he was a bit surprised at and proud of this achievement, as he had always thought himself a demanding, selfish, impatient person (though he recognized and never liked these aspects of himself); he took to heart the positive change. *I think I like the new me,* he thought, and, *Maybe Brig-Wallis has been good for me,* for even in his most contented, blissful moments, Peter always seemed to feel a nagging wonder about "other schools" and "other choices" or whether or not Brig-Wallis was *good* place.

On another little aside from this brief overview of Peter's summer, it must be noted that Peter had several occasions—both waking and in his sleep—on which he could *swear* he saw Headmaster Visconti. Twice, these apparitions occurred on the busy sidewalks of Manhattan, once on Fishers Island, and even once at Emil's family compound in Delaware! Whether these incidents were real or imagined, Peter was not bothered, only surprised. And curious. *If that was really the Headmaster, why didn't he come over and talk to me?*

Otherwise, Peter would have said that his summer had been... successful. But as much as he enjoyed his summer "alone"—as much as he enjoyed being able to follow his own rhythms and the successful practice of his self-discipline—Peter found himself *very* excited when September came around—*very* excited at the prospect of returning to school.

8

SECOND YEAR, FALL TERM

As Brig-Wallis had evolved since its foundation in 1815, it had formed some distinctly different traditions for its students. One was that the first-year experience would be one of getting to know the self through "going within." This is why the first-year experience was so very cloistered and isolated from the rest of the world. Seclusion, meditation, introspection, and unveiling of one's own personal interests were considered the foundation points of the first-year experience. Despite this pattern of focus, trust, dependability, and open cooperation were also traits that were heavily cultivated in that first year.

The first year was also intended to get the individual students familiar with ways in which one might structure a balanced and productive daily life. It was hoped that these patterns might prove so healthy and satisfying to the particular kind of boy that the admissions team worked so hard to try to recruit for Brig-Wallis that they might fall into similar rhythms for the entirety of their adult lives.

There is one odd distinction that separates Brig-Wallis from most other Western schools: a first-year student at Brig-Wallis is precisely that: one who is entering the school as a student for the very first time. This distinction helps to account for the disparate ages of the incoming first-year students. Each and every new student entering Brig-Wallis came in as a first-year student, regardless of his age. For example, Harry Hagen came to Brig-Wallis as a sixteen-year-old. Emil Frederick and Thomas Russell came to Brig-Wallis as thirteen-year olds—though they both turned fourteen during the fall of their first year. Peter and the others all came as fourteen- and fifteen-year-olds and were now fifteen and sixteen. All students attending Brig-Wallis for the first time go through the exact same curriculum and structure of their day. All students returning to Brig-Wallis for a second-year experience a different curriculum—one that is skewed from the schedule and courses of the first-year students (in order to minimize the interactions between the two).

Contrary to the reclusive and comfortably regular rhythms of the first year, the second-year experience was fraught with having to test oneself "out in the world." While the first year tested the individual against himself—or rather, challenged the individual to get to know himself better—the second-year focus was more of a test of the individual against the world, to figure out how he might "fit" into the world.

To an outsider, the daily schedule of the second-years looked similar to that of their first year, and the course names also looked similar. But the entire curriculum was actually set up to try to "test oneself" against all of the temptations that the outside world presented. Cell phones and personal laptops were allowed to second-years (though with limited access, of course). There were more gaps in the daily schedule during which the boys were encouraged to "reach out" to the world and try to offer "service."

An ambiguous word to begin with, "service" could, and did, take on many creative interpretations—especially in the new computer-Internet age—even at Brig-Wallis. These included product or book "reviewer," blogger, "troll" ("I'm offering devil's advocacy for people who are stuck in their belief systems," rationalized the offending student), travel agent, offering online real- and delayed-time counseling or sex "advice," even producing and posting instructional videos on a hugely wide variety of topics of "expertise." Originally, the concept was that the students would offer their physical and/or mental support outside the school walls, most typically, within the surrounding Brig community but, as times changed, the staff felt obliged to adjust and adapt, so, a lot of the second-year students' "community service" work was now performed via the Internet. The Headmaster knew this was risky. But he was also rather excited about the potential learning opportunities that might come from the fallout and consequences of such risk-borne adventures: that is, another kind of "test" for his "special" students.

Though all eighteen first-year students were invited back for a second year at Brig-Wallis, two chose not to return. Harvey Belin chose to stay in the United States, where he was allowed to enroll at Phillips Andover, close to his Boston-based family. Unfortunately, as is often the case with Brig-Wallis transfers, Andover would not allow all of Harvey's Brig-Wallis credits to transfer, so they had Harvey start the year in the freshman class. Luckily, he performed so well on placement exams that they quickly restored his age-appropriate status as a true sophomore.

Benji Hartono was the second student to notify the Headmaster that he would not be returning for year number two. Benji's rather acerbic letter—which was, in fact, written by his father—cited Brig-Wallis's "unproven" and "questionable" curriculum, its "poor graduation rate," and its "disappointing acceptance record" to prestigious colleges and universities, as well as its "racist practices" as reasons for their decision to withdraw.

Too bad, thought the Headmaster. *That one had potential.*

Unfortunately, as the Headmaster learned long ago, recruiting among the Orient's nouveau riche—straying even slightly outside the time-tested bloodlines—was a risk. Though the Hartono family commanded great wealth and power, and came from a fairly reliable Chinese bloodline, the Asian psyche is...different.

A third student, Californian Nathan Ambrose, informed Headmaster Visconti sometime in the midsummer that he would not be returning to Brig-Wallis for a second year—a decision that was reversed upon the sudden and unexpected arrival of Headmaster Visconti on the Ambrose doorstep in Pasadena. It turns out that Nathan had felt that he didn't fit in, that he was so out of place—"out of my league" to use his own words—with his classmates that he felt that he lacked the experience and worldly knowledge of the others—not to mention their tutors, private summer camps, and private school training—and, thus, felt "undeserving" of his place there. Divining that this last sentiment was at the core of Nathan's decision, the Headmaster was very quick and concise in convincing the boy that he did, in fact, deserve his place at Brig-Wallis—"more than he knew." He even went so far as to say that he, the Headmaster, saw "qualities and strengths" in Nathan that made him "perhaps one of the most deserving" of the students at Brig-Wallis (which was true).

Embarrassed and flattered, Nathan conceded. He would come back for the second year.

One of the attractions of returning to Brig Wallis for a second year were the dances—or, as the circles of the wealthy elite call them, "balls." The first dance of the year is always held in the Richemont Room of Lausanne's Lausanne Palace Hotel and Spa, a large rectangular room with access to a patio above Lac Léman via its beautiful south-facing French doors.

This year, the sixteen Brig-Wallis second-years arrive via train (their own first-class car) and then limo van. Messieurs Garibaldi and Montechenin accompany the boys as chaperones.

When the group arrives, it is dusk. The huge lake is calm, shimmering with the beautiful colors of the post-sunset sky, as are the snow-covered mountain peaks to the south and east.

The hotel and spa is teeming with life, as many of the students from other schools in the area have booked rooms for the weekend. To them, the dance (or "Bienvenue Ball," as it is being called by the adults) is just one event for their weekend of fun—though the year's first and second-to-last galas are especially noteworthy for the scope of their attendance.

Some of the schools present are coming just for the evening. Like the Brig-Wallis boys, they are going to be taking late-night transportation home after the dance.

Peter and his classmates have all been to dances and formals and lavish weddings before, so the glitz and glamour of these events aren't anything novel, shocking, or overwhelming. This relative comfort allows the boys more energy to be able to focus on the people who have chosen to come. (It is later learned by one of the boys that several of the schools represented at these dances offered their students a choice of whether or not they wanted to attend. Brig-Wallis offered no such choice.)

Everybody in Peter's group seems to know several people at the ball. Peter himself notices—and nods to—several kids he knows from other parts of his life. One boy, Nicholas Armbruster, practically accosts Peter with the enthusiasm of his greeting. "Peter!" he shouts as he crashes into Peter as if he were tackling him on a football field. Barely managing to keep his balance, Peter cordially laughs off Nicholas's greeting as several of his Brig-Wallis classmates, who have chosen, so far, to remain mostly together, look on.

"How's it hangin', Peter?" asks Nicholas with genuine enthusiasm. It is immediately obvious to everyone that Nicholas has been drinking.

"Things are good, Nick," Peter responds. "How are you doing?"

"Great!" he says. "I'm at Beau-Soleil, you know."

"Really?!" Peter says. "No. I didn't know. Are you liking it?"

"Yeah! It's great! You know, snowboarding every day." Then sidling closer, he says in a conspiratorial voice—though loud enough to be heard by Peter's classmates—which is obviously his intent, "And the chicks are *so* easy!"

"That's awesome," Peter says with far less enthusiasm than his adjective might convey.

"Yeah-ah!" Nick says. "And the schoolwork's not too hard—which is nice."

"Yeah," Peter answers.

"How 'bout you, Peter? Where'd you end up? I know your folks were hoping you'd end up at Exeter—you being a legacy and all."

"Yeah. I ended up at Brig-Wallis."

"Where? Never heard of it."

"It's small. Not far from here. On the Simplon Pass to Italy."

"Hunh!" says Nick, looking bored and distracted. "Nope. Never heard of it. I'll have to ask around—see if anybody else has heard of it."

"Yeah."

"You like it?"

"Yes. I do."

"Listen to him—sounding so prim and proper—like a grown up!" Nicholas says. "But seriously. Isn't Europe the best? I am so glad I'm not in the States right now. Man, what a shit storm that is!"

"Yeah."

Nicholas eyes another friend across the room. "Well, okay," he says. "'S'great to see you, Peter! We'll talk later, 'kay?"

"Sure, Nick. Later."

And Nicholas is off with his same reckless abandon.

"*He's* been into it!" says Emil.

"Yeah," says Peter.

"I'd like to find some alcohol," says Jimmy.

Coming from "Cowboy Jimmy," this doesn't necessarily surprise Peter, but it does provoke some thinking. *Interesting*, Peter notes as he recalls many instances in middle school in which alcohol or drugs were being used or offered to him. But *never at Brig-Wallis*!

After an hour or so, once the DJ has been spinning and spitting his magic for a while and the sunlight has long since left the sky, Peter's band of brothers find themselves scattered. Several have gone off in groups of two or three to seek punch or snacks or head out of the ballroom for bathroom use. Peter himself had been slinking in his Peter way, clandestinely, behind the students who were, in fact, taking advantage of the music and satisfying their urges to dance. He even took a stroll outside, onto the patio for a bit. The air outside is a little cooler than he expected and the stars had just started to repopulate the sky. *The lights around the lake are pretty*, he observes. *I'm glad we're in these tuxes*, he thinks to himself as he decides to return to the warmer confines of the ballroom.

He walks in and begins his usual slow stroll behind the clusters of more animated kids lining the edge of the dance floor. Looking at faces, he finds himself assessing the authenticity in their expressions and their voices, making notes of their attire. There are hundreds of kids: all his age.

As he nears a corner of the room opposite the stage occupied by the DJ and his sound equipment, his eyes connect with another set of eyes across the dance floor: a girl in a 1950s-looking, mint-colored dress stands poised, just at the edge of the dance floor, staring straight at him. Peter reacts with the reflexive "look around" to make sure it is, in fact, *him* that she is looking at. When he returns his gaze to her direction, he finds himself quite surprised and not a little disconcerted to find that her countenance has remained firm and unchanged.

She's looking at me! There's no mistaking it!

The girl in the green dress's large almond-shaped eyes—*Egyptian eyes*, Peter remembers thinking—are staring straight at him.

As he locks eyes and stops looking over her very cute though eccentric-in-a-way-that-betrays-confidence-beyond-her-years appearance, he begins to experience something quite unforgettable: it is as if a tunnel has been created, connecting him with her, a tunnel that draws them closer, that draws Peter *into* her—or rather, into a place in which he is suddenly flooded with a rapid-fire display of pictures, scenes (*memories?*) of her—scenes which he knows, without doubt or hesitation, are not of this world, of this time period, of this lifetime. *Past lives?* he thinks to himself. *What the heck is going on here?* In what he is sure is the space of an instant—certainly no more than a few seconds—Peter feels as if he is experiencing lifetimes of memories—and in all of these "memories" (for he can think of no better word to try to explain it) *her eyes* are at the center.

Feeling a bit self-conscious, as if he might get caught in his vulnerable state, Peter finally breaks eye contact with the girl in green. Taking stock of his brain, his emotions, his body, he notices that he is experiencing a very strong physical discomfort, a kind of disorientation. Dizziness. Even nausea.

He does a quick double take back to where the girl had stood, but she is gone; she's no longer there. Scanning the area, the crowd, he can find no trace of her.

No longer able to ignore his strong feelings of dizziness and nausea, he decides to try to find a bathroom. He skirts the crowd, walking along the walls to the other side of the room, where an exit gains him access to a hallway—a hallway that he knows will lead him to a bathroom.

Coming around a corner at the end of the hallway, he sees the flow of traffic in and out of the two bathrooms there. He enters the men's bathroom. Not needing to relieve himself, he heads straight for one of the washbasins, where he turns on the cold-water faucet.

Cupping his hands beneath the refreshingly cold water, he nearly swoons. He closes his eyes in an effort to steady himself but instead is immediately flooded with visuals from his brief encounter with the eyes of the girl in green.

What was that? he thinks in an almost panicky way.

He opens his eyes and sees that he is standing in front of a mirror, in a bathroom, with his wrists under a faucet flow of cool water. He splashes some water onto his face, then towels off before leaving the brightly lit room.

Outside the bathroom he pauses to let his vision adjust to the dimmer lighting in the hallway. He looks across the hall toward the women's bathroom, where he suddenly sees the girl in green emerging from the doorway opposite him. She sees him, and once again their eyes lock. In her look, in her eyes, Peter sees playfulness, a deviousness—teasing—yet also extreme wisdom and unbound confidence. He also sees the smile—not so much on her lips but in the corners of her eyes.

Peter breaks eye contact and turns as if to return to the ballroom. He feels overwhelmed with a need to create some time in which he can try to make sense of this strange sequence of events, this strange connection, this strange girl—but suddenly she is standing right in front of him, obstructing his path, face and body only inches from his. In fact, the bottom of the skirts of her dress is touching the fabric of the legs of his tuxedo trousers—of this he is ever-so-acutely, intimately, and, he is embarrassed to admit, erotically aware.

Their eyes again lock, but this time the girl in the mint-green dress's eyes are conveying a playful and sly kind of shy demure. "Hi!" she says. "Remember me?"

This time Peter does swoon: his dizziness causes him to feel so disoriented that he starts to lose his balance. Her hands grab his arms, steadying him. *Small hands,* he remembers thinking. *Strong hands.* Then, *what does she mean?*

"Have we met before?" he manages to ask out loud.

She smiles. *So much knowing in there,* he thinks.

"Many, many times," she answers in a very relaxed tone.

What!? Where?! I don't remember! He thinks he says this out loud but can't be sure, as he is feeling so disoriented, while at the exact same moment a throng of students flowing toward the bathrooms engulfs and separates them. (The DJ is taking a break.) Stumbling backward, Peter is saved from falling down by the hallway wall behind him. As he begins to feel as if he is regaining his composure, he opens his eyes to find that the girl in the green dress is gone.

"Peter!" says Emil, who is suddenly in front of Peter. "You gotta get back in there!" he says, somewhat out of breath—and, Peter notices, looking a little disheveled and sweaty. "You gotta see Harry dance!"

Before following Emil and Zi back toward the ballroom, Peter tries looking around among the crowd once more, to see if he can find...her—to no avail. Nor does he have any luck during the remainder of the dance. It's as if she just disappeared. Or never existed.

Did I imagine that whole thing? he can't help but ask himself.

When it is time for the Brig-Wallis contingent to depart, Peter finds himself distraught, almost panicky. *Where could she have gone?*

During the entire two-hour trip back to Brig, Peter finds himself unable to relax. So haunted is he with the strange events of the evening—with the mysteries of the girl in the green dress—that he is unable to participate in the lighthearted and enthusiastic telling of stories that occupies most of his classmates, though he is present enough that he does notice the inebriated or stoned state that several of them are in. Instead, he finds himself poring over the incredibly vivid memories of every single second with the girl in the green dress: every nuance of light and color and feeling, every word exchanged in their brief encounter, every possible meaning of every single word, look, or feeling. Over and over, his mind works and reworks the information.

When the train does pull into Brig Station around two thirty in the morning, Peter discovers that he has fallen asleep. He knows that even in his sleep he has been thinking about her, replaying their encounter, even, somehow, redoing or changing the course of events from those that he knows *really* happened. His first impression upon awakening is, in fact, that he had actually found her and that they had danced and he had touched the skin of her arm—had felt the texture of her skin, the contour of her upper arm and elbow—that they had exchanged more words.

"You said we met before," he remembers saying.

"I did," she responds.

"Where? When? I don't remember."

"It doesn't matter," she says soothingly. "What matters is that we're meeting now."

Only, the dress she is wearing in this sleep-induced version of their encounter is dark red, not the pale green that he is sure she was wearing tonight.

The walk back to the school with his comrades and two teacher-chaperones is loud and raucous. Messrs. Giorgiadis and Montechenin have fun making light of the substance-affected students. Even the intoxicated boys pick up on it and go with it—exaggerating their behaviors or responses to better accommodate the teachers' barbs.

To Peter, the middle-of-the-night air is cool, even brisk, but invigorating. He might even go so far as to use the old cliché that "he had never felt so alive" as he did on that walk home from the train station.

He dreamt of her almost every night. In every dream, they would meet again: at the dance. Only, each time it seemed as if the dance was in a different venue, a different ballroom. And she would be wearing different dresses and different hairstyles in each dream. Sometimes it almost seemed as if she was an entirely different person—a different ethnicity, a different age, in a different era of human history. And yet the eyes! The eyes remained constant. He would always recognize her by those eyes. And each time he would look into those eyes, he would experience the same feeling as if he were being sucked into them—sucked into a different dimension as the features of what people called "reality" around them would melt away and cease to exist, sucked into another world—a world of their own private reality.

And each day he would wake up feeling both exhilarated for having been with her again and then crushed because it was only a dream. He was never really with her. It was all a dream. And his frustration would only deepen as he understood that he could not be with her—might never be with her—until he found out her name—which, he knew, was impossible at this point.

The school's next social excursion—which occurs at the end of October in the form of a Hallowe'en Ball—arrives with incredibly high expectations attached to it for Peter. Since most students attending the ball are boarders, there is no expectation of it being a costume ball. But this does not stop many students from trying. Most commonly seen at the ball are masks, but some people even manage to come up with fairly creative (or fairly planned and expensive) half or mock costumes.

The ball is held, as it is every year, in Montreux at the world-famous Château de Chillon. This is the castle that not only served as a regional prison for torture and deprivation for the dukes of Savoy during the sixteenth century but was one of the inspirations for Mary Godwin Shelley's timeless novel *Frankenstein*—which seems only fitting for a Hallowe'en extravaganza.

Peter knows that not all of the year's dances are going to be held in the Lake Geneva (Lac Léman) area as was the first one, so he thinks himself lucky that this one is. But, as it turns out, luck is not with him on this night: she is not there. And he should have known, as the turnout for this dance is far smaller than the previous one—probably due to the cold, wet weather (rain turning to snow).

One outcome of the Hallowe'en Ball that Peter did not foresee was the sudden increase in risky, aberrant behavior from a majority of his classmates. Peter's preoccupation with his own personal "mission" was probably the reason that kept him from both noticing and being a prophylactic for some of his closer friends' foolish choices. It also, no doubt, played a significant role in his obliviousness to the same temptations that were being dangled before his very eyes. Alcohol, drugs, and, this time, gambling and sex were the fancies to which he watched his peers succumb. The real problem came when what might have been forgiven as one-time acts of curious experimentation turned, over time, into serious problems for the students—and the school.

Enrique, Fabrice, and Michael all got caught with dangerously high doses of both marijuana and cocaine in their systems. As it turns out, two of the three had been closet cocaine users, and Michael had been a prescription drug stealer (from his parents), as well as a master of hiding the drain on Mom and Dad's liquor cabinet for some years. Only Fabrice had entered the night as a relative innocent.

Loïck, Joe-pa, and John had been coaxed into joining a group of students who attended the local school, Monte Rosa, for a walk into town. On their promenade, they proceeded to get very drunk on a wide variety of alcoholic beverages purveyed from a variety of Montreux bars. ("Funky Claude's fucking oysters" was a repetitive theme of conversation on the train ride home that night.)

Robbie Somerset, Adam Quattrone, Bryce Packer-Speares and Jimmy Perry were caught in a bedroom in an off-limits area of the castle with a quartet of coeds performing a variety of illicit sexual acts—with video footage captured on the girls' cell phones. (All of the culprits involved were under age.) And Harry and Thomas were found in a room with five other boys engaged in a high-stakes card game. (Each "chip" [the boys were using pieces of paper they had obtained by shredding a poster they had taken from the castle's entrance hall] was being valued at one million dollars!)

In total, twelve of the sixteen second-year students were caught, guilty of "going rogue" during the Halloween Ball. Emil, Zi, Peter, and Nathan Ambrose were the only four who remained at the party—though Emil was guilty of going for an unauthorized ("forbidden")—and very exciting—exploratory walk around the castle with a new "friend" he made from L'École Lémania by the name of Sophie. It was all rather innocent, and they had returned to the ballroom long before Herr Giorgiadis came around to collect everyone for the walk back to the train station in order to catch their 12:49 return, so, no harm done.

The most embarrassing outcome of the night's debacle was the fact that Herr Giorgiadis could not find all of his students at the designated departure time. No one seemed to know where John, Loïck and Joe-pa had disappeared to, which caused the teacher to have to make the safe decision of placing the "found" students on the train home while he stayed behind to wait for the others. It was just before 6:30 a.m. when he and the three stragglers finally walked onto the school grounds.

The sad aftermath of all of this was that Robbie, Bryce, Michael, and Jimmy all began exhibiting new and unusual behaviors. It turns out they were each hiding off-campus "binging" escapades and drug and alcohol purchases through increasingly frequent off-campus "walks" (some of which were unauthorized). Robbie was orchestrating drug-accompanied sex encounters with a wide variety of partners of the paid kind, both local and called in. Bryce and Jimmy were suddenly best friends, sneaking out several nights each week to pursue adventures in alcohol, girls, and, eventually, drugs. "The Headmaster wants us to socialize!" they would spout off as their rationale while they shared their exploits with their classmates. And cool, quiet, reserved Michael Paine simply chose to self-medicate all by himself—sneaking illicit substances onto the campus, hiding them, and then sneaking around at odd hours to take quick samples of his treasures. When it came time for Michael to own up to his behavior, the Headmaster found himself rather impressed with both the sheer number of hiding places Michael had devised and also with the high level of strategic planning that he had employed in order to have quick and frequent access to his stashes. Accordingly, the Headmaster fought hard to keep Michael.

The Headmaster, of course, recognized the escalation in aberrant, dissociative behaviors. His policy, as had always been his policy, was to wait and watch: to observe how the individual student handles his "problem." Those students who seem strong enough to recognize their problem and either seek help or find success with the quick application of extreme self-discipline—which was always hoped for and expected from any student that he had admitted to Brig-Wallis—would have "passed the test"—tests that he knew all men might have to confront in their lifetime.

If truth be told, the "test" of addictive behaviors was one that the Headmaster had fully designed to be part of the second-year "curriculum." Drugs, sex, gambling, alcohol, competition, anger, greed, covetousness, and even love were all among the many "obstacles" that the Headmaster counted as undesirable to his goals as shaper of men. Watching promising, good-natured young men self-destruct was not something the Headmaster enjoyed—which is why he would not give the addiction too much time to rage before confronting it. He would call a student into his office, and he would ask the student straightaway whether or not he recognized that he had a problem. If this was denied—even once or even hinted at denying—the student would be dismissed immediately—the parents telephoned then and there while the student sat and watched. If the student was quick to admit to his problem, show sincere remorse, and then successfully convince the Headmaster of his desire to conquer it, then the student would be asked what plan he proposed to use in order to defeat his addiction. The Headmaster is, here, looking for particular coping skills, mechanisms, techniques, and styles—one of which is asking for help: asking for help from friends (classmates) and family, strangers and professionals. The other is instituting healthy replacement activities and pursuits as replacement for the void that will occur with the removal of the particular stimulus provided by the particular addiction (or addictions). The real signs of potential success that the Headmaster looks for is a strength of will—unearthly, steely discipline—and spiritual discipline.

As it turned out, both Jimmy and Bryce were deniers. Consequently, their parents each received "the call," and the boys were sent home around Thanksgiving time with the knowledge that they would not be returning. Mercifully, the Headmaster did offer recommendations to each boy's parents as to suggested courses of action—counseling and the like. And he wrote positive letters of recommendation that helped them both get into the successive schools that they attended.

Michael and Robbie were both "contritionists": they both freely admitted to their "problems." The Headmaster, observing the amount of relief that being found out gave both boys, helped them put together "recovery" plans that involved counseling, a buddy system with another classmate, and a rigorous plan for self-discipline. While Michael proved worthy of the second chance, Robbie did not.

This last statement is not accurate. Robbie went through the motions of "recovery" and self-discipline, but, through several discussions, the Headmaster came to realize that Robbie was floundering. The boy was lost. He was unsure about himself, about the world, about everything. All of the signs of intrinsic motivation, interest, and curiosity were gone, lost, in hiding. The Headmaster helped Robbie to recognize his own deep lack of compass, and when the school let out for Christmas vacation, it was understood that Robbie would not be returning. His mother seemed devastated, while his father could not seem to care less. Mrs. Somerset soon recovered, however, as Robbie was soon admitted to Eton for the Lenten Half.

Thus, the aftereffects of the second outing, the Hallowe'en Ball, were strongly felt among the Class of 15-18. It was as if a bowling ball had been thrown into the group of sixteen, with several members being struck. Some teetered and tottered and eventually fell: three classmates gone by the New Year, sixteen down to thirteen. Peter finally began to understand where all the upperclassmen had gone. This insight only steeled him to try harder, to focus more intensely, to hone his self-discipline and commitment to Brig-Wallis life.

Near the end of the Autumn Term, in mid-December, came the last dance. It was thrown as a kind of celebration, after all of the area's boarding schools had run their semester exams. Predictably, attendance was small at this dance. This might be due in part to the fact that the ball was held in the Swiss capital, Bern, which was not as endearing a location for the wealthy elite as other Swiss destinations; but, more likely, it was due to the fact that boarders didn't want to hang around after exams; they wanted to go home (or to whatever exclusive resort destination that their families had chosen for the holidays). Though the dance was touted as a "Yule Ball," the promise of seasonal magic could not keep people from going home.

Peter, however, was one of the holdouts. He had, of course, his motives. Fueled by his comfort with the rhythms of his life at Brig-Wallis, he had also made the decision to stay on at Brig-Wallis over the Christmas Break. This decision was also motivated by a secret fear of succumbing to the pitfalls of some of the temptations facing kids of his age and ilk face out in "the real world." When the Headmaster reasoned with Peter that there would be no classes and no regular daily events, and that many of the resident staff would also be leaving for all or a part of the three-week vacation span, Peter would not be swayed. He wanted to stick to his Brig-Wallis rhythms: they had become his foundation; they were his rock.

The Yule Ball proved uneventful. Only sixty to seventy kids showed up. The usual temptations were waved in front of Peter's face, but he resisted them all without effort. To his great disappointment, the girl from the first ball failed to show up again.

Peter began to give up hope. The girl in the mint-green dress seemed to be fading from his memory; even her appearances in his dreams were becoming less frequent. Rather than dwell on something over which he had no power, he decided to throw his energies over the holiday break into his meditation practice and his "thought energy" work.

9

CHRISTMAS AT BRIG-WALLIS

Christmas vacation surprised Peter quite a little. The campus was so quiet. And yet, with the absence of his classmates and the usual fullness of the daily academic schedule, he found himself noticing things that he had never noticed before—such as the art and architectural nuances all around the campus, as well as the personalities and personal histories of some of the school's staff.

During the first week, he found himself spending a lot of time hanging out with Meneer van Oort ("Willem, please!" the musicologist insisted when alone with Peter). Peter soon realized that, though it was a real treat, and he always learned a lot in Willem's presence, the elder man's almost obsessive focus on his instruments and all things musical made any length of time spent with him a bit tiresome. So, though he visited daily (and continued his exhaustive exploration of the school's instrument collection), by the second week, he found himself looking for excuses to shorten his visits.

Peter found particular delight in getting to know the Groundskeeper, Mawlawi ("Ali") Pahlavi. Pahlavi is always busy before dawn and after sunset making sure the school's paths and sidewalks are clear of ice and snow, so those are the times to find him. It turns out that Ali had been a student at Brig-Wallis in his youth. Apparently, he loved the school and its rhythms much in the same way that Peter did—so much so that he had decided to dedicate his life to whatever work he might contribute—just so he could go on living here! This little tidbit of information planted the seed of an idea in Peter that caused him to consider more seriously the possibility that he, too, might seek a position on the school staff after graduation—or after college.

Peter also found himself engaging in several interesting and enjoyable conversations with Chef Novelli while going through the meal lines. Ever an admirer of the school's food—and, in particular, the artistry of the kitchen staff's work—Peter proceeded to volunteer his help in the kitchens over the course of the second half of the break. "Wherever I can be useful," he offered—though this ended up being more time spent in the dishwashing department that he anticipated.

Another treat Peter enjoyed was Morning Chapel. From the start of the break, he had decided to keep to the school's daily schedule, even to the point of making sure that he arrived at the Chapel by 6:30 a.m. Occasionally, Peter would find himself in the company of a teacher or other staff member—or even the Headmaster—though the Headmaster was traveling for the majority of the break—but it was the rare occurrence of his being alone in the Chapel that prompted a new adventure for him.

The first time he found himself alone, he got the sudden inspiration to sing: alone and loudly! He had great fun playing with the Chapel's acoustics, projecting his voice in a wide variety of sounds and pitches to the plaster-covered stone walls in all kinds of different directions and volumes. And then one day he was caught. Playing with the "feel" of the interaction of multiple sound waves cast in multiple directions, Peter was so engrossed in his "work" that the entrance of the Headmaster went completely unnoticed to him. Interestingly, the elder man chose to freeze in his footsteps and remain standing in place, watching Peter at work, for over twenty minutes. When Peter did finally discover his interloper, he was mortified. "How long…?"

"A while," is the Headmaster's stoic response. He walks down the center aisle toward Peter. "Will you sit with me, Peter?" he says, motioning to one of the pews. Peter is still reeling a bit from being caught in his reckless play—but more, from being addressed as "Peter." *That just didn't happen! Not from the Headmaster!*

"Yes, sir. Certainly, sir!" he answers aloud, scurrying to sit down.

"How are you getting on, Peter?" He clarifies himself by adding, "I mean, you're the only student here. For two weeks now. It must be a little boring. Or at least lonely."

"What?! No, sir!" he says a little overenthusiastically, almost defensively. "I *love* it here!"

"So, what have you been doing? With all of your time?"

"Well, I've been getting to know the school—its art and architecture. And, of course, more of the musical instruments with Meneer van Oort." Peter went on, unchecked, talking about all of the things he'd been doing, for over ten minutes. The entire time, Headmaster Visconti was doing his best to listen, but he couldn't help but see more deeply into Peter—to see his genuine and unbound enthusiasm for the school—for everything! *Such a remarkable boy!*

The Headmaster had long thought of Peter as one of the top candidates, a possible future member of the Order, but now he suddenly finds a new and different thought seeping into the back of his consciousness: *He's so much like me!* Which then leads to his musing, *Is he the one?*

When Peter finishes his detailed chronicle, the Headmaster has another question ready for him. "And this?" he asks, his eyes arching around the interior of the Chapel. "Your sound experiments in the Chapel? Would you care to let me in on that?"

Peter hesitates. He thinks very carefully of what he might say—what the Headmaster might understand. Looking for a prolonged moment into the old man's eyes, he decides to throw caution to the wind. "I was testing the effects of multiple vibrational waveforms on my body's metabolic, cellular, and subatomic patterns."

The Headmaster finds himself reeling. But he keeps his outward composure. "And what did you find?" he manages to say.

Peter has caught none of the Headmaster's internal reaction; he is just so excited to have someone to tell his theories and results to.

And so, he spouts. For fifteen minutes Peter elaborates on his findings. He even goes so far as to backtrack to some of his early steps on this path. The Headmaster takes it all in—understanding quite a lot more than any onlooker might suspect, but all the while thinking, *He's so much like me!*

When Peter finishes, he asks, "So, what do you think? Am I on the right track?"

The Headmaster knows that, yes, Peter is on the right track, but he also knows that there is so much more he needs to learn. *Is he the one?* he asks himself once more before adding, *I should be teaching him.*

"Yes, you are," he says—which causes a stir of excitement in Peter's countenance. "But you might want to try a slightly different perspective."

"Sir?"

He can tell he has dumbfounded Peter. "Yes. Up until now, all of your efforts have been focused on seeing or feeling the effects on your own body—am I right?"

"Yes, sir. That's right."

"Might I suggest that you turn your focus on other things *outside* your body?"

Peter is suddenly dazed. He cannot believe what he's just heard. *Of course! Why didn't* I *think of that?*

"Are you going to breakfast, Peter?" the Headmaster says as he stands up and stretches his long body toward the arched ceiling. "I am suddenly finding myself quite famished."

"Hunh?" Peter is still deep in his thoughts. "Yes. Of course," he says as he gets to his feet.

Together they walk to the Dining Hall, both keeping to their own thoughts.

Peter isn't sure at first if he is reading the signs correctly, but it seems to him that the Headmaster has taken a liking to him. Suddenly, since their "connection" at the end of Christmas Break, the Headmaster is frequently showing up to meals and asking to sit with Peter and whomever else he might be sitting with. Their walk from Chapel to the Dining Hall for breakfast becomes a rather private affair. And the sly and witty banter that passes between the two over the course of the two hours of Philosophy Class simply cannot be ignored. It doesn't take long for his classmates to figure it out.

For a week or so they tease Peter, but this quickly melts away as Peter's fellow students—his friends—begin to understand the real significance of this relationship: the Headmaster has chosen Peter! He has chosen Peter as his *protégé*! And Peter is stepping up to the call!

Thus begins a relationship that finally squelches the already dying fires of his "infatuation" with "the girl in the green dress." This new relationship is one that feeds Peter as he had never been fed before. Peter is really enjoying their banter, enjoying their shared meals. The Headmaster has always been cordial, relaxed, and open with the students, but Peter feels as if the Headmaster is treating him as *an equal.* As a matter of fact, Peter realizes that they seem to feed off each other—whatever one says, the other tries to top it, embellish it, humor it, or add deeper inference or innuendo. Peter cannot compete with the Headmaster's erudition, but it proves to be a thing he relishes, something he secretly aspires to, a source of endless mental replaying in his private time. And Peter begins to take on the challenge the Headmaster gives him—though he struggles with how to access, how to be respectful and unobtrusive to others while still testing his techniques.

He throws himself into studies of anatomy and physiology, into particle physics and quantum theory. He even starts to read some of the odd books in Herr Garibaldi's classroom that he had, until now, dismissed. He becomes familiar with and contemplates the concepts behind terms like "radionics," "electromagnetic" and "bioenergy" fields, "chakras," "dualism," "Taoism," "field theory," "collective unconscious," and even "implicate and explicate." And yet, it is all a turgid mystery to him. He feels as if he were sticking his hand into a cloud while hoping against hope that he can somehow pull out a bird.

Then one day, at breakfast, Peter privately divulges to the Headmaster his frustrations. He pours out a detailed synopsis of all the work he has been putting into his "project." When he finishes, he looks down but not despondent; in his eyes, the Headmaster can see Peter's sincere frustration. But he can also see Peter's resolve and unflinching determination. The fire of curiosity burns strongly in his eyes.

"I might be able to help you," the Headmaster says.

"You?!"

"Would you be interested?"

"What?! Lessons from you?"

"Just enough to get you started, but, yes, 'lessons' we'll call them."

"Wow! Headmaster, you are so kind! But, I couldn't *pos*sibly trouble you. You're a busy man! You've got lots of *way* more important responsibilities than piddling around with a little second-year!"

The Headmaster raises a hand. That's all it takes to stop Peter's nervous, excited chatter.

"I'm offering one visit. One 'lesson,'" he says. "To see where it takes you. That's it. We'll play it by ear from there. Okay?"

"Okay! Yeah!" says Peter effusively.

"Will Sunday, say, at one o'clock work for you?"

Peter's mind is spinning. *One o'clock. Sunday. That's during Repose! But it's Sunday. Our free day.* "Yes! That'll work," he says. "But where?"

"In my offices."

The remainder of that day is a blur to Peter as he works excitedly over the many questions he plans to have ready for the Headmaster. *Sunday.* He can hardly wait. *I'll have my questions written and ready.*

When the day arrives, Peter is so excited for one o'clock to come that he is almost sick to his stomach. He has already pored over his notes many times over. He has even gone for a long walk into town and back in an effort to distract his mind—to no avail. He is nervously excited.

When he arrives at the door to the Headmaster's office, he finds it open. Headmaster Visconti sees Peter and rises to his feet and comes out from behind his desk to greet Peter. "Peter! Come in, come in," he says, closing the door behind Peter. "Come sit on the couch over here with me," he says as they move to the Quad-side end of the room and sit down upon the couch.

"So, I have gathered some materials together for you to read; only I would ask that you only read them here in my offices."

"Sir?"

"Well, if truth be known, I don't really want other students to see them. You know, jealousies and the sort." Peter still looks quizzical. "The journey I'm setting you on is one that I cannot expect every student to be ready for. Usually it takes a fourth-year student or, on the odd occasion, a particularly advanced third-year for me to open my private resources."

Am I an advanced student? Peter is thinking, but he asks, "But this is *your* office! Would there be certain times I would be allowed access to the materials?"

"Oh! Yes!" the Headmaster says, looking slightly embarrassed. "Excuse me for being incomplete! You will have special permission to spend any of your free time or Study Hall time in here with my materials. Even if I am not here, so long as the door is unlocked, it is yours to use."

"Really?!" Peter is shocked at what he is hearing—until he sees a book on the small table next to the Headmaster's shoulder titled *A Treatise on Cosmic Fire* by Alice Bailey. The headmaster notices Peter's distraction. He picks up the book and handles its rice-paper pages with loving care.

"Have you read this book?" he asks.

"No."

"Have you heard of Bailey?"

"I'm not sure. Maybe. But I've never read anything by her."

"I'd like you to slowly become familiar with her writing style—it can be quite obtuse and feel outdated, but once you get used to her vocabulary, it flows a little better. Also, I'd like you to continue your studies of anatomy."

"Human anatomy?"

"Any kind of anatomy. Human, atomic, solar, bioenergetics—whatever kind of anatomy you feel most drawn to study. It should feel interesting. It should feel important. It should feel relevant to your work."

"Yes, sir. Of course."

"Have you read any of the Neale Donald Walsch books down in Maestro Garibaldi's room?"

"No, sir. I thought their titles looked a little hokey."

"Read those. At least the first five in the series."

"Yes, sir." Peter finally finds a space in which to insert his questions. "Headmaster? How do I—how does one direct energy into another object—one that is outside you?"

"Have you not figured out where your mind projects its will, Peter?"

"From the Third Eye?"

"Precisely," the Headmaster confirms. "When you feel or see the effects of vibrational waves on your organs, cells, or atoms, where is it that you are viewing from?"

"I'm not sure, sir. I just thought it was my eyes."

"Are your eyes open?"

"Well, no, sir. They're not."

"And you can claim to 'see' the effects, correct?"

"Yes, sir."

"And when you project these same effects, these waves, into specific aspects of your body, where are they coming from?"

"My mind. My thoughts."

"But is there not a point, a source from which you feel you have a vantage point?"

"I guess I always thought it was my eyes."

"And yet your eyes are closed."

"I see your point. My 'vision' must be coming from somewhere… just not my physiological eyes."

"Your Third Eye."

"So, is that the point from which I should practice projecting thought waves to other objects."

The Headmaster nods.

"But what if I harm them? What if the ripple effect of one of my thought bombs sets off a chain reaction of pain or damage?"

"Ah! Excellent question—a question that reveals to me that you are truly ready to undertake this new direction in your studies." The Headmaster looks upon Peter with moistened eyes. He looks happy. "There is a process by which we can prepare ourselves for the journey we are about to undertake that will align and attune your innermost being to the highest of intentions for yourself and the being or entity that you are hoping to interact with. In fact, I call it the 'Alignment and Attunement Process.' Practice it with sincere honesty and respect, and it will prevent any 'bad' from happening to either you or your target practice site. Would you like to learn it right now?"

"Yes, sir!"

"Okay," says the Headmaster. "Close your eyes. Visualize from that place in which your mind resides, the Third Eye, that you can see, or even feel, the energy flowing into and through your heart. We'll call it the 'Heart Center.' This is a vortex of energy flowing into and through your body. It is a flow of energy that is flowing to and feeding every cell, every atom, every quanta, of your body, but like the Third Eye, it has a point of centrality, a focal point that you can find use—"

"Where?!" Peter sounds a bit panicky.

"Ah, I go too fast," responds the Headmaster. "Okay. Let's slow down a bit." There is pause as he collects himself. "The *where* of a thing is not as important as the concept behind it. If you think 'Heart Center' or 'Third Eye,' that is enough. Spirit knows your intention. Your intention is by far the most important thing.

"With your practices thus far, you have learned to trust your imagination. Yes?" asks the Headmaster.

"I guess so," is Peter answer.

"Of course you have! Otherwise how could you have gone on pursuing further experimentations? You have observed things, effects, in a world that most people would say is imaginary because it cannot be scientifically validated. I mean, what scientist would credit you with the claims that you make about causing changes in the viscera or in molecular structures or at the atomic levels? No one! And yet you, with your practice, with the development of the 'muscle' of your Mind's Eye, you have seen these things!

"All humans—all beings of consciousness—have the same ability that you have discovered within yourself. Not all of them *use* the abilities of their Divine Creative Force; not all of them are allowed or taught or made aware of these abilities. And yet, you have been: you are growing in awareness of abilities that are granted to all of God's creatures. You are also using your knowledge of anatomy—human, molecular, atomic, and subatomic—to cast your experiments. I am here to tell you that you are on a valid and useful path of discovery. But you are also only in the beginning stages.

"You may have heard me say the axiom 'energy follows thought' before."

"It's been talked about in relation to our school motto," says Peter.

"Yes. Good," the Headmaster says. "The school motto: '*A posse de esse, mens agitat molem. Fiat lux.*' 'From possibility to reality, mind creates matter. Let there be light.'"

"Or, as Maestro Garibaldi would have us think, 'Everything is an illusion; we create our own reality, and let's party!'" Peter laughs.

"Maestro Garibaldi is an advanced student."

Peter sobers up.

"Think about it, Peter. 'Energy follows thought.' Isn't that the very principle behind your sound and thought experiments? Every 'wave' or effect you create is the result of a thought, a command, a desire, a wish."

"Yeah. I guess so."

"Well, the alignment and attunement process follows this same principle—the principle that intention is the most important matter in any creative process. When you create a link between you and another person or thing, you want to ask that that link be sacred, that it be accomplished or allowed *only* and *if* that link, that union, is mutually agreeable according to the will of both of your souls, if it is agreeable to the Will of the Cosmos—and that all things that transpire be according to the absolute Highest Good.

"Does that make sense to you, Peter?"

"I think so."

"So. Let's try an exercise. We're going to try to link the Heart Center with the Soul Center with the Third Eye in a kind of triangle."

"The 'Soul Center,' sir?"

"More on that later, but suffice it to visualize it as a point hovering about eighteen inches above the head. Can you try that? Remember, it's the in*ten*tion that is the most important. Believe me: there are many people who practice these principles who have never had a lesson or clue in anatomy of any kind. We of the West are just more familiar with visual types of maps and relationships. Let's try it.

"Close your eyes. Bring your attention to your Third Eye with the intention that that will be the point of your inner vision and the point from which you will focus the force of your Will—"

"Force, sir?"

"Yes, an unfortunate word that I cannot help. Think of it as 'benevolent force' or 'benevolent will,' as, remember, we are aiming to align and attune with the forces of the Highest Good."

"So, attention in the Third Eye. From the Third Eye visualize that you can draw a line of connective energy from your Heart Center, through your body and up to the Soul Center above your head. Try to feel the connection you've just made. Heart to Soul. You are asking them to be in alignment, to be in accord.

"Now draw your energy from the Soul Center down to the Ajna, the Eyebrow Center, your Third Eye. And then, finally, complete the triangle by drawing energy up to the Ajna from the Heart. Now

Heart, Soul, and Mind are all connected and aligned. You are operating with sacred intention.

"Now choose another human being whom you want to connect with. Better yet, choose me. Just call my presence into your field. Remember: energy follows thought; if you can imagine it, if you think it, it will be; it will become manifest—it will have energy.

"To do this, you will draw a line connecting your Soul Center with the Soul Center of the other being—in this case, with me."

"Sir? Does everyone have a Soul Center?"

"Yes! Not only everyone but every single form in Creation. If you can imagine it, then it exists, and it now has a Soul Center."

"But, sir! I don't get it! Do you mean to tell me that atoms, subatomic particles, even thoughts and ideas have souls?"

"Yes, but not in the way that we're used to thinking of them! The souls referred to in religious traditions are different. Strange, limited, and limiting creations created by limited, unseeing minds. The soul in the context of our purposes here is really just another name for the Spark of Creation—the Spark of the Divine that exists in any and every form that enters the realm of Creation. How could a thing exist without the animating force of God? It is impossible! Nothing can exist outside of God—not any one single thing. Otherwise, we would be limiting God; we would be diminishing the All-ness of the Oneness, the Source. Anything—everything—that enters Creation is the result of God's assistance, God's permission and, most importantly, God's presence."

"I get it!" Peter says rather calmly. "That's why everything is an illusion! 'Cuz it's all still a part of God! The illusion is that it somehow exists outside, separate from God—which is an impossibility!"

"Yes, Peter! God allows the illusion of separation to exist. So She can experience the imagined experience of what it might be like to exist outside Himself."

"Wait a minute. You said 'She' and then 'Himself.'"

"Yes," admits the Headmaster. "Damn pronouns. God doesn't really deserve to be cast into either category, for He-She-*We* is it all. And She is nothing."

"Why not make up a pronoun for God?"

"What! For whom?"

"Well, how about for us?"

"Okay. Let's do it. *You* do the honors, Peter. It's your idea."

"Okay. How about *xi*?"

"But that's a sound used in other languages. Chinese and Greek," the Headmaster points out.

"But not English," says Peter. "And, I'm assuming, we're going to be talking in English. So, if we want to create a new set of sounds for a word to be used in English, why not seek them from outside?"

"Okay," concedes the Headmaster, "but it still feels too base, too limiting, too strongly filled with human arrogance."

"Well. We are human, aren't we, Headmaster?" Peter asks rhetorically.

"Yes, Peter," the Headmaster responds, rather absently, even rotely. He is deep within his thoughts, praising and appraising this young sixteen-year-old boy sitting next to him. *Is he the one?*

"Are you okay, Headmaster?" Peter asks, sounding concerned.

"Yes, yes, I'm fine," the Headmaster answers. "I was just thinking. You *are* remarkable."

Peter blushes.

"Shall we continue with this little exercise? We've almost reached the pinnacle of what I was trying to share with you."

"Yes, sir. Alignment and attunement."

"Exactly. So, eyes closed, connect Heart Center to Soul Light—"

"Soul 'light'?" says Peter, interrupting. "I thought you said—"

"Yes, yes. A slip of the tongue. 'Soul Center' we're calling it. All 'centers.'

"So, Heart Center to Soul Center, Soul Center to Eyebrow Center, Heart Center to Eyebrow Center: the Triangle of Alignment. Now project a *questioning ray of connection* to the Soul Center of another—in this case, me. Don't question its place or existence; just call it forth and it will be there! Then ask for permission from my soul, for the highest good of me, Vittorio Visconti—or whatever you choose to call me—and the Cosmos.

"Now, on a rare occasion, you may feel the resistance or outright rejection of your request. Don't take this personally. It just means that this particular time is not a good time for your two souls to work together. That is, after all, part of the reason we *ask* for permission to work with the other entity: to receive permission. If we don't receive permission, it's okay. You will probably receive it later—in another attempt. Perhaps that soul is particularly occupied on a path of choices from which it does not want to vary. Perhaps the ego is feeling contrary or full of self-pity and is blocking any and all inputs or help from the Spirit world—"

"Excuse me, sir, but you keep referring to this as 'soul work' and 'soul connections.' But I find it hard to act as if I am doing 'soul work' or working within a 'spirit world' when I don't even have a grasp on what those things are. What is a 'soul'? What is this 'spirit world' you refer to? How do I fit into this scheme of things? Do all of the Brig-Wallis students get to this point? Are we all in training to do 'soul work'?"

"Excellent questions, all, Peter," answers the Headmaster with a look of paternal care. "But, if you will please allow me the benefit of your doubt to *not* answer these questions at this time—with the promise that all of these questions and many, many more will be answered in due time—I would instead like to set you free to both read some of the books I have suggested to you and practice the alignment and attunement process with things and beings of your choice. Remember: so long as you hold yourself and your target 'soul' in the Light of the Highest Good, you cannot do any harm. Will you do that for me?"

"Yes, sir. I can, sir. Thank you, sir. I hope I'm not being a pest—and that I prove worthy of your trust and confidence."

"You'll practice?"

"Yes, sir."

"And come back to read when you have time?"

"Yes, sir."

"Shall we plan on meeting again, face to face, to see how you're managing, say, the same time next week?"

"Yes, sir! Thank you, sir!" Peter says. They both get to their feet. "I think I'll see if I can get one of the Neale Donald Walsch books from the Psych Room."

"If Herr Garibaldi is around. If not, come back here and you can have my copy."

"Yes, sir. Thank you, sir." Peter says, starting for the door. In the doorway, he stops and turns back to face the Headmaster. "Headmaster?"

"Yes, Peter?"

"Thank you so much for doing this for me. I can't tell you how much it means to me to have not only a little guidance but someone who believes in me—someone who validates the work that I've been doing."

"Peter, it is, in all sincerity, my pleasure. This is precisely the kind of development and initiative that Brig-Wallis was founded to try to nurture and encourage."

And with that Peter turns and leaves.

He could be the one! is the thought dominating the Headmaster's brain as he watches the human form calling itself "Peter Vandenhof" walk away from him and into the shadows. *Finally!*

10

LA BONNE ANNÉE BALL

Over the next week, Peter works on exploring the source materials and concepts the Headmaster shared with him. But there seem to be so many distractions. Classes are a distraction. Classmates are a distraction. Sleep is a distraction. Though he skips a few, even meals are a distraction. And then there is a ball! The Bonne Année Ball in Montreux.

As usual, the entire second-year class (the thirteen who remain) is required to attend. The first ball of the New Year, it is talked about by the staff as if it is a nice one—perhaps the fanciest one of the year. Apparently, the Salon de Quatre Saisons ballroom at the Grand Hôtel Suisse Majestic is quite opulent with its mirrors and crystal chandeliers and baroque decor. Peter is bothered and distracted, but, as the train approaches Lac Léman and he sees the lights of the lake's outlying homes and villages and towns, he begins to feel some excitement. *If it's meant to happen, it'll happen,* he finds himself thinking—about the girl in the green dress. *No expectations,* and, *Just go with the flow,* he finds himself repeating.

As the limousine van approaches the beautiful hotel, Peter finds his stomach aflutter. It is a spectacular building, fully lit for the evening's event. Inside, the ballroom is a large oval-shaped room with striking gilded gold over porcelain-white wall-and-ceiling ornamentation. Crystal and mirrors seem to sparkle from every nook and cranny. The electric lights are dimmed low, with faux candlelight emanating from the wall-mounted fixtures between the mirrors, doors, and windows.

Peter is suddenly shaken from his admiring gaze by the sound of a piano—a beautiful, full-length, grand piano. After a few measures, he recognizes that he is hearing perfection, that it is being played by a true master of the instrument: nothing sloppy or overembellished, nothing labored or pretentious; it is all perfectly concise and...*spiritual.* That is the only word he can come up with to describe what he feels, what the effect of the playing is having on him. The effect is like that of his harp. *God-speak.*

Just as Peter is about to start moving closer to the stage from which the instrumentalist is casting his spell, the pianist is joined by strings. *A string quartet!* And, he can see by looking around the room, this is probably going to be the sole source of music for the night. Peter can hardly contain his excitement.

He takes a moment to close his eyes, to turn his gaze inward, and to "watch" the response of all of his being to the beautiful, heavenly music. *Beethoven,* he recognizes in a state of utter bliss.

Suddenly, he is startled out of his *sentiments élevés* by a tug on his sleeve. He opens his eyes to see a petite girl in a stunning ball gown with billowing opalescent white skirts looking at him. "Would you like to dance?" she asks.

Swept up in the moment, he says yes without thinking and then over theatrically sweeps his partner up and out onto the floor.

Peter does not think of himself as a very good dancer—though, like for most of his peers, ballroom classes had been a requirement in his middle school years. He can still hear the voice of his mother claiming, "You'll need it for when you're an adult!" But he had hated every minute of dance lessons and resisted learning any of it. Or so he thought. But tonight, under the spell of this music, he feels uplifted and light on his feet, rhythmic and confident, enthusiastic, and surprisingly social. He surprises himself when the phrase, *I am a conduit of Light and Love,* passes through his mind. *I'd like to remember that one,* he thinks to himself. *I am a conduit of Light and Love,* he repeats.

And so Peter passes the first hour of the dance, dancing with one partner after another—all excited to ask him as, he feels, *I must be glowing!* And *I'm Fred Astaire!* Some of his partners are quite pretty—though he wouldn't care what they look like, so caught up is he in moving with the music, allowing the music to move through him—through him and through his hands into his partner. He feels as if they could not but *help* but be as one, as the power of the music, the power of Light and Love flowing through him, make him feel invincible, *inviolable.*

After what feels like a dozen partners—Peter has lost track—the quintet stops to take a break. Part of his being feels relieved, for he is beginning to feel his muscles screaming for a break, yet he also feels an intense disappointment, as he doesn't want it to stop—doesn't want to lose his momentum.

Water, he finds himself thinking, his cells communicating to his unconscious.

As soon as he turns to head toward one of the refreshment tables, he sees her. It is *her.* Leaning against a wall, against the window curtains, just to the left of one of the refreshment tables—almost as if she were purposely hiding among shadows of the heavy silk brocade curtains—It's the girl in the green dress, the girl with the Egyptian eyes, the girl who has occupied his dreams over the past months. Once he sees her, he is certain it is her. And she is wearing a dark-red dress! The same dark-red dress he saw in the first dreamlike vision he had of her on that train ride back from the Bienvenue Ball in the autumn.

Peter assesses his body and emotions as he stands watching the girl and her Egyptian eyes. He is quite surprised by the sobering effect her sudden appearance has on him. The ecstatic high of the music and dancing is still resonating in his atoms and cells, but his body feels heavy, his soul…cautious.

Finally, her eyes meet his. This time—though the rest of the world falls away, ceases to exist—like before—Peter is not overcome with nausea.

She, on the other hand, appears more reserved, even guarded—though her eyes are as locked and unflinching as before. And yet, her body language is more…*reserved* is the only word he can come up with. *Perhaps she is tired,* he thinks. *Or* sick. "You come to me," her being seems to be saying to him.

He approaches her feeling confident, bold. Then, all at once, he is there.

As he stands directly in front of her, their eyes still locked, she continues leaning against the wall, holding a crystal punch glass in her gloved hands.

"Remember me?" he says, purposely playing with the words she had used in their previous encounter.

"Of course," she says, continuing to look into his eyes, though, he notices, occasionally darting down to look at his mouth.

"There was a time when I couldn't get you out of my head," he finds himself saying. *What am I saying? I didn't practice this!*

"I know," is her response.

"You do?!"

She nods.

Such a beautiful, elegant move, he finds himself thinking.

"You've been in *my* dreams, too," she says without guile or shame.

"What is your name?" he blurts out almost panicky, as if something might suddenly rip them apart—like before.

"Meela," she says.

"What an unusual and beautiful name!" he thinks out loud. Realizing he's revealed something more than he intended, he blushes.

"Aren't you cute," she says, half-teasing, half-touched.

This only adds to his discomfort. He squirms and blushes more deeply.

She reaches out a hand to touch his arm, saying, "I'm sorry! I didn't mean—"

"No! No! I'm just…not used to…this—"

"What? Girls?"

"Yeah, well, yeah," he confesses, a bit relieved.

"It's okay," she consoles a little flatly. "You're doing fine." She seems distracted.

"Are you okay?" he asks genuinely concerned.

"I'll be fine," she says. "Just…you know. Cramps."

"Oh," he says before comprehending the fullness of her disclosure. *Oh! Shit!* Now he *real*ly turns red.

"Sorry," she says, genuinely apologetic but obviously tired. "Fact of life," she adds.

"Can I get you anything?" he asks, mostly out of awkward desperation.

"Aren't you sweet," she says, touching his arm again. "My knight in shining armor."

Please don't take your hand back! his soul is screaming. Oddly, this time she keeps her hand on his forearm, resting there, almost as light as a feather, and yet, somehow, *linked*—feeling so warm and connected to him.

Increasingly self-conscious of the growing and awkward silence befalling them, Peter nervously blurts out, "Would you like to dance?"

She perks a little, looks around them. "But there is no music."

His head is screaming with the agony of embarrassment at his blunder and blatant stupidity. The tumult roiling inside him prevents him from speaking—prevents him from finding words.

"But, yes, I would love to dance with you when the band starts back up again."

Saved! his mind is shouting again. *Thank you!*

He turns to face the dance floor, pretending that finding out whether or not the band is getting ready to start back up again is important to him.

All the while, Meela's hand has remained resting gently on his arm. *Attached. Married.*

He plops his tailbone back against the wall, just next to the girl in the red dress. *This is nice.* He can feel her subtly scooch up against his side.

"Mmmm," she purrs. "You're warm."

Instinctively, he places his arm behind her back and draws her into his chest. She is nearly his same height, he notices. *But then, I'm only five-eight,* he thinks.

"Thank you," she says as she snuggles in without a fight. Peter feels as if she is melting into him. Soon, he senses that she might even be falling asleep.

Suddenly, he notices that the musicians are reentering the room. He straightens his spine slightly, which causes Meela to stir from her warm torpor. That's when he notices her lack of shoes.

"Cindermeela! Whatever have you done with your shoes?"

"Oh, those stupid things! They got ruined in the slush at the bottom of the stairs of our dorm. By the time I got here, my soaked feet were icy cold. I left them…at the front desk. They said they would try to dry them."

"How?" Peter asks, drowning in the mellifluous sound of her voice combined with the inexplicable feeling of her touch—begging that it never stop.

"I don't know," she answers. "A hotel as nice as this one? I'm sure they'll find a way." And then she adds, "It probably happens all the time."

"Probably."

I think I love you, he finds his mind saying. His ego recoils, thinking, *So glad to not have leaked that one out loud,* as he stiffens his body and self-consciously removes his arm from behind Meela. *This is ridiculous!* his ego is shouting. *You're not even sixteen! You're a kid!*

I know, insists another, far calmer, voice. *This is different. This supersedes time.*

WTF! screams the ego. *What does that mean? What is 'supersedes'?*

"What are you thinking?" Meela asks just before suddenly straightening up and twirling to face him. "What is your name, Mister Knight in Shining Armor?"

He smiles. *She is* ex*traor*d*inary!* he thinks. "My name is Peter," he answers. "And I was thinking how extraordinary you are."

Their eyes lock again for several seconds. The music starts up again, this time with a solo viola leading the way. A collective swoon passes through the room as many of the teens in the dance hall recognize the song. Debussy. *String Quartet. In G…minor. Will they play the whole thing?* Peter wonders.

While not feeling the adrenaline response of his first exposure to the night's quintet, Peter is quite happy to perform the universal motion of offering his hand in order to formally accompany his partner to the dance floor. She responds appropriately, allowing him to lead the way.

They inch up to one another to get into starting position for the first movement of this *tempo rubato* suite. Peter's hand initiates their movement, guiding Meela firmly through his pressure in her midback. Their dancing is effortless and easy despite his hyperawareness of the combination of his shoes and her bare feet.

It's different, Peter finds himself thinking. *Now there is thinking and decision-making,* whereas before he seemed to feel as if the *mu*sic was telling him what to do.

This music seems to be taking him through an entire spectrum of emotions and speeds. In the soft, delicate parts of the second movement, Peter feels compelled to go faster, to spin, like a Russian ballerina or a Sufi dervish, only he has this extension of himself.

That's it! He thinks. *She is an* ex*ten*s*ion of me! And I of her!* For that is truly how he feels: when they are touching, it is difficult for him to discern where he ends and she begins. Even on the molecular level: everything is cooperating in perfect unison, in perfect harmony, in perfect and absolute joy and comfort.

As the quartet moves into the third movement, Peter is unsure of whether or not to continue dancing. He stops and looks up at the stage. Many of the dancers around him are dispersing. This is the moment when Meela chooses to wrap her arms around Peter's back, nestling her head into the crook between his head and shoulder. Without thinking, he envelopes her body and slowly rocks and sways with the slow, delicate music. Meela steps onto Peter's shoes, whispering into his ear, "Does that hurt you?"

"I feel nothing," he says, though he is lying: he feels utter bliss, profound peace, and absolute joy.

They continue to find ways to tighten their embrace as Peter rocks back and forth to the music, feet never moving, never leaving their place on the floor. Chins, cheeks, ears, shoulder, chests, stomachs, hands—all subtly moving, trying to find ways to get closer, to merge. It's such an odd feeling—odd to observe for Peter—as nothing like this has ever possessed him before, and yet nothing has ever felt so natural, so right.

The quartet finishes the third movement and stops. The piano begins to introduce the next piece—Brahms's Quintet number 34. Peter decides to take Meela off the dance floor. He wants to talk—to find out more about her—to find out how they can correspond, how they can get together again.

"I could dance with you forever," Peter says, "But I want to know so much about you—I want to talk."

"That's fine," Meela says. "We've danced before, you know."

Where does she get these things? he thinks, remembering her cryptic greeting from their last meeting.

Peter grabs Meela by the hand and leads her out of the ballroom, into the hallway, and eventually to the hotel lobby. "I thought we'd check on your shoes."

"My shoes!" she says as she pitter-pats up down the hallway and up to the front desk.

"*Excusez-moi, Monsieur,*" she says, leaning her forearms onto the high desktop. "*Avez-vous mes chaussures? Sont-elles déjà sec?*"

The hotel desk person turns and goes into a back room. Less than a minute later, he returns to the front desk carrying a pair of medium-heeled velvet red dress shoes. He is wiping them clean with a snow-white hand towel. "*Voilà! Je suis désolé, Mademoiselle!*" He hands Meela the shoes. "*Elles ne sont pas propres.*" Meela smiles, curtsies, and says, "*Merci très très beaucoups, Monsieur Mon Champion! Vous-êtes mon héros!*" before turning and running back to where Peter is standing in the middle of the lobby.

Peter has been thoroughly enjoying every second of Meela's performance, every nuance of her movements, every inflection and *r* in her beautiful French. But, he notices, he is ecstatically happy that she came back to him.

"Shall we sit down? To see if they fit?"

"We shall!" she teases, scurrying on her tiptoes to one of the lobby's plush settees, where she plops herself down.

"Are they dry?" asks Peter as he sits next to her.

"Better than when I arrived, but, no, they're still damp. And they've shrunk. Throwaways!" she says as she drops them beside her before falling sideways, wrapping her arms around Peter's arm. "Tell me a story, Peter!"

Peter's brain freezes. *A story?* He can't think of one. Finally, he starts ad-libbing. "There once was a girl in a mint-green dress—"

"Mint green? How do you know it was mint green?"

"Well, I don't," he smiles. "I'm calling it 'mint green' because it seemed to me the exact same color of my favorite flavor ice cream—mint chocolate chip."

"You like mint chocolate chip ice cream?"

"Yes, though I like it best mixed or covered with marshmallow topping."

"Hmm."

"Do you like ice cream?"

"Oh, yes!" she says. "Don't get me started on ice cream!"

"Why not?" Peter says, very much enjoying their light banter.

"Because there's one kind of ice cream that everybody should have—'cuz it's the *best*!"

I love how she says "best," he thinks before saying, "And what flavor is that?"

"Blackberry." Peter raises his eyebrows in feigned surprise. "But it has to be blackberry ice cream from the merry-go-round at Watch Hill. It's the *best*!"

"Watch Hill?! Rhode Island?!"

"Why, yes! How *did* you know?" she says, overacting her reaction.

"Because, Miss Dorothy, it just so happens that I have *been* there."

"You have, have you? Then perhaps we *have* met before."

Peter is suddenly putting their previous meeting into a whole new context. *Have we met before? Was she being quite literal before, or was it as layered as I thought?*

"Have you ever been to Kansas?" she adds, obviously adding to their play on *The Wizard of Oz.*

"No. Have you?"

"Actually, no," she says in a more flattened voice. "Have you really been to Watch Hill?"

"Have we actually met before?"

Meela does not respond immediately. Instead she leans in toward Peter's face and stares deep into his eyes for a full twenty seconds. "Yes, we have definitely met before."

"At Watch Hill?" Peter asks.

"Is that where you're from?"

"No, but I've visited there. I've actually ridden that merry-go-round before."

"Did you ever get the brass ring?" She's acting little-girlish again.

"I don't remember." Peter ruminates. "I don't think I ever tried." Still thinking. "I didn't really get the whole merry-go-round thing," he admits.

"I got it five times in a row!"

Peter tries to look duly impressed—though he doesn't really understand the relevance.

"Where are you from?" He decides to change the subject. "I mean, originally. Where were you born? Where do your parents live?"

"I was born in Westerly, Rhode Island. I grew up in Mystic and Stonington. My parents live in New Brunswick. I go to school here, in Montreux, at Surval—"

"I've heard of that!" Peter interrupts.

Meela turns her face toward Peter with one eyebrow raised high above her right eye. *She has serious scars in both her eyebrows!* he notes before adding, *This girl is a handful!*

"How can I see you again?" he blurts out, quite under her spell.

"Well, if you're anything like me, you'll probably be seeing quite a bit of me for a while—in your dreams!" she laughs.

"No, seriously!" He is struggling with his words—wary of saying more than he can handle—more that he really knows the meaning of.

"Well, that depends on many factors." She is thinking while looking upon his face. "Do you ski?"

"Yes, but not here."

"What? You ski—you live in Switzerland—but you don't ski *here*?!"

"Actually, that's right."

"What kind of a school do you go to? A military school?"

Peter hesitates, unsure as to how to answer. "Yeah. Kind of."

"So…they don't let you out very often?"

"Kind of."

"You're kind of freaking me out here." Then she adds suspiciously, "Who are you?"

"Peter! I'm Peter! Swear to God!"

"What's your last name, Peter Swear-to-God?"

"Vandenhof."

"Hmph." She breathes. "Means nothing. Don't know any Vandenhofs."

"It doesn't matter," says Peter feeling a little down at this turn of events.

"Aww. Don't sulk, Peter Vandenhof. We will be together again. *That* I *know!*"

There, she's doing it again!

"I just don't know when or how."

"What do you mean?" asks Peter—almost pleading.

"Well, what I know is that you and I have known each other before. We've danced many, *ma*ny times before. And I believe we both came here again to be together again. I just don't know the timing of it all." And then, looking straight into Peter's eyes, "But I do know that it's *all* in divine order!"

"What do you mean? You keep saying the weirdest things! I don't understand." Peter leaps to his feet. "No, it's *you* who's freaking *me* out!"

He starts to walk briskly away, his mind addled and way overstimulated.

Just as he's rounding the corner to head back down the hallway that accesses the ballroom, M. Montechenin practically runs into him.

"Peter!" says Montechenin. "Just the chap I was hoping to find." He looks around as if for more familiar faces. "It's just about time to leave, Peter, and I was hoping you would help me round up the others."

"Sure," says Peter a little numbly, feeling a sudden rush of relief—thankful for the distraction.

"Aces!" says Montechenin. "You take the ballroom, and I'll check the bathrooms and hallways."

"Yes, sir. No problem."

"Great! Meet you all in front of the cloakroom. Wait there."

"Sure thing!"

A few minutes later, the music has stopped, the lights are up, and members of the hotel staff are moving around, beginning the process of cleanup. Peter has gathered together ten of his compatriots and is trying to get them to move as a unit to the coatroom near the front lobby.

As they reach the coatroom, M. Montechenin happens to be arriving with the other three stragglers. They all procure their coats—Montechenin tipping the clerk lavishly—and then they parade out the front door to the awaiting limo van.

Peter, of course, is peeling his vision for one last—*any*—glimpse of the girl in the red dress. Meela.

It does not happen.

Then, on the drive to the train station, he thinks he catches a glimpse of the back of her walking up a hilly side street. The most suspicious evidence is that the girl in question is stutter-stepping up the cobblestone street with the heels of her bare feet sticking out of the back ends of her shoes.

We shall meet again, Meela of Surval School in Montreux, he thinks. *Next time maybe I'll be ready.*

Then the weirdest thing happens: he swears he catches a glimpse of the girl in the street turning around to look toward him and wave, while, at the exact same time, he hears an unmistakable voice in his head saying, "*Á la prochaine, mon autre!*" He shakes his head vigorously, prompting glances from several of his classmates.

"Anything the matter, Peter?" asks Emil.

"Something spookin' you?" chimes Adam.

"No. I'm fine," he responds.

"So, who was that girl you were dancing with there in the second half, Peter?" asks Loïck.

"Yeah! You guys looked tight!" Adam says.

"Did you suck face?" Michael prods.

"No one," Peter says. "Just a girl." Then he adds, "I danced with lots of girls tonight."

"Yeah, but not like *that* one," leers Loïck.

"Yeah. Did you know her?" Joe-pa asks. "An old flame or something?"

"No! Nothing!" Peter erupts. "Please stop with the questions!"

"Okay, cool! Just askin'!" Joe-pa backs off, then turns his attention to a different compatriot. "What about you, Loïck—"

The rest of the trip home is fairly uneventful—except for Peter's fixated mind. Try as he might, he just can't stop replaying every second of every minute from the night, even the dancing before his encounter with Meela. *What a night!* And *What to make of that girl—that strange and schizoid girl?* His mind wanders, various scenes replaying themselves, eliciting a panoply of emotions: smiles, embarrassment, bliss, utter confusion, stark fear, overwhelm.

The replaying of the night's memories proves so exhausting that Peter falls asleep before the train is fifteen minutes out of Montreux. When the train arrives at the *bahnhof* in Brig, M. Montechenin respectfully awakens his charges, but Peter finds himself feeling exhausted, numb, and shredded.

On the walk home, he can't stop thinking of that last scene: "*Á la prochaine, mon autre!*" *What the heck does it mean?* Even while performing his preparations for bed, while crumpling up under his down comforter, while drifting off to a deep sleep, his mind is reeling with questions and confusion.

11

DOWNWARD SPIRAL

Peter doesn't sleep well that night. He sleeps through Chapel and breakfast. When he does rise, he feels groggy and not his usual self.

He goes downstairs to the yogurt-and-granola bar in his pajamas. He then decides to eat in one of the comfortable lounge chairs in one of the living quarters of the first-year students. Facing the fire in the fireplace, he slouches in his chair, spooning his breakfast mix into his mouth. He loves this lounge. *So many good memories here…things were much simpler then.*

The current tenants flit in and out of the room from time to time—at first choosing not to bother their upperclassman interloper—whispering their musings as they pass by. But then a first-year stops.

"Are you all right?" he asks.

"Yeah," Peter says, then adds, "Girl problems."

The first-year chuckles.

"Don't ever get involved with them," Peter says. *That was dumb!*

Left alone, finished with his breakfast, Peter gets lost in another montage of memories from the previous night: the highs of dancing, the music, the confusion set off by the girl, the awkwardness of the ride home, the extraordinary feeling of peace and calm when he and she were touching, her weirdness, her beauty, those *eyes*!

The remainder of Peter's morning is pretty much a waste. He tries dressing but nothing feels good, so he keeps on his pajama bottoms and throws on a T-shirt. *Thank God it's Sunday!*

Meditation goes nowhere. He tries a walk, but it's raining. *In January!* Still, the rain feels good on his face and hands.

When he gets back, he showers and dresses and then tries to get focused for his Sunday appointment with the Headmaster.

The visit goes badly. He explains to Headmaster Visconti that the week was too busy for any practice with alignment and attunement and, though he did manage to get a copy of *Conversations with God* from Maestro Garibaldi's classroom, he had not had time to get into it—all of which are lies—which makes Peter feel worse. But the biggest "lie" weighing down on Peter throughout his visit and over the course of the following weeks is his concealment of his encounter with Meela.

A few days later, Peter is able to admit to himself that she had "rocked his world"—though not necessarily in a good way. His meeting her had thrown him off course. He cannot help it. Try as he might, Peter has trouble focusing, has trouble with his mind frequently wandering. He finds himself losing track of classroom discussions or conversations at the meal table, and he most certainly has trouble with meditation and working on his thought-transmission experiments. He just can't seem to focus—and it really bothers him. Self-discipline, focus, and concentration are all things that he had prided himself on. They used to come so easily. And now he feels as if he has lost them.

Over the course of the next few weeks, Peter becomes increasingly withdrawn, distant, and irritable. Everybody notices. But everybody decides to give Peter his space.

Except Emil.

Though Peter would say that he felt the same degree of friendship with *all* of his classmates, he is more aloof than he knows. All the boys like him. Nobody dislikes him. But he is self-involved. Emil Frederick, however, had become quite devoted to Peter. Not in a pesky, annoying way; just in a kind of 'silent shadow' way. And so it is Emil who finally tries to get Peter to talk.

He decides to confront his friend in the private confines of Peter's room—which is where Peter has been hanging out a lot lately anyway.

"Peter. Could we please discuss what it is that's been bothering you?" Emil asks.

Peter looks up at Emil as if surprised that someone else is in the room. It is obvious from the look on his face that he didn't hear what Emil said.

"I know something's bothering you," Emil says, pressing on. "We *all* do. You've been so different—so distant and…well…so grumpy…" *Since the dance,* he wants to say but can't manage it.

"What do you mean?" Peter responds, feigning innocence. "I don't understand."

"You've been…different," says Emil, unable to find a new or better word.

"Have I?" Peter continues hiding. "I'm sorry." He puts his head back into the book that he'd been trying to read.

Emil decides to bulldoze ahead. "Ever since the ball." He watches as Peter's body suddenly stiffens. Lips pursed, he turns to Emil, fixing a piercing stare upon him.

"Is it the girl? The girl from the ball?" Emil presses further.

"No," says Peter emphatically.

"I can't think of anything else. I *know* you didn't drink or do drugs—"

"It isn't the girl," Peter says, his voice causing a sudden chill in the room.

"Come on, Peter," Emil pushes on. "It's okay to talk about it. You don't have to do this all alone—"

"Please leave now, Emil," Peter says. "I don't want to talk about it. I don't want you here right now." The strain of trying to keep his emotions under wraps is audible in his voice.

"Peter." Emil plods along. "You can't go on like this! It's not healthy! You're not *you* anymore—"

"*Get the fuck out of my room,* Emil!" spews from Peter's mouth.

Emil visibly recoils.

"You don't know what the fuck you're talking about, and why would I share anything with a little fuck like you?" Peter practically yells—feeling the flood of remorse and regret as soon as the words come tumbling out.

He turns his head and looks away.

Emil stares at Peter a moment. Seeing no change—no softening or retraction coming—he gets to his feet and retreats slowly from Peter's room.

Peter continues going through the motions of daily routines. He shows up for everything (except for music during evening free time) but is only half-engaged in any activity. His attempts at meditation are all fuzzy and blank, or else they are filled with spiraling thoughts of self-loathing, paranoia, and fear. His attempts at physical exercise slump into daily habits of walking aimlessly around the streets of Brig—sometimes not returning until well after suppertime. He is completely oblivious to the new absence of his former "shadow," Emil. And, though he continues upholding his commitment to visiting the Headmaster's office on Sundays, it is all just show. His replies to any of the Headmaster's inquiries into his health or reading are always curt and vague. "Fine," and "Haven't had much time," or "It's interesting," are pat responses—though, in fact, he is making no progress in any of his extracurricular "studies."

The Headmaster, for his part, has long noticed the change in Peter. As is his habit, he chooses to watch—to observe the ways in which the individual student chooses to deal with his "crisis." Though he knows nothing of the cause of Peter's distress and distraction, he knows from close observation and through the input of others that Peter is not battling with an addiction. Still, he can see that Peter's conflict with his "inner demons" is not going well.

So one Sunday he chooses to confront Peter during one of their regular meetings.

Peter realizes he is in for a reckoning as soon he sees the Headmaster close the office door behind them. He takes a seat on the couch at the opposite end of the room from the Headmaster's desk and braces himself. Quickly, he recognizes that part of him welcomes this.

"Headmaster," Peter is the first to speak, surprising both of them. "I've got something that's been troubling me."

Headmaster Visconti looks on, eyebrows raised, saying nothing.

"A while ago—back in the fall," Peter begins, "at the Bienvenue Ball, as a matter of fact, I met a girl."

The Headmaster sits back against his desk.

"It was the weirdest thing that's ever happened to me," Peter continues. "It was like—when we met—the rest of the world disappeared. Like it just ceased to exist! Like the only real thing in the...*u*niverse was us and our connection. As a matter of fact, in those moments that we first locked eyes, it felt like eons—lifetimes—many, many forms and places—passed by—right in front of my eyes! It was the weirdest thing: so unsettling and confusing! I can't explain it—can't do it justice. It was just...so...unexpected! And so unlike anything that's ever happened to me before." He stops to look up. Seeing the Headmaster's attentive gaze, he forges ahead.

"And then I would dream about her. Every night! And each time she'd be dressed differently. And sometimes she'd be in different bodies, at different ages! But the eyes...the eyes were always the same.

"Anyway. I didn't see her again at any of the other balls. So, gradually, the excitement and curiosity of that first meeting just faded away. The dreams stopped coming. I was back to normal. But then, at the New Year's Ball, she was there. We connected again. We danced. We talked. And she was so weird! She said the weirdest things! It freaked me out! And then I ran away from her! She was just freaking me out! I had to get away! And then we came home." He looks up into the Headmaster's eyes. "But I can't get her out of my head. There were things that were so weird...but *wonder*ful...and then there were things that were so weird that they scare me to death!" He changes his tone. "Well, not to death. Only to...distraction."

The Headmaster looks on a minute, again choosing not to speak, choosing, instead, to listen.

"And now," Peter recommences, "I've gotten stuck in these loops of vision and words, and I'm not here—I'm always in my own head! I'm not paying attention in class. I'm not doing *any* work with *this* stuff," he says while holding up the Alice Bailey book he brought with him. "And I'm shutting out my friends. But I can't help it! I'm feeling so *ang*ry! So alone and frustrated!"

Headmaster Visconti continues looking on, waiting patiently. Seeing that Peter has reached the end of his confession, he speaks. "And how do you feel right now?"

"Tired. But good," he responds. "It feels good to have let it out. To have shared it."

"And why is it, do you think, that you've not been able to share this with anyone before today?"

"'Cuz it's so weird!" Peter responds. "The stuff she said. The dreams. They're not normal! These aren't the kind of things that happen to normal people!"

"So, then, you are thinking that you are not normal?"

"Yeah. I guess," he says. "I *know she's* not normal. I'm not even sure she's human! Or real! I could be imagining the whole thing! Maybe I'm going crazy."

"I'm curious," starts the Headmaster. "What are some of the things she said?"

"Oh, I don't know," Peter says. "Like, 'Remember me?' the first time we met!" He looks sharply at the Headmaster. "And, no! We had never met before!

"Then she said something about us having met many times before and, later, that she didn't know why or when but that we 'came here' to be together 'again.'" Then, looking straight at the Headmaster again, he adds, "And I don't think she was talking about the ball or Montreux but about Earth! And about other lifetimes! Like we'd been together in past lives!"

"And is that something that troubles you?"

"I don't know. *Yes!*" he answers. "I don't know anything about past lives! I've never had anyone in my life *talk* about them before. I know we've talked about some weird stuff in Psych Class—alternative time lines and universes and out-of-body experiences and stuff. And your meditations definitely leave open all kinds of possibilities—but past lives? And all in a look? In dreams? In the words coming out of a teenage girl?"

The Headmaster is smiling. "New information can arise from the most unexpected places," he says.

"So you think I'm right? That she's talking about past lives?"

"That, my dear boy, is for you to discern. But I do know that first encounters with new information can provoke very defensive responses in us—especially if it is information that is far out of our previous knowledge or experience base."

"Do you believe in past lives, Headmaster?"

The Headmaster hesitates, weighing the possible effects of his response choices. "I do, Peter," he answers.

"Do you know your past lives?"

"Some," is the Headmaster's initial response. Seeing the flood of questions on Peter's face, he decides to expand. "It is my belief that past lives and alternate versions of Self are made available to the individual according to his readiness and/or need."

Peter looks lost.

"I have had the good fortune of being made aware of alternate 'stories' of my Self that seem to offer information that has proved helpful or appropriate to this, Vittorio Visconti, version of my Self."

"When you say 'version of yourself' you are meaning past lives?" asks Peter.

"That which you and I are calling 'past lives' is one form of information that can prove useful to our growth and progress here on Earth."

"So, what do you think I saw in her eyes—in our connection?"

"What do *you* think it could have been?"

"It feels like it was a history. A superfast video replay of all our history."

The Headmaster looks on with his eyebrow arched. He says nothing.

"But how?" Peter continues. "And how could a teenage girl know about stuff like that?"

"Aren't *you* a teenager with special insights, special talents?"

"Well, that's different. That's scientific."

"Which is another way of saying 'repeatable information flow.'"

"I guess—"

"Which may be what this girl is doing."

Peter pauses for a moment. "But her information—her way of talking was so…natural, so matter-of-fact. It was like she *knew*. She had no doubt, no question. It was all so familiar and comfortable to her."

"Isn't your world of directed thought waves familiar, comfortable, natural, and matter-of-fact to you?"

"No. Not like her. With her it was like she was *born* with this knowledge. As if she came to Earth knowing…*ev*erything!"

"Have you attempted to contact this girl? Since the ball?"

"No. I don't know her name," he lies. "Or where she lives." Once again Peter feels immediately self-conscious and guilty for his act of concealment.

The Headmaster senses Peter's guile. "Perhaps you will see her at the next ball."

"Maybe," he responds. "Truth be known, I'm pretty scared to see her again."

"And why is that?"

"'Cuz of the way I behaved last time. You know, running away like I did." He pauses, looking from his hands to the Headmaster. "She freaked me out!"

"Does her insight and information still 'freak you out'?"

Peter takes a minute to consider. "No. Not really," he answers. "I mean: I'm still a bit freaked out that I know someone who claims to *know* that we're connected. I mean, the implications of that!"

"What implications do you mean?"

"Well, for one: Does this mean I have to *marry* her? I mean, if we're destined to be together, then doesn't that, like, make any other relationships kind of...irrelevant? A waste of time?"

"No, I don't think so. Not necessarily," the Headmaster responds. "If you've heard the term 'soul mate'—" Peter nods. "Then, I will inform you that a soul mate is not necessarily someone that you affix yourself to for all eternity as if there is no choice. One of the points of the human experience is to allow us to try to rediscover or relearn for ourselves that we are *al*ways in choice—that you are *al*ways the creator of the course of your life.

"Also," the Headmaster continues, "the term 'soul mate' is much overused and overinflated. A soul mate is someone who puts you into a place or pattern from which you then have the opportunity to learn important things about your Self and the universe. A soul mate is a representative of the community of spiritual beings with whom your own Higher Self has worked many, many times. A soul mate can take the form of a person who is in your life for a short while—a year, a day, a few minutes. Sometimes that is all it takes for two soul mates to make their impact—to shake up each other's worlds."

"So you think her world has been shaken up, too?" Peter asks.

"I cannot answer that," the Headmaster says. "But I do know that your experience of meeting and interacting with this extraordinary young lady does not seal your fate or 'destiny' for the rest of your life. I cannot impress upon you more that you are *al*ways, *always*, in choice. Every single choice you make comes with its own set of consequences—its own set of learning opportunities—as well as its own set of new choices. There are no right or wrong choices, only new ones to make after each preceding one."

"There is one more thing I'd like to share with you, Headmaster," Peter says slowly. "Something I just can't get my head around." He pauses with a pleading look in his eyes. "Maybe you'd have an opinion."

The Headmaster appears attentive.

"Every time this girl and I…touched—any time we had any kind of physical contact—I was filled with the most amazing sense of warmth, of calmness, of *whole*ness, of carefreeness. It was like nothing else mattered in the world—in the universe. As if that touch, that contact, that connection, was the most important, most liberating thing in the world." A tear streaks down Peter's face. "It was so beautiful, so comforting, so natural. Our touch was like a message that everything else was just little stuff—just petty stuff—just make-believe, and that our connection was the real thing—the *only* thing that was real."

Peter looks up to find the Headmaster gazing affectionately at him.

"It sounds beautiful, Peter," the Headmaster says.

"It was," Peter says as he crumples over, giving way to unsuppressed sobs.

"And you miss it," the Headmaster says, walking over toward the couch, placing his hand on Peter's back.

"I do," comes Peter's muffled response. He continues sobbing, releasing weeks, even months of pent-up frustration and confusion.

The Headmaster stands silently, gently holding his hand in place on Peter's back, occasionally moving it in a rubbing motion.

Eventually, Peter's weeping subsides. He leans over against one of the arms of the couch, pressing a pillow against his chest.

The Headmaster takes a seat at the other end of the couch. "Would you care to hear my recommendations, Peter?"

Peter nods.

"First of all, a nap seems to be in order."

Peter nods again.

"Then some sustenance and maybe some fresh air." He pauses. "Today should be a recovery day. A lazy, take-care-of-yourself day."

Another nod.

"But then I think you have some choices to make," the Headmaster continues. "One would be to try to learn about this mysterious world you've been introduced to—"

"You mean past lives?"

"Yes. You'll find plenty of resources around the school.

"Another option would be to try to talk about past lives and the like with your teachers—even your peers. You never know what kind of exposure they might have had.

"And then maybe you'll want to try to go back to your studies—the things that we know that you love—"

"Including directed-thought experiments?"

"Of course!" says the Headmaster. "Whatever brings you joy! Whatever interests and excites you. And also, I would try to use your meditation time…to go different places. To open yourself up to new… information."

"What do you mean? How?"

"Well. For example, you might try going into a contemplative meditative state after reading some profoundly affecting passage. Or you might try seeing where your meditation might lead you if you hold a particular event or person or thing in your mental embrace." The Headmaster pauses. "Are you still keeping a dream journal?"

"Not really," Peter answers. "I've gotten lazy."

"Start again," the Headmaster insists. "Even daily journaling. There are plenty of insightful things that cross our paths over the course of every single day. Look for them. Write about them. See what turns up."

"That's it?"

"For now," answers the Headmaster. "I think that's plenty. Let's just focus on getting Peter Vandenhof back into the flow of life again."

"Hear, hear to that!"

The Headmaster jumps to his feet, showing none of his ample years. "Well, then. Let's get on with it, shall we?"

Peter nods while pulling himself to his feet with considerable more effort than the Headmaster.

He stretches and yawns. "A nap sounds good."

"I thought it would."

"Thank you so much, Headmaster, for taking this time for me," he says before adding, "And sorry to dump all my problems on your couch—literally!" He laughs.

"I am just glad that you have finally decided to move forward, Master Vandenhof. We've really missed the ever-inquisitive, ever-ready-for-battle Peter Vandenhof."

"Yeah," Peter says absently. "Me, too." And he opens the door and walks out of the room.

12

WINTER INTO SPRING, SECOND YEAR

The Midwinter Ball fell onto a Saturday in the middle of February this year and is hosted by the wonderful country setting of Le Château de Vullierens outside of and in the hills above Lausanne. The rustic-barn feel provided by the château's Dorianna Room is perfect for the youth that it serves. While Peter cannot help but be disappointed by the nonattendance of Meela and the girls from Surval, most of his classmates are able to enjoy themselves. The more folk-oriented music provided for this dance may be less refined than the previous ball's classical quintet, but it seems appropriate, for this dance is far less formal; there is far less dancing but a lot of fun and exercise. There is sledding and sleigh-rides, fires blazing in all of the chateau's hearth-size fireplaces, punch, hot chocolate and fondues, canapés and hors d'oeuvres, breads and fromages, patisseries, and confîtures abound, and, unfortunately, a lot of illicit and inappropriate substances are passed around as well.

Loïck, Adam, and Harry each find themselves the centers of attention at differing times and for different reasons through the night. Loïck's stunning good looks attract a lot of attention—to which the young man's budding ego takes like a duck to water. A problem surfaces when he and two girls are caught in a compromising situation in a darkened basement recreation room. Loïck emerges from the situation all smiles and grins, the girls a little less so.

Harry, too, finds himself attracting his usual share of attention due to his Nordic colorings and athletic physique, but tonight he is coerced into participating in a drinking game outside on the sledding hill that proves awkward when his inebriated state causes a slip in judgment that leads to the crash of a toboggan into a tree. While Harry escapes with only a broken right arm, two of the other riders are not so fortunate. A girl from nearby Brilliantmont School is knocked out cold as she is flung head-first into the tree, and another boy from Beau-Soleil loses three front teeth in the crash. Unfortunately, Harry had been assigned the dubious status of "designated driver" for the fateful ride and receives, thus, the brunt of most of the blame. Needless to say, the headmasters of the two schools have words with Headmaster Visconti over the following days; however, with the high levels of alcohol discovered in the blood of all of the victims, the ire projected onto Harry (and Brig-Wallis) is quick to dissipate.

Adam's misstep, however, proves less benign. Always prone to being goaded into risky behavior, Adam is lured into a group of "worldly" kids who decide to go on a "trip." Their walk off into the woods would not have been so troublesome had they not all decided to preempt their travels with a strong dose of LSD. To make matters worse, several of the students from other schools had the foresight to sneak flasks of high-proof alcoholic beverages to the party—which they shared willingly and liberally. When the group is finally found—at the bottom of a steeply sloped ravine in a wooded section of a property adjacent to that belonging to the château—it is nearly daybreak. Needless to say, the level of panic of all school chaperones involved—not to mention that of the château's management and owners—is high. It turns out that the students involved in this particular outing took a "bad step" on one of the footpaths high on the ravine's slope and had fallen—all seven of them. It was miraculous that no one was killed, but several of the students were rendered unconscious in the tumble, and three experienced significant injuries—including Adam. He sustained a neck injury that might have become much worse had the effects of the alcohol and drugs not rendered him too disoriented and disabled to move. While a couple of the girls who ha misstep and tumble down had escaped with nary a were far too "out of it" to be of any help to the other down and cried until they eventually fell asleep. Lu the group had the dumb luck to convince the others in the group to try to huddle around each other for warmth; otherwise, there might have been some cases of frostbite or hypothermia.

Adam's injury to his spinal cord required a ride out of the woods on an emergency carpet and an ambulance ride into Geneva, where doctors kept him in hospital for the next four months. The Brig-Wallis boys were allowed to visit Adam on two different occasions, but the time and logistics of the trip proved challenging: the school year had to move forward.

When Adam was well enough to move, he was flown home to New York City, where he remained with his family for the ensuing months of convalescence. He did not return to Brig-Wallis.

Though the Midwinter Ball had its drama, it was an overall success for the Brig-Wallis boys. All had thoroughly enjoyed themselves. Peter, Fabrice, Nathan, Enrique, and Emil had even lucked into the company of a delightful set of girls from Lausanne's L'École Lémania. Though dancing was not the big focus of the night, the small group—who had all met at the fondue and hors d'oeuvres table quite early in the evening—enjoyed a lot of laughs, memorable conversations, and furtive glances this way and that over the course of the night. The "crises" of Harry's crash and Adam's missing party even had the benefit of providing excuses for hugs and hand holding for Fabrice, Enrique, and Nathan—which then prompted an endless barrage of teasing from Peter and Emil on the trip back to Brig-Wallis. *What goes around comes around*, is the rationale Peter uses for his sophomoric behavior. But, in the end, it is all in good fun. Harry recovers fine and is soon back "in charge" of the Workout Room. Loïck, however, takes a turn in behavior: he becomes more distant—both from his classmates and from his commitment to the Brig-Wallis classes and activities. Peter is surprised to notice how much Loïck's new attitude ects group morale and even group dynamics in classroom projects. It makes him a little nervous.

Peter finds himself rather shocked when March's "Welcome, Spring!" soirée ball is announced. With their recent "track history," he had fully expected that the school would discontinue allowing the second-years out on these enticements of worldly risks and dangers. But, when he hears it is going to be in Montreux, he can't help but feel grateful—and, as one can imagine, excited. As it turns out, Peter's excitement is unfounded as, once again, Meela is nowhere to be found among the attendees. As a matter of fact, there are *no* Surval girls present at the dance—which Peter finds puzzling, since the girls' boarding school is located in Montreux.

Held in the Salle des Fêtes at the Fairmont Le Montreux, it is apparent to Peter and his classmates that this pleasant but small excuse for a dance has come with lower expectations for attendance than any of the previous dances. Peter imagines that a lot of schools are on vacation. ("Last weekends for skiing," is another, slightly more accurate, theory.) But, as the boys had learned from the previous dance, small numbers are no excuse for not having fun. Despite slim pickings with regard to members of the opposite sex, the boys find no shortage of excuses for laughter and silliness—including a rather spirited walk down to the lakeshore and back. Though marijuana and alcohol are available, on the sly, the boys return home sober—both their bodies and reputations unscathed.

Spring Break goes by without a hitch. Peter is fully reengaged in his "imaginary" world of energy and thought. And when the third and final term of the year begins, he finds himself in a groove, back into enjoying his in-class banter with Headmaster Visconti, as well as their Sunday visits; but more, his staff-aided "researches" seem to be making great headway. "Bioenergy work," as he is now calling his directed-thought experiments, is proving very entertaining and enjoyable. He can feel that he is on a very special path to…*some*thing (he does not know what). Also, the suggestion by both the Headmaster and Meela to try to bring someone else (her) into his meditations is proving fruitful. In fact, on several occasions, Peter can swear that he feels Meela's presence—her feelings, her thoughts—but he also finds himself totally confused by the challenge of trying to distinguish whether or not the incoming information is coming from the "current" Meela or from a "past-life" version. Still, it is exciting.

In the Brig-Wallis community, the phenomenon that is generating the most excitement is the sudden and quite drastic change in the weather. What had been a seemingly long winter seems finally over. The snow is gone, and flowers and grass are popping up everywhere. During his daily walks around Brig, Peter loves seeing the increasing number of occupied flower boxes outside the windows of people's homes.

When the next ball, the so-called La fête des fleurs, comes around in late April, Peter is in high spirits—and, it must be added, high hopes. Held in the gorgeous candlelit ballroom at Lausanne's Beau-Rivage Palace, this event is very well attended. There are, in fact, several schools represented that Peter has not heard of before—and a lot of new faces. However, the girls from Surval are not among them; Meela is, once again—for the fifth time (yes, Peter is counting)—absent.

Frustrated but quick to let go of any disappointment (what can he do?), Peter decides to enjoy himself. The music is wonderful. Peter's dancing is once again transported by the music. He is so popular on the dance floor that he scarcely has a chance to sit much less enjoy some punch or finger foods.

One cute little brunette in a beautiful spring gown seems to take a real fancy to Peter, as she asks him to dance on three different occasions. She even persuades him to take a break in order to take a stroll out onto the patio. But when she tries to corner him for a little hormonal interaction, he quickly and rather abruptly breaks free and runs back into the dance hall.

While Peter sees the jilted girl a few times over the course of the night, he feels no remorse or regret despite her attractiveness—and despite the natural allure of sexual experience. "It just didn't feel right," he says later in the confidence of his reacquired friend, Emil.

Peter finds himself most pleased with the way the night turns out for his friends. Fabrice and Enrique are able to reconnect with two of the girls that they had befriended at the Midwinter Ball, and Emil finds himself occupied by a strikingly cute girl for almost three-quarters of the night. Between the successes of his friends and the wonderful time he has dancing to the wonderful music, Peter is able to almost totally forget about the absence of his own heart's desire. Almost. *Only one ball left,* he realizes when they return to Brig-Wallis and he sees the schedule for the rest of the school year.

On another positive note, the Brig-Wallis boys come away from the "Fêtes des fleurs" yet again without incident and with school and individual reputations untarnished. *Quel miracle!* (What a relief!) And so, with winter past, and spring well underway, the boys head into the home stretch of their second year at Brig-Wallis.

Academically, the third or "spring" term of Brig-Wallis unfolds differently for the second-year students than the previous two. Though the daily schedule remains the same, the course offerings change slightly. The most conspicuous change is the new focus in history class on war and genocide. Over the course of the twelve-week Spring Term, the students are exposed to a wide variety of source materials that expose the students to the facts and legendary accounts of many of the world's most well-known conflicts, with particular emphasis on those that exhibited more advanced attitudes of ruthless, heartless aggression, and depravity. The theme of the horrors and atrocities instigated (and perpetuated) by the ever-swaying balance of resource control, economic need, and the material greed of a few is quite prevalent. Also obvious in the lessons are the facts pointing to the intentional manipulation and propagandist sway or "brainwashing" that wealth and power have been orchestrating in order to create a more submissive general population. As a matter of fact, the masterful control of information, security, basic needs, and resources by the wealthy appears to be the key to the unleashing of many of the most violent events or movements in history; conditions of deprivation and enslavement over the masses seem to have been orchestrated with increasing precision and mastery over the course of human history. Fear, intolerance, and re- or misdirected vengeance have been used by the controllers, the "masters," as motivational tools for thousands of years.

The lessons of historical topics are taught through the most graphic and personal source materials possible: journalistic accounts and/or videos, personal diaries or testimonials—from both sides of a conflict—as well as a field trip to Srebrenica, in the Bosnian Republika Srpska.

Srebrenica is the site of one of Europe's most recent atrocities. The lessons of actually standing on-site, seeing the mass graves and bombed-out buildings left behind by the crazed behaviors that humans can perpetrate on one another, is powerful, to say the least—especially when these are reinforced by dozens of printed and videographed personal accounts, hundreds of photos and artifacts, and hours of before-and-after visuals. Up to this point in the boys' young lives, one would be hard pressed to cite any event or academic course that has had a greater effect on their psyches than this one.

Not coincidentally, the guided meditations that the Headmaster leads during the Morning Meditation portion of the boys' Chapel time during Spring Term seem to focus much more than usual on elements of peace, calm, and forgiveness.

Another pedagogical shift that occurs for the second-years' final term is a new focus in Ecology Class on the role humankind has had on the ecological health and balance of planet Earth. The revelations of human-induced ecological shifts, climactic changes, and species extinctions, when compared to other natural disasters like asteroid collisions, volcanic activity, and ice ages, is also quite alarming and eye opening. But there is one particular lecture and discussion that all of the boys find slightly disconcerting for its being strangely out of the usual contexts: this being Wo Chou-chen's lecture on the history of Earth and its tectonic plates. To hear of Earth's tectonic plates described as something as fragile and ephemeral as the film that forms on the surface of a cup of hot chocolate is difficult to comprehend, but the "fact" that the ever-moving, ever-shifting tectonic plates that provide the land surfaces of Earth's "continents" have been able to support biological life for over 250 million years is astounding. The effect of this revelation unleashes a flood of questions.

"So where does human life fit into that equation?" asks Thomas.

"This current form of intelligent hominid life that we call *Homo sapiens sapiens* has been walking on the planet for about two hundred thousand years."

Gasps and numerous outcries of "What!?" greet Mr. Wo's proclamation.

Emil, who has a penchant for numbers and math, quickly figures out that this means that his species has only used "eight *ten thousandths* of the time that life has been possible on the surface of the planet."

"That sounds about right," Mr. Wo affirms.

"But what about the other…two hundred and fifty million years?" asks Rique.

In true Brig-Wallis fashion, Mr. Wo answers, "What do you think?"

"Is it possible that it took humans that long to evolve?" Nathan wonders aloud.

"Our first bipedal ancestors seem to have appeared about seven million years ago," remarks the teacher.

Everyone looks automatically to Emil.

"Two point eight *hundredths* of the time!" he spouts out.

"Whoa!" breathes John Marchaud. "We've been around not even three percent of the time of our ancestors."

"So humankind has only been evolving for less than three percent of the time in which biological life has been possible on land?" asks Joe-pa.

"Yes."

"So, how long has there been life—actual, documented life—on the planet?" asks Michael.

"Microbial life," Mr. Wo begins, "for more than four billion years."

Audible gasps can again be heard from several members of the class.

"Multicellular life, eight hundred million years ago," Mr. Wo continues. "Fishes and sea creatures: four hundred forty million years ago." He pauses. "Land-based life-forms—plants: four hundred thirty million years ago."

"Now things are moving!" blurts out Loïck.

"Earliest land reptiles: three hundred five million years ago," Wo presses on.

"Oh! So humans couldn't have existed more than three hundred million years ago," Emil states.

"Definitely not," answers Chen before continuing. "Two hundred fifty-one million years ago, ninety-six percent of all of Earth's biological species died off in the Permian-Jurassic extinction event."

"Whoa!" breathes Fabrice.

"What caused that, Mister Wo?" asks Zi.

"An asteroid hit the planet," is Wo's answer.

"Ouch!" says Thomas.

"First evidence of mammals occurs one hundred seventy million years ago," he continues. "Disappearance of the last dinosaurs: sixty-six million years ago.

"Appearance of the first meat-eating mammals: sixty-three million years ago.

"Appearance of the first *Homo* species…"

Everyone laughs.

"Two million years ago."

"But mammalian life has been present for, what? A hundred and seventy million years?" asks Loïck. "Why is evolution so slow?"

"Is this slow, Master de Rothschild?" responds Mr. Wo.

"It sure seems like it to me," Loïck answers.

Then Emil says, "So species that are potentially human have been around for two million years?"

"That is correct, Master Frederick."

"So, have there been other species of humans on the planet?" Emil continues.

"That, Master Frederick, is open for debate," Mr. Wo answers. "There is fossil evidence of no less than sixteen subspecies in the *Homo* line of development—all of which have either died out or been incorporated into our own species' DNA."

"What does that mean, 'incorporated into our own species'?" Emil asks.

"It means that, for example, forty thousand years ago, the last of the Neanderthals disappeared. Yet many members of our current population—every member of this very room—can be shown to have between one and four percent of their DNA makeup coming from Neanderthals."

"We mated with them?" asks Michael.

"There is also evidence-based theory that we exterminated them," responds Mr. Wo.

"Genocide?" Thomas asks.

"Killed off our own relatives," comments John in disgust.

"It happens all the time," says Mr. Wo. "Even today we kill off members of our own species. Both intentionally and passively."

"Srebrenica," Michael mutters.

Distant, sober stares and small nods pervade the room.

At the end of the term, there comes a day when Headmaster Visconti stands in front of his History Class near the end of the allotted time period and makes the following speech:

"Many of you are probably wondering why we have spent this semester studying history with such a focus on war and genocides. You've been exposed to a much harsher side of human nature than your privileged backgrounds have seen before. And you must know that this was all done intentionally—even so far as the level of graphic and written detail. And so, I image that you are all asking yourselves, 'Why?' Why have we chosen to do this? The answer to this question is twofold.

"First of all, we are trying in*tentionally* to desensitize you." The Headmaster pauses for effect. "In order to continue on to a third year at Brig-Wallis, you will need to begin getting used to—to begin learning how to detach from—the horrors of the human experience, the evils of human agendas.

"The second reason for the exposure to all of this horror and brutality is to be able to inform you that everything you've seen, everything that has happened in the past two thousand years, has been part of a plan." The Headmaster pauses briefly, studying the faces of his students. "All of the horrors and atrocities committed by humans upon each other, upon other species and ecosystems, upon the host planet itself, are all demonstrations of the success of a grand scheme." Again he pauses. "While individual events were not planned, the behaviors that allowed them to occur are, I assure you, part of the plan.

"The Earth-based human experiment that you and I call *Homo sapiens sapiens* was created with the specific and expressed objective of seeing how far into ignorance, fear, and depravity a complex, self-aware creature of the Cosmic Scene could be taken. As my staff and I have tried to illustrate over the past three months, those depths of depravity have been quite successfully achieved. No species in the history of this host planet has ever been able to achieve willingly and knowingly the same depths of cruelty and self-declared impunity, depravity and denial, rationalization and arrogance as the species into which you were born." Another pause. "You are members of the most deadly, destructive, and self-centered four-dimensional biological species ever—and all of the film and videos and firsthand accounts and journalistic reports and history books have been presented to you as proof of this fact."

"Are we supposed to be, what? Proud of this?" interrupts Joe-pa.

"No, because you do not yet understand *why* this could be a source for pride," responds the Headmaster, nonplussed.

"Yet?" Harry asks.

"That is what you will begin to discover in your third year at Brig-Wallis. And that is why I speak to you as a group today. In case you have forgotten—or, in case you've never quite realized it—your commitment to a Brig-Wallis education is a choice. You have no obligation to be here. You never did." The Headmaster pauses, beginning to slowly walk around the room. "Some of you may have started here because you were flattered. You were surprised and excited at having been noticed, at having been wanted, having been sought after. As I've said on numerous occasions, each and every one of you was recruited to join the Brig-Wallis program because you seem to fit the profile of the kind of people who find great success in the "service leadership" roles that Brig-Wallis graduates fulfill. We've taken a great chance on inviting you to join us here. Some of you have shown us that we were wrong, that you weren't the type of individual who could succeed on the difficult path that Brig-Wallis graduates travel. Those students have left.

"I now ask that you each take some time over the next few days to reflect on a few things. Before the time comes for you to depart for your summer holiday, we'd like you to have considered a few things that will become very important to your ongoing success at Brig-Wallis.

"The questions I would have you ask yourself include whether or not you like it here; whether or not you like, enjoy, and trust your surroundings, your teachers, the Brig-Wallis staff, your classmates, the school's daily rhythms, as well as the educational process as you've come to know it here.

"Do you like the people here? Do you enjoy your days, classes, and interactions here? Do you feel safe, respected, and nurtured here? And, most of all, do you enjoy, like, and trust the person you see yourself becoming? Do you like yourself? Do you think that the people and patterns and methods are working for you—helping you to grow and feel more confident, more powerful, more passionate, more engaged in life, more in control of your choices. Is Brig-Wallis helping you to become a person that you like? Can you look back upon your two years here and say that you are better for it? Can you look forward with excitement to another year here—because, if you cannot, then we have some talking to do—some issues to confront."

The Headmaster holds up a piece of paper with some printed boxes on it. "I'm going to pass this sign-up sheet around the room. Please put your name into a box representing a time on Thursday or Friday that you would be open to sitting down with me to talk. You will see that the times I've made available are all one-hour blocks—which should be more than adequate for our talk—and that they run from one to nine p.m. with two hours blocked off for exercise and supper blocked off. Twelve slots: one for each of you. And you may rest assured that everything you and I say in the confines of this meeting will remain totally and completely confidential."

He passes the sign-up sheet to the student sitting closest to him.

"Thank you, and class is dismissed."

13

END OF YEAR BALL

The final dance of the school year, slated for the first weekend in June, is to be held at the Grand Hôtel du Lac in Vevey on the northern shores of Lac Léman, just west of Montreux. Peter is heading into the event with virtually no hope or expectations, as he knows, from looking online at the Surval school calendar, that Surval's school year ended at the beginning of May. Still, he can't help but feel a little of the nervous butterflies as the limo van pulls up to the front steps of the Grand Hôtel.

It is gorgeous. It has been a gorgeous day. The scenery on the train ride from Brig has been gorgeous. The sun has been staying up till almost ten o'clock. Even the other arriving students look gorgeous. He can't explain it, but Peter finds that he is feeling very high, almost euphoric. Second year is drawing to a close. He has survived and surmounted some heady obstacles and come out stronger than ever. He is going back to Westchester for the summer. Things are good. Life is good.

As the boys are taking their turns emerging from the limo, Peter notices the steady stream of vehicles lined up to drop off their charges for the dance. "This is going to be a big one," he says to Harry, who is waiting just next to Peter still inside the van.

Inside the hotel lobby, the boys take their time as Maestro Garibaldi does his best to hold them together so that he can orient them around the hotel. "We're meeting here, in the front lobby, at midnight," he announces. "Now, off with you." Then, shouting after the fleeing boys, "Have fun and represent Brig-Wallis well!"

The hotel's Viennoise Ballroom is exquisite if a little snug for the number of guests in attendance. Peter notices a lot of now-familiar faces but just as many that are unfamiliar. He nods in greeting to a few and is quite pleased to watch several of his classmates rush off to join acquaintances made at previous dances.

Suddenly, he finds his vision being obstructed by a pair of white-gloved hands reaching around from behind him.

"Guess who?" sounds a familiar voice. Peter feels his heart virtually leap out of his chest. He spins around, and before he knows it, his arms are wrapped around the waste of his beloved Meela, and he is lifting her into the air, spinning around and around. His joy is so overfull that he finds himself choked to the point of being unable to speak. He brings Meela down to the ground and pulls himself into a tight embrace with his chin tucked tightly into the crook between her neck and shoulder. Tears begin streaming down his face. He feels embarrassed at the prospect of being seen like this—it is, after all, still broad daylight—and yet he cannot contain himself.

"Where have you been?" he whisper-sings into her ear.

"What do you mean?"

He pulls away from their embrace so that he can look into her eyes and face.

"Well, I've been coming to these 'balls' every month—"

"Aww! You've missed me!"

Peter blushes. He embraces her again. "I have."

"I've missed you, too," she whispers back.

Eventually the two calm down and compose themselves long enough to stop hugging and groping. "Let's walk," Peter says.

"*Avec plaisir,*" Meela says as they head outside, hand in hand, through the ballroom's open French doors, onto a patio.

"So? Why haven't you been coming to the dances?"

"Well, Peter Vandenhof. If you must know, Surval offers a lot of chances to travel!" Meela professes. "To places I might never get the chance to go again."

"What? I don't get it."

"There are, like, weekend, or week-*long*, field trips. Like, I just got back from three weeks in Japan—"

"Three weeks!"

"Yeah, well, not all of it was school related," Meela says, amending her statement. "My daddy met me over there for the last eight days, and before that there were trips to London and Amsterdam and Kenya and Morocco and, of course, tons of day trips around Switzerland—"

"Okay, okay. I get it," Peter says, placating her. "And that's why you've only been to, what, two—now three of the year's eight balls?"

"I guess," she says, trying to not feel guilty in the umbrella of Peter's hurt. "Look. I didn't know we were going to meet *now*. For all I knew, it could've happened twenty or forty years from now."

"But you knew? You really and truly knew we'd meet?"

"Yep."

"And you're sure it's me—that I'm the one…that you're supposed to meet?"

There is a twinkle in her eyes. "There is no doubt whatsoever."

"How? How do you know?"

"I don't know. I just do. Just like I remember events and conversations—word for word—from when I was in my mother's belly. The same way I know when we're anywhere near a landfill or a power grid or an electric blanket. The same way I can see people's thoughts and moods and baser instincts and patterns by just looking into their eyes."

"You can? You can do all that?"

The arch of her eyebrows is her only response.

"You, you see or know past lives?"

"No, but I know that *we* have a lot."

"Together?"

"Sometimes. Not always. We've always had to fight *really* hard to be together. And more often than not, we've been defeated."

"What do you mean?"

"That forces have kept us apart; that we've been killed or separated more often than not. But it's okay. They're just games—just roles we're playing in order to provide lessons to others."

"So, if these are just 'games,' as you say, what's real?"

"This," she says as she lifts up their interlaced hands. "This," she says, connecting their eyes—which has the immediate effect of making their surroundings melt away and stars and light and a thousand faces and backgrounds parade before his mind's eye.

"I've never felt anything like this," Peter says looking down at their interlaced fingers. "It's the most profound comfort and joy I've ever felt." He spins on his feet to directly face her. "Which reminds me, I want to apologize to you for wigging out on you last time: I was really getting freaked out by your cryptic meanings. I just wasn't ready."

"And things have changed?"

"Yeah! I've been studying up on past lives and stuff—hearing tons of stories and testimonials." Peter starts getting excited. "There's this one book—by Michael Newton—it's called *Destiny of Souls*—it helped me understand, and, more, while I was reading it I felt as if I were growing up! It all made sense to me—all this stuff we go through in these human bodies—"

"I like these human bodies," she says while mischievously rubbing Peter's thigh and raising one single eyebrow.

"Yeah, okay, well…" Peter finds himself flustered, speechless, blushing.

Meela laughs.

"How old are you?" he asks but then suddenly swoops in for a kiss—which is met willingly, receptively, even enthusiastically.

"That was nice," she says after Peter has pulled away.

"Mmm," Peter responds. "I've never done that before."

"Felt fine to me!"

"There's something about being with you—being in your company—just touching you—that fills me with the most profound comfort, ease, joy, and security. It's like the world could fall apart around us—we could be being tortured—but it would be all right, it wouldn't matter, so long as I'm holding your hand."

"I understand."

"Seriously, a kiss is nice—I mean, it presents a whole bunch of other feelings and complications—"

"Complications!"

"Just let me finish, please," Peter pleads. "But this—just holding your hand is the best, most real feeling I could ever imagine. I neither want nor hope for more."

"But I like these bodies," Meela says in mild protest. "So long as I've got one, I'm going to enjoy it!"

"I understand all that. That's part of the 'game' as you call it—fun and games—but 'this'"—he again holds up their intertwined hands—"this is real. This is everything. This is enough—*more* than I or anyone could ever hope for.

"What am I saying?!" he changes direction. "I never *hoped* for this! I had no clue that 'this'—that these kind of feelings—were even possible. I expected, I think, to go through life like every other zombie schmuck. But now! Now, I am awake! I am alive! I *know* what is available. And, personally, I don't ever want it to go away again."

"Okay," starts Meela. "I understand what you're saying. And, believe me, please, I'm feeling the same things you are. But, we've made a commitment—"

"A commitment?!"

"Yeah, a commitment. To play the game—the Earth human game—and there are certain rules we have to abide by in order to play—"

"Rules? What are you talking about? Let's make up our *own* rules!"

"Yeah. We *could* do that. But…I have a feeling that we came back to Earth for *more* than just being together."

"What?! What could be more—"

"I get what you're saying, but listen. Please, Peter. Just let me talk. This might be the hardest thing for you to hear—and it's not going to be easy for me to say, so please be patient with me.

"I did not have to come back," she begins in complete earnest. "I've done my work. I've used the Earth-based human forms to the ultimate benefit of my spiritual growth. I've passed all the tests, risen to the place where Earth experiences are of diminishing returns for my growth—kind of like a kid who's been playing gin rummy for a long time. There comes a time when you get bored—when you've learned just about all there is to learn from that particular game—and now it's time to try a new game.

"I was at that point that the Earth-based game had served me about as well as it could. I was getting ready to try a new game. But then you came along and asked me—ever so sweetly and ever so persuasively—if I would mind coming back down here one last time—just to help ensure that you would finish your own work. And I said, 'yes'!"

"So you're here just for me?"

"No. I'm here to sup*port* you. *You* still have to do the work. I'll just kind of check in from time to time to make sure that you're staying on course."

"And what course is that?"

"I don't know! Whatever course it is that will get you to the place where you feel, 'I'm done. I'm ready to move on—to the next game.'"

"I'm sorry."

"For what?"

"For having been so selfish as to ask you to come back here for me."

"No! Don't be! The human experience can be so much fun! Especially when you *know* that it's a game—when you know it's not real and that it's all a series of little tests trying to drag you down and suck you in."

"Suck you into what?"

"Into thinking that it's real!"

"So, now that you've shared that with me—now that you know that I know the secret—what's the point of staying?"

"To enjoy the ride! I mean, if this is our last trip to this particular playground in these particular vehicles, don't you want to take advantage of all the rides?"

"Metaphor," breathes Peter. "I see what you're saying. But some of the rides seem…dangerous."

"Then don't do them. Or don't let them be dangerous. I mean, what's the worst that could happen?"

"Oh, I don't know. How about *death*!"

"Oh, that old thing! How can you say that when you know this place, these bodies, are all just illusions?"

"They don't feel like illusions."

"And your dreams? Your fantasies? Your thoughts?"

"I'm not following you."

"Just think of your life, your body, your Peter Vandenhof self, as a big dream, a big thought."

"I'm still not following you."

"The only difference between a thought or a dream and our lives in these bodies is that our lives have been going on a lot longer—the information we've created, absorbed, and processed has had time—*lots* of time—to be repeated and reinforced so that now these patterns feel real. They feel solid. Life is just a dream that has calcified."

Peter is dumbfounded. "How old are you?"

"Why? It doesn't matter—"

Peter leans in to kiss Meela again.

"I feel so free, so limitless, so uninhibited with you."

"I'm so glad!" They kiss again. "I can't wait to feel your skin… against mine."

Peter is speechless.

"Oh!" Meela gushes excitedly. "I almost forgot! I didn't finish making my point! You distracted me, you silly boy.

"My point was: you came back to Earth because you still had work to do—'unfinished business,' as they say. And I don't even know what that work is. Only *you* can discover that for your own self. In the meantime, I'll be around—on the planet—if and when you think you want or need me, but just 'cuz we found each other so early, so young, it doesn't mean we're supposed to stop living our lives."

"I don't get it! What more could one want than *this*?"

"I get what you mean, Peter, but *this* isn't what you asked me to come back with you for. You asked me to come back with you in hopes that my support might help you complete your unfinished business."

"What unfinished business?"

"I told you: I don't know. That is for *you* to figure out. And then *fin*ish it."

"So what happens? What do we do now? Do we just go back to our previous worlds and forget about each other?"

"Of course not. Unless you want to."

"What does that mean?"

"That means that *that* is an option. You always have a choice: keep me in your life or...not! Go back to your previous patterns or not. The question is, where do *you* think your work lies? Is there 'unfinished business' with me?"

"We haven't even started!"

"Or is there unfinished business with yourself, your school work, your studies, your career, your other relationships?"

Peter is silent. He understands.

"Tell me about your school. What drew you there? Why do you stay? How is it serving you?"

Unexpectedly, this simple set of questions sends Peter into an excited frenzy of descriptions and details, vignettes and personal discoveries. At the end of his little outburst, he realizes that Meela is right: he has "unfinished business." There is a whole world of self-discovery that he has just started. Though he feels Meela will be a part of it, he knows that Brig-Wallis and his personal journey are inextricably intertwined, that the journey he has begun at Brig-Wallis is crucial to his success.

"Sounds like a pretty amazing place."

"It is." Peter suddenly feels a need to move. "Hey, Meela. Would you care to walk?"

"I would *love* to walk!"

The remainder of the evening Peter and Meela spend walking, at first just around the hotel ground sand patios but then on into the town. They walk and talk, taking turns telling one another stories from their pasts—of their families, of their travels, of their schools, of their likes and dislikes—all the while tightly and inextricably bound by their intertwined hands—and interestingly oblivious to the amazing scenery of sumptuous houses, flower gardens, lake views, and sunset colors.

"It's going to be really hard to leave tonight," Peter says at one point on their walk. "This—holding your hand—is all I truly desire."

"Then we could walk and hold hands forever. But then we'd die—and you might not have accomplished all that you set out to do—and, believe me, I had to throw quite a tantrum just to get permission to come back just *this* time. I *know* I'm not going to be allowed to come back another time!"

"What do you mean? You had to 'get permission'?"

"Well, not really 'permission,' but, you know, all the guides and teachers and counselors and other spirit beings depending on you to work as a team to help each other grow—they're all waiting for me to have this 'one last vacation at the Earth playground' while they prep for the next group project."

"Which is?"

"Which is what?"

"What is your 'group's' next project?'

"Oh my God!" Meela jumps a 180-degree turn around to face Peter in a crouch. "I'm *so* excited! I'm going to be working with planetary weather systems! It's kind of an intro-level training ground for the big job of planetary logos."

"What the hell is 'planetary logos'?"

"Oh! It's…it's…the conscious ensoulment or animation of a planet!" Then she adds, "Or a star."

"What! Do you mean that planets and stars…have *souls*?! That there are conscious beings…possessing—"

"Wearing."

"What?"

"It's more like 'wearing.' Like they've put on the clothes that make up a star or planet."

"Really?! Really?"

"What?" Meela asks in total sincerity.

"You're really trying to tell me that you were about to start training for the eventual 'ensoulment' of a planet?!"

"Or star."

"Really."

"Yeah." Meela looks at Peter, trying to figure him out. "Actually," she continues, "if you want to know the *whole* truth, part of me is doing the training right now—"

"What?! Now you've com*plet*ely lost me."

"Yeah! Didn't you know—haven't you come across in your readings and explorations—that spirit beings rarely put one hundred percent of their energy and attention into their human host experience?"

"Well, yeah. I guess I did come across that stuff—"

"Well, what do you think the rest of me is doing while, say, fifty percent of me is invested in this critter?"

"I don't know. What? And don't refer to yourself as a 'critter.'"

She laughs. "Okay. Anyway, the answer is that the rest of me is continuing to work in other realms, on other projects, including prepping for planetary-weather-systems work. Only, the rest of my team wishes I were there, more fully invested in the project."

Peter looks on in wonder and disbelief.

"So, are you…what? An alien?"

"Of course! But, then, so are you! So is everybody! They just don't know it yet—or more accurately, they've all chosen to forget it for a while."

Peter is silent. Meela senses his resistance, his reluctance, to believe her—or, perhaps, his overwhelm from all of the information she has been gushing.

"Wanna see what I can do?" she asks playfully.

Peter decides to play along. "Sure. Show me what you can do." He stands, waiting, watching Meela.

"Did you feel that?"

"Feel what? What was I supposed to feel?"

"Let me try it again," she says. Again, Peter stands still, watching, waiting. A little gust of wind tousling his hair is all he notices.

"Did you feel it?"

"Feel what, Meela? What am I supposed to be feeling?"

"The wind!"

Peter is dumbstruck: in utter shock. *Could that breeze* really *have been her? Can she really manipulate…the weather?*

"You expect me to believe that *that*…little breeze was…you?"

"Yeah."

"No way."

"You want me to do it again?"

"Sure."

"Which direction do you want me to send it from?"

"I don't know. How about straight down on top of my head," he says rather flippantly.

"Okay, Mister Doubting Thomas."

Suddenly a *whoosh!* of wind descends upon Peter as if from straight above him.

Impossible! he thinks. "You did that?" he says.

She nods while hopping and dancing in a happy circle around him.

"You expect me to believe that you can make wind?"

"I told you: I'm studying planetary weather systems. But, no, to answer your question: I expect you to believe nothing. I place absolutely no expectations on you, Peter Vandenhof. I love you too much to ever do that."

Once again Peter is reeling. He plops down on the grassy lawn next to the sidewalk upon which they had been traveling.

"You can manipulate the weather," he says flatly—more to himself than to anyone else.

"I'm only beginning," Meela says, continuing to dance around. "Wind is easy. I've been working on clouds, too. But the problem is that there are other forces much bigger than me out there working it, too. So I don't always get my way. As a matter of fact, I've been learning lately that most of the time I *don't* get my way. My little wishes and whimsies have to somehow fit in with the larger designs of more advanced beings than me."

"Wow!" Peter says as he flops back onto the grass. "Fuck me," he says in exasperation, again, as if to himself.

"I thought you'd never ask!" says Meela playfully as she practically jumps on top of Peter. "This feels nice," she says grinding her pubic bone into Peter's.

"Meela," Peter says rather flatly.

"Yes, Peter," Meela meets his serious tone.

"What are you doing?"

"I'm rubbing *my* 'little bits' against *your* 'little bits,'" she answers in a playful tone. "Only, yours isn't so little anymore, is it?"

"Meela! We're on the lawn of some stranger's house! In public!"

"So? What's the worst that could happen?"

"So! It's illegal! We could get arrested!"

"That would be exciting," she teases. "Oh, all right," she rolls off him. "You're no fun!"

"There's a time and there's a place."

"You sound like a stodgy old man."

Peter tries to contain himself but then bursts out laughing. "You are the craziest person I've ever met, Meela," he says as he rolls over, back on top of her. "Hey! I don't even know your full name."

"Ludmilla Gregorovna Rostropovich."

"What?" Peter straightens. "You're Russian?"

At which Meela begins spouting off sentence after sentence of Russian epithets and indignations. The she stops. "No. I'm not; I just *love* Russian!" she says, smiling mischievously. "Ludmilla Gregorovna Rostropovich is just the name I made up for myself—you know, if I ever have to pretend I'm someone else—"

"Have you had to use it?"

"I don't think I've ever *had* to. But it has come in handy a couple of times. You know: awkward traveling experiences. Especially, believe it or not, in the States."

"Oh, I believe it! American men can be such bastards."

"And it's not just the men."

"Oh, really!" Peter laughs. "So, what is your real name? And, by the way, what are you doing here right now? I looked it up and the Surval school year is finished! Why aren't you home?"

"Home? In New Brunswick? Are you serious? You think there's anything to do in New Brunswick?"

"Oh, I don't know. I think there's probably mischief *you* could get into anywhere. You just have to put your mind—"

"Oh, shut up and kiss me," she says pulling Peter's face down to meet hers. When they come up for air, Peter whispers, "Vaht ees your name," in a mock-German accent. "Eef you do not tell me, I vill haff to continue zees torture." He kisses her again.

In that case, I may *never* tell!" she says, pulling him down again.

"Peter?!" comes a voice from down the sidewalk. "Peter? Is that you?"

"Shit!" Peter breathes. "That's one of my classmates."

"Yeah, Joe-pa!" he answers, rolling into a seated position on the grass beside Meela.

"His name is *Joe-pa*?" Meela says, trying to suppress her snickers.

"Holy shit, Peter!" says Joe-pa running up the sidewalk toward them. "We've been looking all *over* for you!"

"Why? What time is it?" asks Peter.

"It's twelve thirty! We were supposed to be gone by now. Maestro Garibaldi refused to leave until we found you. He said it was part of 'team building.' 'No man gets left behind.'"

They all laugh as Joe-pa finishes closing the distance between them.

"I'm so sorry, Joe-pa. I had *no* clue that so much time had passed." He notices Joe-pa staring down at the now-seated girl in the yellow-and-white dress.

"Oh. Sorry," Peter says. "George Paul Taylor. Meet Mee—Ludmilla Gregorovna Rostropovich."

"Rostropovich? Like the cellist?"

"Yes," Meela says in a fake but passable Russian accent. "He is uncle."

"Whoa! I've seen him in concert! He is amazing—"

"Yeah, well," Peter interrupts while getting to his feet. "We should probably get going—especially if there's a shit storm waiting for me back at the hotel."

As the three begin their not-too-long walk back to the hotel, Meela manages to sneak her fingers between Peter's, seemingly unnoticed by their "third wheel"—who is busy filling Peter in on the great lengths the Brig-Wallis contingent had been going through in order to try to find him.

"'Five blocks,' Garibaldi said, no further, and then we were all to turn around and come back to the hotel—that's how he would ensure that all of us would stay pretty close and return at nearly the same time," Joe-pa is saying as they reach the hotel.

The rest of the group is already there. The variety of looks Peter and Meela receive from the Brig-Wallis gang is quite interesting. Meela can't help but let out a little laugh.

"I am seriously so sorry, guys, Maestro Garibaldi," Peter says. "I meant no disrespect. Time just...got away from us."

This evokes several suppressed sniggers.

"I better go," Meela whispers into Peter's ear. His look of panic betrays his profusion of questions as yet unasked and achingly unanswered. He looks over to Maestro Garibaldi and asks, "Could I please have a minute here? To say good-bye?"

"Make it snappy, Master Vandenhof. You have inconvenienced us enough already."

"No inconvenience to me," can be heard from Michael Paine.

"Paine! Don't be a...pain!" Maestro Garibaldi retorts, unintentionally setting off a round of full-out laughter.

"Come on, Vandenhof. Get it over with!"

"Yes, sir! Thank you, sir!" he says before grabbing Meela's hand and leading her in a run up the stairs of the hotel and into its lobby.

"When will I see you again?" he asks. "Do you need a ride home? What is your name? How do I get ahold of you?"

"Sh-sh-sh-shh!" she says using her finger and then her lips to stop his mouth.

"Meela Zane," she says breaking away from their kiss. "You know how to find me. We'll make it happen when it's supposed to happen."

"Arghh! I hate your pithy sayings," he says. Then, settling down, "But I *love* you. Every cell, every atom in my being, knows that: they're all screaming in agony at the prospect of leaving you, and yet at the same time they are infinitely grateful for having met you—for having had the opportunity to be with you, to be in your presence."

"Don't forget that feeling," she says. "Take it with you. Tap into it when we're apart."

"You're sounding like my headmaster."

"He sounds like an amazing man."

"He is." Then Peter asks, "Do you need a ride?"

"No. I'm all right. It's a beautiful night. I have lots to think about on my walk home."

"Don't let the wind blow you down," he says with a wink. "I love you," he says before they kiss one last time.

"I love you," she says as they pull apart.

As Peter exits through the front door, he keeps his eyes glued on Meela. Even as he descends the stairs backward, his eyes never leave her. His last impression of her is that of her smiling, tear-streaked face on her tilted head, with a small, gloved hand waving slowly, almost imperceptibly.

When Peter finally reaches the thirteen others, they are just finishing loading into the limo van. This time there is no teasing, no barrage of juvenile questions aimed at embarrassing Peter. The van pulls away and, once again, the distinct and chilling presence of Meela's voice "appears" inside his head, "*Je t'aime, mon amour.*"

Je t'aime, he thinks—broadcasting it sloppily out into the universe.

This trip back to Brig is peaceful and joy filled as Peter and his classmates ride back in the silence that abounds (but does not really exist).

14

YEAR-END INTERVIEWS

The Headmaster's end-of-year interviews with the second-year students go slightly awry. The Headmaster had formulated a list in his mind of the students who he thought were true Brig-Wallis material and a list of those whose ethics and/or psyches are "questionable." From the former group, he had determined that there were seven, while saw that there were five on the latter "list."

The first two interviews go smoothly: Li Zihou and Fabrice Takazaki had both proved Brig-Wallis stalwarts. They are both hard-working, intelligent, unpretentious, and even-keeled individuals who keep low profiles. Their respective commitment and contributions to Brig-Wallis life are undeniable. Though they both have some "growing" to do, they both belong; they both deserve a chance to continue to prove themselves against the "tests" of the third year. And, as expected and hoped, they both "sign on" for their return.

The Headmaster knows that his third interview is going to be tricky. Loïck came to Brig-Wallis the twenty months before as a small boy with what seemed a rather shy demeanor. Vittorio Visconti watched the shyness peel away as Loïck had proceeded to grow a significant amount over the first- and second-years. Now, at the end of the second year, he stood as the tallest student on campus—almost as tall as M. Montechenin and Mennen van Oort, who both top two meters. With that new height came a newfound popularity—especially among the opposite sex. Loïck had metamorphosed into an exceptionally handsome young man with a head of curly white-gold hair, slender face and body, and stunning blue eyes. Headmaster Visconti had watched with disappointment as Loïck's new status provoked the growth of a newfound cockiness to match. Loïck's attention to his appearance—and to who might be looking at him—proved to have become such a distraction that all of the school's students and staff noticed his gradual withdrawal from all things scholastic—except for off-campus events: that is when one could see Loïck shine.

The interview goes well. Loïck is the first to admit that his "investment" in the Brig-Wallis curriculum had "slipped." He also admits to Headmaster Visconti that he looks forward to his summer vacation back in Paris with more anticipation than he expected. Upon the Headmaster's probing review of each of the individual questions he had asked the boys to "think over," they are able to reveal that Loïck has, in fact, felt a growing distance between himself and his classmates and a loss of "regard" for the daily routines of the school. While he still enjoys the learning and educational styles of the school, he feels ready to make a "transition"; he informs the Headmaster that he will be leaving to find another, "more social" educational venue. *The Rothschild family will be disappointed,* the Headmaster knows, but they'll get over it. *Perhaps he'll become a member of the Order later in life,* he speculates—though, deep down, he believes otherwise.

Edmund "Joe-pa" Taylor proves to be a more difficult customer. The Headmaster had watched Joe-pa fail to mature. The affable young man has not been able to grow out of his attention deficit issues. He is a poor concentrator, a distracted meditator. Yes: he is friendly enough—and eminently well liked among his peers—but, worries the Headmaster, when the going gets tough, would he come through as a "team" player—as someone the others can depend on? Headmaster Visconti senses that the answer to that question would be "no," yet most of the trust- and team-building "tests" are traditionally saved for the third year of attendance. Still, Joe-pa did perform well through all of the social "tests" (the balls). He neither dabbled in nor fell to the temptation of any of the addictive habits that were intentionally dangled in front of the boys.

In the end, the Headmaster knows that he has to give Joe-pa the benefit of the doubt and let him move forward—trust that his important "growth" is yet to come. Despite his best efforts, he cannot get Joe-pa to see any advantages of going elsewhere: Joe-pa likes it here, loves his friends and teachers and the school routines; he cannot wait for third year. Still, the Headmaster ends that meeting with a feeling of doubt. *Oh, well,* he thinks. *We always need examples for the third-year students of the kind of behaviors that do* not *necessarily serve the Brig-Wallis family well.*

Enrique Osario also proves to be a tough one. While coming from great stock—Enrique's maternal grandfather was a Brig-Wallis grad and has served the Order for decades—and his mother is a very strong woman—"Rique" also had never really blossomed, had never really fulfilled any potential. He is present, but he is not assertive. He came to Brig-Wallis lacking in self-confidence, and he seems no better now. The school seems to have failed to help Enrique discover his own talents and enthusiasms. A likable enough boy, he just has… nothing to offer! Yet he has done nothing wrong. He has performed adequately. He has contributed regularly, though never brilliantly—he never "wows" his teachers or peers. He is just "there," no more and no less. Rique is far from a "leader in service."

In the end, however, the Headmaster has to admit that there is nothing about Enrique that makes him objectionable or a "detrimental" member of Brig-Wallis. It's just that he will probably never make a strong candidate for membership within the Order. During the interview, Enrique makes it clear that he "likes" and is happy with everything about Brig-Wallis. He will be returning. Time will tell where he might fit. The Headmaster gives in to his hope that some experience in the Brig-Wallis curriculum will spark an "awakening" in this rather passive human being.

Emil is a shoe-in. No question, no argument. He wants to return—a great way to end day one of the interviews.

The next day proves more interesting—starting right off with the first interview. Peter comes in presenting the case that maybe *he* isn't good for Brig-Wallis. He tells the Headmaster that he feels that he has been disruptive, selfish, and self-absorbed, and not entirely "on board" or "in line" with what he himself had determined was the "ideal" Brig-Wallis student.

"And what, pray tell, is it that you think makes up the 'ideal' Brig-Wallis Student?" prods the Headmaster.

"Well," Peter begins, "the way I figure it, it's the natural and unfailing allegiance to everything about the place: the grounds, the people, the curriculum, and the traditions. I watch the staff and the few upperclassmen I get to see, and I see this attachment and reverence for each other, for you, for the Brig-Wallis practices and traditions. I don't think I'm there. I don't think I'm one of you. Don't get me wrong. I love it here; I love everybody here—I can think of no better place on the planet—and definitely no other place I'd rather be—no place I love more. But I don't see me as your guy. I'm too selfish—too self-absorbed. I'm not friendly like Joe-pa. I'm not the life of the Brig-Wallis party type of guy like Bryce or Adam or Jimmy or Harry. I'm not a giver like Harry or Zi or Nathan or Emil. I'm a taker. Brig-Wallis thrives on givers."

The Headmaster is dumbfounded at Peter's astute reckoning of both the school's successful chemistry and his own self-assessment. "Once again, Master Vandenhof, you have caught me off guard." He takes a moment to collect himself. "I had thought that you liked it here—"

"I told you: I do," Peter asserts.

"And yet, if I hear you correctly," the Headmaster continues, "it sounds as if you think that I should…excuse you from returning for your third year."

"It would be a waste of the Brig-Wallis money and resources," Peter states flatly.

The Headmaster is silent a moment, considering his own options in this unexpected scenario. "Well, Master Vandenhof, I must admit that your assessment of your own shortcomings is spot on," he says. "And yet we both know that you have had some extenuating circumstances that may have, shall we say, retarded your growth here for a bit. But we both also know that you have turned yourself around, that you have been a much more engaged and collegial-minded community member over the past few months."

"Thank you, sir. That is kind of you to say. But I still see myself as being distant and arrogant. I am not an asset to this community."

"I'm afraid, young Master Vandenhof, that I am going to disagree with you there," the Headmaster says. "I base my challenge to your assertions on what I see as the continual and ongoing realization of tremendous potential. You forget, Peter, that you are still young. At sixteen, a young man still has a lot of growing to do—and I don't mean just physically. You still have a lot of experience to gather and a lot of mastery as yet unaccomplished. I think that this, coupled with my own wisdom and years of experience, should necessarily disqualify you from being the final judge of your valuation to this community. I think that you belong here. I think that you are, in fact, an asset to this school community and, the way you are developing, I think you may grow to become an even greater asset." He pauses to gather his next words. "It is my most sincere hope and desire, Master Vandenhof, that you would reconsider and decide to stay on at Brig-Wallis. I think you will be happy if you do. The third-year experience is one that might help prove to you that you are more valuable here than even you can imagine."

"Thank you, sir. I will take your counsel under advisement," Peter says with such formality that one half expects him to stand and salute the Headmaster. While he does stand, he does not salute.

"When do you need to know my final decision, sir?"

"Well, Peter," the Headmaster says, trying to de-escalate the formalness of their encounter. "I would say that any time over the summer will do. Even as late as September, if that is what you need."

"Thank you, sir. I will be in touch," he sticks out his hand to shake.

"Yes, well, thank you, Peter," responds the Headmaster uneasily, shaking Peter's hand.

"Good-bye, sir."

"Good-bye, Peter."

"And, Headmaster?" Peter turns before exiting the room. "Thank you so much for all you've done for me. Your guidance and tutelage have been invaluable to me." Then, softening a bit, he adds, "We both know I wouldn't have made it without you."

"Now, I wouldn't go that far, Peter—"

"I would. I know it to be true. So, thank you."

"You're welcome, Peter."

Peter walks out—leaving the Headmaster with one of the most disturbing feelings of uneasiness that he has known in many a year.

In retrospect, the Headmaster realized that the remainder of Friday's interviews passed by in something of a haze. He was less than fully present in the interviews that succeeded Peter's, and, therefore, he knows that he did not truly get his way with each student as he had planned: Harry Hagen and Nathan Ambrose both fully deserve to be at Brig-Wallis. Though both students eventually succumb to the Headmaster's 'pressure' to reenroll, Vittorio feels that he did a rather poor job of making them feel as worthy and valued as they both, in fact, were.

And then there are his three "mystery boys": the devious, quietly narcissistic Thomas Russell—whom the Headmaster does not truly trust, and yet in whom he has observed growth and still sees potential; the quiet, mouselike, nearly invisible, yet unobjectionable John Marchaud; and Michael Paine—whom the Headmaster admires for his self-determinism and for his showing the self-discipline to climb out of the rut of the addictions he had succumbed to in the autumn but whom the Headmaster still feels is lacking of some inner strength and inner compass or inner security necessary to matriculate into the fold, into the "team."

In the end, all three commit to their return for a third year. Yet Vittorio Visconti is left empty—reeling from the prospect of losing his star pupil, his "protégé." He finds himself feeling quite unsettled with regard to the stretch of time that he will have to endure until Peter contacts him with his decision.

Is there anything I could be doing over the summer to help sway him? is his last thought in bed that night before putting his mind to rest.

15

PETER'S SOCIAL SUMMER

Peter goes home for the summer feeling lost, without a compass. Those last three weeks in Switzerland had really shaken him. He had spent hours analyzing his motives, his values, his morality. Then he would calm down, relax, have a good meditation or walk. But then it would all start again: doubt, questions, self-recrimination. He knew he did not want to play a role in contributing to people's (or the planet's) suffering, but, then, *what role? How would or could one live among humans and not play some role in the chaos of human degradation—even if it were passive and unconscious?* These are the kinds of questions that plagued Peter during those last few weeks at school—the questions and thinking that made him present himself in his end-of-year interview with the Headmaster as he did.

The one good thing that happened before Peter left school was that he received a letter from Meela. With his recent acquisition of her full name, he had been able to send her a letter care of the Surval School. After struggling for hours, through multiple drafts, he sent a letter that was simple and straightforward: "I love you," and, "Is there any chance we might see each other over the summer?" Meela's reply was even more condensed: "I've booked a flight home through JFK on Monday, August 8. Love, Meela" followed by the pertinent flight information.

August! I have to wait until August? is Peter's initial reaction, which is then followed by, *I get to see Meela in August!*

For five weeks Peter's mind—and his life—seem as mercurial as that reaction to Meela's letter. His moods swing radically from one extreme of the emotional spectrum to the other in the space of seconds: from frustration to excitement, optimism to pessimism, self-love to self-criticism, and so on. What he thought would be an easy transition back into his routines from the previous summer at the family's Westchester compound proves to be something else entirely: he is simply unable to get a handle on his anxiety, his perpetual state of antsiness. So, surprising even himself, he moves around a lot. He tries Fishers Island, but that is definitely not the scene for him. Remarkably, he finds himself feeling social—but not in the country club kind of way. He wants to see people. And art. Culture. So, he ends up spending most of July in Manhattan at his parents' apartment house on Eighty-First Street. With eight beds and eight bathrooms and multiple sitting- and entertainment rooms in this full-floor residence, Peter can have his privacy, when he wants it, but he can also have immediate access to all of the art and activity that New York has to offer.

It is indeed such a strange feeling for Peter to feel such a desire to be with people—and it keeps growing. He finds himself far more interactive and far more interested in people watching than ever before. When he goes out, he loves hanging out in Central Park or outside—or inside—the Metropolitan Museum of Art. He goes to visit Adam in the hospital. He has John Marchaud and Emil spend overnights with him. After what starts out as a sluggish, scattered, first couple of weeks of vacation, Peter finds his busy social calendar to be quite satisfying—quite the cure for his tentative start.

One thing continues to remain unresolved: his final decision about whether or not he is going to return to Brig-Wallis. More often than not, he suppresses brooding over the topic. When he is with his school friends, they all act as if there is no question that they will all be together again as third-years. But, alone, Peter continues to have his doubts. Even a letter from Headmaster Visconti does not help sway him one way or the other. It isn't time. Deep inside, Peter knows that a lot hinges upon his rendezvous with Meela.

When August 8 finally arrives, Peter finds himself feeling uptight. He did not sleep well, as he tossed and turned over the details and decisions and myriad possibilities the day ahead might reveal. *Take the limo or a taxi? How to dress? How much time will we have together? Will the flight be on time? What if it isn't? What if she misses her flight? What if her plans have changed? What if they change the receiving gate? What if she doesn't have any time between her flights and can't come out of the TSA restricted areas?* Et cetera, et cetera. Peter cannot get out of his head long enough to enjoy any part of the day.

When he arrives at JFK Airport two hours early (he takes a cab), everything seems to be going smoothly. No flight delays. No cancellations. Normal flow. Great weather.

Meela's flight arrives on time. (Swiss Air is pretty dependable like that.) She emerges from the restricted area with all of the other passengers from the flight. Peter sees that she sees him—they wave through the glass—but she is a little preoccupied, he can tell. It turns out that she is helping another passenger—an elderly lady who looks very first class and couldn't be a day younger than eighty-five years old. Meela is helping her to manage her two carry-on bags.

As they emerge from behind the glass doors, Peter can hear Meela saying, "See, Miriam? This is the young man I was telling you about. Isn't he handsome?"

The cute old lady, who is no taller than a ten-year-old girl, looks up into Peter's face and says, "I'll say, honey. As a matter of fact, if I were a little younger, I might give you a little run for your money with this one!"

Peter blushes.

"Peter," Meela is saying, "I'd like to introduce Missus Miriam Grosbeck to you." Peter bows graciously. "Miriam, this is my friend,

Peter Vandenhof." Mrs. Grosbeck holds out her hand for him to kiss—which he does obligingly.

Then Meela moves forward and into Peter's unusually formal embrace.

"I'm just going to help Missus Grosbeck get her bags, if that's okay," she says, pulling back from Peter's airport hug.

"That's fine," Peter says. "Is there anything that I could carry," he asks, brimming with joy at being in Meela's company.

Meela is focused on orienting herself within the airport.

"Miriam!" Meela suddenly spouts. "Our baggage carousel is going to be this way," she says as she tries to guide the unsteady lady toward the baggage claim area.

Once they have all secured their bags and Meela and Peter have helped get Mrs. Grosbeck and her luggage to a taxi, they finally have time to focus on each other.

"So! What do you want to do? How much time do we have?" Peter begins.

Meela drops her bags to the sidewalk and, saying, "First things first," walks into Peter's arms and kisses him—a long, fully engaged, attention-gathering kiss. When they separate, Meela just stands there: composed, smiling slyly, never taking her eyes from his. Peter, on the other hand, breaks away amid feelings of self-consciousness interrupting his euphoria. He finds himself wondering what he has done to deserve this...bounty, while, at the same time, feeling painfully aware of the visible bulge in his trousers.

"I felt that," says Meela playfully. "What're we going to do about *that*?" she asks—which makes Peter feel even more awkward and uncomfortable.

"We start walking," he says, picking up one of her bags with one hand and grabbing her hand in the other. "Let's go!"

"Where to?" she says, grabbing her purse and her other carry-on bag.

"I don't know," Peter answers. "Just not here." He heads back toward the interior of the terminal. "How much time do we have?"

"How much time do you want?" is Meela's reply. Peter stops dead in his tracks, frozen, searching her face for meaning. "Would the rest of our lives be too much to ask?" is his flirtatious answer.

Meela squeals and sidles up to him. "I like the way that you think, Peter Vandenhof."

"But, seriously," Peter continues. "How much time do you have?"

"Well, school starts back up on—"

"No! Seriously," Peter interrupts, enjoying her playfulness but wanting to get something started.

"I told my parents I was going to spend a few days with a friend in New York."

"What?! Seriously?!"

Meela's raised eyebrows are the only response he gets.

"You're serious?"

"Mm-hmm."

"I get to, like, take you home? Take you into the City?"

"If that's what you want to do."

"I don't know *what* I want to do! I *never* expected *this*!" he says. "I thought we'd have minutes or, if I was lucky, an hour or two—here, at the airport—before you'd have to catch your connecting flight!"

"Nope," Meela says nonchalantly. "Next flight is…whenever."

"Oh my God!" Peter starts spinning around—with Meela's bag in his outstretched hand becoming a danger to other airport travelers. "Oh my God! I can't believe this! I am in *hea*ven!"

"So, what are we gonna do?"

"What? Umm. Let's go! Let's go into the City!"

"Okay," she says.

Peter starts heading back toward the taxi pickup zone. Meela is looking at the overhead signage. "Let's take the subway."

"What?!"

"Yeah! Subways are so exciting! You meet the greatest people there!"

Peter is thrown a bit. "I don't know *how* to catch the subway from here—or even *if* the subway comes out this far."

"It does," Meela says, pointing to the signs above them.

"Okay, then," Peter swallows. "Subway it is." And they begin the long—extraordinarily long—walk through the most bizarre setup of convoluted underground walkways in order to get to the Howard Beach sub stop at the west end of JFK airport.

The walk is made much more tolerable by their companionship; their conversation is able to keep them distracted from the demands of the tenuous walk. Peter finds out that Meela has spent the entire summer at Surval. She'd been recruited as a counselor for the school's six-week summer camp—which amazes Peter because of the enormous responsibility such an assignment places upon a sixteen-year-old. So most of the walk passes quickly as Meela relates story after story from her summer camp adventures.

When they finally get to the subway station, Meela proves to be the more savvy at procuring their subway tickets from the A train into Manhattan.

Once they have gotten Meela's suitcase and carry-on into the train car and have secured two side-by-side seats, she asks, "Where are we going?" They're both looking up at the subway map on the train car's interior wall.

"Looks like we can take the A train all the way to Penn Station and then transfer over to Grand Central and then up—"

"Can we take the Lex? I just *love* the Lex!" says Meela.

Peter hesitates, looking at the map, seeing the possible routes and their transfer station names. Inside, he continues to find that the thought of taking the Lex is a bit unsettling—as if some negative childhood experience is associated with it. "Sure, okay," he says. "We can change at Fulton Street," he adds, knowing that that's an okay neighborhood. "That way we only have to change once."

"Yay!" Meela squeals, her body wriggling like a child.

They fall into a spell of quiet as they watch the passing scenery. (The train is above ground for a good portion of the trip into Brooklyn.) The rustling vibrations of the lumbering train on the rickety tracks also have a lulling effect. But for Peter, he is just happy being able to sit next to Meela, just being able to hold her hand.

Eventually the car begins to fill. At first some of the boarding passengers look rather business typical. Some you can tell are from a different class as they step on in various forms of service uniforms: nurses, maids, security guards.

The train suddenly moves into the darkness of the underground. At the very next stop, Rockaway Avenue, an overdressed older lady barely manages to get on board with an overabundance of overstuffed plastic and canvas bags. She does not look at Meela and Peter as she collapses into a seat directly across from them, letting her bags take up the extra space on both sides of her.

She looks tired. She peeks ever so furtively at the young couple before shrinking back into a guarded, hypervigilant posture that reminds Peter of a scared rat.

"Hi!" Meela says to the lady, startling Peter out of his slumbering state of passive observer. "What's your name?" she asks in a voice intoning perfect innocence.

To Peter's shock, the woman answers. "Ladonna," she says. Peter notices that there are a few teeth missing from her mouth. "Ladonna Crane."

Meela leans forward. She reaches across the narrow aisle separating her from Ladonna and gently takes hold of one of Ladonna's hands. She cradles it in her own, studying it as if she were a palm reader. "Ladonna. You have the most *beau*tiful hands!" The woman is obviously caught off balance. She does not, however, remove her hand from Meela's grasp. "Why, Miss Ladonna Crane!" Meela says. "Did you forget to put your lotion on your hands this morning?"

Ladonna squints her eyes, the ratlike wariness back.

"Your hands are so *dry!*" Meela says, gently placing Ladonna's hand back in her lap. Meela sits back and begins foraging through her considerably sized brown Italian-leather purse. "I know I have some lotion in here…" she says before pulling out a small vial of Lancôme hand lotion. "Ah-*ha!* I knew I had some!" Then, scooting back across the aisle, she perches herself on her knees, on the floor of the train car, at Ladonna's feet. Meela begins applying her lotion to Ladonna's hands, one at a time, massaging each one as she does. "I'm sorry for that *aw*ful smell," she says.

"It's all right," are Ladonna's soft words.

"You and I both know, don't we Ladonna, that there's nothin' worse than *ashy* skin!" which evokes a cackle from Ladonna. "No, no, no," Meela goes on, shaking her head exaggeratedly as she continues her manual ministration, "No ashy skin."

"Girl! Where'd you learn to talk like that?"

"Why, Miss Ladonna," Meela breaks into an exaggerated Southern belle accent. "I thought I learnt it from you!" which provokes another series of laughs from the older lady.

"Girl! You are a *trip*! I ain't laughed like this in a *long* time!"

"I'm glad," says Meela, switching hands. "Laughter is *such* good medicine!"

"You got that right, young lady!" responds Ladonna studying her benefactor intently. "I have a feeling that *you* is good medicine, little darlin'."

"Why thank you, Miss Ladonna," Meela responds. "I am flattered."

Ladonna continues studying Meela as Meela finishes the second hand and places it back on Ladonna's lap.

Peter is thinking that this is probably the most relaxed—and loved—that Ladonna Crane has felt in a long time.

As Meela finishes putting her bottle of lotion back into her purse, she falls back on her heels and looks up to the lady sitting in front of her, still fixated on her hands. "Those hands have seen some hard work," she says. Then, looking up to Ladonna's face, "What is it that worked those hands so hard?"

Ladonna looks down on Meela as a tear streaks down her face. "Young missy, I don't know what I did to deserve such a blessing today, but you are gift straight from God Almighty!"

"As are you, Miss Ladonna Crane. As are you."

Meela gets back on the seat next to Peter, though her eyes remain transfixed on her new friend across the aisle. “Ladonna, when was the last time you ate something? Something that tasted good, was good for you, and filled you up?”

Ladonna reflexively draws back, looking like her former rodent self. Then, with effort, she relaxes a bit. “’S’been a while,” she says.

“How ’bout you and me and my handsome knight in shining armor here get off at the next stop and find a place to have a nice healthy meal. Would you like that?”

Peter squirms a little—obviously a little uncomfortable with Meela’s proposition.

“Why, Peter and I have nowhere special that we have to be,” turning to Peter, “Do we, honey?”

“Umm. No,” is Peter’s limp reply.

“By the way, my name is Meela. And this is Peter.”

Nods are exchanged all around.

“Besides, Ladonna,” Meela launches ahead, “I have a feeling that I’m gonna enjoy hearing your story. And this,” indicating the train car, “is no place to hear a story. What do you say? Will you let us take you up for a meal?”

Ladonna takes a moment before answering. Her eyes move from Meela to Peter to her surroundings in the train car and back to Meela again. “You sure you got the right person, Miss Meela?” she asks. “I’m thinking that you and your handsome young man got plenty o’other things better to do with your day than hang around with some—”

“Nope!” Meela interrupts. “Like I already said, we got nowhere to be and no schedule. But we’re both hungry,” turning once again to Peter, “Aren’t we hungry, Peter?” at which Peter nods his head: he does have to admit that he is hungry.

Ladonna waits another few seconds before answering. “Well,” she begins, as Meela visibly claps, “if you two is serious—and seein’ that you two has got to eat anyway. You sure you wanna do this?”

"Yes!" says Meela almost beside herself with excitement. "Don't we, Peter?!"

"Yep!"

Meela is quick to move forward. "Let's see...the next stop is... Fulton Street."

"Perfect," says Peter.

"Perfect!" Meela exudes. "Oh, I'm so excited. And so hungry!"

And, so, Peter and Meela spend the next couple of hours in the company of Ladonna Crane. Despite the burden of having to cart Meela's luggage around with them, Peter finds himself relaxing and truly enjoying the experience—particularly Meela's amazing gift for easily disarming and coaxing people out of their shells. Her guileless ways are so bewitching that they are contagious: even Peter finds himself joining in on the banter that is, he recognizes, an outpouring of love—*for that is what it is,* he articulates in his mind. *Meela is simply, unabashedly—fearlessly—loving everyone who is lucky enough to cross into her world.* As a matter of fact, Peter recalls, Meela has this same effect of lifting spirits on everybody. From Mrs. Grosbeck back at the airport—whom Peter had assumed had been an old family friend but, he found out later, had only met Meela on the plane—to Dixon the ticket taker at the subway station, to Charlie the flower vendor outside Central Park, and to David, the front-door man at the entrance to Peter's parents' apartment building: they were all treated as equals—or better, more accurately, treated as the most interesting, most important person in the world while they were in the loving bubble of Meela's attention.

"You are unbelievable," Peter finds himself saying when they are finally alone in the guest bedroom that he knows his absent parents would find acceptable for Meela's stay in their home.

"Thank you," she says. "You're pretty wonderful yourself." She launches herself into the air to fall back onto the bed, whereupon she makes hand motions signaling her desire to have him join her. Peter finds that his initial reaction is one of hesitation. *My parents' home!* he is thinking. But then, realizing that they are away at their

Fishers Island "cottage" for the next two weeks, he decides to join her.

When they emerge from the bedroom an hour or two later, Meela is wearing a different outfit, and Peter, after first sticking his head out into the hallway to scope out the situation, tiptoes with only a bath towel draped around his torso down the hall to his own bedroom.

At dinner Peter watches in amusement and amazement as Meela works her magic on the servants. Cook, it turns out, is named Annette and was born in Belfast. The serving maid, Vanessa—a woman who had worked in Peter's family's home for over thirty years!—had successfully raised and put through college three sons! *Why didn't* I *ever think to get to know these amazing people?* he asks himself with no little pangs of conscience. He soon finds a little self-forgiveness in the realization that he had simply been following the lead example of his family in the way they had always treated *every*thing and everyone in their lives.

After dinner Meela takes Peter on a tour of wonder around his own home. She notices things around their home that he had never noticed or had taken for granted for years—though he does surprise himself with the amount of knowledge he possesses regarding quite a few of the objects that catch Meela's attention. This little awareness serves to help him remember and appreciate how curious and inquisitive he had been as a child.

At one point in the evening, Meela turns abruptly to Peter and says, "Let's go out!"

"What?" he retorts, once again caught by surprise. "Where?"

"I don't care," she says. "For a walk!"

"But it's nearly nine o'clock! That's three a.m. in Switzerland. Aren't you tired?"

"Not yet. I feel too alive! Come on," she pleads. "Just a little walk—around the block. That's it."

Peter acquiesces—though he suspects, based on their afternoon's adventures, that something as seemingly little as "a walk around the block" has a high probability of turning into a life-changing event.

They grab jackets despite the likelihood of a hot August night but are glad that they did, as a brisk breeze has picked up since the afternoon. Their stroll proves to be fun and not too filled with delays, as the streets are fairly busy. A lot of people, it turns out, take evening walks—and not just for their dogs—which Meela finds quite fun to meet and pet: each and every one. Peter had never realized how a human's pet can serve as such an easy gateway into getting any person to engage and open up. Thus, he becomes a witness to a long string of Meela's new "best friends" or, as Meela puts it later, "wealthy pets and their humans."

Over the course of their first few hours together, Peter realizes that Meela has a special way of treating everybody the same: it doesn't matter if they are old and rich, young and shady looking, homeless or working class, handicapped or disabled, eccentric or cool and reserved. To Meela they are all just people, and, as people, they just wanted to be loved—a service that she provides with ease and without artifice.

When they get back to Peter's parents' home, Meela leads Peter straight to his bedroom. She disrobes and gets under the sheets before Peter has a chance to protest.

A little while later, as they are lying in each other's arms, Meela opens a new conversation. "Tell me more about Brig-Wallis," she says. "Why are you there? How did you find it? I'd never even heard of it. No one has."

"I didn't find it. They found me."

"That's weird," she says. "How?"

"I don't know. Someone just showed up. Here. Knocked on the door unannounced."

"How did they get past David?"

"Good point. I don't know."

"Are solicitors always given such easy access to your front door?"

"No," Peter answers, deep in thought. "No, they're not. Security is *very* strict here."

"Then he must have been expected."

"Yeah. You're probably right. Just not by me."

"Your parents?"

"Maybe."

"What does your dad do?" asks Meela.

"I'm not totally sure. I know he's in the financial world."

"Hmm. Anyway. They found you."

"I guess."

"What do you think they want? What do you think they see in you?"

"I don't know. Perhaps good followers."

"Why do you say that?"

"'Cuz the twelve of us that remain are good, obedient, make-no-waves type of guys."

"And you're going to be a junior?"

"Third-year."

"Whatever," Meela quips. "By the way, that's weird, too."

"I think it's pretty common outside the American system."

"Hmm. And no girls—no women—anywhere in sight?"

"Not on campus, but we have free access to the town. And dances."

"Yes, thank you, Jesus, for the dances." Meela kisses him.

"What about you and Surval?" Peter asks. "How did you end up there?"

"Parents thought an all-girls Swiss boarding school sounded good. We weren't born rich like you. Money's only been a fairly recent phenomenon. But, suddenly, there's a lot of it. And my parents, I think, like the idea that their daughters might marry Kennedys or a son of a European billionaire."

"Is that what Surval is known for?"

"Not totally. It's a school for sheltered rich girls. It's meant to teach us about how the rich are supposed to have fun and how rich wives do philanthropy work."

"Really?!"

"Mm-hmm."

"Do you like it?"

"Yeah. It's okay. I love skiing. And running and biking and swimming."

"You sound like a triathlete."

"Yeah. I've done a couple half tris."

"Whoa!"

"I just like to be outside. And Surval lets you be outside a lot. And travel."

"I guess."

"Plus, any place is better than New Brunswick!"

"Yeah. Tell me about that. How'd your family end up there?"

"Boat building. My dad's a naval engineer. He builds expensive private yachts for rich people. The Irving family is paying him to build a luxury yacht for them at their old shipyard."

"How long does that take?"

"About three years. More with sea trials and retrofittings and makeovers."

"And how long have they been there?"

"Almost three."

"So they're getting near the end of the project."

"Yeah, but the Irvings will probably want him there for a couple more years."

"What're you going to do after Surval?"

"Next year?"

"What?! You're going to be a senior?"

"Yep."

"But I thought you were sixteen."

"I am. Birthday's in September."

"Oh!" says Peter, thinking. "I'm in love with an older woman!"

"Get over it," Meela says. "In forty years who's gonna care?"

"Forty years…sheesh. Where'll we be—what'll we be doing forty years from now?"

"This…" Meela begins playing with Peter's "toy," as she likes to call it.

In their next wakeful interlude, Peter focuses his questions on the future.

"What do you think you'll do after Surval? College?"

"Yeah. Probably."

"Any idea of where? What do you want to study?"

"I don't know. I haven't really given a lot of thought to it. I figure that's for this coming year."

"Do you think you'll be going to school back in the States? Or Canada?"

"I really don't know. We'll see. What about you?"

"Wow! I hadn't really thought about it. The Brig-Wallis experience is so 'here and now.' I don't even know what Brig-Wallis grads do."

"They must go to college. You said the school's called a prep school. Aren't prep schools to get you ready for college?"

"I don't know. I've never been to one before."

"Smart-ass!"

"But seriously. The program's kinda weird. Intense. They keep you super busy. We never travel. We even go to school six days a week."

"What?! Six full days?!"

"Yep. One just like the other. Sunday is our only rest day."

"And you never travel?"

"Never. 'Cept to go to the dances," answers Peter. "Last year I don't remember ever leaving the school grounds except for vacations and a few walks around town or hikes up into the hillsides."

"So do you get *any* exercise?"

"Yeah! Tons! Every day. And there are tons of choices. But they're all pretty much on campus. Runners or hikers and walkers leave campus but not for too long: our exercise time is built into our suppertime."

"That's weird. So do you study normal stuff? Languages, literature, history, math, and science?"

"Kinda, but not really. I mean, yeah, we touch on all of those, but our topics vary a lot. We kind of create the topics as we go along. And then the teachers guide us with questions and research projects."

"That sounds kind of interesting, actually. A lot better than boring old lectures and textbooks."

"Yeah! I think so, too!"

"So you like it there?"

"Actually, I love it. Learning has never been so...*fun*! And it never seems to stop. From the moment we start our day to the moment the lights go out, it feels like we're learning. And it's almost *ne*ver boring!"

"Wow. You sound lucky. Maybe that weird school of yours has got something."

"Yeah, maybe." Peter pauses. "Only, I'm in a bit of a dilemma right now."

"What kind of a dilemma?

"I'm not sure if I'm going back."

"Why not?"

"Well, when I look at all the other people there, I really wonder if I fit in."

"Are you bullied?" Meela asks.

"Oh, no! It's nothing like that! It's like...I'm different. I'm...selfish. Self-centered. I'm not as social or friendly or engaged in 'team' activities."

"And everyone else is?"

"It's hard to explain. It's like everyone else there—including the teachers and staff—they're all living as an easygoing, perfectly balanced, and healthy unit. An organism. And then there's me."

"Are you a troublemaker?"

"No! I just don't...fit in. I don't *na*turally contribute. It's not natural—not automatic for me—to think of others—to think of the whole, the collective. What I'm trying to say is that I'm too preoccupied with my own shit!"

"You're a teenager! Aren't you supposed to be all caught up in your own shit?"

"Maybe. But it seems as if the others...aren't. They've already figured out or risen above their stuff. I'm still dealing with mine."

"So this makes you think that you don't want to go back?"

"No! I *want* to go back. But I wonder if my motives are impure. I'm so selfish!"

"But if you went back, aren't the chances pretty good that you can figure your stuff out and continue to benefit from the school?"

"I suppose."

"And—excuse me for questioning your judgement, but I find it hard to believe that a bunch of teenage rich boys have all achieved perfection—"

Peter laughs. "No! I didn't mean to say that they're all perfect—"

"Well, then. Good. Neither are you. So, what's the problem?"

"I see what you're saying...but there's this other little thing..."

"Which is?"

"You."

"What?" she says with a laugh. "I'm no 'little thing,'" she snaps back. "*This*," she says as she fondles Peter's flaccid penis, "is a little thing."

Peter laughs. "Yes. You're right. That is a little thing. And, yes, you are really a big thing."

Meela looks at Peter. "I already told you, didn't I? We're young. Yes, we'll be together. We're together now. But being together is *not* the number-one reason you came back here. You have work to do! I came along—at your request—to hold your hand or kick you in the butt—whatever it takes to help you stay focused on the work you want to accomplish while you are here. And by 'help'—if that means leaving you alone so that you can focus, then that's what I'll do. I will not be the distraction—the excuse for you to drop out or avoid doing the work you set for yourself."

"How do you know all this?" Peter asks. "How do you have such clear confidence?"

"And why don't you?"

"Well, yeah," Peter mumbles.

"It's because I'm not as invested in the goals and results for my own personal growth as you. I told you: I've already used the Earth

School for all the learning I set out to learn. This trip is like a free ride for me. I'm here to play—to have fun. And help you if I can."

"So how are you helping me right—oh, never mind."

"Thank you. I thought you were going to try to suck me into your little pity party."

"Pity party?! You think I'm feeling sorry for myself?"

"Sure sounds like it to me: 'I'm too selfish.' 'I'm not good enough to go back.' 'They're all so perfect.' 'I should just quit and hang out with Meela.'"

"I never said that!"

"No, but I can tell you're thinking it. You were putting out feelers to see if I'd bite. You're caught in 'Disney princess mode': you meet your one true love, kiss, and give up everything to be together—happily ever after, of course."

Peter is stewing.

"Peter," Meela continues. "I love you. I've *al*ways loved you and I always *will* love you. But I love you so much that I won't let you stop trying, stop growing—I won't let you give up your dreams and goals just to be with me—"

"But what of *that* dream? What's wrong with dreaming of being with you?"

"Trust me. If you make that your number-one goal right now, forces will tear us apart. You haven't done the work yet—on yourself. You haven't *earned* the right to a happy, smooth-sailing life yet. You have a plan of which I am a supporting part, but I am *not* the main reason you came back."

"But then, why? Why did I come back?"

"I cannot answer that for you. And I won't. That is part of your work: self-discovery."

"And self-realization," Peter says flatly.

"Yes. Very good."

"Are you self-realized?"

"What do you think?"

"I don't know."

"Let's put it this way: I have mastered the rules and laws of the Earth School but there is *so much more* out there. This little playground we call 'Earth' is like for young schoolchildren."

"I don't know. It seems pretty hard to me."

Meela is silent a moment. "You're right. It is difficult. It all is. But it doesn't have to be. It all depends on how much importance you choose to attach to things."

"That's weird," Peter muses. "Just now you sounded just like my headmaster."

"Well, maybe he's a pretty smart guy," she says. "But I bet he's not as good at this," she says as she rolls on top of him to deliver a long, full-bodied kiss.

The next day Peter and Meela spend out and about, walking, spending a big chunk of the day in the Metropolitan Museum of Art as well as a lot of time in Central Park. Peter enjoys his day with his companion to no end—their hand holding and easygoing exchanges of affection—as well as the incredible strength and confidence and fearlessness he feels in her presence—yet he finds himself inwardly distracted. His decision to return to Brig-Wallis for his third year has gained resolve, and he is obsessing internally with how best to convey his decision to the Headmaster.

Peter manages to enjoy his day with his "spirit bride"—for this is how he has come to think of Meela—continuing to marvel all the while at her truly astonishing gifts for disarming and winning over the trust and love of every single person she chooses to engage with—which happens to be just about everybody, he realizes. And, despite his preoccupation, he finds himself emboldened by her example to "risk" more himself, the rewards being tremendous and uplifting.

At the end of the day—after they are in bed together, after they've made love again in their fumbling, playful, and even, at times, humorous, way—Meela announces that she will be leaving the next day. Peter is not surprised. He is actually more surprised to find how little disappointment or sadness he feels at her news. But he does manage to broach one last topic of sensitivity with her.

"Will we see each other again? This year?"

"I don't know," she answers.

"You know I want to," he says.

"I know," she responds. "I cherish every single moment I get with you. But they are not expected. They are not essential to my happiness or well-being. Just knowing that you are on the planet, knowing that you are on your path, knowing that you are safe, happy, and healthy—"

"I'm happiest with you," Peter interrupts.

"I love you, too," she says. "But I do hope that you will come to realize your own happiness—that endless fount of happiness that resides within each and every one of us—it's neither dependent on or controlled by anything or anybody outside of us. Your happiness is not dependent on me."

"I understand your words, Meela, but…it's like when I read these books that the Headmaster gives me: I understand their concepts, but I can't seem to see how they apply to me and my life. I mean, my experience level has not yet accumulated enough information to validate them."

"I understand. And you're kind of saying something that I've been trying to communicate to you: our love, our relationship, will take on far deeper, far greater meaning as you continue to follow your own path. The experiences that will help you to understand yourself, your place in this world, and my place in your life will become more apparent as you gain experience. You just have to live them on your own—on your own terms, in your own time. No one else can do it for you."

"I got that." Peter pauses a moment before speaking again. "Thank you. I'm so glad—so lucky that you give me this time—that you and I met this year."

"Really? Are you sure?"

"Yes," he asserts. "First of all, if everything happens for a reason, then there was a reason we met now instead of in twenty or forty years, right?"

"Yes," Meela affirms.

"And *I think* that reason is to show me how much further I have to go until I de*serve* you—until I catch *up* to you."

"It's not a race!"

"No, but, obviously, you are much farther along the spiritual path than me."

"It's okay!" she says. "You just got sucked in a little deeper than me."

"What?!"

"I think it's a guy thing," Meela asserts.

"What?! I'm not following you."

"Oh, nothing," Meela says. "I've probably said too much, anyway. Besides, this is our last night for a while—maybe a long time. I think we have more work to do," Meela says as she rolls over on top of Peter.

In the days after Meela's departure, Peter is surprised to find that he is not filled with sadness or brooding. Instead, he feels himself incredibly energized. Meela's fearless altruism has infected him. He finds himself on the move at all hours—mostly walking the streets—even at "risky" hours of the day and into areas of the city that he knows are generally considered "unsafe." These areas, however, usually are the ones that spawn the most rewarding experiences. Constantly testing his new mantra, "What would Meela do?" leads him into all kinds of joyful and empowering encounters.

In the middle of this, Peter manages a phone call to the Headmaster—or, at least, to the Headmaster's answering machine—on which he leaves the Headmaster the message that he "would like to come back" if he's still allowed. And wanted. A couple of days later, he returns home from one of his excursions around Manhattan to be greeted by the housemaid, Vanessa, with the message that his school's headmaster had called, and that "he had received your message and was looking forward to seeing you in September." While Peter stands in place, processing the significance of this message, he notices that Vanessa, too, has remained in place and is looking at him with a patient, yet expectant, look.

"Yes, Vanessa? Is there something else?"

"Well, Master Peter. I was just wanting to relay a message from Cook and me—about how much we enjoyed that new friend of yours, Meela. We do hope we'll be seeing more of her."

Peter smiles. "Me, too, Vanessa. Me, too."

At the very end of Peter's unusually social summer, Peter receives a phone call from Meela—a late-night phone call. "A lullaby," Meela calls it. They talk for nearly an hour, she to relieve her boredom and he to thank her for all of her wisdom, guidance, and inspiration—which takes him about twenty minutes to accomplish.

"So, what did you decide?" asks Meela, to which Peter mischievously replies, "I decided that I like it much better when you are here in this bed with me."

"You mean, on top of you?" Meela teases back.

"Well, that, too," he says embarrassedly. Then, composing himself again, "But, anyway. I'm going back to Brig-Wallis. I already informed the Headmaster."

"Good."

"Is there any chance we'll run into each other this year?"

"Are you coming to the balls?"

"Sadly, no. That's only for the second-years."

"That's so weird," Meela says. "Your school is just too weird."

"I know."

"Well, then, I'm not sure," Meela says. "That certainly makes it more difficult."

"Yes, it does."

"Well, then. We'll just have to wait and see."

"See what?"

"See what the Universe provides."

"Okay," he says, not consoled, after which they spin into the spiral of good-bye routines and rituals that have served young lovers from time immemorial, before finally hanging up.

16

THIRD YEAR, AUTUMN TERM

All third- and fourth-year students and most of the school staff at Brig-Wallis live in Merchant House. The teachers and some members of the staff live on the ground floor, the third-year students live on the first floor, and the fourth-year students live on the second floor, with their rooms overlooking the town below from its north side and, to the south, the Quad and hills and mountains leading to Simplon Pass.

The third-year living situation is yet again an adjustment from the previous two years. The eleven returning boys have the run of the floor in this rather "open" floor arrangement. The kitchen and commons area are in a large room that takes up fully half of the floor plan, with bedrooms and bathrooms reaching through a wide hallway to the west. Before the school acquired the building in the early nineteenth century, these were the original living quarters of the merchant family who owned and ran the place; while their businesses were downstairs, the children and extended family slept upstairs. The living area, sitting rooms, and lounges of the first floor had long since been converted to simpler bedrooms (six), and the one large commons area that includes the kitchen now served as both the eating and studying areas.

Though third-year students still had full access to all services and meals in the Dining Hall, the boys of 15-18 found that they very much enjoyed the newfound freedom of having their own food prep and eating area. At first it seemed as if independent eating behaviors far outweighed any dependencies on meals in the Dining Hall, but, as the new school year's rhythms began to unfold and settle, the third-year boys were quite often found in the Dining Hall for the Midday Meal (Chef Novelli's meals are difficult to top).

In their own kitchen, culinary aficionados Zi and Fabrice begin to enjoy an ongoing competition to see whose ethnic food style is most popular among their peers. (In all fairness, though, Fabrice is at quite a disadvantage due to his challenge of sourcing the quality and varieties of seafood desired for his Japanese-styled dishes.) Michael and John, in particular, take great interest in "the battle," because both had developed rather highly refined gourmet inclinations at very young ages. Though the fun of the foursome's nightly kitchen skirmishes is not lost on the others, they just have less weight invested in the outcomes. Rique and Harry have fairly bland, colloquial food preferences that have been dictated greatly by the fare they grew up with in Brasil and Germany, respectively, and Joe-pa has acquired the fairly bland palate that is most typical of the British population from which he came—though, ironically, Indian curries are forever a source of interest and excitement.

Nathan, Thomas, and Peter seem to gravitate toward various forms of vegetarianism, though each in his own style and for totally different reasons. Nathan's vegetarianism is totally driven by a life-long aversion to meat—in truth, to fat. It makes him gag. Ever since he can remember, the act of trying to eat meat has been a chore—and this includes both poultry and fish (though his antipathy to fish is due more to the taste and to the fear of swallowing bones). Chewing, chewing, chewing until he could manage an attempt at swallowing has made Nathan a slow and picky eater. As he has grown older, he has become more adept at choosing the least offensive serving of meat, making sure that all his meat offerings are cooked to "well done" in hopes of charring the fat (which makes it more tolerable), and achieving a well-honed surgical skill at fat excision. But Nathan is never so happy at a meal as when meat is not a requirement or option. Thus, he is in heaven at Brig-Wallis, both in the Dining Hall and in the autonomy of the third-year kitchen, for the absence of any and all expectation that he eat meat.

Thomas is an unusual vegetarian in that it might be more accurate to describe him as an ascetic. Always pale-skinned and without an ounce of fat on his small, boney frame, Thomas just never has much of an appetite. He is not sickly or one of those unfortunates afflicted with a tremendously sensitive digestive system; he just doesn't seem to require much input in order to keep him going. It probably helps that Thomas does not put very high demands on his body; it might even be said—by a social psychologist or the like—that Thomas does virtually everything with a tremendous economy of motion. Were it not for his exceedingly active mind, it might be surmised, then, that Thomas burns far less energy than the typical human and, therefore, must not require as much input to fuel his simple needs. But Thomas's mind is seldom at rest.

Another observation one might make about Thomas and meal times is that he uses these down times in the day for study: Thomas appears to be in a constant state of hypervigilance; it would seem as if nothing could or would be able to escape those ever-watchful eyes. In fact, Thomas's mind is driven to accumulate as much information as possible about his surroundings and, especially, of the biological creatures in his surroundings. He is in a state of constant Darwinian analysis: assessing any and all potential threats—real or imagined—to his well-being, as well as assessing every human being for his or her potential as a competitor—looking for weaknesses—weaknesses in character, weaknesses in physical makeup, weaknesses in psychological makeup—any chink in a person's armor that he or someone that he could manipulate might be able to take advantage of, if he ever need to. Where this pattern of constant suspicion comes from one cannot be sure, but Thomas was raised by surrogates: nurses and governesses and boarding schools and summer camps, while his parents traveled the global circuit of the wealthy elite. Provisional, conditional, even false or counterfeit love is all he ever knew, so perhaps his distance and almost-paranoid cynicism are understandable, even forgivable. He really is not a violent or vindictive child—never would he ever really act upon the wild fantasy schemes that his defensive mind contrives. It is purely the way his mind developed. And his eating habits are a perfect reflection of this: need or require nothing, and nothing can hurt you. This is why the temptations of addictive substances or habits hold no attraction to or sway over him. It is also why he does not easily earn or attract friendships. This is probably why the odd friendship that he and Harry Hagen have so awkwardly and, it must be admitted, ironically developed serves as such a source of interest to Headmaster Visconti.

The Headmaster was inclined at first to suspect that Thomas's motives were less than altruistic, more likely exploitative. Thomas is taking advantage of the German boy's size and strength, affable popularity, and genuine good nature, as well as his insecurities at being automatically assumed to be a "dumb jock"—or so the Headmaster thought. But, as time went on and he had watched the ebbs and falls, the give-and-take struggles between the two boys—as they, too, tried to figure out why and if this "friendship" could work, much less if it were authentic and genuine—he has found himself surprised to think, to believe—or was it only hope?—that the relationship has proven to be healing and strengthening to both of the boys. He has watched as Harry's self-confidence and self-assuredness have improved as he has learned to stop giving power to his projected perceptions of others. And he has watched the defensive paranoia in Thomas's eyes recede and disappear—has seen glimmers of his forgetting himself in moments of laughter and increasing social interaction. Thomas, the fear-motivated, rodentlike observer, has relaxed, has come out of the shadows and grown into a more trusting social creature.

It is all the Headmaster had hoped for. He has watched as these two major obstacles to these boys' being able to reach their full potential have dissipated. Still, he worries. *The tests that the third year pose could prove unraveling to the progress of* both *boys.* Yet, he chooses to remain optimistic. *Both boys possess superior strength of will. That will get them through,* he thinks, hopes.

The vegetarian lifestyle chosen by Peter Vandenhof is different still. For Peter, eating has always seemed like a waste of time—precious time. *Eating is a necessary evil,* thinks Peter, but he hates it for the time it takes away from other, more important things that he could be attending to.

Peter learned at a fairly young age—probably from *Animal Planet* or some other science-related show—that all our energy needs come from the indirect and inefficient conversion of the Sun's energy into burnable and/or storable energy in the human body. Plants are the best, most efficient solar energy convertors and storers. Animals eat plants and plant by-products for their possession of the Sun's energy. Carnivores eat vegetarian animals, going after the digestive organs first for their higher concentration of ready-made energy. So, Peter would ask, why can't humans just learn to directly convert and store the Sun's energy—light—as plants do? This is the question that has perplexed and occupied Peter's mind since he was about eight or nine years old. Some of Peter's strongest and most dominating memories come from his efforts, while sitting in the Sun, to try to absorb and convert and store the energy ("heat," he had thought) into the cells of his body. He had watched animals—they seemed to do it: cats and dogs, snakes and lizards. This probably helps explain his unusually developed awareness and familiarity with his body—as well as his facility and obsession with the effects of sound and thought vibrations on his systemic, cellular, and even atomic makeup. It also helps to explain his vegetarianism.

Peter is not necessarily a healthy vegetarian. His food choices always include the fastest, easiest caloric delivery system. Restaurant and school cafeteria food always work fine, because they are ready made. The same can be said for the food prepared by Chef Novelli or by Peter's family's cooks back home. On his own he almost always chooses quick-fix choices: whatever is fast, easy, ready-to-eat. Thus, Peter is as likely to choose a bag of chips or cookies as he is the chef-prepared omelet or salad. In fact, he pays so little attention to *what* he eats—to taste even—that it makes virtually no difference to him what he is shoveling into his mouth, so long as it satisfies any hunger pangs (which he thinks of as depleted energy stores, of course). Consequently, Peter has a very highly developed acuity to his points of satisfaction: when he feels as if his temporary needs have been met, he simply stops eating (and usually leaves the table to return to his most pressing mental preoccupation). This serves him well in that he rarely overeats and effortlessly maintains a svelte physique. But it may also work slightly against him in that, depending on the nutritional values of his chosen "energy source," Peter might find his inner alarm of "depletion stage" sounding more frequently on a junk-food diet as opposed to on a more desirable three- to five-meal day that might come from more nutrient-rich "healthy" foodstuffs. The advantage of the third-year experience with its more autonomous food choices is that Peter is able to perform some experiments that help him to gain some insights into which foodstuffs prove more sustaining and satisfying than others and, thus, keep those stocked for himself. (Third-year students are given the option of shopping and stocking their own foods in addition to food-preparation independence.)

It turns out that the point of greatest contention among the third-year "commune" revolves around getting the dishes washed. Though the consensual rule is "You use it, you wash it," this does not prove sufficient under circumstances in which a particular student or group of students takes it upon themselves to share the fruits of their own labors. Aside from Nathan, all of the boys have been spoiled in having been raised in homes where all sanitation "inconveniences" were performed for them by other, often hidden, services and servants. Thus, some of the responsibilities that come with the third-years' new freedoms have proven taxing, to say the least. Interestingly, it is the duo of Harry and Thomas that seems to have the most difficulty, which results in the pair of them splintering off a little more than ever before—taking all of their meals in the Dining Hall and spending more of their time away from the third-year commons area.

Another new "freedom" granted the third-year class is the relaxation of any expectation for them to attend or participate in Morning Chapel, Exercise, and Music or Choir. It turns out that this age-old practice was instituted precisely to "test" the third-year students into showing (and self-discovering) which parts of their daily life patterns have become so comfortable and/or valued that the boys would maintain them outside of requirement or expectation. Nearly all of the students take advantage of these new lax attendance expectations, but it ends up that third-year participation in all three extracurriculars averages about 95 percent. Even concerns about Thomas's participation in daily physical education and Enrique's precarious commitment to a strong, formal meditation practice prove unwarranted. (Thomas has become quite an avid martial arts enthusiast, and Enrique has an entirely different, surprising excuse: "It's so easy for me," he would say. "I meditate all day long in everything that I do!"—which seems to please Headmaster Visconti to no end.) Peter's loss of enthusiasm for musical exploration and participation causes a little concern to the staff, but again concern proves unwarranted. Both he and Enrique recognize the power of "group energy" while Thomas notes that "a healthy body makes a healthy mind."

The other huge transition to the routines of the third-year class comes in the form of their curriculum, as there are shifts here to both content and structure. Traditional sit-down, classroom-bound learning "classes" suddenly become less structured and less defined. There is a formal gathering in the morning after breakfast, in a classroom, in which a teacher, other school staff member, or occasional guest speaker shows up to initiate a discussion, research project, or other activity through his release of some provocative information. What Peter and Thomas are quick to recognize is that each day's activity seems to be built around problem-solving, yet the outcomes of the class's findings or reports are never graded or criticized. The students are never even talked about; instead, the day's adult leader(s) guides the group into another discussion of "what worked and what didn't" or "where they could have saved time and/or resources and still come up with the same solutions." The result of this unusual focus is that group projects have become more streamlined, more efficient. The group as a whole has become more cognizant and appreciative (and reinforcing) of the particular strengths and talents of its individual members. At the same time, the individuals have become more conscientious of their own personal "shortcomings." Some choose to yield to these discoveries and get out of the way so that others with better skill sets can step in and help the group achieve its finished product. Others stubbornly or diligently place more of their energies and attentions outside of class into improving upon these "weak areas."

Frequently, these projects that are initiated in the mornings will spill over into the afternoon block or even into multiple days of work before the group feels "ready" to present its "solution" to the administering adult. On several occasions, the presenting adult intentionally provides the class with unresolvable projects—just to see how long it will take the class to recognize and report, in the usual consensus format, that they were unable to come up with a viable solution. The ensuing discussions oftentimes prove to be more animated and more revealing than other solution-bound offerings.

On days that the group comes up with an early or quick delivery and reflective discussion, they might be released to the supervision of Herr Giorgiadis for some "Mentastics" exercises that prove to be far more complex than any they have received before. Or they might find Herr Garibaldi stepping into their classroom to lead them into some mind-expanding lecture, video, or exercise. Once in a while, the Headmaster might be waiting for them in order to lead them into a discussion of current world events, their implications and historical contexts.

It is interesting to report that all of the boys have noticed a rather odd disconnect between the Headmaster's discussion topics and the aim of the discussions he leads. It is as if he is more concerned—or, at least, more concerned than ever before—with the opinions and comments of each individual in the group—not with the words or grammar students would use, or even their accuracy or command of the facts, but with the ethics and values being conveyed. At first the students find the Headmaster's more aggressive, more personally targeted tactics alarming and unsettling. But, gradually, they begin to understand and recognize them for the concealed gifts of self-awareness and self-knowledge that they are. Nearly every individual present is able to comprehend that what the Headmaster is trying to do is to help them to discover their own limitations, their own boundaries. He always chooses to offer praise to the individual—not only for submitting to the "exercise" with fortitude and courage but also—more so—for being able to exhibit growth beyond previously held perspectives. The boys soon grow to understand that this is always the Headmaster's ultimate goal: to challenge them to branch out, to experiment, to explore new perspectives. "Even a slightly different perspective might mean all the difference between frustration and emotion or freedom and detachment," he is fond of saying, as well as, "Attachments to beliefs and values and expectations can and will *only* serve to lead one into emotional entanglements."

I get it! thinks Peter. *He's trying to teach us detachment! Detachment from everything!*

This realization, in turn, spurs Peter on to trying to apply these "new" terms of "perspective" and "detachment" to everything he does—even his bioenergy experiments and meditation practice—which are merging more and more into one practice. Though he is sure that the Headmaster does not intend a practice of detachment to translate into "not caring" or apathy, Peter does find himself struggling a little. So he decides to take his questions and concerns to the Headmaster himself.

It is early November when this falls into place. The Autumn Term well over half-finished. Peter and Headmaster Visconti still have not reestablished their "Sunday visits" from the previous year. Peter is unaware, but the Headmaster is leaving the dynamic of their relationship entirely in the hands of his young ward. He is making this choice not out of punishment or disinterest but out of patience and, yes, detachment. He has no desire to rush or force or unnaturally influence a student's individual growth and progress (at least, outside the classroom environment). Thus, he treats Peter no differently from any of the other students—whom he is surprised to find that he is enjoying tremendously—even Thomas, Enrique, and Joe-pa! But he has determined that there is absolutely no benefit in trying to force himself or his own private agenda upon Peter or anyone. Instead, he decides to stick with the tried-and-true pushes and prods that are provided quite naturally by the Brig-Wallis curriculum. If a student is going to "rise to the top" (though "self-actualize" might more accurately portray the Headmaster's viewpoint), the time-tested curriculum will make that happen. So, when Peter asks for a private audience, the Headmaster welcomes it without pretense. They schedule it for noon on Sunday.

When the appointed time arrives, Peter shows up calm and relaxed. The Headmaster is as gracious and affable as ever, yet something is different. *He is detached!* is Peter's delighted realization.

"What can I do for you, Peter?" asks the Headmaster, opening the conversation from a seated position behind his desk. Peter finds himself momentarily distracted by the beautiful lighting emanating from the stained-glass windows behind the Headmaster: the blues are particularly light and cerulean, but the amber of the yellows is what really catches his attention. "I forgot how beautiful those windows are," he says out loud.

The Headmaster turns around to look, saying, "Yes, they are." He follows that with, "Thank you for that reminder, Peter," before resuming his august position. "So, how may I be of help to you?"

"Yes! Sorry! I know that you must be busy," says Peter rather hurriedly. "Headmaster, I think I figured out what you're trying to teach us this year."

The Headmaster shows an interest that is genuine.

"You're trying to help us all to let go of our expectations—to expand our abilities to see from new and different perspectives," Peter says. "You're trying to help us learn detachment."

"Very good, Peter! And why do you think I would want you to learn those things?"

"Well. I've been thinking about this for a while…and quite intensely this week. The way I see it, it's all a natural progression within your desire or attempt to see if we're all the right stuff for those special leadership roles you mentioned during our first year."

"Go on."

"Well, I think the first year was aimed at getting us all to know and like ourselves—to see if we could feel comfortable here—if we felt as if we fit in. And then second-year was all about testing ourselves against adversity—especially against temptations and bad habits. And now, the eleven of us who remain are being taught to learn and master detachment."

"To what end?"

"Of that I'm not quite sure, Headmaster. But I've been thinking for a long time—about a couple of things you said in our previous years. I remember you using a term—"service leadership," or "leadership in service"—which, at first thought, seems like a koan or conundrum or even an oxymoron, as leadership generally implies an exertion of force—or at least will—upon others—a leader who both leads and serves…well, let's just say that that is a real unusual combination.

"Then I couldn't help but associate Bailey's use of the term 'ego,'" Peter continues. "The way she uses it, it makes me feel as if it's an evil thing—or at least something that inhibits or limits our true potential. And I look back on the students who didn't work out here—and the commonalities among those of us who remain—as well as of the staff and upperclassmen I've watched—and there are very few selfish, egocentric people here. The ones who were—even in the slightest way—are gone.

"And then I look at my own struggles—how my own ego has taken me into places that made me feel like I didn't belong here. I was a selfish, conceited, self-important 'man on an island.'" Then, looking straight at the Headmaster, he adds, "You know how I struggled with my decision to return here."

"I do," answers the Headmaster. "But what I *don't* know is what changed. What led you to make the decision to return?"

"Well, I guess it was realizing that there was nowhere else I'd rather be. That, coupled with the realization that I did not like this conceited, isolated person that I had become—that I wanted to try to change that person."

"And has that worked for you?"

"Yes and no. Yes, I made many more efforts to be social, to enjoy the company of others. I felt almost compelled to do so. And I do! People are really so amazing if you just give them the chance. I spent hours and hours just walking the streets of Manhattan, trying not only to trust the Universe and the goodness that I believe is at the core of all human beings but to trust in myself—to trust that whatever I might do or say with another human being—be it stranger or friend—was for the highest good of both me and that other person."

The alignment and attunement process, thinks the Headmaster.

"And it worked. I mean, it was really quite magical. I had encounters in subways—that was the best place to subtly 'force' interactions. I talked with homeless people and street musicians, old people and foreigners, even children—man! Can you learn a lot from children! And in the end, I began to feel...interested. Appreciative. I even came to the conclusion that I virtually fall in love with every single person I meet! I mean, if you give a person a chance, you can meet—or, maybe 'see' is the better term—the best in them—the most beautiful, lovely parts of them.

"And so I began to like even myself—to feel better about myself—to realize that all that time I spent in my head or in my own little world was not healthy—that I was creating an imbalanced, opinionated, self-righteous, and self-absorbed creature. And then I realized that I could make it work at Brig-Wallis—that all of these amazing, interesting, and beautiful people here at Brig-Wallis were exactly the kind of people I wanted to be like—were exactly the right kind of people for me to be around, to learn from in order to become a better, more well-rounded and complete human being.

"And now I see that this 'letting go' and peeling-away-the-layers process that you teach is intended to serve us all in this journey—to help us learn to see ourselves for who we've become, to dismantle any attachments we've come to so that we can be free to fulfill our potential as loving, interactive, responsible human beings."

"And the 'service leadership' aspect?"

"Well, I know we're not a Christian or religious school, but it seems like Jesus was a leader in service to...the world. His example, his mind-expanding lessons, allowed people to see and aspire to bigger versions of themselves, which was a consciousness-raising gift or 'service' to humanity. He led because he attracted followers! He never really aspired to be king or most popular or most powerful. He wanted to help humanity step up and realize new and better versions of themselves—to help promote the realization of human potential. And that, I think, is what you'd like us all to become: people who help others achieve the most in human potential."

The Headmaster looks on: pleased but, he realizes, somehow not surprised. "And so, Peter, what can I do for you today?"

"Am I right?"

The Headmaster considers for a moment. "You have successfully unraveled much of our intent here. You are not finished, but you are well on your way."

There is a brief pause before Peter gathers his thoughts—remembering why he came in the first place. "So, Headmaster, I am struggling with this concept of 'detachment.' How far is it safe to detach? I mean: if one took it to its extreme, one would stop trying, stop moving, waste away and die—"

"And that would *not* be a wrong choice," declares the Headmaster.

"What?!" Peter is shocked. "Really?"

"With a certain perspective—a certain knowledge—no, there would be nothing 'wrong' or 'bad' or 'scary' about that choice."

"You sound like Meela," Peter finds himself saying under his breath.

"Excuse me?"

"Oh, nothing. Sorry. Just talking to myself."

The Headmaster decides to let it go, though his curiosity is piqued. "I'm sorry, Peter," he says instead. "I interrupted your line of inquiry."

"It's okay. I was just saying that I'm really clueless as to how to apply this concept of detachment. Exactly what are we supposed to try to detach from?"

"My answer to you, Peter, is that it is best left for you and your process to figure it out. I assure you it will unfold as the year goes on."

"I've been trying—"

"I can see that. I guess a better answer for you is that there are no right or wrong applications of detachment. I will leave you with this statement: with the ultimate application of the law of detachment, we would be leaving the world of Illusions and rejoining our original state of Unity Consciousness from which there would be no here and there, no this and that, no need or want—and thus, no possible opportunity for attachment."

Peter is silent for a while. "Headmaster, I still don't get why we even choose to come here—to Earth—to occupy these human bodies. I mean, what's the point? How does this job—or adventure or whatever it is—how does it help us on that trip back to Unity Consciousness? Why aren't we just focusing on detachment—on trying to return to Unity Consciousness? It seems like this place, this Earth School, is just a playground for infants—a place of distractions that are really just diverting us from the real goal."

The Headmaster is silent a minute. "You are not wrong about the Earth-based human experience being a diversion, a trip in the direction away from Unity Consciousness…what is difficult to explain is that this part of the Journey of Spirit into Form—of which we are active participants—is to help explore the farthest reaches of Creation—to help explore the deepest depths that the Grand Illusions of Duality make possible. The Earth-based human experiment is a very bizarre yet contrived, distant, and dense step away from the joy, freedom, and beauty of Unity Consciousness. But, for whatever reason, here we are. Our Oversouls—our Higher Selves—have decided to participate in this brave and bold—and, yes, scary—journey. We are serving the Cosmos by helping to actualize the imaginative possibilities of creative potential. And all I can say to your question of 'Why?' is the answers that God might give: Why not? For the experience! To say that we did!"

Peter can tell that the Headmaster is a bit angry—that he is venting. And yet he can tell that he's not venting at him, Peter, but at God or at someone else. *He's angry at…his job?* Peter wonders. At that moment Peter feels a very deep sympathy for the Headmaster. He finds himself trying to put himself in the Headmaster's shoes and is shocked to find that the Headmaster must have a very difficult job.

"I'm sorry, Headmaster," he says. "I'm sorry to have wasted so much of your time." And then, getting up, says, "I should be going."

The Headmaster is unresponsive—deep in his own thoughts, surprised at his release—more surprised at the empathetic response of this boy. *Is he the one?* he finds himself thinking for the first time in a long time.

Peter leaves the Headmaster's office in a daze. His mind is in a frenzy as he's bombarded with a procession of all of the things he could have said—could have, should have said differently. This gives way to a new parade of thoughts and memories, things heard and things imagined, of all that might have been inferred during their conversation.

He decides to seek some fresh air, to go for a walk. The fresh air and time away from anything resembling academia helps—a lot. Eventually, he returns to Merchant House. He plops down in a couch in the third-years' commons room, still deep in thought. Fabrice and Zi are squabbling, as usual, behind the island sink and food prep area. John and Emil are working quietly, both writing, at a distant study table. Joe-pa suddenly emerges from the bedroom hallway.

"Hey, Peter! What's up?" It is the same thing the ever-convivial Joe-pa would say to anyone he might encounter upon entering the commons room. But things unfold a little differently today.

Peter looks up. He likes Joe-pa but realizes suddenly that he's never given Joe-pa much credit—rarely talked with him. He decides, for some reason unknown—even to himself—to change that.

"Do you really want to know?"

Joe-pa stops, looks down at Peter, and realizes that this is a first: Peter Vandenhof is offering to let him, Edmund George Paul Taylor, into his very private and complex world.

"Yeah," he says, stopping to sit down on the couch next to Peter.

"Okay," Peter says.

Peter begins to unload. The extraordinary oddity of this occurrence even draws Emil and John into Peter's audience. Two years of questions and theories, answers and conversations—mostly with regard to his findings about the school—come pouring out of Peter. The others sit dumbfounded, thoroughly astonished at hearing all that they had never known was going on inside Peter during the course of their association.

"Whoa! Peter! You've got a busy mind," is Joe-pa's first comment when Peter has finished.

"It can't be healthy to have been holding all that inside for this long," says Emil.

"I'm sure you're all just as busy in your own heads," is Peter's comeback.

"Not even close!" says an exasperated Joe-pa.

"I'm just glad you shared this with us," says Emil.

"Yeah, but now we have to figure out what to do with it," says John.

"We do nothing," says Peter. "There's nothing *to* do. Unless it upsets you: then you either learn to live with it or you leave."

Everybody seems to take a moment to process.

Peter is the first to speak again. "We learn to use it in our daily awareness," he says. "It's just another level of awareness—'a different perspective,' the Headmaster would say."

The boys' ensuing silence seems to indicate unanimity with this declaration.

17

THIRD YEAR, WINTER TERM

The Winter Term at Brig-Wallis opens with yet another shift in the curriculum. Maestros Garibaldi and Giorgiadis announced on the first day of classes that the focus of the Winter Term's learning activities is to be called "Group Dynamics and Mutual Aid." They explain that the boys will be set forth into activities that will require "team building," the conquering of personal fears, the testing of one-another's comfort zones, and the learning of trust and *inter*dependency in order to achieve successful problem solving. They also say that there will be assignments given that will not and *cannot* be completed without the successful cooperation of each and every member of the group. While some of the assignments will be hypothetical or virtual (i.e., computer simulated), most of them will be "real." Many of the exercises will be easy for some while harder for others—and some will be specifically designed for specific individuals with the design of trying to help them conquer specific fears.

The first assignments are given that day. The boys are told that they are expected to plan, prepare, and clean up after a full seven-course meal. The meal is to be sufficient to feed the entire school community, and it is to be served as the main meal on Sunday—*this* Sunday. They are told also that they will be able to use all campus resources and facilities but that on the day of the meal, they are to be alone in the kitchen, with no Chef Novelli and no staff.

Needless to say, the news of this assignment excites some of the boys, while it upsets a few of the others.

Herr Giorgiadis quells all dissention with the declaration: "*Ev*erybody is expected to contribute and participate in *all* phases of the meal—from planning and procurement of the necessary ingredients to preparation and cooking to service and cleanup." He then looks to his coteacher before adding, "You are expected to leave the place as you find it."

Before the boys are set loose on their initial planning discussions, Maestro Garibaldi passes around a tray of medical specimen jars. "Each of you please take one," he instructs while the tray circles the room. "You are each to return with a semen sample tomorrow," he says, raising all sorts of noises. "Do not come to class without it. And, yes, it must be your own semen."

The sudden, awkward silence in the room lies heavy with emotion as most of the boys find themselves feeling embarrassed or even angry at the "assignment." Eventually, the boys are able move on to focus successfully on their meal planning.

The next day, the boys all return to the classroom with their semen samples—which Maestro Garibaldi ceremoniously lines up on the table in front of him. "Very good," he says. "Now, I think we can all admit that everyone here knows how to masturbate," which leads to some tension-relieving laughter. "We're all human. We're all males of our species." Then he adds, "I hope some of you were even able to enjoy yourselves," which leads to a few more laughs.

Maestro Garibaldi then proceeds to open each jar and pour their contents into one jar that he leaves standing on the table. The others he moves to the lab sink behind him, where he rinses and washes them. When he finishes, he sets the ten cups on the counter top to dry and returns to the one cup that now contains the sum total of the group's semen.

He takes out a Sharpie marker from his shirt pocket and makes a horizontal stripe to mark the top level of the cup's fluid contents. Then he pours the cup out into the sink, rinses and washes it before setting it back on the table in front of the class.

"So, how goes the dinner planning?" he asks, releasing the mesmerized group into a relieved frenzy of sharing and discussing their progress and obstacles.

"Well, you have the rest of the morning to continue trying to work out your issues. Good luck!" says the teacher before stepping out of the room.

The boys get to work, with all kinds of animated voices and excited behaviors on display. At the end of the period, before releasing the boys to the Midday Meal, Maestro Garibaldi brings the class back to his attention. "I have two more assignments for you to work on. First: let me announce that, on Monday of next week, you will all be going snow skiing."

This news elicits several enthusiastic cheers. "It is a third-year-only field trip."

"Sir?" Rique's meek voice interrupts his classmates' cheer. "I don't ski."

"You don't ski, Master Osario, because you don't like to or because you don't know how?" asks the teacher.

"Because I don't know how," Rique answers. "I've never been skiing."

Rique's response evokes several, "What?!" and "You'll love it!" comments.

"Are you willing to learn?" is Maestro Garibaldi's response.

"Yeah. Sure. I guess. Why not?" is Rique's less-than-easy answer.

"Good," Garibaldi responds. "It is your classmates' job, then, to help prepare you—to help teach you how to ski."

"All right!" bursts out of the general class members.

Zi's hand goes up. "I don't know how to ski either," he says.

"Okay, Master Li. Are you willing to learn?" asks Maestro Garibaldi again.

Zi hesitates. “I have a fear of heights,” he says before pausing. “Bad,” he adds.

Everybody hushes.

“Is it something you’re willing to work, Master Li? In order to try to conquer?” asks Maestro Garibaldi.

“Yeah,” answers Zi. “I guess. But I don’t know how. I was born with it. I’ve always been afraid of heights.”

“How ’bout it, boys?” asks the teacher, scanning his class. “You think you can help Master Li learn to ski despite his fear of heights?”

There is some subdued discussion.

“Well, believe it or not, that is part of your assignment: help Master Osario and Master Li learn how to ski,” states Maestro Garibaldi rather flatly. This leads to more discussion, this time more animated, which results in encouraging words and hand slaps issued toward both boys.

“Oh! I almost forgot!” says Maestro Garibaldi, attracting the group’s attention once more. He holds up the plastic specimen jar. “You are to return this tomorrow. Filled up to this line.” He uses his finger to indicate the line he had drawn.

“With sperm?!”

“Yes, sir!” the teacher answers. “And everybody—*ev*erybody contributes!”

Maestro Garibaldi’s unusually authoritarian decree is met with a deafening silence.

“Got it?”

Several deflated “yeahs” escape from the group.

“Here, Master Ambrose. You’re in charge,” says Maestro Garibaldi, handing the cup to the mortified boy. “Class is dismissed.”

The next morning the group returns. Nathan squeamishly places the cup on Maestro Garibaldi’s teaching platform. It is full to the line, as assigned.

“Very good,” says Maestro Garibaldi. “And, just to check: everybody contributed?” His eyes pass carefully over the boys in the room.

Each boy in turn acknowledges his inquisitive gaze with a little nod or look of embarrassment.

"Maestro Garibaldi," inserts Michael. "No disrespect intended, but what the *fuck* is the point of this 'exercise'?"

The teacher smiles. "Well, gentlemen? What do *you* think is the point?"

"To teach humility."

"Equality."

"Shame."

"Guilt."

"Embarrassment." These are some the answers ejaculated into the room.

"Very good!" responds Maestro Garibaldi. "The answer contains a little bit of *all* of those."

"Detachment," adds Peter.

"Yes! Very good!" The teacher spans the class with a sweep of his eyes. "The ultimate goal of this little exercise—and, truly, all of the exercises like this that we give you—is to help you learn *detachment*—detachment from all of these self-limiting emotions, detachment from feelings of shame and guilt and embarrassment and the like. We are all equal. We are all human. We all have weaknesses and shortcomings, fears and insecurities. But why? From where did they come? What purpose do they serve except to limit us—to make us feel smaller than we could be?

"We are all of us—each of us—occupying a human body," Maestro Garibaldi continues. "Each of these human bodies has biological needs that are natural, even essential to their form and function. Why should we feel ashamed or embarrassed about these needs and natural functions?" He pauses. "The answer is, we shouldn't."

The boys look convinced, even bolstered by this little pep talk.

"So, how goes the planning and preparation for Sunday?" asks Maestro Garibaldi. "Have you spoken to Cook? Do you have your ingredients list? Do you know what you need from the market?"

This, in turn, sets off a flurry of multiple discussion threads.

Both the Sunday meal and the Monday ski outing transpire without hitches. The boys are even applauded by the rest of the school community at the end of the meal on Sunday, and both Rique and Zi so enjoy themselves on the mountain at Rosswald that they each go for multiple runs. The boys are quite proud when, on Tuesday morning, Maestro Garibaldi leads the group in a review discussion on what they think they learned from the events. At the end of class, Maestro Garibaldi announces to the group that the Winter Term will culminate in a two-week trip to the Greek island of Crete—which is received with great enthusiasm all around. "But," the teacher continues, "there are a few skills that all boys must master in order for that trip to take place." All of the boys must learn how to drive—which evokes quite an unexpected reaction of fear and anxiety within Peter—and they must all learn to swim—which sets off a near-panic within Thomas, who, it turns out, has quite a deep fear of sharks, fish, and deep and open water and who has, thus far, totally avoided learning to swim.

So, for the next several weeks, the boys are ushered off three days a week to the luxury pool facilities and mineral hot springs at the nearby Brigerbad Spa and Resort to learn and practice swimming and water-safety skills. Here it becomes the group's challenge to try to coax Thomas and any other weak swimmers into attaining competency and, hopefully, comfort in water. Then, on the other three days, a local driving instructor is brought in to teach road and vehicle safety rules and regulations while the boys are granted unlawful and, therefore, clandestine use of the school's two cars and three Solex model mopeds. The staff try to make clear, once again, the importance of the group managing as a team—as a unit—in order to help each member become comfortable and competent at the necessary basic skills and knowledge base that goes into every task that they are given.

Several other "learning tasks" are rather surreptitiously demanded of the third-year class over the course of the first half of the Winter Term. A course or series of hide-and-seek "games" using the school grounds is presented without warning, preparation, or exception.

The first couple of rounds are performed in daytime conditions so that the players have a chance to get comfortable with the rules and this new perspective of the school's campus. After the first week of day trials (one of which lasts five hours and costs the boys a meal), the game moves to nighttime. At first the boys are allowed to use flashlights or headlamps in the pitch dark of the campus after "lights out," but they are gradually graduated to candles and, then, to nothing at all. The major challenge of the after-dark games is that the boys are not allowed to be finished—that is, they are not allowed to go back to bed—until all eleven classmates have been found. Needless to say, these night games leave the boys quite tired—and with several new black-and-blue marks from unexpected night obstacles.

Then comes the night that they are awakened by M. Pahlavi and told that they have to find Enrique. The heaviest sleeper of the group, Rique had been transferred onto a stretcher, carried around the campus by staff members, and left to sleep in some godforsaken corner of the school's boiler room—all while still sound asleep! This same version of the game is attempted several more times, using other students' bodies—several of whom wake up at various stages of their extraction and transport but are able to be gently calmed and coaxed into "playing the game"—even falling back to sleep once they have been relocated.

Then there is the "trick" version in which the third-years are awakened in order to try to find Michael. What the group fails to consider is the possibility that Michael had never been moved (which proves to be the case). Because Michael happened to be the odd man out when room pairings were assigned, he is the only member of the third-year who occupies a bedroom all to himself. Consequently, the boys spend a very frustrating night scouring the campus grounds and turning up nothing. When breakfast time comes around and the hungry, exhausted boys decide to report to Maestro Garibaldi and "give up," they are indecorously informed that "giving up" is "not an option." Unfortunately, for the teaching staff—who are all desperately suppressing their amusement at the scene—a hungry and bewildered

Michael happens to stumble into the Dining Hall at nearly the same moment that his defeated classmates are about to exit in order to continue their "search mission."

"Where've you guys been?" asks the sleepy Michael as the other ten exuberantly circle, hug, and cheer their "missing" compatriot. When the boys hear about Michael's "hiding place," they are so startled that they unleash a stream of fatigue-induced complaints and vitriol. Maestro Garibaldi's shrugged shoulders and raised eyebrows make them soon realize that it was their own shortsightedness and comfort zones that had allowed them to overlook the resultant possibility.

As it turns out, this is just the beginning of the staff's "cruel and sadistic" hiding places. New hiding places even entail the use of mild sedatives to help ensure that each night's "victims" remain calm and docile. While the Headmaster is away on one of his rare off-campus trips, Peter is found in the Headmaster's bed. Joe-pa is found in bed with a first-year student (whom he had never met). Fabrice is found in a cabinet in the kitchens in Engineering Hall, Harry in a cot that had been suspended by ropes from a set of rafters in a dark hallway (no mean feat!), Zi standing asleep (drugged) in the closet of a second-year, John buried in a sleeping bag in the dirt of the herb garden in the Quad, and Thomas in a cot that had been taped to the underside of a wooden table in the Psych Room. Obviously, there is more than one sleepless night involved in these nefarious "manhunts." The staff and the rest of the student body enjoy many laughs.

"Why don't I remember this stuff from last year or the year before?" asks Fabrice during one of their postgame meals in the Dining Hall.

"'Cuz this is the largest class of third-years they've had in a while—at least since *we've* been here," answers Peter. "When we were first-years, I counted only three third-years. Last year there were only two." And then he adds, "My guess is that they have different sets of 'learning exercises' for each year."

"Maybe they rotate them so things don't get stale," says Nathan.

"Or just adjust them to different-size groups," says Emil.

The driving, swimming, and skiing lessons all go well, with each of the beginners becoming proficient and, eventually, comfortable, despite their former anxieties. Even Thomas is getting to feel more trusting of the aquatic world—though he clearly realizes that a pool is quite different from an open ocean. Still, he finds his spirits bolstered by the support and trust he receives from his peers. Peter and his aversion to driving eventually sort themselves out. Manhattan life has both gotten him used to other people's providing transportation and built up his fear for road travel—due, in part, to the number of car accidents he has seen and heard about. Once he has mastered the basics and has practiced a little, he becomes quite confident—so much so that he even asks one day if he can use the school sedan for a road trip to Montreux.

He is denied.

"You are being given the skills and knowledge, but the government will not issue driver's permits before the age of eighteen," he is informed by Maestro Garibaldi. "Even an international driver's license would not allow you to drive here until you turn eighteen."

"Darn!" says Peter. Feeling bold, he can't help but persist. "How 'bout a moped?"

The response Peter receives is in an assignment form: he is to calculate the investment of time and money that a moped excursion to and from Montreux would entail. When Peter starts to arrive at numbers for these figures, he realizes the stupidity of such a request—though he does find out that anyone over the age of fourteen can acquire a moped license. Still, he understands the futility of his chase and gives it up as unrealistic.

As it is winter, the school provides the third-year class with a few other eventful outings. A skating party at the Saas-Fee skating rink proves more challenging than expected, as the students' instructions at the time of drop-off in the morning are, "You will not be allowed to come home until *all* of you can do a full lap around the rink unassisted." Initially, the boys think that this should be an easy test for them to pass, as most of the students have grown up in a four-season northern climate, but then they find themselves confronted with the reality that Enrique and Nathan—and even Fabrice and Thomas—have had little exposure to ice and its recreational uses. Ankles, shins, thighs, and glutes do not develop overnight. Instead, they tend to get tired, weak, and shaky. However, with appropriate breaks, rest, hydration, and helpful coaching from seasoned veterans Joe-pa, Harry, and Peter, the goal is accomplished, and the boys are brought back home (though this 'threat' or condition of completion almost backfires on the Brig-Wallis staff because Saas-Fee is quite a fun resort town with lots of winter activities and lots of young people with whom the boys rather enjoy interacting).

A second skating party is brought to the more local outdoor rink. This time the boys are told that they all need to master backward skating with the same requirement of being able to complete an unassisted lap before they are permitted to come home. This proves a little easier for the boys to accomplish, as the Brig Stadtplatz rink is considerably smaller than the one at Saas-Fee, the distractions (of other people) considerably less, and the skills of the boys considerably better than those of their previous outing.

The next winter 'test' the boys are put through involves a second trip to Saas-Fee, but this time to try their hands at the six-kilometer toboggan run that takes them from Hannig, 2,336 meters above sea level, down to the Alpine village—a descent of 536 meters over the length of the six-kilometer road. The boys have all been sledding before (rewind to last year's outdoor fun at the Midwinter Ball at Le Château de Vullierens above Lausanne); however, Switzerland is host to several mountainside sites at which summer roads are rendered inaccessible to car traffic during the winter months. These roads—sometimes miles in length—are banked, fenced, and groomed for sledding. A ski lift, cable car, or cog train takes a group up to the top of the sledding hill, where the single-person dual-runner sleds are let loose. While this is exhilarating fun for most people, there are a few among the eleven Brig-Wallis boys who find themselves anxious, even fearful. For Zi, of course, it is another test of his fear of heights. For

Rique, Peter, and, to a lesser degree, John, it is their discomfort with speed and the feelings of loss of control that come with high speeds. All students, however, survive and, in fact, again make multiple runs.

The next outdoor "exercise" put before the boys is a winter campout. Some of the boys have been camping before; Michael, Harry, and John have even been winter camping.

"It's easy and fun!" they assure the others.

"Two nights," they are told as they are dropped off at an Alpine hut in a wooded area near the tree line within the Landschaftspark Binntal, which is east of the school a few miles. They are outfitted with two compasses, food, water, sleeping bags, ski goggles, headlamps, ropes, and first-aid kits ("just in case") and told, "Head west and you'll be back at school on Sunday. Follow the footpaths as best you can—they'll make it easier. And beware of avalanche areas." What the boys aren't told is that they are to figure their own way home. Though as the crow flies they are no more than fifteen kilometers from the school, the winter conditions and mountain terrain make it seem more like thirty or thirty-five. Of course, it is also assumed that the group will only return "as an entity of eleven." Much of this is revealed to them in an instructional letter that is found as if by accident in one of the pockets of Harry's coat as they unpack for the night. Fortunately for the boys, the weather patterns over the weekend are fairly mild, posing no severe challenges—though they do wake up to a fresh ten centimeters of snow on Saturday morning.

It is a good thing that Alpine hiking in Switzerland is such an actively pursued pastime year round, for the well-marked trailways are not very difficult for the boys to negotiate. Actually, it is the meals and sleeping conditions that provide the most difficulties for the boys, as the elemental, "barbaric" conditions prove to be snapping points for several of the boys—especially on the second night. The boys' nerves have, of course, been made a little more fragile by the fatigue of a whole day's hiking—as well as the general discomfort of this, the most severe of their tests thus far. Still, after they have had their appetites sated and their sleeping arrangements satisfied, they all manage to sleep like babies and awake fresh and ready for the "final leg" of their adventure. In fact, as the boys walk through Termen and Ried-Brig and onto the campus, their puffed-out chests and loud, laughing voices betray a bravado and pride that is quite unlike the "normal" that is expected from Brig-Wallis students. But, to give them credit, this is probably their greatest accomplishment as a collective unit—thus far.

The week before the Crete trip, the boys are informed that they are being taken on a field trip to Genoa to visit the Natural Historical Museum there. What starts out as a scenic bus ride through the Italian Alps and Peidmont to the scintillating blue Mediterranean Sea turns into a bit of a horror experience for one Japanese boy from Peru. By now, the boys know to be suspicious about any off-campus adventure, and this one proves to be no exception, for when the group arrives at Genoa's Natural Historical Museum, they very soon find themselves entering an exhibit of snakes and reptiles—live ones. To make matters more precarious, several museum staffers are perched in the wide hallway of the exhibit sporting a variety of serpents wrapped around various body parts—hands, arms, shoulders, and necks.

"Man!" breathes Fabrice. "The school has thought of *every*thing!"

"What do you mean?" asked Emil.

"I swear they've somehow figured out each one of our greatest fears—our Achilles' heels—which they test us with," says Fabrice, pointing to one of the museum staff members, who is playing with a small orange snake on his hand. "Snakes are mine," he says, visibly recoiling from the people carrying the slithering reptiles.

None of the boys are truly comfortable with the animals presented them by the herpetologists, but each unfailingly takes a turn handling one or more of the snakes presented. Several boys even surprise themselves with unexpected feelings or sensations they're confronted with. "Hey! They're not slimy!" squeals Enrique, and "They're amazingly trusting and docile," comes from Emil; "This is cool!" says Joepa, and "I never thought I'd find myself doing this!" adds Harry.

Fabrice, however, proves to be a very tough sell. But with the help of John, Emil, and Zi—as well as the seasoned museum staffers—he is able to ease into first touching and then petting and, finally, even holding one of the smaller snakes. "That is a Sunkissed corn snake," announces the museum aide helping Fabrice. "It is beautiful," whispers Fabrice, trying to breathe calmly as the snake perches calmly on the back of his hand.

At the end of the day, even Fabrice is wont to admit how much his former fear has been eased and diminished by the little exposure and experience the visit has provided. Plus, the boys are treated to some downtime in the beautiful Italian city, with its harbors and beaches and old medieval quarter built along the hillside. On Piazza Invrea, the boys and their Italian-speaking chaperone, Maestro Garibaldi, stumble into a beautiful restaurant that is housed within an ancient sixteenth-century palazzo, where they have a fabulous meal.

"This rivals the masterpieces of Chef Novelli!" exudes Rique.

"Yeah, but not *our* masterpiece!" says Michael, reminding the group of their cooking project from the first week.

"It's been quite a winter!" says Joe-pa.

"Yeah! I'd say we deserve a break!" says Fabrice, still coming down from his accomplishment of earlier in the day.

"Good thing Crete's coming!" adds Zi.

"Anybody ever been there?" asks Nathan.

"I've been on a cruise to some of the other islands," says Harry. "Never to Crete, though."

"Me, too," says Michael.

"I can't wait," say John and Emil, almost in unison.

When the group return from their Genovese field trip, they head immediately up the Merchant House stairs to their apartment. The first person into the apartment is Michael. His "*Fuck!*" reverberates down the hallway to the others. They come running to join him.

There, on the maple-block countertop of the kitchen island of their commons room, are the familiar plastic specimen jars from the first part of the term: eleven of them. The note lying on a piece of paper on the floor in front of the cups reads, "You have ten minutes. You know what to do."

The very next night, the boys are awakened after midnight by Wo Chow-chen and Señor Avarti.

"I thought we were done with this shit," groans Michael.

The boys are led to one of the communal shower rooms at the southeast corner of the first floor of Aubrey Hall, where they are told to strip and shower.

"You have ten minutes," they are instructed.

As they enter the showering area, they are shocked to see the same eleven plastic cups lined up in a perfect circle on the floor in the middle of the shower room.

"Fuck!" Michael yells. "Fuck! Fuck! Fuck!"

"This is really humiliating," says Joe-pa, picking up his cup.

"Detachment!" Peter yells, picking his up. He turns the word into a medium for a mock-operatic song. The others soon join in: as they, too, do their duty.

The rest of the week goes smoothly. No surprises, no 'tests.' The boys aren't sure about their assessment, but they remark that Chef Novelli's meals are among the best they've ever had in their three years at Brig-Wallis. "Maybe they're just spoiling us," says Joe-pa.

"Yeah. Fattening us up for the slaughter," says Harry.

"I hope not!" says Rique. "I'm hoping Crete is a vacation."

18

CRETE

It turns out that Crete is part vacation, part "final exam" for a term of exhausting ordeals and torments. The school booked suites for the boys at the Kalimera Kriti Hotel and Resort on the island's north shore, about forty kilometers from the airport at Heraklion. The five-star resort is beautiful and the weather relatively warm when compared to the Swiss Alps in March. Though the trip and arrival are fairly uneventful, the boys have no idea what is in store for them.

The first day's "test" is fairly benign, as the teenage boys are "forced" to spend the day at the resort hotel's private beach. This would not be such an ordeal were it not for the presence of a number of topless female bathers—some of whom are nearly the same age as the boys. The real test, however, proves to be the open water. The beach at the Kalimera Kriti is a comfortable mix of sand and small peastone pebbles, while the gorgeous aquamarine water proves quite enticing—especially as the day's surf is rather sedate with one- to two-foot rollers gently making their way to the shore. Thomas, however, finds the gradual-yet-insidious increase in water depth as one moves away from the shore quite unsettling. Up to this point, he has been able to handle almost all of the "tests" with stoic restraint and self-control. This is the first time his classmates have ever seen him close to abject terror.

As the urgings and beckons from his brethren wanting him to join them in the water increase, Thomas seems to withdraw proportionately. Finally recognizing their friend's distress, Harry, Peter, Emil, and Rique come back onto the beach to talk to him.

"What's up?" asks Peter.

"I can't do it," Thomas says. "I just can't do it."

Harry motions the boys away. "I have an idea," he whispers to his three classmates. "Wait here."

In a few minutes, he returns with the rest of the boys—all ten of them. Harry leads them in forming a tight circle around Thomas—who remains seated on a beach towel. "Thomas," Harry begins. "What if we go out there with you—*all* of us, just like this: ten bodyguards circling around you at all times. Anything that might be in the water will have to get through us—through our circle."

"Here," says Zi, kicking off his rubber-soled nylon surf shoes. "You can wear these so you don't step on anything."

"And we can grab one of those boogie boards so you can float on top of the water," says Michael.

"We'll stay with you. Everywhere you go," says Fabrice.

A tear falls from Thomas's eye.

"Do you want a mask?" asks Emil.

"How 'bout a wet suit?" Zi offers.

After this last suggestion, Thomas's eyebrows flicker. "Okay, okay," he says, getting to his feet. "I'll do it." He brushes some of the sand from his bathing suit. "And I like the idea of a wet suit."

"You can rent them in the beach house," Harry says as the gang moves in unison toward the palm-covered hut at the back of the beach. Fifteen minutes later, the band of eleven can be seen returning to the beach, Thomas and Peter in arm- and legless neoprene "shorty" suits. As they approach the shore, the circle tightens around Thomas. Harry hands Thomas one of the boogie boards the boys had rented at the beginning of the day. Peter, Zi, and Rique each have one of their own banded to their wrists.

"Here we go," says Harry as the eleven-celled "blob" moves into the water.

"Feels nice," says Thomas. "Not as warm as the pools at Brigerbad, though."

The others laugh in agreement.

"Yeah," says Zi. "The temperature is awesome both in and out of the water," he says, referring to the nineteen-degree Celsius temperature of both the water and air.

The group remains tightly circled around Thomas for a good fifteen to twenty minutes as Thomas experiments with walking, wading, floating, and resting on his boogie board. Finally looking like he is relaxing some, he blurts out, "Okay. I'm ready to try *that*," as he points to a group of kids riding their boogie boards amid the incoming waves—some making it all the way to the shore.

In the space of ten more minutes, one can see all eleven of the Brig-Wallis boys atop boogie boards, bodysurfing to shore. Michael and Rique have discovered that having flippers on enhances the success rate of "catching the wave" and riding it all the way in to shore. After a quick but hearty lunch in the club's food cabana, the boys are back at it—this time with flippers and boards—for the entire afternoon.

Emil, it turns out, is the ultimate savior of the group for insisting that they apply and reapply sunscreen to their skin several times over the course of the day. Even so, scalps, ears, backs of the knees, and tops of the feet do not escape sunburns over the hours of exposure during the day. Evening aloe vera applications following showers and a leisurely evening meal out beneath the stars cap their remarkable day. Everybody sleeps well that night.

The next morning the boys are awakened with the information that they need to be dressed and ready to go in one hour for a field trip to a local orchard. The tired boys all groan in protest of both being awakened "too early" and being taken away from the beach.

"I thought we were supposed to be on vacation," John complains.

"Tomorrow!" says their chaperone, Herr Giorgiadis—who, it turns out, speaks fluent Greek, as his parents had emigrated from Greece to Switzerland back in the 1970s.

A private bus takes the group westbound along the coastal road for about a half hour before turning off into the parking lot of a market petrol stop on the north side of the road. The boys are told to get off the bus and gather at the back side of the small market building after they've "stretched and used the bathroom."

Behind the store Herr Giorgiadis instructs the boys to "suit up" into a pile of white beekeeping suits. "Five in the first group. Six in the second," he continues as he grabs one of the suits and begins dressing himself.

"Are we going to work with some bees, Herr Giorgiadis?" asks Michael excitedly as he begins donning one of the suits as if he's done it before.

"Yes, Michael, we are," the teacher responds before adding, "It looks like *you've* done this before."

"Oh, yeah!" Michael says. "My grandmother keeps bees back in Suquamish."

"Good. Then you'll be a real asset," says Herr Giorgiadis. "Has anybody else done this before? Or seen it done?" he asks.

Several hands go up. "On video," "in the movies," and "on Animal Planet," are a few of the verbal responses.

"Good!" Herr Giorgiadis says. "Suit up! With six suits, we need six of us in the first group. The rest of you can go in the second wave."

Peter, Emil, Zi, and Fabrice step forward and begin suiting up.

"Where's Harry?" Thomas asks, noticing his friend's absence.

"He stepped into the bathroom," Herr Giorgiadis answers. Finishing with his own suit, he turns to help the other boys with theirs.

Suddenly, John falls to the ground. He has fainted. Herr Giorgiadis goes right on with his focus on assisting Michael and the others with the straps of their thick cotton suits. "Someone help John, will you?" he says, oddly nonchalant.

"Herr Giorgiadis! He's fainted," Rique says.

"Just hold him up. He'll be okay," says Herr Giorgiadis. "John's just nervous about bees," he adds.

"Holy shit!" breathes Fabrice with a little anger in his voice. "Another fucking test!" he says standing stiffly, eyes ablaze, looking as if he might be trying to provoke the school's representative.

Either Herr Giorgiadis doesn't notice Fabrice or he has chosen to ignore him because he seems focused on helping his five cohorts finish the final adjustments to their suits.

Just then, John begins coming back to consciousness.

"John!" speaks Herr Giorgiadis sharply. "Do you want to come with us to the hives or wait here for the second wave?"

"I'll wait here, thank you, sir," John answers a little flatly.

"You know we're doing this for you, don't you, John?"

"Yes, sir. I get it."

"We know you're not allergic to them—isn't that right, John?"

"Yes, sir. That's right. I'm not allergic to bees."

"Is anybody here allergic to bees?" Herr Giorgiadis asks the rest of the group.

"Not as far as I know," says Joe-pa. "I've never been stung," he adds. "So, officially, we don't really know yet, do we?"

Herr Giorgiadis smiles.

"Okay," he shouts. "First wave. On the truck."

The six white figures, who look like they might be escapees from the Brig-Wallis insane asylum, climb up onto the back of the small pickup truck and are soon whisked off into the orchard fields spreading out before them.

A little less than an hour later, the group returns. The five boys are hootin' and hollerin'.

"That was *so* awesome!" yells Zi.

"Amazing," seconds Emil.

"Look what we brought back!" shouts Fabrice, tipping a five-gallon plastic bucket so everyone can see the thick amber-colored liquid inside.

"Okay!" shouts Herr Giorgiadis, jumping down from the truck bed, helping to fast-release the straps and snaps of the other boys' suits.

"We can't find Harry!" says Joe-pa.

"He probably went back inside the bus—"

"No! We checked! He's not there! We can't find him *any*where!"

"Don't fret, Joe-pa," Herr Giorgiadis says. "He'll turn up. It's not like he could have gone anywhere," he says, sweeping his arm across the panorama of field after field of olive and citrus trees. "Even if he went wandering off for a walk, he knows to come back here."

Changing his focus, he looks straight at John. "You ready to do this, John?" he asks as four of the next five boys begin to suit up.

"I guess so," he answers.

"You'll be fine," Herr Giorgiadis assures.

"Yeah! It's really not a big deal," says Peter, trying to be encouraging.

"Eeww! Gross!" Rique says. "Michael, you *soaked* this thing!"

"Sorry," says Michael. "I got hot out there!"

Five minutes later the next group of boys are suited and loading into the back of the truck. The truck takes off in a different direction from the previous foray as the boys wave to each other.

"I'm parched!" says Michael. "Me, too!" agree the others as they move around to the front of the station store. Inside they carefully keep an eye out for their missing compatriot as they take turns purchasing bottles of water or soda to quench their thirst.

"I wonder where Harry could have gone off to," says Michael when they return outside.

As far as the eye can see—even on the mountain hillsides—it looks like orchard trees.

"What a landscape," remarks Emil.

"I wouldn't want to live here," says Peter. "But I sure would like to get back to the beach!"

"Yeah. Hopefully tomorrow," Zi says.

"Yeah," Emil seconds.

They sip on their drink bottles as Peter leads them across the highway into an orchard field.

"Where are you taking us?" asks Fabrice.

"Nowhere," answers Peter. "Just wanted a little closer look at these olive trees."

A lazy minute crawls by in which absolutely no traffic passes on the highway. The air is almost eerily quiet.

Suddenly, Peter stiffens. "Hey! Did you hear that?" he asks, looking sharply across the road.

"What?" ask the others.

"Shh!" he says.

Everybody is still.

"It's coming from over there," says Emil, pointing to the orchard back on the other side of the highway—off to the southeast of the gas station.

In an instant, the boys are crossing the street and running into the orchard.

"It's Harry!" says Zi as they get closer to the source of the sound of the muffled shouts of a male voice.

The boys slow down as they get close to what they are sure is the source of the yells.

"Harry?" Peter yells between shouts. They freeze again, listening.

"Peter?" Comes the muffled return.

"It sounds like he's right here!" says Michael.

Suddenly, Fabrice stumbles and nearly falls into a hole at his feet. The circular hole is less than a meter in diameter—just big enough for a man or animal to fall into.

"Harry?" he calls down into the dark hole.

"Fabrice?" comes back. Then, "Hey, guys! You gotta get me out of here!"

"*Where* are you?" asks Michael. "How the hell did you get down there?"

"I don't know! I just woke up here five minutes ago. But you gotta get me out. I'm freakin' out down here!"

"What is it? How far down are you?"

"Are you hurt?"

"No! I'm fine! It feels like it's an old well. I've tried climbing up the sides, but there's not enough to grab hold of. It all crumbles as I try."

"Harry. Can you see my face?" asks Emil.

"Yeah."

"How far do you think we are from you?" Emil asks.

"I'm guessing five, six, maybe seven meters."

"Shit!" Michael exhales.

"We just need some rope," Peter says.

"I'll go back to the station and get some," says Michael.

"Go with him, will you, Emil?" asks Peter.

"Sure," says Emil.

The two trot off together.

"Okay, Harry," shouts Peter down the well. "Michael and Emil have gone off to get some rope. You got water? Are you thirsty?"

"I'm very thirsty," comes the response.

Peter grabs one of the leftover soda bottles from Zi. "I'm gonna drop a soda bottle down. Get ready. Protect your head! One. Two. Three. Here it comes—now!"

"Ouch!" yells Harry.

"You okay?"

"Yeah. I just bent back a finger. And it still hit me on the head." There is a pause. "But thanks," he adds, obviously having taken a sip.

"So, how did you get down there?" asks Peter.

"I have no idea," Harry responds. "All I remember is going into the snack store at that petrol station we stopped at."

"We're still there," says Peter.

"What? Really? I thought for sure I'd been kidnapped."

"Probably just another fucking test," Fabrice says for Peter's and Zi's ears only.

"I heard that, Fabrice!" says Harry. "I think you're right."

"Is there something about this that you've got a phobia about?" asks Peter.

"Yeah! Claustrophobia! Luckily, it's dark enough down here. It's not as bad as it could be. If I was like squeezed in—like, in a coffin, like that girl in *Kill Bill*—that would be bad!"

"In the coffin?" says Fabrice in horror.

"Yeah," Harry says.

"That'd freak me out, too!" says Fabrice.

"What's taking those guys?" asks Peter, looking back toward the petrol stop.

"Maybe they can't find any rope," says Zi.

"They gotta find something! Even if we have to tie our shirts together, we need about twenty feet of something—something *strong*," Peter says. Then, leaning over the hole, "Harry? How much do you weigh?"

"About eighty-two kilos," comes the answer.

"Kilos. What's that in pounds?" Peter asks looking to Zi and Fabrice.

"I don't know," Zi responds.

"Where's Emil when you need him," says Peter.

"You sent him off with Michael—" answers Zi.

"Yeah, I know. I'm just kidding," Peter says.

"How long would our three shirts make?" asks Zi.

"I don't know," answers Peter. "Not long enough. Maybe six feet with good, strong knots."

"What if they don't find rope?" Fabrice says. "Even with their two shirts, we'll only make about three meters."

"Guess we'll need everybody's shirts," Peter says. "If it comes to that. But it won't. They'll find something. Or Herr Giorgiadis will."

Peter leans over the well opening. "Harry? We're going to sit over here, under this nearby olive tree. It's too sunny to be standing out here. We won't be far. We just can't do anything until the others come back. So, sit tight."

"I'm not going anywhere," Harry yells back up.

"Is there enough room for you to sit down?"

"No. I'm pretty snug in here with my shoulders."

"How the hell did they get him in there?" Peter asks Zi and Fabrice as they walk over to sit beneath the nearest olive tree, about ten feet from the hole.

"I wish they'd quit fucking with us," says Fabrice.

"Yeah," says Peter. "Have they got everybody?"

"No," says Fabrice, "not Nathan or Michael or Joe-pa yet."

"I think Thomas got it the worst," says Zi compassionately.

"No doubt!" says Fabrice.

"What was Emil's?" Peter asks.

"The camping!" says Zi.

"Oh, yeah," remembers Peter. "That was bad."

"He was freaking out!" says Zi.

"Lucky there're so few wild creatures here in the Alps. I mean, it's not like it's the States, where bears, mountain lions, or wolves might show up," says Peter.

Twenty minutes later there is still no sign of anybody coming down the road.

"Should we head back to look for help?" asks Fabrice.

Suddenly, the boys see a dust trail off to their left. It's the beekeeper's truck tearing through the orchard on its way back to the gas station.

"Shouldn't be long," Peter says before repeating his statement a little more loudly for Harry.

"I hope so," comes the voice of Harry. "My mind is starting to play some strange games!"

"Try meditation," yells Peter.

"What do you think I've been doing?" Harry responds.

"I don't know. It sounds like you're talking with us," Peter quips. Zi and Fabrice laugh.

Five minutes later the gaggle of seven boys are running toward them at top speed. Nathan is the first to reach them.

"Where's Giorgiadis?" asks Peter, sounding a little perturbed.

"He's going to try to call for help," Nathan answers.

"Fuck that!" Peter says as the others all finish arriving. "Everybody!" Peter barks, "Take off your shirts! We're going to make a rope out of them."

"Yeah, sorry, Peter," pants Michael. "That lady at the gas station was no help. Even Giorgiadis couldn't get anything out of her."

"It's okay." Peter looks at John. "How'd it go, John? With the bees? How're you doing?"

"Okay," John answers. "It was nerve racking. But I made it."

"Awesome," Peter says, patting John on the back.

"Those bees are amazing!" spouts Nathan.

The boys take turns sharing their enthusiasms as they finish tying the last of the shirts together.

"Okay!" says Peter. "Let's see what we've got. Stretch it out."

They do.

"Really stretch it! We need every inch we can get!" says Peter, pulling like tug-of-war from one end of the "rope."

"Six meters," announces Rique. "*If* we're lucky."

"Shit!" Peter spits.

"We've *got* to try it," Thomas says.

"Yep!" Peter steps up to the edge of the hole. "Harry! We're gonna send down our rope. Let's hope it's long enough."

"Anything! Just get me out of here!"

They start to lower it. As it gets near the end, Emil says, "We've got to keep a chunk of it here for us to be able to have a good grip."

"Yeah, but it should stretch a little," says Michael.

"Especially with Harry's weight," Thomas adds slyly—causing a little ripple of laughter—which helps reduce the tension the boys are feeling.

"You got anything yet, Harry?" yells Peter down the hole.

There is a pause. Then, "Yes! Yes! I've got a hold of the end—"

Peter is lurched forward by a pull from the other end of the "rope." "Whoa! Big guy!" he panics, trying to maintain a hand- and foothold on the top end. "Don't pull so hard, Harry!" he yells. Then, turning to his classmates, "Guys! Help me out here!"

Michael, Emil, Thomas, and Fabrice jump to help grab hold of Peter's end of the rope.

"The rest of you grab us from behind," Peter commands. "We don't want to get pulled in!"

The other five boys respond accordingly, grabbing hips and arms, wrapping arms around ribcages and leaning back.

"Okay, Harry," Peter says. "What can you do?"

"I'm going to try to climb the walls using my feet and butt to alternate upward movement."

"Okay. Good luck," Peter says. "We'll do our best to do our part."

"I think it'll get much easier once we all can get both hands and our body weight on the top side here," says Michael.

"Ready?" sounds the voice of Harry.

"Ready!" shout back the boys at the top.

"On three, Harry!" shouts Peter.

"Yeah! Okay! On three...one...two...three!"

A tremendous tug is felt from the top of the rope, causing all ten boys to lurch forward toward the hole. They recover, just, and regain their footing—this time digging in even better now that they know what to expect.

Thomas leads the recovery with a shout of, "*PULL!*"

"I wasn't ready," shouts Harry. "Try it again!"

"Okay," says Peter. "On three, Thomas?"

"ONE...TWO...THREE—*PULL!*" Thomas yells in a voice the others have never heard from him before.

They gain a few inches.

"ONE...TWO...THREE—*PULL!*"

A little bit more.

"It's working!" Harry yells up from below.

"ONE...TWO...THREE—*PULL!*" bellows Thomas.

They've gained a meter. John, Zi, and Rique swoop in to claim some of the newly exposed "rope."

"ONE...TWO...THREE—*PULL!*"

They gain another half meter.

"ONE...TWO...THREE—*PULL!*"

Another half meter.

"It's working, but my hands are getting tired."

"Are you lodged into the walls? Feet and back?" asks Emil as the others rest and reconfigure their grips and foot placements.

"Yeah," comes the panting reply.

"If we gave you back some of the rope, do you think you could tie it beneath your butt—at the top of your thighs?" Emil asks.

"Like we do in ropes course—" says Michael.

"Or rock climbing," says Emil.

"Yeah! I think I could!" yells Harry from below.

"Okay, guys," says Emil. "You heard him. He's lodged in, so we can give him back a little."

"How much?" asks Zi.

"A meter should be good," Emil says.

They comply, giving time for Harry to both loop and tie while they all adjust their positions and grips on the shirts.

"Okay!" he yells. "I think I'm ready."

"Okay," says Emil. "Thomas?"

"On three," Thomas bellows in a voice that still seems so surprising to all of them. "ONE...TWO...THREE—*PULL!*"

They gain a good meter in just one pull.

"Whoa!"

"That was awesome!"

"Yeah!"

"Ready, Harry?"

"Ready!"

"ONE...TWO...THREE—*PULL!*"

This time, with all ten boys pulling with their fullest strength, they start pulling and just keep on going until they see Harry's head appear and his arms fly out of the hole to straddle the surface around it.

"One more pull, guys!" he shouts.

"ONE...TWO...THREE—*PULL!*" screams Thomas as they lurch forward, pulling Harry's rear end up and over the lip of the hole.

Harry springs to his feet—a little wobbly at first—and runs into the celebrating arms and cheers of his classmates.

A minute later, as they begin to pull themselves off the ground from what has become their victory pile, Peter cries out, "All right! I want my shirt back!"

The others laugh.

"Yeah! I want mine back, too!" shouts Michael.

Between the highs and lows of the morning's honey-gathering adventure and the Harry rescue operation, the boys are pretty exhausted when they get back to the resort hotel. An afternoon excursion to the ancient ruins of King Minos's Palace at Knossos is fascinating and enjoyable—prompting many minotaur, labyrinth, and "Midas touch" jokes, gags, and references—but the highlight of the day, without a doubt, has been the tremendous sense of satisfaction and camaraderie gained from the collective effort that went into the "rescue" of Harry. As a matter of fact, it might be said that of all the events these boys have been through over their thirty months together, this one has proven to be the most transformative. The gains in mutual respect and care have achieved new heights.

When they return to the resort, Herr Giorgiadis has to awaken the boys, as they had all fallen asleep on the bus ride back from Knossos. When he finally manages to get them off the bus, he introduces them to their "new best friends": the school has rented eleven Solex mopeds for their exclusive use over the next ten days.

"This is why they made us take driving lessons!" shouts an elated Michael.

Though it is strongly recommended that the boys not use them until the next day—or at least only use them in the safety of the private grounds of the Kalimera Kriti, where they are staying—none of the boys can resist taking their new "toys" for a spin at that very moment.

About half the group recognize fairly quickly that they are far more tired—and hungry—than they had realized and quickly abandon their bikes for the alternative: food and rest. While those boys retire to the confines of the interior of the resort, the other half can't resist the temptations that the mopeds present; Zi, Fabrice, Joe-pa, and Rique, led by Michael, continue to play with their new toys. At first they just use the resort's parking lot, grounds, and infrastructure of private streets. Eventually, however, they find themselves venturing out on the main road and even into the nearby town. Zipping around street corners, playing "chase" or "follow the leader," is all fun and quite innocent, but when they come across a well-lit restaurant from which some loud music and crowd noises are emanating, Michael can't resist stopping.

"I don't think we should go in," cautions Rique. "It's late and you don't know what Herr Giorgiadis has in store for us tomorrow."

"Aw, come on," Michael says, taking his helmet off his head. "It won't hurt to just have a look." Looking at his companions, he says, "Don't you want to at least see what local life is like here?" Then, leaving his helmet on the seat of the bike, he begins walking into the yard of the restaurant. "You guys can wait here if you want," he says over his shoulder. "I'm just gonna go check it out." And before anyone can stop him, he's down the steps and in through a side door.

"Hey! Wait up!" Joe-pa yells as he runs after Michael.

"We should probably at least keep an eye on them," says Rique.

"Yeah. Make sure they come back out," adds Zi as the three remaining boys get off their bikes, prop up their helmets, and follow Michael's path into the restaurant.

Four hours later, after a considerable amount of beer, wine, and the local specialty, *tsikoudia*, the boys emerge from the restaurant, stumbling up the path to their parked mopeds. Even the normally restrained Zi is bobbing and weaving his way to his moped, slurring some words and singing some of the contagious Greek folk melodies that he has picked up.

"That was fun!" admits Fabrice as he straddles his bike, waiting for the others to get ready.

"Yeah!" says Rique. "Greeks can party almost as good as Brasilians!"

Joe-pa is happy just floating in and out of his own collage of melodies and Greek words and phrases he's picked up. "I liked Kiria Kopanakis," he says, slurring his words a bit. "I would've fucked her if she asked."

"Her family was right there!" Rique says.

"I don't care," Joe-pa says. "She liked me. She was beautiful."

The boys laugh. Only Michael is quiet, even sullen looking. As he starts his moped and turns out into the street, the others yell from behind, "Hey, Michael! Wait for us!"

The other four struggle to keep Michael in their sights the whole way home. Several times it looks as if he is in danger of being hit by passing traffic as he stubbornly refuses to yield the pavement or at least go over to the right edge of the road, as is proper moped etiquette. Cars come up from behind, brake, and honk before having to pull around to pass him. But they make it back to the resort and into bed—though not without waking some of the others.

The next day is given to the boys—designated a "free day." They are allowed to explore the area on their bikes or go back to the beach—or both, as some manage. The only rule imposed upon the boys is that they are required to "buddy up" with at least one other classmate in whatever they do—especially if it involves water or leaving the resort compound. This works rather well, as all five of the "party boys" are paying sorely for their exploits of the previous night: they sleep in, and, when they do finally wake up, they find themselves suffering from horrible hangovers.

"You need to pound down the water," preaches Herr Giorgiadis. "And sweat. Exercise will help get the toxins out of your system."

"My uncle always said the best thing for a hangover was a morning beer," says Michael as he orders a Bloody Mary from the poolside bar.

Meanwhile, Thomas, of all people, is trying to recruit as many takers as he can muster for a return to the boogie boards. Harry, Peter, Emil, Nathan, and John are quick to sign on. The six of them stay out there, in the ocean surf, for the better part of the day, while the others pretty much wallow around the pool, taking brief swims and long naps in the shade over the course of the day.

After dinner Michael is gung-ho to go exploring: on moped, outside the resort. He is met with total rejection. Everybody is either too tired from a full day in the sun and water or too shell shocked from the previous night. So he goes off to his room to sulk—or so everyone thinks. When everybody does turn in for the night, they are quite surprised to find that Michael is nowhere to be found. A quick count of their moped inventory reveals that one bike is missing.

The boys are visibly concerned. Michael's "lone wolf" behavior seems so contrary to their new *esprit de corps*. Peter worries about a relapse into some of the addictive behaviors that had beleaguered him during the fall and winter over their second year. So, when Michael does finally return around 1:30 a.m., Herr Giorgiadis and a few of the boys rouse themselves to greet and confront him. Michael is evasive, defensive, and eventually, belligerent. Herr Giorgiadis has the good sense to de-escalate the situation by insisting that everybody go to bed—saying that "things will look different in the morning."

Morning comes. The boys are all a little on edge. A few skip quickly out for an early breakfast, thinking that Michael will probably be sleeping in, but most stay in the lounge area of Michael's suite. They can all sense that something important is brewing. So, instead of slinking off to take part in some of the many activities offered by the resort (it is raining outside), they all choose to hang around playing cards and board games or watch stupid shows on the television.

When Michael does finally emerge from his bedroom around 11:00 a.m., he looks disheveled, slow, and light sensitive.

"You guys missed a good time last night!" he says before walking into the bathroom to urinate. "There were girls at this place!" he says over his shoulder. "Lots of pretty, young girls. Like *our* age—not like the old hags from the night before."

As he turns around to exit the bathroom, he realizes that all of the boys are here—all ten of them—and that he is the center of attention. "What?!" he says. "Never seen a guy who just got laid?" He grins slyly.

Comments of "No!" and "You didn't!" greet his revelation.

"Yes, I did! And why not? This is supposed to be our vacation, right?" his eyes fall upon John and then Harry. "Despite the tricks they keep playing on us."

"We're supposed to stay together, Michael," Peter says.

"What?!" Michael acts surprised. "You heard me! I tried to get you guys to come with me. Anybody. But nobody would."

"We were tired—" says Fabrice.

"What about consensus?" Emil prods.

"Fuck consensus!" Michael explodes. "This isn't school! We don't have to practice all that bullshit out here—in the real world." He looks indignant. "Those are just games they make us play when we're *there*. Well, we're *not* there. We're *here*. And here we get to make up our *own* rules. Or, at least, take advantage of the ones that the big wide world has for us."

There is a pause. Everybody seems to be sitting on pins and needles.

"Besides. Who're we kidding! How the heck are we supposed to apply all those games—all these Brig-Wallis rules—to the big picture? And, seriously, you think we—us little know-nothing nobodies—are gonna become '*leaders*'? *Fuck!* No way! We're not leaders! We're all followers."

"No, we're not!" Fabrice yells out.

"What!" Michael focuses all his venom on Fabrice. "You, little Fabrice? Little Jappo rich boy? You think your daddy's gonna let you run anything? Really? Can you really imagine your big powerful billionaire dad grooming you to take over his empire? Or any of you here?" he says, passing his eyes over the group. "Ask yourselves that—all of you mild, meek, follower types. You really think your rich daddies have a place for you? Hell no! Maybe in the accounting department! Or in the company choirs!" He laughs at his own joke. "We're all worthless cannon fodder being trained to serve the Man just like everybody else. Only you have a leg up: you're all rich boys who'll never have to work a day if you don't want to—"

"I'm not!" protests Nathan. "I'm not rich."

"Oh, you probably are and you don't even know it, little Miss California Golden Boy." Michael pauses. "You're adopted. You don't even know who your real parents are: probably some daughter of a mega-rich guy who got pregnant and gave you up for adoption. Point is, there's nothing special about any single one of us. Except we come from rich families. If you think otherwise, you're deluding yourselves. The Headmaster's just succeeded in brainwashing you with his do-goody bullshit.

"Hell! If you ask me, the guys who're really gonna make it—the guys who're gonna make a difference in the world—they're already gone. Bryce. Jimmy. Harvey. Loïck. Benji. Somerset. Even Adam. They were the best of us. They're the ones who're gonna make an impact—be leaders—take over their daddies' empires. Not us."

Michael turns away from his stunned audience in order to walk back into his dark bedroom. Behind him he is waving his hand as if to cast off the group. "I'm outta here," he says in disgust. "I am *so* outta here."

Five minutes later he emerges with his suitcase and backpack. "See ya," he says heading for the door. "Have a nice life, losers," he says as the door slams shut behind him.

"Holy shit!"

"What do we do?"

"I don't know."

"Do we go after him?"

"Was he serious?"

The boys remain where they are, still half-stunned. Ten minutes later Herr Giorgiadis enters the room. The boys look up expectantly. "Michael has decided to leave us," he says with little emotion or fanfare. "We probably won't be seeing him again."

"Even at school?" asks Rique.

"I wouldn't bet on it," Herr Giorgiadis says. "But then, stranger things have happened," he adds beneath his breath.

And now they are ten. Once again the boys are reminded of the fragility of their little group.

Later that evening, after the boys have had a slow, lazy day, they are gathered in the same bedroom of the morning's fiasco, talking very little, looking dazed and a little shell-shocked.

Herr Giorgiadis walks in to tell them the next day's schedule.

"Herr Giorgiadis?" Fabrice speaks up. "Do you think Michael could be right? That none of us will ever amount to anything?"

The teacher looks over his flock with compassionate eyes. "What did you imagine your life would be like *before* you came to Brig-Wallis?" he asks in return. "Think about this. And then take stock: are your plans and dreams different now than they were then?"

The boys are silent a few minutes before a discussion begins to unfold. Nathan is the first to speak. "I know I'm in a place that I never dreamed possible for myself three years ago," he says. "And I really like who I've become, where I am. Though, I have to admit, I have no idea where this is taking me."

"I've loved my time here," Harry says. "And I really love all you guys."

"Aww! Harry likes us!" and other cutesy jabs pop out before someone leaks the inevitable, "Harry's gay!" which results in an all-out pillow-fight-cum-WrestleMania reenactment.

The remainder of the two-week trip is full of peaks and valleys. The boys are still riding the crest of their new "team" spirit—especially Thomas and Harry—and yet Michael's drama-filled departure had taken some of the wind out of their sails. The boys still enjoy themselves a lot, zipping around the north coast and into the foothills of the mountains on their mopeds, as well as swimming, beach walking, boogie boarding, and even enjoying some good-natured fraternizing with some girls they meet in the resort. They even try snorkeling and sailing on the small two- and four-seat sailboats that the resort has sitting on the beach. The only real "test" the boys have—besides the continued test of sticking to the buddy system and continually improving Thomas's comfort level around the water—occurs when the boys are informed that they will be going sky diving. Though Zi is the group's only true sufferer of acrophobia, several others find themselves a little queasy at the prospect of jumping out of an airplane and having to depend on a parachute. But they all manage it—and are much the better for it.

Two other events manifest themselves that were never really meant to be "tests" yet end up turning into "educational" experiences that the boys really enjoy. Both events are the result of chance discoveries made while on group moped exploratory treks along the north coast. The first occurs just east of the town of Malia. The boys are drawn to a Minoan archeological site—which turns out to be kind of boring—when Rique sees a sign for "Patomos Beach." This long, fairly empty sand beach, despite its size, is made more fun for the fact that a mountain river empties into the sea in the middle of the beach. This intersection of cool fresh water with the salty Mediterranean Sea proves to be quite a fun place for the boys when Zi and Fabrice—rather unconsciously—start a "dam project" that gets the entire crew highly involved.

The two boys start "relocating" rocks and handfuls of pebbles that had been naturally distributed along the edges of the mouth of the river into a more "organized," "man-made," "engineered" structure. What starts as a few stones being piled at the edge of the river—presenting the curious outcome of affecting the flow of the water, causing some new ripples and eddies—very soon turns into a whole-group effort at a rather serious attempt at damning, or at least diverting, the stream. When the boys' efforts of several hours' unbroken work finally result in the creation of a new "tributary" around their rock pile, the boys feel their work finished—which is good thing, as the sun has just set, and daylight is fading fast. But the reward and satisfaction of that full day of concentrated teamwork serve again to further cement the silently growing bond between the boys.

The second synchronous event that affects the boys in an educational way is their chance stumbling upon a group of girls sunbathing on a small beach cove to the east of their Kalimera Kriti Hotel and Resort. Following the beachside dirt roads east of Milatos Beach, past the old windmill and past the "end" of the road at the Ekklisia Agios Nikolaos, the boys continue on, exploring the motorbike paths and footpaths along the rocky coastline. Not two hundred meters beyond the little old church, the boys happen upon a narrow strip of rocky beach on which five teenage girls are sunbathing—*au naturel.* Caught ogling at this unexpected boon, the boys are startled when the girls begin waving to them—and, it turns out, these girls are not just waving *at* them but waving as if to beckon them over!

"I don't know," says a nervous Emil.

"Come on!" Joe-pa says. "They're just girls!"

"They're *naked*!" John adds.

"So?" questions Joe-pa.

"They're calling us over!" says Fabrice excitedly.

"I say we check 'em out," says Joe-pa, dismounting from his moped.

Joe-pa, Rique, Fabrice, Zi, and Nathan park their bikes and start to walk the fifty meters to the girls. Peter and the others decide to watch.

Seeing the boys reach the girls, talk a bit, and then settle onto the pebbly beach in seated positions, Emil and John run off to join them.

"Suit yourselves!" says Thomas, yelling after them. Then, turning to Harry and Peter, he says, "What do we do?"

"I guess...we join them," concedes Peter, finally getting off of his moped.

The events that unfold next are really rather innocent. The naked sun worshippers—who, it turns out, are from Sweden and who speak very good English—are totally unapologetic and unselfconscious about their *joie de vivre*—which the boys find intoxicating and infectious.

When the girls create one particular occasion to get up and run down to the water for a quick cool-off, one of them asks, "You are coming with us?" The boys look to one another before jumping to their feet to strip off their clothes. Soon even Peter, Harry, and Thomas are frolicking in the water in their birthday suits.

Later, the boys discuss how surprising it was to them that sexual thoughts were the absolute furthest things from their minds. They share openly their amazement and appreciation of the joy and exhilaration of the experience, of the sense of camaraderie and innocent trust that seemed to pass so easily among the whole group—and how liberating being naked felt. Needless to say, this "accidental afternoon" proves to be yet another "peak experience" for many of the boys.

As the boys are dressing to leave—to "get back to the resort"—the girls invite them to come dancing that night. "We're at the Radisson Blu Beach," the leader, a cute thing with dark hair and tomatoes for cheeks calling herself "Hanna," says. This proves to be a whole other educational experience as, during the course of the evening, it is revealed that the only one of the Brig-Wallis boys who is still a virgin is "cute little" Nathan—which Maja, Linnea, and Tuva are more than pleased to help him with.

"Lucky bastard," Joe-pa is heard to say, which prompts Hanna and Vera to both take him by the hands and escort him off to a place of their own.

"Is it really that easy?" discuss John and Fabrice between sips of their fruit drinks while the others enjoy themselves on the dance floor.

The long, fragmented trip home is made much more pleasant by the individual time spent in silent reminiscing; the ease of banter among glowing, youthful smiles; and the many brief opportunities to catch up on sleep. By the time the ten reach Brig-Wallis, they are refreshed and ready for the final leg of their third year.

19

THIRD YEAR, SPRING TERM

"Hey, Peter! Emil! Come look at this!" shouts Nathan from his seat in front of the tabletop computer in the third-year commons room. "Do you think there could be anything to this?" he asks the boys as they arrive and look at an article on the computer screen entitled "The 13 Bloodlines of the Illuminati."

The boys scroll down the list of family names.

"Loïck is a Rothschild!" says Nathan. "He used to talk about it all the time!"

"Robbie used to say he was 'royalty,'" recalls Peter.

"That's right!" Nathan says. "He said he was a Plantagenet!"

"Thomas's last name is 'Russell,'" says Peter. "Do you think it could be *that* Russell?" he asks, pointing to the name on the list. "He's from England, just like this family."

"And Zi's last name is 'Li,'" adds Nathan.

"Yeah, but Li's gotta be like Smith or Johnson," says Peter. "One of the most common names there is in China." He looks at Emil. "Emil? You all right?"

Emil is standing stiffly, his face drained of blood. Nathan turns to see, too. "Geez! What the!"

Emil finally speaks. Slowly. "I'm a Du Pont," he says, pointing to the list.

"What?!" Peter exhales.

"No way!" Nathan says. "Holy shit!"

"Yep," Emil adds. "My mom's the daughter of Pierre Du Pont the Fourth's daughter, Elise."

"Really?" asks Peter. "You never said anything."

"I didn't think it mattered. My family doesn't go around broadcasting it—though they do get invited to Du Pont family reunions and stuff."

"Is the home I visited you in—in Delaware—is that a Du Pont property?"

"Yeah, I think so," answers Emil. "I mean, it's just *al*ways been our family's summer home. I never even thought to question how or why we go there. We just always have."

"And those other kids around," Peter continues. "Are they Du Ponts?"

Emil pauses, wracking his brain. "I can't think of any of them with Du Pont last names. But they're all cousins of mine. Or, at least, that's what I was taught to call them."

Peter turns his attention back to the computer. "What made you look for this, Nathan?" he asks.

"I haven't been able to stop thinking about some of the things Michael said on that last day of his," Nathan responds. "Or, rather, some things he said got me asking questions about what might make us special to Brig-Wallis. And I was Google-searching 'bloodlines of the rich' when this came up.

"Do you think it could be true?" he asks, looking at Peter and Emil. "That we're all members of these wealthy bloodlines?"

"What about you?" asks Peter. "You're not."

"No. Probably not," Nathan says. "But I *am* adopted. I don't really know anything about my biological parents—other than the fact that they obviously had some Asian blood in them. Like Michael said, maybe my mom was a victim of a teenage pregnancy. For whatever reason, we know she couldn't keep me. What if she or my father were from one of these bloodlines?"

"Is there any way you can find out?" asks Peter.

"Maybe," answers Nathan. "My parents might know. But they've always been pretty hush-hush about it. I'm not even sure that *they* know any of the details."

"What about you, Peter?" Asks Emil. "I mean: it's obvious that your family comes from some *seri*ous money. I mean, that apartment in Manhattan—and the 'family compound' up in Westchester. Those are the kind of things that have been passed down for generations."

"What's your family history?" asks Nathan.

"I don't recognize any of the names on the list," Peter answers. "But I know my parents and grandparents always said our family is one of the oldest in New York. 'Among the founding families of New Amsterdam'—which is what New York was originally called when the Dutch settled it."

"So your last name isn't German? It's Dutch?" asks Emil.

"Yep."

"One of these families is Dutch," Nathan says, referring the trio back to the computer screen. He presses the link to the article from the "Van Duyn family." The boys pore over the text. "'Founding families of New Amsterdam'!" shouts Nathan excitedly. "Do you think…?"

"That our name could've changed?" Peter finishes Nathan's sentence. "I don't know. I'll ask my parents."

"What about the others?" asks Nathan. "Do we know any more about the bloodlines of the other guys?"

"I don't," says Peter.

"Me either," seconds Emil.

"If there's any *slight* possibility that even a *part* of this could be true—that bloodlines are a determiner of how Brig-Wallis students are found and recruited…" says Emil out loud. "How would the Headmaster know?"

"Or *why*?" posits Peter. "What's the point? Why would our bloodlines be important to what this school teaches?"

"Questions for the Headmaster," says Nathan.

The boys continue scrutinizing the information on the website, taking time to click on the link to each family name, reading carefully through the convoluted and often disorganized texts. Many of the references within the articles point to principles of Satanic worship as organizing factors or motivations. There are also a lot of references to various religions and societies that have supposedly been formed by the families in question in order to be used as shields or smoke screens to distract the world from the deeper motives and goals of its members. Freemasonry, Mormonism, Jehovah's Witness, and Theosophy are mentioned by name, as well as other, lesser-known groups.

"This is depressing," says Nathan.

"The author was definitely biased," says Peter. "He's like a paranoid witch hunter."

"Yeah," says Nathan. "This is all about the evil agendas of these families."

"I wonder what his sources are," asks Emil.

"I think we should ask the Headmaster about it," says Peter. The other two look at him. "Tomorrow: in class, with everyone else there. You guys game?"

"Yeah!" says Nathan.

"Yeah, sure," adds Emil a little more cautiously.

The following day, after the Midday Meal and Repose, the third-year boys gather in the classroom in Châtelaine Hall that has been designated for a new class that is entitled, "Political Science." It is one of two new classes that the boys have for this Spring Term, the other being a morning "Bioenergy" class taught by their old Science and Ecology teacher, Wo Chow Chen.

At 2:00 p.m., Headmaster Visconti saunters into the Poli-Sci classroom with robes flowing behind.

"Welcome back, boys," he says, greeting the boys in his usual affable way. "I trust you all profited from your adventures on the ancient isle of Crete?" he asks, scanning the tanned faces of the boys. "I am sorry about the news that Master Paine has decided to leave us," he says before adding, "But I think it for the best."

"Why?" asks Peter. "Why do you think Michael's leaving us is 'for the best'?"

Headmaster Visconti studies Peter for a moment before answering. "I sense that something is amiss," he says. "Is something bothering you, Master Vandenhof?"

"Yeah," Peter says, charging full steam ahead. "We want to know why we're here. Why us? What made you choose *us*?"

"We *know* you were very deliberate," Emil jumps in, "very careful in who you recruited—"

"We were handpicked!" adds Nathan.

"But why?" asks Peter. "And why is it 'for the best' that Michael is gone?"

The Headmaster looks on with marked interest, choosing to wait patiently for the boys to finish speaking their minds.

"Is it true that we were all picked for our bloodlines?" asks Emil. "For our wealthy families?"

"Are we Illuminati?" asks Nathan.

"Are you training us to become Freemasons or Illuminati or Satanic worshippers?" adds Peter.

The Headmaster's furrowed eyebrows suddenly relax, a glint of humor sparkling in his eyes.

"My, you are curious!" he says. "Whatever did Master Paine say to you in his departure?"

Nathan jumps to answer first. "That we were all chosen for the rich families we came from."

"Yeah." John suddenly joins the barrage. "And that we could never seriously hope to become 'leaders'—as you say we are. That the *true* leaders have already left us."

"I'm not sure I'm following you there, Master Marchaud," admits the Headmaster.

"He said that Loïck and Bryce and Jimmy and Benji were the best of us," John says, trying to clarify. "That *they* would be the ones to go on and take over their family empires. That we were going to end up as meek little accountants—if we were lucky."

The Headmaster takes a moment before responding. "You know, I believe Master Paine was onto something," he says. "I can see why he might have thought that the classmates who entered Brig-Wallis with you nearly three years ago might go on to succeed in the world of material attachments. And they may do exactly that! They *are each* on their way to obtaining e*xact*ly the kinds of winning and attention-grabbing qualities and characteristics that one typically associates with our history's rich and powerful. But, no, this is not the hope we hold for the rest of you." The Headmaster pauses again, looking around at the faces in the room.

"Master Paine is also correct in pointing out that you—the remaining ten students of that original eighteen—you are different. And, yes, I will admit it now that you were *all*—all eighteen of you—exceptional enough to have attracted our attention—to have provoked us into meeting and pursuing you for attendance here. But let me assure you: We are *not* the Illuminati! We are not representatives of a religious or Satanic cult. Nor are we a training facility for such. We are not the Society of Cincinnati, White Lotus, Triad, Gen-Yosha, Yacusa, Knight's Templar, Freemasons, Opus Dei, Skull and Bones, Rosicrucians, Zionists, Bilderberg, IMF, WTO, or WTF. These societies mentioned—of which there are many, *ma*ny more—are *all* manmade. They are *all* fueled by human emotions, by human motives, by the flawed and limited perceptions of the human ego.

"The founders and sustainers of Brig-Wallis," continues the Headmaster, "are not bound or allegiant to any Earthly society or agency. The founders and sustainers of Brig-Wallis are all volun*teers.* And yet, we are all committed, contracted, obligated to help carry forward a *spirit*ual plan—a plan that was designed *long* ago and that has a higher purpose or objective that, I'm sorry to say, you boys are not yet ready to understand." Headmaster Visconti pauses again, looking at the boys. "But, yes, *you were* chosen for your potential to become carriers of the torch. All of you here have all of the skills and gifts necessary to become leaders in the service of the Grand Plan of our Spiritual Masters."

"I'm sorry, Headmaster," says Thomas. "I appreciate your trust in divulging this little bit of information to us, but I have to say, it's all sounding pretty cultish to me."

"And scary," says Fabrice.

"Yeah," echoes Zi.

"I mean," Thomas continues, "where's the proof that there *is* even a race of spiritual 'masters,' as you say? How and when are you going to be able to *prove* all of this to us?"

"A very good question, Master Russell," responds the Headmaster. "I understand your frustration with my continually pushing off into some distant and seemingly far-off future each of your inquiries. But I am going to do so again here. I am sorry."

"No!" bursts out of Nathan. "You can't just close this conversation! Not this time! You have to answer at least *some* of our questions."

The Headmaster focuses his attention on Nathan, looking both surprised and amused. "Okay, Master Ambrose. Let me see if I am able," he says, speaking in a calm, deliberate tone. "What questions do you have for me?"

"Am I," begins Nathan, "are we all from special...bloodlines? Is that how we're chosen?"

"Yes."

"Me, too?"

"Yes, Nathan," says the Headmaster with compassion. "You, too."

"But...how do you know?" asks Nathan, looking and sounding exasperated. "Do you know who my parents were? My real, biological parents?"

"Yes, Nathan. I do."

"And...they're...from one of these...special bloodlines?"

"Yes, Nathan. They are. Or rather, your mother was."

"Michael said I was probably the result of some rich girl's teen pregnancy."

"Master Paine was not far from the truth."

"Is my mother—my biological mother—still alive?"

"I'm not sure if I should answer that, Nathan, as you must surely understand. But, if it is truly important to you, I will seek permission from your parents to provide you with more information."

Nathan is quiet.

"Do you know all of our bloodlines?" asks Zi.

"Yes, Master Li."

"Every student here comes from one of these bloodlines?" asks Peter rhetorically. "But...but why? What difference could it make?"

"That, my dear Master Vandenhof, is a question that I am going to use to launch into a topic of great relevance and importance for your continued progress here at Brig-Wallis," says the Headmaster. "Who here can recall the words I often use at the end of some of our guided meditations at the end of Chapel?"

"'I have a body, but I am not my body—'" chimes in Fabrice.

"Yes! Very good, Master Takazaki," says the Headmaster, looking quite animated. "And the very end of that little declaration?"

"'I am a spark of the divine—'" continues Fabrice.

"'—a wave in the great ocean of cosmic creation—" joins in half of the rest of the group.

"'—an individuated point of pure consciousness,'" the boys finish as a whole group.

"I am impressed!" exudes the Headmaster proudly. "And, of course, there are other variations," he adds. "My point is that we are *all* individuals—"

"Playing the game of life in the imaginary—no, il*lusory*—field of four-dimensional Earth!" interjects Peter.

"Very good, Master Vandenhof," says the Headmaster. Then, projecting back to the whole group, he says, "Each of us is a point of consciousness. We each have a perspective, a point of view that, we believe, is different or separate from everyone else. We each are living in a conscious mind that makes us believe that we are separate from each other—that we have these 'solid' bodies that are made up of solid things like skin and organs and cells and molecules and atoms. But—"

"None of those are real," blurts out Peter.

"Thank you, again, Master Vandenhof," says the Headmaster. "Yes. We are all living inside a mind, a localized point of view, a lens of consciousness that we have all agreed to use under the pretext that we are separate, independent individuals." He pauses. "And yet, we know from our lessons in physics and philosophy and psychology and quantum mechanics that none of this is real. Not even *a*toms are real. They are all fabrications. Creations. Illusions. Of our mind."

Thomas speaks up. "Then why do we all have the same or common perceptions," he asks. "Like this room, these walls, these bodies, this temperature, these colors?"

"Yeah," John joins in. "And why can't we walk through walls?"

"Ah, but you can, Master Marchaud," responds the Headmaster. "And we do! *All of the time!*"

"What?!" sounds John, looking confused.

"Yes," begins the Headmaster. "Every time you find your mind wandering to a memory or a daydream or a night dream or a picture in your mind conjured up by something you're reading or hearing—these are all examples of what is called 'bilocality'—the ability to be, to imagine ourselves, in more than one place at a time. For example, you can drive a moped or eat your meal or keep your body in an erect sitting posture, completely aware of your 'immediate surroundings' and yet be fully engaged in a totally different place. And time!

"And, yes, Master Russell," continues the Headmaster. "We *do* share many of the same common perceptions, though I would argue that no two of us see, feel, or experience *anything* exactly the same as another. But, the point is, we have common sensual and linguistic experiences because we have agreed to participate in a world that was created with and for such common structure and rules. And here I want to point out a new significance to this word 'we.' I would like to have you all get used to using and thinking of 'we' in a new and different context: By 'we' I in*tend* to refer to the collective of individual entities that animate, or 'ensoul,' these human bodies that we think we have. Remember: 'we' are *not* these bodies; 'we' are *not* these emotions; 'we' are *not* these thoughts or belief systems; 'we' are spiritual beings who are using these human bodyminds for experience—for adventure—for the testing of our 'selves' against a long list of experiments and goals that we our*selves* create in advance of these lives.

"It's like volunteering to participate in a stage play or a choir performance: we all go into that experience knowing that there will be a fairly unified agreement in the use of a certain set or script or sheet of music that has been commonly predetermined—or that we have helped to determine. This is the same with our core beings. The mind, the point of view that can enjoy bilocality, is a watered-down version of a higher, more etheric, non-Earthbound mind—which is then yet a*nother* step down or away from even higher and less-contained, less-restricted perspectives."

The Headmaster sees a bunch of blank stares in his audience.

"I am sorry, boys, that these concepts are a bit overwhelming to you," he says. "I am here to tell you that this very topic will be the principal focus of this term's learning." He pauses. "It *will* get easier. It *will* become familiar. And you *will* be provided with plenty of proofs to support these new ideas and information."

"But you still haven't answered the question, Headmaster," interjects Peter. "Why us? Why these bloodlines?"

"All right. I shall try." The Headmaster takes a deep breath, composing himself.

"The ancient bloodlines from which you all come have proven, over a great length of time, to create a higher percentage of self-disciplined, goal-oriented, hard-working human beings than *o*ther bloodlines. The obvious proof of this fact is in the ability of these families to achieve high degrees of mastery over human information and Earth resources. Many of your families have been successful as masters of men, and as masters of Nature, for many generations. But this is only a small part of the equation of success. More important than this is that We—and, again, here I want to try to get you used to thinking of yourselves as something bigger than your body, mind, and ego—We, the Spiritual Beings who volunteer—yes, *volunteer*—to take on the commitment to step down and into the illusory world of Earth-based human nature—we at Brig-Wallis have also taken on a far more serious commitment. Each of you, believe it or not, entered the human experience—this version of you—a human being—with the promise to *at least try* to serve the fulfillment of a far larger mission. You decided—*long* before you made this commitment to come to Earth in a human host—to offer yourself up to the in*credibly difficult* task of helping to continue to guide humanity on a certain course of history, a course that was designed and supported by all of Us—by all who have chosen to participate in the experiment."

"Excuse me, Headmaster, but, what 'experiment'?" asks Joe-pa.

"And what 'course of human history'?" asks Thomas.

"The experiment to which I refer," says the Headmaster, "is what we humans currently occupying the planet call *Homo sapiens sapiens.* The course of history to which I refer—the one that our collective of spiritual beings have all chosen to design, support, and participate in—is the pursuit of the deepest, darkest, yet illusory world that We are able to imagine and realize—a world that is replete with the extremely fearful illusion of separation from Divine Love, Spiritual Power, and Unity Consciousness."

Again, the boys all look dazed and confused.

"As I thought," says the Headmaster. "This is all too much for you at this point." He straightens his body and takes a deep breath before continuing. "As this final term of your third year unfolds, I am hopeful that my point will become more clear. And I am hopeful that the progress of this term will help you to acquire a common language so that we will all be better able to communicate about these complicated truths."

"Are you saying, Headmaster, that we are all," begins Peter, stumbling through his thoughts aloud, "that all of humankind, at some level, is...aware...and cooperating—willingly—in an experiment of darkness and fear?"

"Yes," says the Headmaster. "And nearly eight billion individuated Spiritual Beings have insisted on being allowed to participate in this adventure. All at one time."

"And the ten of us—here—in this room—are supposed to help them—what? Achieve destruction?" asks Peter. "Mass orgy?"

"The ten of you are not alone," corrects the Headmaster.

"That's true," Peter says. "I forgot. Sorry. There are a number of us each and every year."

"And many, many out there who serve the cause as well," amends the Headmaster.

"'The cause,'" snaps Thomas. "Now there's a scary word."

"Yeah," adds Harry. "It sounds cultish to me."

Several more "yeahs" come from other class members.

The Headmaster is silent. He stands patiently, looking resolute.

"So," begins Peter, thoughtfully, "we 'spirits'...decided to descend into the corrupt illusion—or 'game'—that we call the material world—Earth—where we use these human...bodies...to influence other humans." Then, looking to the Headmaster, he says, "So, what happened to our spiritual intelligence—to our awareness of the fact that this is all a game?"

The Headmaster decides to answer in a language that he knows Peter will understand. "Submission to the 'wearing' of certain veils of ignorance is one of the conditions to entering a denser realm of vibration," he begins. "Then, the bombardment of conditional information helps to inform the contextual field of our illusory world. Our new 'reality' begins to become familiar. We begin to see and feel patterns. We begin to experiment with techniques and tactics that seem to work within the flow of these patterns, that create feelings of comfort or ease or satisfaction or happiness or pain and suffering and fear and isolation. Over time—typically not much more than seven or eight years—our new human bodyminds begin to accumulate enough familiarity with Earth's rules and human patterns to figure out how to 'survive' and flow through."

Seeing that even Peter is in over his head, the Headmaster stops and changes the direction of his speech. "As I hope you will see, this course in political science will unfold in a way that will help you to become better able to understand this information. It may sound dense and foreign to you now, but, given time, I assure you, it will become familiar to you.

"So, if you will *please* extend me the mercy of your trust yet one more time, let me turn your attention to the course syllabus." This he begins to pass out. "As you can see from the syllabus, there will be certain books that will help inform our daily and weekly discussions. Please do your best to try to get these books read before the dates listed next to them. There will be time in our class period for reading, though most classes will, of course, be occupied with discussions.

"For tomorrow I'd like you to try to get as far as possible into one or both of these two books," he says while holding copies of *Ishmael* by Daniel Quinn and *The Red Tent* by Anita Daimant in his hands. "You may come get your own copies here, and you may be dismissed to begin reading them."

The boys rise from their chairs to file through the line to access their own copies of the books.

Peter looks over the list while leaving the classroom. *Ishmael, The Red Tent, Das Kapital, Escape from Freedom, The Tao of Physics, Quantum Healing, Vital Lies, Simple Truths, Healing Words, Communion with God, The Matrix, Quantum Psychology, Destiny of Souls.*

Should be interesting, he thinks to himself as he tries to decide which of his favorite reading nooks to hole up in for some reading.

20

END OF THE THIRD YEAR

Peter is sitting on the couch in the third-year commons room, looking over his notebook from Headmaster Visconti's Political Science class. He is bothered by a deep-seated question: *What's it all about? What is the point? What is the object of this school and its approach to education?* Something tells him that this notebook, with its list of the titles the Headmaster gave to each and every gathering of his Poli-Sci class, hides a clue—maybe the answer.

Below each 'title' Peter can see the invariable scratchings and doodlings of his note taking. Something is telling him that these are unimportant, that the important clues are in the titles.

Starting from the beginning, he pages through his notebook, reading each headline. "Political Science." *The science of politics?* he thinks. *Or the politics of science? "Polis" meaning "city" and "science" coming from the Latin word for "to know" and/or the Greek "to split, rend, cleave" or "to separate one thing from another." The Illusion of Separation!*

He proceeds through the pages. Titles like "Patriarchy and Matriarchy," "Takers and Leavers," "Parasites and Viruses," "Masters and Servants," "Slavery and Enslavement," and "Mutual Aid" remind him of how, each week of the term, the Headmaster had framed the discussions of each of the week's six class periods around a particular book or film, how each of the names of each of the six discussions had been generated from the source material. He is reminded of how

Karl Marx's *Das Kapital* fueled a succession of discussions that the Headmaster titled "Masters and Servants, Slavery and Enslavement, Part 2," "Feudalism and the Working Classes," "Capitalism: The New Feudalism," "Darwinism and Eugenics," and "Communism, Socialism, and Anarchism." Daniel Goleman's *Vital Lies, Simple Truths: The Psychology of Self-Deception* generated some fascinating discussions on the human mind and ego—which worked under such titles as "Fear Is the Mind-Killer: The Autonomic Nervous System and the Biology of Fear," "Indoctrination, Propaganda, and Brainwashing: The Manipulation of Information," "The New Normal: Terror, Denial, and Escapism," "Escapism and the Magic of Entertainment," and "Addictions Are Our Friends." Rachel Carson's *Silent Spring* led to discussions entitled "Gaia: The Living, Breathing Organism," "Rape and Rape Mentality," and "Technology, Overpopulation, and Biodegradation." Erich Fromm's *Escape from Freedom* inspired some deep discussion on "Man's Fear of Freedom," "Democracy, Fascism, and Oligarchy," "The New World Order," "Imperialism and Globalization," and the relationships between food systems and human health (called "Where the Rich Were Once the Obese, Obesity Is Now the Realm of the Poor and Impoverished"). With the pair of books, Gary Zukov's *The Dancing Wu Li Masters* and Stephen Wolinsky's *Quantum Consciousness: The Guide to Experiencing Quantum Psychology* came "It's an Observer's World," "Mind Over Matter," and "Implicit and Explicit Order," with eight days of "quantum psychology" exercises. From Neale Donald Walsch's *Communion with God* arose several impassioned days of discussions around the Grand Illusions and the so-called War Against Spirituality. Out of the 1995 film *The Matrix,* the Headmaster deftly orchestrated discussions on "Illusion and Reality," "Devolution and the Constitution of Man," "Joy and Suffering and Choice," "Form and Individuation," and "Ego and Personality."

Control! Peter finds himself thinking. *The pattern I'm seeing here has to do with control! Control and submission: control of information, control of humankind, control of the course of human history. I remember the*

Headmaster saying, "Humankind is descending deep into the Illusions," deep into ignorance and fear and the illusion of separation. Are we *supposed to be the guides for this 'descent'?*

Meanwhile, Wo Chow-chen's Bioenergy class proves equally fascinating—especially in the way it seems naturally, almost miraculously, to grow out of information and topics that the boys had previously been exposed to in Maestro Garibaldi's classes—and by the way it seems to dovetail with and reinforce many of the topics brought to light in the Headmaster's Political Science class. Excerpts from the likes of Alice Bailey, Douglas Baker, Brenda Johnston, Barbara Briner, Alan Oken, Randolph Stone, John Upleger, and Michael Newton continue to help expand the broadening perspectives of the boys.

On the last day of Spring Term, late in June, the third-year boys have been through their morning routines: an exhilarating sing in Chapel followed by a serenely satisfying meditation, as guided by the Headmaster; an extraordinarily lively breakfast; an enjoyable game of 'Tower of Babel' in Montechenin's Language Lab; a deeply satisfying morning of Chakra Tai chi, Sufi dancing, and Esoteric Healing practice in Mr. Wo's Bioenergy class; and a fine celebratory feast at the Midday Meal, *grâce à* Chef Novelli and his dedicated crew. The boys are riding such an 'end of term' high that none of them chooses to nap, much less slow down, during the rest portion of Repose. Instead, they join together for a spirited, laugh-filled game of hacky sack out on the Quad. When it comes time to attend their afternoon class with the Headmaster, they are coasting atop a wave of contented fulfillment.

As usual, they enter the classroom in Châtelaine Hall as a unit. There the boys are greeted, also as usual, with the large chalk printing of the day's discussion topic on the blackboard. Today's topic, written in large block letters is the word "DÉNOUEMENT."

The smiling, ever-congenial Headmaster welcomes them and waits for them to take their seats. He then begins speaking.

"Well, boys. Today's the day," he says rather nonchalantly. "You have made it through three intense, demanding years at Brig-Wallis.

Today is the day that I reveal to you the heretofore obscure reason for your being here at Brig-Wallis—the real purpose of the educational process used here."

The boys look alert and enrapt.

"Though we have had discussions in which layers or facets of the Brig-Wallis mission have been divulged, none will have been so complete as today's. I have waited until today for this declaration—this dénouement—because, until today, you were not ready to receive and fully appreciate it. Yes, as I hope you will soon see, even yesterday would have been too soon for such a disclosure.

"There are many things for you to think about over your summer holidays—one of which will be whether or not you wish to return to Brig-Wallis for a fourth year." This declaration causes a little stir of mumbling, which the Headmaster plows over. "As most of you have turned or will be turning eighteen years of age this year, you are considered 'emancipated' in most first-world cultures. I, too, release you today with the belief that you are your own person—that you have all of the skills and knowledge necessary to make intelligent, heartfelt, and informed decisions regarding any and every aspect of your life." He pauses a moment to let this sink in. "A decision to return to Brig-Wallis for a fourth year is neither a hope nor an expectation. The fourth-year experience here is one of stark contrast to your previous three years. The commitment of a fourth year at Brig-Wallis is more similar to a commitment to a year of life in a monastery. It is isolated, focused, and intense—far more intense than your previous years. It is *not* for everyone. I will repeat that, for it is important: the fourth-year experience is *not* for everyone. So, please, consider carefully and deeply any decision regarding such a commitment.

"For those of you who choose not to return to Brig-Wallis for the fourth-year experience, there is a wide world of choice opening up to you—a world that we can help you to negotiate and which I will get into in further detail later in my talk.

"By the way, I apologize for delivering this information to you in a lecture form instead of our more usual Socratic discussion format, but this, as I hope you will see, serves both me and the information… better. There will be plenty of opportunity for questions and discussion when I have finished, so thank you for indulging me.

"As I was saying, the Brig-Wallis curriculum is not an easy one to put up with. Our demands of you have been severe, at times even harsh or questionable in their humanity or civility. Ours has been—as you so wonderfully guessed in your first year, Master Vandenhof—a process of attrition. We found you and recruited you. You chose to come here and have continued to do so for three years now. I hope that you will look back and feel that it's been worth it." The Headmaster again pauses, organizing his thoughts.

"The Brig-Wallis curriculum, its campus, its courses, its extracurriculars, even the way the day and week are structured, are all set up intentionally as a means to test you. We have been testing the individual human beings who walked in through those gates from Polenstrasse those three years ago in order to see whether or not you belonged here. And now I salute you. I salute you for each and every day that you rose to the challenge, for each and every day that you passed the tests we threw at you, such as: 'Can I wake up six days a week in the dark?' 'Can I wear a uniform?' 'Can I fit in?' 'Can I find nourishment and meaning—even joy and satisfaction—in singing? In meditation? In making my own food and exercise choices?' In the strange and unusual information we bombard you with? In group dynamics and multiple languages and cultures? In social and private functions, inter- and intrapersonal situations? 'Can I find comfort and satisfaction in these rhythms?' 'Can I understand and love myself?' 'Can I make sense of the world and still love and enjoy it?' All of these and many, many other tests are we placing in your face each and every day. And here you are. Apparently, you've been able to find enough 'yes' answers to the questions and challenges we've forced upon you to stick it out. I hope you're still here not just because you've no place else to be or because you didn't know you had a choice but because you like it here, you like our ways, you like each other, and you like yourselves and who you've become. We'd like to think that's why you're still here. If this is not the case, then I think you have some serious thinking to do over the summer."

The Headmaster pauses, glancing at the chalkboard.

"Onward: 'dénouement'—as it says on the board.

"As I've said, we found you, we recruited you, but you chose to come—you chose to continue coming to Brig-Wallis despite our tests of you. Thus, there must be some kind of fit, some kind of commonality that we all share—we being the sum total of Brig-Wallis staff, both past and present, as well as you, the matriculating human being. I hope we have been able to help make clear to you that we believe the human experience to be a voluntary one—that each and every one of you came to Earth to occupy the human body that you possess by a choice that was all your own and that the force of consciousness that animates your human bodymind is one of a spiritual nature. We also hope that some of our attempt to prove to you that the four-dimensional Earth-based reality that you have chosen to participate in is illusory—is, in fact, a fabrication, a contextual field that a spiritual community of which we are a part created—has made sense to you. Whether or not you believe this or at least trust us in our sincere effort to try to convince you of the veracity of such a belief may have a strong bearing on any decision you make to move forward within our little fraternity. The key, however, to your continued investment of time and energy into our enterprise rests in the concept behind a subject that was only recently exposed to you: that is, the topic of 'devolution.'

"As we discussed on the day that topic was introduced to you, there is no such thing as 'devolution.' Evolution is evolution whether it is so-called backward or forward, descending or ascending. But we use the term with respect to Alice Bailey's presentation of information in which she refers to one of the directions of spiritual evolution that is *away* from, or more *sepa*rate from, our God-Source Consciousness.

"Remember when I used my own teacher's analogy of the deep-water diver to help describe Bailey's concept of 'devolution'? The deep-sea diver represents the feelings of isolation and deprivations and seemingly tenuous connection to our Source—our oxygen. Like the deep-sea diver, there are many, many variables in depth and location that one can choose from when one chooses to participate in the Tao, in the Great Ocean of Cosmic Creation, the Grand Illusions. Well, I'm here to tell you that we are all members of a particular group of spiritual beings who have chosen to focus on the exploration of a very specific manifestation of deep-water diving in a very specific area of the Ocean: the human experience—or, more specifically, the current version of humans—*Homo sapiens sapiens*—on a very specific place—little blue Gaia—within a very specific contextual field of potentiality: twenty-first-century Earth. What has *not* been revealed to you before—until now—is that this particular 'experiment'—this particular variation of the Earth-based four-dimensional human host 'vehicle'—has been devised and modified for the express purpose of creating an experiential 'stage' or platform for very extreme use of the Grand Illusions—very, very deep-sea diving. It's as if we're exploring the ocean floor of the Marianas Trench.

"Does anyone have any idea of what this might mean?" the Headmaster asks.

Nathan is the first to respond. "I guess it would mean that we're about as far away from God as possible."

"Which would mean?" prods the Headmaster.

"Bad things!" says Rique, inciting laughter from his classmates.

"Yes!" says the Headmaster. "Can you all see that the creation of such a world would naturally prove conducive to conditions of disorder and disconnect and…disease—even darkness?"

"And so, you're saying, Headmaster," begins Peter, "that this is by de*sign*? According to some plan?"

"Yes! Exactly so!" The Headmaster is excited. "This—this world in which we live—is the fulfillment of—the manifestation of—a plan! A Grand Design created expressly for the purpose of exploring the Grand Illusions to the ex*treme*—to their *deepest* depths!"

"So, we…humans…are supposed to be…bad?" asks Zi.

"Yes!"

"No way!" says Joe-pa. "I'm not buying it!"

"And that, my dear Master Taylor, is pre*cise*ly one of my points," says the Headmaster enthusiastically. "You don't *have* to buy into it! You are *al*ways in choice!"

There is a brief silence.

"So, are humans inherently good-natured or not?" asks Emil.

"That, Master Fredericks, is open for debate. But I would first like to remind you of a more fundamental decision you have to make: Is human nature materially driven or spiritually driven?"

"Well, spiritually, obviously—" begins Peter.

"Even for those caught in the belief that *this*—that the world around us—is the true reality?" interrupts the Headmaster. "For those living under the veils of ignorance, illusion, and ego?"

"Well, no," concedes Peter. "To them, human nature probably seems pretty…evil."

"Or whatever their surroundings are informing them," continues the Headmaster. "The veils of ignorance and ego are thick with familiarity and comfort. The distractions provided by ego and emotion can easily keep a person blinded to the spiritual truths for an entire lifetime!"

The silence in the room is stifling.

"What if I were to tell you that this is *part* of the Plan—part of the Design—part of a way to test Ourselves—our spiritual selves, I mean—to see if We can rise above the distractions and chaotic dissonance that We have purposely set up—or, maybe more accurately, to see how much time it takes Us to rise up and rediscover Our spiritual nature—which is why it often takes multiple incarnations to pass the test."

Everybody looks a little stunned.

"So," Peter begins slowly, "You're saying that we keep coming back—we keep playing this 'Game'—until we figure it out? Until we figure out that it *is* a game?"

"Yes! Exactly!"

"And then what? Find another game to play?" Peter asks half seriously.

"Yes!" the Headmaster answers sincerely. "Or else we come back to try to help others to find their own way back."

"Like Jesus," says Rique.

"Yes, like Jesus," responds the Headmaster. "And many, *many* others. Many of whom have had their words and intentions misconstrued or manipulated in order to serve the designs of others."

"Others?"

"Those who would have us stay ignorant and base," the Headmaster says.

"So, are we being trained to be helpers?" asks Thomas. "Like angels?"

"Not in the way you're probably thinking, Master Russell. This is probably the most difficult concept for you young men to grasp—as evidenced by the number of times we return to it. In the world of God—and, even to a lesser degree, in the world of Spirit, there is no right or wrong, no good or evil, no better or worse." The Headmaster stops, letting the class stew over his words for a moment. Then he continues. "There is only temporary self-consciousness within a Field of Pure Potentiality with all of its infinity of possibilities. Everything—*everything*—provides experience. And experience, if you remember, is what it's all about."

"So, war, rape and murder, greed and hunger. These are not bad things?" asks Rique.

"Who is asking, Master Osario?" the Headmaster asks with laser-focused eyes. "The ego or the Spirit?" Rique only looks confused. "If it's the ego that is asking that question, then of course belief and value systems that are based upon human- and Earth-based realities are informing your question. If it is the Spirit Being that animates and is using this human bodymind as its vehicle in a contextual field designed for experience that is asking, then you will be less interested in the answer to that question."

"You mean it doesn't matter what we do—what actions we take in these human bodies?" asks Peter. "That it's all okay in the end? Because it's just 'experience'—more experiences?"

The Headmaster takes a moment before answering. "I guess I do mean that, Master Vandenhof," he says slowly. "As a matter of fact, be it known that some us choose—and *plan*—lives on Earth with the expressed purpose built into them of performing so-called harmful or deplorable acts upon others—or our own selves—precisely to help provide specific experiences and learning and growth opportunities for *others* to work with as well as for ourselves!"

Headmaster Visconti stops a moment to collect his thoughts.

"Remember that concept of 'spiritual contract' that we've talked about?" he continues. "The idea that we plan our lives on Earth with other Spirit Beings? Well, we can plan these lives and the goals and means to achieving those goals in amazing detail—with multiple opportunities programmed into our lives for the presentation of these learning opportunities for ourselves and others. My point being, these are multiple souls working together each for their own benefit as well as, and at the same time as, for the benefit of others. And all—*al*ways—with the goal of providing learning and growth experiences for one another. This is where that element of sacrifice—of giving of yourself for the benefit of another or a cause—that we discussed before comes into play. Sacrifice comes out of an expression of honoring all that is sacred, all that is Godly, of honoring the Beauty, Love, Truth, and Joy that is within each and every one of us, each and every event and experience—that arises equally out of the Beauty, Love, Truth, and Joy that is Pure Potentiality."

The Headmaster again pauses, allowing the boys time to try to digest what they're hearing. Most of the boys look deep in thought. Almost all have their eyes looking blank and their brows furrowed.

The Headmaster decides to continue. "Keeping this in mind, I will now share with you the part of the Plan that all of you volunteered for—that all of you and many, many others came to Earth with the intent and open-mindedness to participate in. It is the reason you chose the families you chose to come into. It is the reason we were able to find and convince you to come to Brig-Wallis. It is the spiritual mission, the purpose you had in mind when you committed to coming to planet Earth at this particular time in history. And, I will add, the job you volunteered to see if you could do is *not,* and never was, a foregone conclusion. The human ego has ways of reshaping our paths once we're here. But the Brig-Wallis curriculum was created and perfected to enable and ensure our ability to identify individuals who are truly interested in the job they signed up for.

"I do want, here, to try to convince you that you all have, in fact, signed up for this particular job—because this is no ordinary job. This is a job that very few have the heart and fortitude, strength and self-discipline, concentration and resolve to take on. And yet it is a job that many of your ancestors and forefathers within your own bloodlines have taken on and served. In fact, your particular bloodlines are among the few who, early on, committed to—and remain committed to—this particular cause. It is also one reason we look to these bloodlines for the 'new conscripts' such as yourselves, as well as the reason *you* chose those families for your entry point to this particular Earth-based human experience. These bloodlines are proven supporters of the cause. You knew this coming into your present human life. You wanted to try to see if you were capable of contributing to that cause, that particular course in human history. Even those who have 'failed'—those who chose to enter the human experience within these bloodlines but who might not have proven strong enough to reach the point you ten boys have reached—and I'm not referring here to *on*ly your fallen classmates but to any soul choosing to occupy a bodymind within these families and this echelon of human socioeconomic status—they *all* are playing their parts—their *very* important roles—in the Grand Plan. You, however, have proven yourselves capable of handling a different, more specific role in the play out of this particular course of human history—which is, may I remind you, designed to take four-dimensional experience to levels of submersion into the deepest depths imagined for the use of the Grand

Illusions. You have proven yourselves worthy of being entrusted with the continued guidance and facilitation of humankind's descent into the most depraved versions of the Illusions of Ignorance, Separation, Need, and Isolation."

The Headmaster sees ten blank faces looking up to him.

"Do you mean we're supposed to make sure humans are…evil?" asks Fabrice.

"We're devils," proclaims Thomas under his breath.

"It has been the responsibility of our kind to try to ensure that the 'test'—the road to spiritual awakening and Self-realization—is difficult—is prolonged for as long as possible."

"How?" asks Joe-pa.

"We manipulate money, information, and resources—or *use* money, information, and resources to manipulate the thoughts and behaviors of humans," responds the Headmaster.

"So that they remain distracted and confused for as long as possible?" asks Harry rhetorically.

"Yes! Exactly."

"And somebody planned this?" asks Joe-pa.

"Yes. We did," responds the Headmaster.

"That is one fucked-up plan," says Fabrice.

"You and I, Master Takazaki, and every spiritual being engaged in this enterprise we call 'humankind,' has had a say in the creation, manifestation, maintenance, and perpetuation of this plan. Your very presence here is proof and endorsement of that fact."

Another hush.

"I know it does not sound like a glorious or praiseworthy plan," the Headmaster goes on. "But, again, if you can look at it from a spiritual perspective—from the detached perspective that says that there is no right or wrong, no good or bad, no better or worse, then, perhaps, you will be able to see its merit—to see just how sacred this undertaking is. We are manifesting a heretofore only i*magined* set of possibilities—possibilities using the Grand Illusions to their greatest extent.

"And, again," the Headmaster goes on, "this task, this job, this undertaking, is *not* for everyone. Even some of you here may find yourselves shirking from or even outright rejecting any kind of role in this operation. You have that right. You are always—*always*—in choice." The Headmaster hesitates for a moment before rushing into his next disclosure. "Some of you may even turn out to try to oppose us—to try to use your power and knowledge to deter or expose or bring us down!" He pauses, watching the looks of astonishment blossom on each face. "And that is okay, too! It is a chance we are willing to take. Believe me: it is even a *planned* for, even considered a de*sire*d, aspect of the Grand Plan." Again, there is a pause. "But we think, we hope, that through the rigors and tests of the Brig-Wallis experience, you will be able to handle this information and that you will be able to *at least* consider and imagine yourself playing an active role in helping to see the Plan forward."

"I have a question, Headmaster," says Thomas.

"Yes, Master Russell?"

"Does this plan involve the eventual extermination of our species?"

"Of course!" is the Headmaster's sober response. "*All* species—*all* things in Cosmic Creation—run their course and adapt or perish. That includes planets, stars, black holes, and dark matter."

"Even gravity?" asks Emil.

"Good question, Master Fredericks," says the Headmaster. "Who remembers the spiritual perspective on gravity?"

"Gravity is a force that exists to remind us that everything is one—that everything wants to move back to Unity and Oneness," answers Peter.

"Excellent," says the Headmaster. "So, then, would gravity as a primal force ever come to a point in which it would not exist? In which it had served its purpose?"

"Sure!" explodes Zi. "When all things have returned to Unity Consciousness."

"When God decides to close up shop," Joe-pa adds.

"Yes!" says the Headmaster, openly displaying delight in the boys' displays of comprehension. "When *We* decide as a collective that *We* are finished with Our experimentations with the Grand Illusions. So, yes: even gravity and light have restrictions on them."

"What about thought?" asks Peter.

"Thought is *also* an expression of the Illusions," answers the Headmaster. "If there were no need for the use of the Illusions, there would be no thought. Unity Consciousness, while pregnant with the infinite possibilities of Pure Potentiality, does not need to be active or projecting itself 'out' into a world of Illusions if there is no world of Illusions! 'Divine Content' is a state in which Need, the most basic of the Illusions, is not being used—is un-needed."

The boys laugh at the Headmaster's unintentional play on words.

"So you want us to think over the summer about whether or not we want to participate in this 'grand plan'?" asks Harry.

"Thank you, Master Hagen, for getting me back on track," says the Headmaster. "You are already participating in the Grand Plan. My question to you is whether or not you wish to play a very specific and very challenging role *within the manifestation* of the Plan—a role that your Brig-Wallis experience has shown us you are fully capable of playing. And let me be honest with you: I'm a little nervous offering this information—this 'offer'—to ten of you." The Headmaster pauses again, casting a very serious gaze across his field of ten boys. "It has been a *very* long time since Brig-Wallis has had this many young men make it to this day. And let me also try to make clear that I understand the tremendous burdens that playing this role in shaping human history presents. Watching the horrors and terrors humans can inflict upon each other can be disturbing. Knowing that it is your intention, that it is your express purpose, to ensure that this barbarism continue, that it *es*calate, *that* can be a deeply disturbing psychological burden. And yet, we think that what you have shown us here at Brig-Wallis makes you a strong and viable candidate to handle such a burden. You have all exhibited successful investigation and analysis with spiritual perspectives as well as with varying degrees of application of the law of detachment. Though your life-long success is by no means guaranteed, your chances of mastery and steadfastness are high."

"Headmaster," opens Nathan. "You said the others—the other boys born into these bloodlines—will also be doing work to help carry out 'the Plan.' Do they know this?"

"A very insightful question, Master Ambrose," acknowledges the Headmaster. "No. They probably don't understand that their roles are contributing to the fulfillment of the Plan—though *some* may discover it. Some may a*chieve* spiritual awareness to such a degree that they eventually figure it out—but none to the degree that you are now aware. As I've tried to tell you, you each and all have a very special awareness and control that has enabled you to get to this point. Now it is up to you to decide how much further you'd like to travel."

"The path is now ours," notes Nathan. "Before, it really wasn't."

"Yes and no," responds the Headmaster. "As I've tried to convince you, at some level—deep in your conscious mind—in places that have been shut out by the inputs of Earth 'reality' and ego constructs—you have known. You knew long before you came to Earth. Only now are you finding yourselves able to reaccess those information centers. Which leads me to add: over your summer, if you choose to maintain a mediation practice, try to go deep within, try to shut down or shut out the voice of your ego and listen for the voice of Spirit. Even ask It questions. And remember to phrase your questions and prayers in affirmations; leave out the negatives or self-limiting words or phrases. The ego is limiting, fear based. Spirit is limitless and love based."

"Headmaster? What exactly are our options? What kinds of 'jobs' are we eligible for from this point on?" asks John.

"Unfortunately, Master Marchaud, that is a very difficult question to answer, particularly because the answer would be different for each and every one of you—and because each of you has different interests and different talents."

"Will we continue working together? The ten of us?" asks Harry.

"That will be entirely up to you," answers the Headmaster. "Obviously, we have made great efforts to nurture the bonds you now share. And I think we've been fairly successful. While I can see over the long term you boys working together in some capacity or other, I cannot tell you specifics or probabilities. Those will unfold with time—as your individual journeys continue. Plus, they are, of course, highly dependent on your personal efforts. So, I guess my answer should be, 'You will be the determiners of that possibility.'

"Now, back to Master Marchaud's question for a moment," the Headmaster says. "I will tell you that any interest in coming back here to Brig-Wallis should not be predicated on social factors or filial loyalties. A fourth-year student here leads a very solitary and isolated life."

"I've noticed!" says Peter.

"Yes, I'm sure you have," responds the Headmaster. "Master Vandenhof is, of course, referring to our one fourth-year student currently on campus."

"We don't see a lot of him," Harry comments.

"And he lives in Merchant House like us!" Rique adds.

"No. Master Grossi has been hard at work on his research," says the Headmaster.

"So, fourth-years are doing research?" asks Peter.

"Yes."

"What kind of research?"

"That, my dear Master Vandenhof, is again determined between you and the staff here. Think of it as a year of 'independent study.'"

"On stuff we've already studied?"

"That is a possibility," says the Headmaster. "At a much more in-depth level, of course. But, more often, it is the deep and concentrated pursuit of an issue or topic that is of very specific interest to that particular student and which, of course, will benefit the school, the curriculum, or the cause."

"You've referred to this 'cause' before," Thomas begins. "And yet you deny its connection to any of the organizations or secret societies that we've all heard of—the so-called man-made societies. But is there an organization? A network—for communication purposes and the like?"

"Yes, there is," is the Headmaster's flat response.

"Does it have a name?" asks Thomas.

"Yes, it does."

Everybody waits, expecting a name to be divulged.

"It has a name that shall remain unknown to you at this time. I'm sorry about that. Propriety and decorum, you know."

The boys look and sound dissatisfied.

"So," the Headmaster says, moving on, "do you have any other questions before I release you to go on with your last academic day at Brig-Wallis?"

The boys are so shocked at the sudden finality they hear in the Headmaster's words that they freeze.

No questions are forthcoming.

"Then, you are dismissed," says the Headmaster with a flourish. "Enjoy the rest of this beautiful day and, of course, the wonderful concert this evening." Then, as the boys begin gathering their belongings and awkwardly mill about the room, he adds, "It has been my supreme pleasure to have served you these three years. I shall await your personal contacts over the summer."

Several boys can't resist getting a bit choked up at this dismissal. Nathan, Fabrice, Harry, and Joe-pa sidle up to the Headmaster to give him a hug on their way out.

"I'll see you tonight and, of course, as each of you departs tomorrow," he says in his usual benign, affable way.

On their way out, the Headmaster calls out, "Peter! Could I have a moment of your time?"

Peter returns to the center of the room.

"I just wanted to say," begins the Headmaster, "that I am sorry that we were never able to find the time to reestablish our Sunday study sessions from the previous year. I've missed our talks."

Peter stands staring blankly, apparently having nothing to say.

"I never got the chance to—no. Let me start that over," the Headmaster says, stumbling uncharacteristically. "I never *made the effort* to find out what became of the girl you met last year. She seemed to have quite an effect on you."

"Meela?" Peter responds.

"Was that her name?"

"Yes," Peter confirms. "She's still around. I think. I mean, she's in my life. You know: the occasional postcard."

"So, you're still in contact with her?"

"Barely," Peter admits. "I haven't seen or talked with her since last summer."

"I see," says the Headmaster. "I was just wondering. I know how much she impacted your life last year"

"Yeah."

"And again," the Headmaster adds, "I'm sorry we haven't talked more this year. The third year is so demanding."

"I'll say."

"And how do you think the year went? What do you think of the Brig-Wallis experience?"

Wow! Talk about a loaded question! Peter thinks.

"Well, sir. Based upon what you shared today, I think it was a success. I agree with you that you've been left with ten extraordinary individuals. I'm not sure what you'll *do* with them all."

"Oh? And why is that?"

"Well, as close as we've become, I can't say that I see us all joining a club or going on vacations together, much less forming a *compan*y together. As you said, we still remain, each and every one of us, very different individuals, each with our own talents and interests." For a moment, Peter looks distant. "But I'd have to agree with you: I think Brig-Wallis has brought out the best of us. I really like who we've all become—though there are a few of us who still have a ways to go—"

"That goes without saying!"

"—I'm excited to see where we all go. I think *that* will keep us connected more than anything: watching each of the group members 'fly,' so to speak." Peter looks at the Headmaster, finding him attentive yet somehow distant. "Headmaster? I have a question for you."

"Yes, Peter?"

"Is college an option for Brig-Wallis grads?"

"Of course!" responds the Headmaster. "*Many* Brig-Wallis students have gone on to obtain college degrees. And, between you and me, you *don't* have to be a grad in order to get in."

"Really?!"

"No. You could get into just about any school on the planet right now if you wanted to."

"What?!" Peter recoils. "What about tests and grades and degrees?"

"It's all just busy work," the Headmaster assures. "Colleges are first and foremost businesses. If you have the money and the interest, you can go."

"But a college education is not an expectation of Brig-Wallis grads, is it?"

"Oh, no! By no means! Most Brig-Wallis grads bypass college and go right into business." The Headmaster pauses a moment, collecting his thoughts.

Peter speaks first. "What I guess I'm getting at is that the rest of the world sees education—especially a college education—as a key to, if not an essential ingredient in, success in the world," he says. "You don't share this opinion? I mean, what will happen to us if we *don't* go to college? We're just seventeen- and eighteen-year-olds!"

"Well, Peter. Let me start out by saying that, historically speaking, many of the great minds and achievers in the world found more struggle and limitations imposed upon them within our systems of education. I'll not bore you with a list of their names or their stories, but suffice it to say that the system of education that has been developed for Brig-Wallis has proven to be more than adequate to serve our small target population. Believe it or not, Peter Vandenhof, you, standing here at seventeen years old, are far better prepared to take on 'adult' responsibilities than ninety-nine point nine percent of your species—not just your age group but your species!"

"Seriously? Why is that?"

"Because you know how to take care of yourself. You know how to think critically. You know how to cooperate. And you know who you are and how and when to apply your talents and skills."

"I'm not so sure about that last one, sir."

"Granted, your perceptions and perspectives in *all* of those areas will continue to change and grow. You came here, after all, to challenge yourself."

"Yeah. I hope I'm up to it!"

"As do we, Peter. As do we."

"Thank you, sir. It has truly been a pleasure learning from you—being invited to be a part of such an amazing institution. You've changed my life—and *only* for the better."

"Thank you, Peter."

"And don't be surprised if you see me in the fall."

"I welcome it," says the Headmaster in full sincerity. "Anytime," he adds. "And you know how to reach me? Over the summer?"

"Yes, sir. Got it covered."

"Excellent. Well, enjoy the rest of the day."

"Thank you, sir." Peter says, heading for the door. "See you tonight!"

"Yes," says the Headmaster. "See you at the concert."

21

BROWN

On Saturday, Peter, Emil, Nathan, and John share a limo taxi to Zurich airport with a couple of first-years. The four of them happen to be on the same commercial flight to New York. Though Emil and Nathan are continuing on to California, the four boys secure seats together in a row in the first-class section. On the plane the boys spend some time talking about their respective interpretations of the Headmaster's revelation of the day before and the implications as they see them for themselves. Peter says he sees them all returning for a fourth year. The other boys are not as sure.

"I think I'm college bound," says Emil. "I just feel academia calling me."

"You just want to be around girls," teases Peter.

"What about you? You and Meela?" Emil teases back.

"I don't think so!" Peter says. "I haven't seen or spoken to her in almost a year."

"I'm not sure I want to go through another year at Brig-Wallis," says John.

"What?" and "why?" are the responses he receives.

"This year was *hell*!" he says. "I don't think I want to go through that—or even be *near it* again."

The other three are shocked. They suddenly realize that they've always just pretty much gone along with whatever was asked of them.

"I think I'm ready to be out in the world," John adds.

"What? Work?" asks Peter.

"Yeah. Work!" John answers. "You heard the Headmaster: he says we're ready. Surviving the 'Brig-Wallis experience' has proven that we're able—that we're ready."

"But what? Where?" mumbles Peter.

"I don't know," John returns. "I'll ask the Headmaster. He seems ready to help all of us find the right fit for us."

The other three are stunned. John's little revelation seems to take the wind out of their conversation. After more than a minute of awkward silence, each of the boys finds himself tuning into on-demand movies.

When it comes time for good-byes at JFK, the boys act nonchalant, but all four have new reservations: they know their little bubble of safety, of camaraderie, is bursting, and they can't help but feel a little heavy-hearted over it. But they hide it and go their separate ways—Emil and Nathan to their connecting flight to LAX, John and Peter to their family homes, in separate cabs.

About a week later—after the fourth of July weekend—Peter hears from Emil that John has found a job as an intern or apprentice or something in his father's business offices in Manhattan. Peter makes a mental note to try to check in on him but never does.

As mentioned, Peter had not seen Meela at all over the course of his third year at Brig-Wallis. There had been occasional correspondences—mostly in the form of postcards sent by Meela during her exotic travels to distant lands. As usual, the texts of her letters were brief and to the point: "Miss you," or "I was here and you weren't," or "Hope everything is going well," and "I bet I know where you are. Guess where I am," with Meela always signing her postcards "Ludmilla."

Peter, for his part, tried sending newsy epistles for the first month or so of the year but soon lost momentum and fell into the same pattern of using postcards. He did, however, find himself quite enjoying the process of collecting postcards, for he found immense pleasure and amusement in the ensuing process of making up 'exaggerated' stories of big, extravagant, even romantic, trips for Meela's entertainment—of seeing how much nonsense he could squeeze in his small hand print onto the allotted space on one of those cards. Thus, postcards from odd places like the ski villages of Sees-Fee and Rosswald, the thermal baths at Brigerbad, the skating rink on Brig's Stadtplatz, Genova's Natural Historical Museum, Zurich airport, and, of course, Crete—he bought lots of postcards in Crete—became the source of stupendous (if fantastical) adventures—all for Meela's benefit.

Despite his newfound flair for the melodramatic, Peter always signed his cards and letters, "Peter."

In July, Peter received a postcard from "Ludmilla" from Switzerland that said, "Flying to NYC on August 7 on way to NB. Got time?" with the flight information codes at the bottom. Excited, nervous, slightly bewildered at her frustratingly cryptic wording, Peter could not help but be a little distracted from his normal tasks at hand during the three weeks leading up to the seventh of August. But when that day comes, Peter is waiting at the airport a whole hour ahead of the plane's scheduled arrival. (He'd taken a cab.) This time when Meela comes off the plane, there is no Mrs. Grosbeck. Their joyful reunion is almost ecstatic as they hug, squeeze, kiss, and stare into each other's faces, too emotion filled to speak, tears streaming down both of their faces.

As they finish spinning around and around in each other's arms, Meela says, "I'm so sorry! I only have one night with you!" She looks beseechingly into Peter's face. "I gotta get home to get ready for college! We start next week!"

"Next week, next week?"

"Yeah! Isn't that *crazy*!"

"Like, Monday next week?" asks Peter. "One week from today?"

"Like, drive down Friday, see all the relatives on Saturday, move into the dorm on Sunday, orientation and registration on Monday and Tuesday, classes on Wednesday!"

Peter looks confused. "Hey! I don't even know where you're going!"

"Brown!"

"Brown University?" he asks. "In Rhode Island?"

"Yeah!" Meela says. "It's a family thing. My dad's related to the Brown family."

"Oh-ho!"

"No, no! It's not like that!" she says. "No special treatment or anything."

"I don't care!" Peter says, looking into her eyes, his own still glimmering with tears. "It's so good to see you!" He pulls her into yet another deep embrace.

"It's good to see you, too," she returns. "Again: I am *so sorry* that we only have a day—"

"It's okay! It's okay!" Peter stops her mouth with kisses. "It's more than I expected. I'll take whatever I can get!"

"Really? You're not disappointed?"

"No!" Peter says. "I'm just grateful to even lay *eyes* on you, much less get to touch you."

"You sound like Rumi."

"Who?"

"Rumi." Meela says. "The poet."

Peter's look is blank.

"You don't know Rumi?"

"I don't think I've even *heard* of Rumi," Peter admits.

"Well, there's gonna be an awakening tonight!" Meela teasingly forewarns as she takes his arm and steers him toward the baggage-claim area.

"Of that I have no doubt!" Peter says mischievously.

Meela looks at him sidelong, appreciating his humor. "Hopefully, there'll be a little of *that*, too!"

"What do you mean, 'a little'?" he says, playing along. "I've been saving up!"

"I'll bet you have, you poor little celibate monk, you."

As they reach the baggage area, Meela pulls left as if to go outside.

"Don't you have any bags?" Peter asks.

"Only this," she says, indicating the backpack on her shoulders. "I sent the rest ahead."

"Good thinking," Peter says, a twinkle in his eye, "You won't be needing any change of clothes anyway."

Meela laughs and playfully thrusts her hip into his.

"Let's take a taxi," she says.

"Really?" asks Peter. "No subway?"

"We've only got about eighteen hours together. Do you want to waste time taking the subway?"

"When you put it that way, no. I guess not." They hail a taxi. "But then, there's always *Risky Business*."

"What?"

"Have you ever seen the Tom Cruise movie, *Risky Business*?"

"Yeah. What about it?"

"Remember that scene on the subway train—"

"Peter Vandenhof!" Meela shrieks, playing offended. "You have got a one-track mind!"

"Me?!" he protests. "*Me*?!"

Later in the evening, back at Peter's parents' apartment, after the two have returned from a middle-of-the night excursion to an all-night Greek deli, they are following up their second love tryst with some reading from the Coleman Barks book of Rumi poetry that Meela found earlier at Crawford & Doyle when, suddenly, Meela is struck with a thought.

"What about you? What are you going to be doing this year?"

"That, my love, is an interesting question," answers Peter, extricating himself from his comfortable position of head resting in Meela's lap while she reads and strokes his hair and scalp. Propping himself on his elbow, he continues. "A question whose answer is complicated by the fact that I could be done with school."

"What! How is *that* possible?"

"Well, it turns out that making it through three years at Brig-Wallis is apparently enough. The whole school, according to the Headmaster, is set up to test the boys it finds—to see if they're... 'capable' of serving 'the cause.'"

"The cause? What cause?"

"Well, according to what the Headmaster told us—and get this: he waited to tell us on the very last day of school!" Meela responds with raised eyebrows. "What he told us on that last day in the last class of our third year—a year, I might add, that was really brutal, even cruel, which I can get into more later if you're interested—was that Brig-Wallis grads go on to—that they have *proven* themselves 'worthy' to—continue to work for this 'cause'—a cause whose name he would not reveal but that he says has been set up as a kind of Earthly instrument or agency for protecting or helping to carry out some 'plan' that some kind of congress in the spiritual world has designed for us—for the course of human history."

"Did he mention what the goals of this cause—or, rather, of this design or plan were?"

"Kind of. Not specifically," Peter answers. "He said that we—including me and you—are all volunteers playing parts in a particular course in human history, a course that is intended to play out the very basest of human behaviors in order to test us to see if we can still wake up and figure out our true spiritual nature and then rise above the trappings of the ego and the distractions of the material world."

"That makes sense," Meela says approvingly.

"What?! That makes sense to you?!"

"Yeah! Well, just look at our world," Meela says. "We're behaving in pretty 'base' ways: killing each other, poisoning the planet, killing ourselves. I'm not sure it could get much worse than this, so, yeah: as a test to see if we can rediscover our true spirituality, it's a pretty ingenious one. It's fucked up—I mean, whoever invented it, whoever thought this up, has a pretty warped imagination."

"The Headmaster says that there is no right or wrong, no better or worse, no good or evil."

"That's not what they're saying in the churches! That's not what the government and news media are telling us. And it's *cer*tainly not what the *planet* is telling us!"

"He's speaking from a spiritual perspective. From the perspective of God."

"Oh. Well, in that case, I suppose he's right," Meela says, perhaps tongue-in-cheek. Peter's not sure.

"What do you mean?" he asks.

"Well, from a godly spiritual perspective, it's all a game, right? It's all just part of a painting or a play or a movie. It's all being made up… for fun! For the heck of it!"

"It's so weird to hear you talk that way—to try to *think* that way. I mean, here we are, in human bodies, in a bed, on Earth. It all feels so real."

"It's a good design."

"'Good'…"

"It *works*," Meela amends. "It serves as a nice playground. Or, in your version of things, a good testing ground."

"Anyway," Peter says, deciding to move on, "so the Headmaster goes on to tell us that we chose these lives—we chose these bodies and families—knowing fully that we were aiming for this job—this job of helping to ensure the fulfillment of the plan."

"How? How do you ensure the fulfillment of the plan?" asks Meela.

"That's what I don't quite get," Peter says. "I mean, he said it was by controlling the flow of and access to money, resources, and information. But I'm not sure how."

"Control the flow of money and information. You mean like the UN, the IMF, the World Bank, or the WTO?"

"No. And not like some of the rumored 'secret societies.'"

"Like Bilderberg and Skull and Bones?"

"Yeah," Peter answers. "Not like them. Those are 'man-made organizations.'"

"I don't get that," Meela responds. "Isn't everything here man made?"

"I think what he meant was that they're designed by motives of greed and power and control—which are ego constructs—whereas our orders are informed by a higher source."

"Listen to you: speaking like some snooty-nosed intellectual elite. 'Our *orders* are in*formed* by a *high*er source,'" Meela says, quoting Peter while using a mock-British accent.

"Yeah. Sorry. I guess three years of Brig-Wallis makes you kind of talk like someone from Brig-Wallis."

Meela laughs. "You're so cute! And funny!"

"I'm serious!"

"I know!" she says in defense. "That's what makes it so cute!"

"So, anyway," Peter says, charging ahead. "As I was saying, I have lots of choices in front of me."

"Like what?"

"Well, like returning to Brig-Wallis for a fourth year."

"I thought you said you were done, that you've been 'released unto the world.'"

"I am. But a fourth year at Brig-Wallis is one of my options."

"And what does that serve?"

"I don't know. Maybe it helps give clarity to one's future—or just to one's options."

"Maybe it gives you an inside track to some higher positions?"

"Maybe."

"What else? What are your other choices?" Meela says, sitting up in bed. "Oh, this is so exciting!"

"You're weird."

"What? It's fun hearing a person's choices! So many adventures lie down the path chosen by every one of them!"

"Whatever," says Peter. "Another option, I guess, is to go into 'the business.'"

"What!"

"I don't know. Apparently, the Headmaster will help each of us find a place or role within the cause that might suit us best—as individuals with our own skills and interests."

"Okay."

"Then there's the option of going to collcgc—"

"After three years? You're seventeen!"

"I know. But the Headmaster says it doesn't matter. He says that colleges are businesses first and will take anyone who's got money and interest."

"Which is true…"

"And you know this *how*?" Peter asks.

"Well. Look at me!" Meela says. "I went to this exclusive school for rich girls, where they only let me in 'cuz my parents had the cash."

"I'm sure that's not the only reason they let you in."

"No, but cash is the key ingredient," she responds. "And listen: I did not fit in there. Those girls are messed up! And mean—though they probably don't even know it—throwing their lists of names and possessions and places they've been around like it's so important."

"How did you handle it?"

"I just loved them. I just helped them understand that there is learning and joy and suffering to be had in *all* walks of life."

"I'll bet you did," Peter says with a big grin. "You took 'em to church." And then, in a more festive display, he says, "Church with Meela! Everyone should be so lucky."

There is a momentary pause before Meela speaks again. "What else? What else?" she asks. "What are your other options?"

"Well, I guess the other main options are to quit—to leave the Brig-Wallis path and go off and lead a normal life—"

"Whatever *that* is."

"Exactly!" Peter says. "He even told us that some of us might even choose to reject all this information—to try to work against the Plan—to try to expose or oppose the flow of the cause—the course of descending evolution."

"Really?" Meela asks, genuinely surprised. "The Headmaster *told* you that that was a choice of yours?"

"Yeah!" says Peter. "I think it was his way of trying to reinforce one last time a lesson that he's been trying to drum into us from day one: that we are *al*ways in choice."

Meela is quiet. She seems suddenly quite distant.

"What's wrong? Where are you?" asks Peter.

"Oh, I was just thinking," she says dreamily. "All you're talking about reminds me of something I've discovered about myself—about my own mission—and my *own* choices."

"Your mission?" Peter asks. "The mission to help me out?"

"No: the other one. You know: weather systems."

"Oh, yeah!"

"Well, I recently got spanked a little—"

"What! What do you mean?"

"Well. You know how I like to play with the wind?"

"Yeah."

"Well, I'm always playing. And, well, I was getting a little cocky—trying to change weather patterns around me then trying to affect larger weather systems."

"What do you mean?"

"Well, like typhoons and hurricanes and destructive weather patterns." Meela looks at Peter. "And, well, first of all it's a *lot* harder than making a little puff of wind ruffle up someone's hair; I can tell you that. And, well, I guess I'm being taught, like you, that death, destruction, and suffering are part of a bigger plan than my own little wishes and desires."

"I'm not following you."

"Well, I got told no," Meela says, "when I tried diffusing or changing the course of a couple of these storms—storms that I knew had some really destructive power."

"Were you told why?" Peter asks.

"Not specifically," Meela answers. "But hearing you talk about these spiritual plans and their human egos I realized that that's it:

it is my human ego—my own empathy and attachment to human happiness—that led me to try to change the courses of these storms. I forgot that my purpose in working with weather systems was bigger than its effects on humans—that weather systems serve the natural health and balance of the planet, which makes it a viable, thriving host for all life, present and future. I got all caught up in the human ego as well as my loyalty to a life-form that is only temporary for me. I was all caught up in the self-serving perspective of little ol' me when I should be working for the health and happiness of the planet."

"Gaia."

"So we call it. I know it as Sanat Kumara."

"I've heard that name before—"

"It's the name humans have been given to use to refer to the conscious being that is ensouling this planet that *we* call Earth."

"Wow! That is cool!"

"Yeah, and humbling. And, as you just heard, a little humiliating."

"You're just an egg," Peter says almost absentmindedly.

"What's that?"

"Oh, just a saying I like from a book I read. It's meant to remind the characters—to remind us—that we're all learning, that we're awakening to new worlds, new perspectives."

"I like it!" effuses Meela. "What book is that from?"

"*Stranger in a Strange Land,* by Robert Heinlein."

"I'll have to look that one up. Sounds interesting."

"It's good!"

"So, back to your choices. What are you going to do? Which ways are you leaning?"

"Until that last day of school, it was a foregone conclusion that I'd be going back to Brig-Wallis for a fourth year. I always assumed it was like a high school, that it took four years to finish."

"And now?"

"Well, I'm not so sure. Of the ten of us who finished the third year together—"

"Ten!" interrupts Meela. "Only ten?"

"Yeah, well, that's a whole different story—one that would take for*ev*er to tell—"

"But I thought there were—"

"Yeah, well, some fell by the wayside. Another time. Anyway, of the ten of us, it sounds like two are going to go to college; two have already entered the work world—taking jobs within businesses or organizations that the Headmaster connected them with; three are traveling; and the rest of us are undecided."

"So, what are your inclinations?" Meela asks, stroking Peter's hair lovingly.

"Well. I don't want to go to some bullshit waste-my-time college—"

"What makes you say that?" Meela asks. "That college is a bullshit waste of time?"

"Oh. Yeah. Sorry. No offense."

"It's okay. I'm just curious about your reasoning."

"Well, I guess there's a part of me that gets it. I get that this is a game, that we're spirits in a material world. I mean, how can one think any other way? Quantum physics *proves* it: everything that we call reality—that we call matter—is made up of ninety-nine point nine percent space and point one percent energy—which is then totally dependent upon a conscious observer for its validation as being real!

"Anyway, my point is: I'm just not ready to hang around with, much less share conversations and beers with, people who are totally immersed in material-reality thinking! I can't do it!"

"But isn't part of your so-called cause to help ensure that people are immersed in all that 'bullshit'?"

"Yeah, but I guess I'd rather do it—if I'm going to do it—from the outside, not from within, from among them." Peter strokes Meela's arm. "By the way, Meela. I think it's so cool that I can talk to you about this stuff—and that you're not freaked out by it all. You even seem to get it. Will you marry me?"

Meela looks long and deeply into Peter's eyes before answering. "You know, Peter Vandenhof—or whatever name it is you want me to call you—that at *some* level we are al*ready* married—that we have been married many times before, that, in fact, we were born into this universe married."

Peter is struggling to make sense of Meela's disclosure. "I believe you," he says.

"Then, yes, I will marry you." She kisses him.

"Really? You will? I mean, you know, I was really just joking."

"But I'm not," Meela says. "I am, always have been, and always will be, your other—your other half. We have a connection that goes back to the beginning and which can *ne*ver be broken. So, when I say yes to your proposal, I am merely acknowledging a condition that already exists, a state of union that we were born with and which will never *not* exist. In fact, it is even silly to consider otherwise, as that would be impossible. It would be like trying to ignore or pretend that half of your own body does not exist—it would be a lie, a deceit, a delusion."

"But we've chosen to live in a whole world of illusions," Peter points out.

"Yes, and that would just be one more illusion that we decide to use: the illusion that we are not bound inextricably by sacred bonds of Joy, Truth, Beauty, and Love.

"So, with this in mind, will you, Peter Vandenhof, marry this Meela-version of your other half?"

"It sounds as if I have no choice!" Peter teases.

"Within the realms of Maya, there is *al*ways the illusion of choice," Meela recites.

"Whoa! That's a heavy statement!" Peter remarks. "And it kinda sounds cynical. 'The illusion of choice'!"

Meela is unresponsive. She persists only with her intense gaze into Peter's eyes from about three inches from his face.

"Yes, Ludmilla Gregorovna Rostropovich, I will marry you."

They kiss rather formally.

"I think you should go back to Brig-Wallis," Meela says, rolling back onto the pillows against the headboard.

"What? Why?"

"Because that is where you will find the most answers."

"I have questions?"

"Peter Vandenhof! You have more questions than any person I've ever known. You probably drove your parents crazy with your questions!"

"I was alone most of the time."

"Then your teachers—"

"I mostly read books."

"My point is," Meela says, at first pretending to be exasperated, "Brig-Wallis makes you happy! You love it there. You've said so. I see how you glow whenever you talk about it. Even when you're complaining about it, it's like you're so *proud* or *glad* that they put you through the crap they've put you through. And I think you really get off on that monastic type of living. Heaven knows it's easy for you: you've spent so many lifetimes in monasteries or in priesthood. Plus, this headmaster dude seems to be the man you most want to be nearest to—the one you want to figure out—the enigma you idolize but want to tear apart and figure out at the same time. And where else are you going to get the chance to study him than at that school?"

Peter is dazed, absolutely dumbstruck by Meela's rant. When he recovers enough to speak, all he can manage are the words, "How? How did you know?"

"It's been so obvious—ever since those three days we had last summer: you are ob*sessed* by that guy. You want so much to get to know him—to try to get into his head. And yet you're afraid. You don't want to discover something that might destroy the illusion of grandeur and greatness you have built around him. *And* you don't think you're worthy. Last year it wasn't the *school* you were questioning your worthiness of, it was the damned *Head*master. You couldn't understand or accept why he had let you into his world—why he had allowed you *deep* into his world. So you threw yourself out. You pretended everything else was more important. But I can hear it, I can feel it, I can see it: you want nothing more than to know *everything you can* about this man, to figure out what really makes him tick. And, even more, to feel what it's like to *be* him, to be as *great* as you think he is. What would that *feel* like? What would it be like to know what he's thinking, to know why he thinks, acts, and talks the way he does. Am I right?"

"Deadly right."

"Then, there's your answer. If you are willing—if you are strong and courageous enough to follow your heart—to follow your *truth*—you know where you're going this fall."

Peter looks ashen. "I'm tired," he says scooting down beneath the covers. "I need to shut down. To process."

"I understand," Meela says. "I'm sorry. I hope I'm not ruining our time together. It's just that I could see you needed a little butt kicking."

"A little! I feel like you chewed me up and spit me back out."

"No, that's later," she teases, trying to lighten the mood. "Let's turn the light out and sleep a little," she says. "We still have lots of time together."

Needless to say, the two enjoy every minute of the rest of their eighteen hours together. To Peter it feels as if every moment is overflowing with intimacy and laughter, oneness and bliss. And, of course, there are the dozen or so new "best friends" that they make through Meela's irrepressible care and compassion for her fellow human being. There is Kaseem, the cab driver who has lived in the United States for seven years and is still trying to earn enough money to get his wife's parents and brothers over here. (Peter tips him handsomely.) And Marie, the part-time bookstore employee and student of literature at Columbia, who helps them find "the best" version of Rumi poems while trying desperately to hide her laughter from her fellow workers as she takes pictures with Meela's iPhone of Peter and Meela's suggestive poses as performed in the bookstore aisles. And, of course, there are David, Vanessa, and Annette at Peter's parents' apartment. In fact, each of them is so excited to see Meela that it takes nearly hour for Peter and Meela to get to Peter's bedroom, as Meela is trying to be polite and play "catch-up," listening to all of the stories about their children and grandchildren. Then there is Adonis, the middle-aged do-it-all cook/server at the all-night Greek deli, whose enthusiasm for life and optimistic outlook despite tragedy and hardship—even at two in the morning—are truly inspiring (not including the fact that he makes one of the best spanakopitas Peter has ever tasted: extra cheesy). And then there is Laris at the United Nations building (a place Meela wants to go to because she is thinking that she might like to work there one day), who is from Kenya and loves her job as guide and interpreter but is sad that her two-year term is nearly up and that she will have to go back to Nairobi soon. And the list goes on.

When Peter escorts Meela back to JFK for her noon flight to Moncton (via Boston Logan), they are both thinking that this will be the last time they'll see each other for a long time. But then Meela happens to inject some thought-provoking possibilities into their good-bye.

"You know, Rhode Island is not too far from here," she says as she backs away from him. "And Christmas isn't so very far away."

"I love you!"

"I love you, too!" she says as she almost stumbles backward through the opening to the TSA check-in.

The rest of Peter's summer correspondence allows him to keep up with some of the activities and plans of his classmates as they unfold. He knows that Emil is off to Princeton. He knows that Fabrice is still traveling in Japan in an effort to explore his "roots"—both his cultural and family heritage. He has heard from the Headmaster that only John and Zi have committed, as yet, to "joining the crusade" and that they have already assumed job positions working in apprentice-like situations under other, more established members of the "SSL" (as Peter enjoys calling it—standing for "Sacred Servants of Leadership"): John in Manhattan, Zi in Beijing. He hears via postcard that Harry and Thomas are backpacking together in India. "For a year."

Not the place I want to go, thinks Peter upon hearing this news.

Adam is fully back on his feet and planning to go back to Hotchkiss for his senior year. Rique is wallowing around Brasil in his family compound, trying to decide what to do. And Joe-pa is so busy with his London social schedule that he has not made any decisions yet (other than the party or social event of the day). And then there is poor Nathan, who is still under the impression that he will have to pay his way in any future undertaking. Luckily, thanks to Peter's insight and intuition, the Headmaster is able to intervene to inform young "Master Ambrose" that any and every expense for the rest of his life would be covered by a trust fund that the backers of the school have created expressly for this purpose.

In the meantime, Peter's heart and mind are telling him that Meela was right: that Brig-Wallis is where he belongs. And yet the prospect of being so far from Meela is heart wrenching. But he also knows that this latter urge is totally ego-driven. They will have their time.

A late-night phone call to Meela finalizes it. Meela is in her own world at Brown—busy as all get out. She is taking eighteen credits of classes, she is rowing on the women's crew team, she is candy-striping at the nearby Hasbro Children's Hospital in Providence, *and* she's been nominated for Homecoming Court. It is obvious that she is completely and fully immersed in college life. Peter feels guilty for even thinking that he might be able to insert himself there.

And so, he makes the call to the Headmaster. He will be returning to Brig-Wallis at the end of the week. He will be a fourth-year monk.

22

THE GRAND PLAN

Thirteen men are seated around a conference table. They are not necessarily extraordinary physical specimens, nor are any of them remarkable for their apparel. In fact, there is nothing that would set these men apart in a crowd. Yet, here they are: the Keepers of the Grand Plan of the Ancient Order of Osiris, the thirteen men charged with steering the course of human history.

Where these men differ is in name, bloodline, job title, and place(s) of residency. What they have in common is *un*commonly strong wills: a dedication to the fulfillment of their mission so complete, so focused and unwavering, that any sense of self, any flare of ego, has long been extinguished—or at least been beaten into such a state of submission that one might think of each of them as "masters of invisibility." And that is indeed what they seek: secrecy, anonymity, invisibility. These are the men who give the orders and who create the money for things to happen. The loans that enslave the world, the funding for the educational policies and media trends that brainwash the masses, the arms and technology that make possible perpetual war and perpetual fear, the political puppets and fanatical religious leaders who help distract people from the real underlying causes in human history all come from decisions made by these men—even the movers and shakers in the drug, alcohol, gambling, sex, slavery, and terrorist trades are funded by these men. It is part of their job. It is the reason they came to Earth—the role they promised to play while participating in the *Homo sapiens sapiens* game.

Though thirteen men fill these seats, hundreds came to the planet with the dream of performing these duties—and many are still serving the "cause" in their own small ways. But thirteen, only thirteen, and always thirteen bodies fill these seats.

At the head of the room, facing the oval-shaped conference table, now standing while being framed by the luminous snow-covered mountain scene in the large window behind him, is a gaunt, steel-gray-eyed man whose pale, wrinkled, papery skin heralds his aged status. It is the man we've come to know as Vittorio Visconti, headmaster of Brig-Wallis Preparatory School for Boys.

The Headmaster steps forward to the edge of the table, and, leaning onto the table with his arms, he begins to speak.

"Fulfillment of the Plan is not yet complete—though there is evidence that we are nearing the end of our Earthly mission. Humankind is mired in fear and disharmony. Sanat Kumara is in the throes of casting us off. Still, we must remain focused; we must stay the course.

"The boys remain the keys to our success," he says as he looks from countenance to countenance. "There are several among this new crop who show great promise. As you know, not all of them will make the grade. Despite the fact that every soul entering our bloodlines knows what it may be getting into, very few will pass the many tests required of them. And this is fine. Even *we* are born into choice. Plus, we only need a few to make it—enough to replace those of us in this room, plus another hundred or so to reinforce and back us up. The others will play different roles, which is fine. We can always use more Hitlers, Stalins, Maos, Pol Pots, Mladics, and Assads.

"The Plan to guide humankind into the deepest possible forms of ignorance, fear, and depravity is ours to orchestrate. We are the means to those ends, the captains of the ship. Some of our children may end up trying to oppose or expose us. As I said, even *we* are born into choice. Be watchful. Be wary. We must steel ourselves to the task of hardening them. Our methods are proven. The system works. You are the proof of that.

"Thank you all for your service."

Headmaster Visconti spends a minute looking one last time into each and every face sitting around that table. Then sits down.

What has been most remarkable throughout the course of the short address is the focused stillness of the twelve other men in the room. There are no nods, no coughs or shifts in facial expressions, not even a shift in anyone's posture as all twelve sit in deferential, disciplined attention. And, by the looks in each set of eyes, every single person in the room is as fully present and fully attentive to the speaker and his words as if nothing else of any greater importance exists in the whole wide world.

The speaker now asks his audience to close their eyes and "focus within and without." It is obvious that this exercise is one with which everyone in the room is familiar.

"I have a body, but I am much more than these organs and cells and atoms that I use in service of the Grand Plan.

"I have emotions, but I am much more than the feelings and reactions that I use in service of the Grand Plan.

"I have a mind, but I am much more than the thoughts and beliefs that I use in service of the Grand Plan.

"I am an individuated spark of the Divine, a wave in the Great Ocean of Cosmic Creation. I am a servant of the Master Plan of descending evolution, an agent of spiritual sacrifice, a proctor of the human exam."

Without word or prompt, the room falls into silence—a very still silence lasting about ten minutes. Again, the degree of stillness created by these men is remarkable.

Eventually, each member opens his eyes, not all at the same time but nearly so; then, looking around the table, each man pushes